Legacy of the Maker

Sharon K. Angelici

Book 4 of The Maker Series

Dedication

For my husband, my daughter and my son. You inspire me and I'm grateful for the minutes, days and years of living this adventure called life. You are mine and whatever part of these characters resides in me is part of the love we live as a family. I have never been so proud to be yours.

For my Aussie family. I cannot imagine my life without you in it. Your courage led me to find my way as a queer woman and I owe you, always. We have done incredible things with all this love.

To my mother, heart and soul this story begins and ends because you inspired me to be more, to chase desires and to live from a place of love. Even after your heart stopped beating, and the days felt impossible, you made me believe. You taught me that love can be like a lion and a lamb and in that spectrum will be joy. If wishes were reality, you'd be here to celebrate this series.

Dad, that you've read a series about LGBTQIA+ people who love first and fight the demons that come, brings me more joy than you could know. I am grateful for the way you loved my mother, for the way you showed me how love could be.

CHAPTER I

KNOCK

"Does it hurt, love?" I asked, holding the cold cloth to her neck.

Shay's forehead was damp with sweat, and her red hair clung to her cheek. Her discomfort went beyond the stranglehold she'd experienced during our shared dream, and I could sense, by the look in her green eyes, that she was shaken.

"I only hurt a little." She reached to touch my neck, and I noticed faint discoloration around the scars on her hands. "What about you?" Shay asked.

"I'm fine. I woke up before—" I stopped to take a breath and relive the nightmare we'd experienced only moments ago.

We were asleep, sharing our dreamworld and dancing in the tall grass of an unknown field. Shay's gorgeous red hair floated, caught by the wind, and my heart was filled with genuine happiness. The joy felt real until I stumbled upon the slatted boards. The taloned fingers and the darkness of someone's ancient grave. Whatever monster was down in the darkness, it wanted us dead, and there was nothing we could do to stop it.

"Wildwood!" Shay yelled my name, and I returned to the safety of our bedroom and to her arms. "Where'd you just go?" Her pale fingertip traced across my forehead to tuck the wild strays of black hair clinging to my face.

"I don't know where I was, but I know I don't want to meet that…*thing* again." I rubbed my throat and stared at the chokehold redness around Shay's neck. "How did we dream together?" I asked.

Shay sat still; the blankets of our bed dropped around her hips. "I'm not sure, but maybe it has something to do with all the events that happened yesterday."

Ah, yesterday, when all the troubles of Bannock came crashing together inside our home. I rubbed my shoulder, where the puncture wound should still be, and remembered the abduction and torture and death. Life in this small town brought death. The memory of our half-morphed dragon-dog squealing in pain and the crippling fear of loss fell heavily into the pit of my stomach.

"Where's Dexter?" The German Shepherd and dragon hybrid had fallen asleep with us before the shared dream, but he wasn't there now.

"He's still laying right here." Shay threw the blanket aside to uncover the animal sprawled along her legs. "He never left our bed. Even after all the weirdness of the dream."

I climbed over Shay's hips to stretch across and lay my hand on the animal. Yesterday, for a time, he was gone from us, and the loss had hit Shay hard. Shay's ten years of law enforcement experience included less than one year with the K-9 in our bed. They were partners beyond the reality of animal and cop. Dexter licked the back of my hand to remind me he was there.

"Hey, buddy." I made kissing noises, and he rolled sideways for a belly rub.

"He seems good, don't you think?" Shay asked as she scooted to rest against the headboard.

"It's kinda hard to know." My cheeks stretched with a smile. "He's just laying here like a lump."

Shay dragged the blanket between us and rolled over to get out of bed, and I pouted at her.

"Don't leave yet," I said as she pulled on a pair of jogging pants.

But I'm not sure she heard me. She was looking at Dexter with concern. "He *is* just laying there, which isn't like him at all." Shay clapped her hands twice and whispered a command. "Dexter, *ante*."

The dog performed a sideways twisting roll to land with all four paws on the floor. He knew more Latin than I did. In my defense, I'm a blacksmith, not an extensively trained K-9 police officer.

"That's a good sign," Shay said as the dog rubbed against her knee.

In canine form Dexter's shoulders met Shay's hip, and when he stood on his hind legs, he was taller than her by almost six inches. I was happy Dex was part of our family and that, if I ever met him in a dark alley, he'd be on my team.

"It's a *great* sign." Surrendering to the fact that we weren't going back to sleep, I followed Shay's lead and put on a pair of sweatpants. "Coffee?" I asked.

"The pot probably turned off." She checked her watch. "It's after ten. We definitely need coffee and maybe even lunch."

"A beer would hit the spot right about now." I heard Stout before I saw him, but I knew exactly where our gluttonous fairy was. It's where he was every day when we got out of bed.

"Really, Stout?" I said more than asked, but it was also comforting to hear his gravelly voice after seeing the torture he'd endured yesterday. Gosh, was it really only yesterday?

"Have you checked the time?" He flew in front of the clock on the wall. The sound of his wing flutter was different, louder if that was possible. "Are you on vacation or something?"

Shay's smile was telling; the rise of her cheek gave me a fluttery feeling in my heart. "We are not."

He hovered in front of Shay, noticing the red marks around her throat. "What is this?" He flew close but didn't touch her skin.

"It's hard to explain." Shay rubbed at her neck.

"It was real?" Stout said as he flew to the refrigerator door.

Shay turned to look at me as she followed the fairy, and I tried to remember if Stout was part of our dream. *"Don't let it touch you."* The voice was clear as I recalled the memory. He was there.

"You were there, too?" I asked as Shay opened a bottle of beer for him.

"We were all there," Stout explained, hovering around the glass on the kitchen table.

His words repeated over and over in my head. *"We were all there."* It made perfect sense that the four of us would experience the dream together because as mismatched as were–dark-haired dusky-skinned me, redheaded fair-skinned Shay, fur-covered dragon-dog Dexter, and loud-mouthed husky fairy, Stout–we were a complex found family.

"Do you know what did *that* to Shay?" I pointed to the marks on her neck.

Stout gripped a straw, poised to plunge it into the pint and consume the frothing glass of beer. "Nope." He put his lips to the straw.

I picked up the glass, covering the top just before he took a drink. "Do you have a guess?"

"Come on!" he yelled.

"Do you have a guess, Stout!" My voice was louder, less patient.

Shay patted my shoulder. "Wil, just give him a second."

She took the glass from me and set it on the counter. Seconds later, the straw plunged into the amber liquid, and Stout sucked the contents of the pint glass halfway down. Our fairy was an interesting fellow, and his beer drinking wasn't about the alcohol buzz. For reasons he'd never explained, beer was the solitary enhancer of Fairy Dust, which was derived from his gooey saliva. It was gross if I thought about it, so I tried to avoid pondering the containers of his dried spit in the apothecary cabinet as much as possible.

"Okay," I said as I touched the straw. "You've had plenty of seconds, so tell."

Stout flittered his wings to hover close to my face. "I have a guess," he whispered. "But —"

"I'm not gonna like it, am I?" I interrupted as I dropped into the chair beside his drink.

"Nope, you're definitely not going to like it."

Shay's hand rested on my own, and the reassuring squeeze gave me a momentary sense of calm. "Yesterday we faced the most powerful demon. We can handle this, too."

"Not the *most* powerful," Stout said as he finished the beer in his glass. He sucked the last few drips and floated to the table in front of our joined hands.

"What do you mean, not the most powerful?" Shay asked.

Stout drifted from the table and hovered at the top of the stairs. "Come with me," he called as he flew down to the workshop.

I kicked into my boots and followed our fairy. His wings were twice as loud as they were before Andrea's torture, and I wondered if previous injuries were the cause for the initial obnoxious sound.

"Brigid's hammer has all the answers." He stood beside my hammer and asked, "You know the Pictish?"

"Yes," Shay answered. "We know the rules of the hammer written on the side."

I picked up the hammer and touched the childlike etched symbols wrapping around it. "This is the rule of keeping guard." My fingertip trailed over the line of text. I rotated the head to see the opposite side. "This is the magick that connects the Maker to the Goddess of Creation."

Shay nodded. "The magick that binds us together comes from Brigid, the fire goddess herself."

"That's not the bit you need to worry about." Stout landed on the back of my hand and pushed it over so we could see the artwork. "That." He pointed to the pixel image opposite to the striking face. "I told you it was the demon component of the hammer's magick."

"Yes, the evil part that balances the good," I attempted to explain.

"Something like that," he said. "The Goddess of the Hammer trapped that demon's power inside."

I squeezed the handle, trying to sense a force that might not be mine. I felt the earth energy rise past my feet until it moved through my body and flowed into my palm. The Pictish symbols lit up a brilliant orange, and I understood this magick was pure goodness.

"I don't feel the demon." My hands trembled. "I only feel Brigid."

"That's good." As he flew closer to Shay, Stout explained, "Kai had power over the hammer. She knew how it felt to be the Maker, but part of her served the demon inside."

I set the hammer on the table and opened my palm. The sigil, a delicate series of images—earth and fire, arrows and moons—burned into my skin, getting hotter as the glow increased and my *ignis* flame burst from my hand.

Shay held her flaming palm beside mine. "Did you call your flame?"

"No."

"There's a ghost inside there," Stout said.

He touched the hammer, and tendrils of energy arced off the steel, shooting the fairy across the room. I heard the thud as he hit the workshop sliding door. His fairy body landed on the pile of empty moving boxes, and Shay jumped over Dexter to retrieve our crumpled friend.

"What the hell was that?" I asked as Stout trembled and twitched in the palm of my girlfriend's hand.

"Perhaps something wants me to keep my mouth shut."

Shay laid him on the table and turned toward the stack of files beside him. She flipped one page after the other; some were notes she'd written, some belonged to her late best friend and former training officer, Regina Benton. She was quiet for a long moment, and I wondered what mystery she was trying to unravel as she moved through the documents.

"Shay?" I touched her arm. "Honey?"

"Mm, hmm." She turned to look at me.

"What are you thinking?" I asked.

Without hesitation, Shay reached for the hammer. There was no arc of power or strange transfer of energy. She was the Magick of Bannock, bound to the Maker, and even if we weren't lovers, this connection entitled her to carry the hammer, but what else did it do?

"I'm thinking that Andrea Peters was the mother of demons all along, and she wanted this." She snapped her wrist a few times, jerking the hammer up and down. "She not only wanted to *find* the monster inside; she wanted to release it."

"Why release a creature that could destroy us?" I asked.

Stout snorted derisively. "Because they want to do exactly that."

"Nope!" I said as I turned on my heels and walked away. "Nope." My hands flew up in surrender. I wasn't ready for ultimate evil. "Nope, nope, nope." I hadn't even had my first cup of coffee yet.

I was aware of my feet hitting the stair treads and my hand gripping the railing as I climbed to the apartment above us. My eyes roamed the kitchen, stopping to stare at the crumpled plastic on the table. The evidence bag held the only remains of our demon battle from the day before. I picked it up and studied the bone whistle inside.

"What next?" I whispered to the empty room. "Why the hell was this left behind? Nope, nope, nope, nope, nope."

I let out an annoyed groan as my forehead hit the tabletop.

"I wish I knew what was coming next," Shay said as she walked up behind me and took the bone whistle bag from my white knuckled tight grip.

"I was honestly hoping not to be destroyed today." My response was sarcastic but also laced with extreme anxiety.

Shay and I had been together for almost a year, and in that time, we'd faced more otherworldly crises than worldly. We lived together in my carriage house apartment. We had a simple life, but when we cuddled up in bed at night, our dreams were clouded with demons and mysterious creatures hiding in shadows.

Shay's excitement over the hammer and the artwork coming to life made me nervous about the reality of our dream. If all four of us had shared the nightmare it was likely a message or a prophecy. *Oh, joy.*

"I think you're safe for today," Stout said as he hovered near the stairs. "Unless you tell me we're out of beer."

His wings made the obnoxious sound of a trading card clipped to a bicycle tire. Yesterday, Andrea had torn the lace-thin wings away from the anchor points on his back. He was healing, but he would scar, though I had noticed some other marks, ones Andrea hadn't left. Stout had obviously been tortured sometime in the past, and my heart ached for him.

"We definitely have beer at the bar," Shay said. "And maybe we can drop in and see Dani at the same time."

"Isn't Dani at the Station?" I asked.

Shay looked at her watch. "Probably, but if we time it right, we can meet for lunch at Slammed."

It was almost noon, and I didn't mind burgers and a beer at the bar that Shay and Dani shared ownership of. The inherited space was home to our secret cellar of archives, witchcraft, and Magick and Maker history. But the questions I had about demon hammer energy and enchanted bone whistles made me want to stay in the comfort of our apartment. The barrier around the building was a powerful spell cast by Shay and me, meant to keep out evil of every inhuman kind.

"I'm not sure I'm ready to face the world," I said as Shay changed from her track pants into faded denim jeans and a Bannock Police Department hooded sweatshirt.

"I know the last twenty-four hours have been difficult," she said, grabbing my hand. "But there's so much we need to know. We can't do that locked up inside the carriage house."

"But I'm not like you Shay," I whispered as I sat on the corner of our mattress. "I still don't know enough about magick and demon fighting. I feel like I'm chasing after safety all the time."

"You know more than you realize, Wil, and one day you'll have as much confidence in yourself as I have in you."

She dropped to one knee in front of me and trailed her fingertips along my thigh. I stared at the scars on her hands and pushed at her sleeve to reveal the old wounds on her forearms. Shay knew a lot about surviving, not just because of our history in the foster care system, but because of the attack she'd faced as a teenage girl. She was also the first girl I crushed on who used the shortened version of my name, and when she called me Wil, I felt the power behind the covenant of her love for me.

"You really are magick, ya know?" Tears collected in the corner of my eyes. "Just one damn touch and—"

"Shh." Her finger brushed my lips. "I know that yesterday was scary. I've never been more frightened in my life, and you know what that means."

My head dipped, and those tears dropped to my legs. "I don't want to lose you."

Shay lifted my chin, making me look at her. "I will fight for you with my very last breath," she whispered. "And we will face all of this armed with every bit of magick I can assemble and the thousands of weapons you promised to forge for me."

I closed my eyes, remembering the vow to protect her with the Hammer of the Goddess. Our magick was bound, and that connection had saved me. We'd saved each other.

"Do you think that maybe this time we can go slow?" I asked hopefully.

Shay's smile was a half-laugh. "Oh, my love, I wish slow was going to be part of this, but it's not."

"Oh, yay! Brutal honesty. My favorite," I said sarcastically, rubbing the tops of my thighs to ease the tension, but there was nothing that could.

"Come on." Her fingers tangled into mine as she pulled me to my feet. "Off with these." She tugged at the elastic around my waist. "We have questions that need answers."

She opened the drawer and tossed a t-shirt and jeans on the bed. I kicked out of my sweatpants and got dressed. Shay waited by the bedroom door with a blue and orange flannel shirt dangling from her hooked finger.

"Thank you," I said, both of us knowing that my gratitude was for more than just the flannel shirt.

"I'm going to give Dani a call." She walked to the kitchen, and I listened to her side of the conversation as I stopped in front of the mirror to finger comb my jet-black hair.

"Hey, D. How's the day going?" She was silent for a beat, listening before she asked, "Are you headed to the bar for lunch? Good, we're heading over in a few."

I laughed at her last comment. When Shay was living on Shay time, a few could mean minutes or hours. I was sure that we would see Dani sometime between the two.

Coming back into our room, she held a hand out to me. "You want to walk?"

The question would be a simple one in any place but Bannock. One of the last times I'd walked through town, I was chased and almost devoured by a gatekeeper demon, a monster nearly twice my size, with fangs and claws and tight skin stretched over its skeletal frame, that was hungry to erase me and my legacy from the earth. Quick thinking and a bit of magickal protection helped me escape. "Is it safe?" I asked.

Shay smiled. "I think after our fight with Andrea, it's a good bet that the demons were only coming after us at her command."

"And now that she's gone?"

"Only time will tell."

Shay coupled her hand in mine, and I followed her down the stairs and out the carriage house door. She paused to rub at the glossy, orange-painted surface. For most of the rest of the world, I'm sure the color red means romance and love, but not for us. Shay's first home was an adorable cottage with a bright orange front door. She'd painted it to stand out on a street full of cookie-cutter style homes. The color reminded her to stay happy when she faced loneliness as a single woman. Our orange door was a reminder to her that she would never be alone in her quest for happiness.

"Dexter!" Shay yelled over her shoulder and the thump of beastly German Shepherd paws fell against the stairs. Stout was close behind him.

"Are we getting beer?" the fairy asked.

"Yes, we're getting the beer," I said, not hiding my smile as we stood together in front of that bright orange door, a family of survivors.

The quaint ghost town of Bannock was properly established in the 1800s and occupies less than four square miles. In the last few years, the council had invited people like me to come help restore the old buildings and revive the dying town. Little by little, tourists were passing through, discovering the curiosity shops and historic structures, putting Bannock back on the map. The transformation of the old buildings mirrored my own, and I reached out to touch the masonry wall of the new pharmacy, admiring the *Opening Soon* sign on the window.

The transition from concrete to stone sidewalk marked the landing place of our bar, Slammed, and I tugged Shay's hand to stop her before we entered. "I love you, ya know?"

She turned, and her back fell against the side of the building. She pulled the two of us together, and I didn't even try to hide the smile on my face. Being loved by Shay Pierce was just about the only thing I wanted for the rest of my life. Stout buzzed beside my ear at the same time Dexter pushed nervously against Shay's leg, whining.

"What's up, buddy?" Shay asked, holding tight to my hip.

"I think it's this." Stout tugged at the cellophane bag in Shay's sweatshirt pocket.

"The bone whistle?" Shay grabbed the bag and hid it. "Let's not show it to the entire world, Stout."

"Dexter is nervous about the alicorn's powers," Stout said, his wings surging, vibrating fast enough to launch him toward the door.

"Alicorn?" I asked, unfamiliar with the term. "What's an alicorn?"

"Dex says it's the solitary horn of Monoceros."

Shay's brow furrowed. "The constellation?"

"Wait, what?" I decided that the tiny bone of a constellation, hidden in Shay's pocket, might actually be a threat of interstellar proportions.

The dog snorted loudly, and Stout said, "Not the constellation—the animal."

Shay removed the bag and turned it until we could see the whistle inside. "There's no way." She pressed the bag between her palms.

"No way what?" They'd lost me at Monoceros, and I was struggling to catch up.

"That isn't a demon bone," Stout said.

"I kinda guessed that from all the constellation talk," I said as I took the bag from Shay. She dropped to one knee in front of Dexter.

"How does he know?" She looked at her dog in amazement.

"He says that the blood of the slain never fades," Stout said, "and magickal creatures like the Monoceros weep for all eternity when they're murdered for their alicorns."

I was done with this conversation, exhausted by the vague references. "What the *hell* are you talking about?"

Shay took the whistle from me as she walked into Slammed and into the office, waving at Amelia, who was standing behind the bar. Once we followed her inside, she closed the door and twisted the lock.

"It's an alicorn," Shay said, and that was the only thing that I knew for sure because she kept repeating herself, but it didn't answer my question.

"So you've said, but what in the hell is an alicorn?"

Shay mushed the sides of the bag, making the whistle more visible. "It's not any part of a demon, like we thought. It's also not part of Andrea."

"Okay, so what is it part of?"

Dexter sniffed, and a puff of smoke burst up between us. Stout landed on Shay's wrist and stepped close enough to touch the bag she was still holding.

"I've been alive for a very long time, but I've never actually touched one before." He whispered in reverence.

"But what the hell is it?" Annoyed at the lack of answers, I snatched the bag away.

Before I could say another word, I saw the truth revealed. The room went black, and one by one, bright points of light pegged the ceiling above me. I recognized the mighty hunter, Orion, and just beside the belt of his stars, I saw the Monoceros pattern appear, one white pinpoint at a time, twinkling in the heavens.

I blinked hard and everything went green. I saw the tall grass quivering against the wind and rain. The rush of imagery made me stumble, and I closed my eyes, falling into the chair behind me.

Four hoofed legs pounded against the grassy lands, kicking up bog and turf, splattering mud against the light brown hair on its legs. The thundering of hoof strikes beat rhythmically against the ground. The animal's muscular legs moved, spots of mud creating a random pattern on its glistening coat. The animal stopped. That's when I knew what I was looking at. That's when a creature out of the outrageous dreams of every childhood became clear.

"It's not possible," I said as I opened my eyes.

"I feel like anything is possible, now," Shay whispered. She was on her knees in front of me, her hands resting on the side of my thighs. "Did you see it?"

"Yes! But no."

"Was it beautiful?" Stout landed on my knee.

"Was it beau—?" I set the whistle on the table. "It's from the horn of a unicorn."

Of course, it was beautiful, but, I wondered, how was it possible?

CHAPTER II

TERRARIUM

"**Y**ou're saying an alicorn is the real name for the horn on its head?" I asked. My finger rubbed across the holes of the carved whistle. The three-inch piece of bone-like material fit beneath my fingers.

"Yep," Stout said. "I've never seen a living unicorn. This is the closest I've ever been to the animal. Legends say they are powerful in battle, even with only one horn as their defense."

"Legends? What legends?" I asked, my shoulders tense.

Bannock was a funny town. I'd lived here for close to a year, but my world had exploded with so much that was unbelievable in those ten months: magick and demons, fairies and dragons. But unicorns were the peak of this far-fetched reality.

"The legend of the Monoceros," Stout explained. "Scottish, I think. What do you know, Red?"

He looked at my girlfriend, and the twitch in the corner of Shay's eye made me smile. She hated when Stout called her Red.

"I know that unicorns have powerful magick," she said. "But I always believed they were folktales to keep children in line."

"Are they mean?" I ask, puzzled. "Do they eat children?" Why would anyone use such a fantastic creature to discipline children?

"Nothing like that." She smiled. "They're kind and represent love and purity and all things good."

"How does that keep children in line?" I asked. It was all I could do to contain my skepticism.

"Kindness, my love."

As a child surviving the foster care system, kindness wasn't something I experienced much. I moved often, which meant new people, unknown places, and measurable compassion for a little-bit of a human like me. Except for Mama Pierce, Gran, Earl and Shay, I didn't have many kind encounters to look back on.

"Kindness would have been nice," I said without censoring myself, and Shay reached for my hand.

"Yea," She squeezed my fingers before pulling away.

"You're saying that unicorns could kill 'em with kindness?" I was trying to be funny and break the ridiculousness of the conversation.

"And they could kill with that alicorn, too," Stout said in a severe tone. "But that's not important now. We need to talk about an alicorn whistle that calls to a fairy. What the hell was that monster doing with it?"

Shay kicked at the corner of the desk and moved the floor panel to open access to the magick apothecary in the cellar. "Let's see what we can find in the archives."

Shay walked down the secret staircase, wearing a smile on her face, and I knew why. She was happiest when she turned pages in a book and gobbled up the magickal, mystical secrets of Bannock. Good thing for her; there were thousands.

"*Ignis.*" I heard her whisper and ducked down to the bottom of the stairs; if she was about to discover the secrets of unicorn behavior, I wanted to be there when she did.

~~~~~~~~~~~

"Nothing." Shay pushed the book into the space on the shelf and knocked the whistle with her finger. "If Benton knew about that thing, she didn't write it down."

"I keep telling you we didn't know," Stout said.

"How's that possible?" I asked.

I picked up the whistle and turned it over, looking for any mark that might lead us to answers. It was the fifth time in the last few hours that I'd played with the whistle and come up short. It seemed improbable that Shay, the master of research, couldn't find a single reference to alicorn horns or whistles made from them.

"We're looking in the wrong place." She dusted her hand on the thigh of her jeans.

"Where is the right place?"

I hesitated to ask again because the last time I had, she said the answer was with Andrea Peters, and the only voice she had would be among the former Assistant Mayor's possessions.

"She had the whistle for a reason. If it calls to a fairy, that fairy has to be wherever Andrea was."

"Okay, superhero. I'm going to let you and Dani manage that research session." I kissed her before walking to the spiral staircase, but I hesitated before climbing. "The former Assistant Mayor is outside of my area of expertise." My boot clanked against the step.

"You'll let D know I'm down here?"
~~~~~~~~~~~

Shay's voice held a tone, and I looked back at her. The tiny wrinkle lines accompanying her smile were telling.

Playfully, I smiled back. "Yes, love. I'll tell her exactly where to find you and then I think I might head home."

She gave a short wave. As I reached the top step, I looked through the tiny peephole I'd drilled in the access door to facilitate discreet entry and exit to the cellar apothecary.

I entered the stockroom after I was certain the coast was clear and entered the bar. Amelia sat at her regular table, shuffling files and papers that appeared to be inventory sheets and invoices.

"Hard at work?" I asked as I rotated a chair to sit.

Her hands paused as she looked up. "This place practically runs itself."

I pointed at the tabletop. "Looks like a hot mess," I joked.

"That's just because every damn supplier has to send me next month's deal of the century." She shuffled the pages into a pile. "Did you see Danielle?" When I shook my head, she said, "She ran to get something for Shay. You must have just missed her."

"Is everything alright?" I asked.

"Oh, you know them. There's always a spell to research or a prophecy to troubleshoot."

I laughed. "Did she find any answers about Andrea and the whistle?"

"Nothing that specific, just access to her office. I think the chief wants them to snug the loose ends."

I thought about all the loose ends left behind by Andrea Peters. She was the Assistant Mayor, whatever that meant. I'd never seen her anywhere but near my girlfriend, harassing the two of us. To me and the rest of my chosen family, Andrea was a monster who'd tried her best to destroy us all. I squeezed my hand, feeling the tension as it balled around the fingerless glove I wore in public to cover the sigil scorched in my skin.

"I think the two of them can run the investigation while I go home and work at the forge," I said.

"You need something to eat before you go?" Amelia asked as she stood from the table. I noticed for the first time she was still on the crutches, and I wondered if the arrow strike permanently damaged her prosthetic.

"Maybe I should ask if *you* need anything before I go. Your leg still hurting?" I knew very little about having an amputation, and asking questions felt like an invasion of privacy, but Shay had used the demon sift on Amelia's wound, and it should have healed.

"Leg's fine. Sometimes I need a break. After all these years, I'm good with or without. You don't have to worry."

"I—" The clipping flap of Stout's fairy wings was loud enough to interrupt the conversation.

"Don't go yet." Stout hovered between Amelia and me.

"What? Why?" I asked and watched the dog exit the office, followed by Shay and Dani.

"We're heading over to Andrea's townhouse," Shay said. "I know you don't want to come, but I want someone to take Dexter home, and Stout is coming with us."

It felt like a fair compromise to take the animal that could transform into a dragon and leave behind the chatty, three-inch, beer-guzzling fairy.

~~~~~~~~~~

Dani and Shay spent most of that evening and the next couple of days sorting through the contents of the building, Andrea's former residence, and office. Every shelf, notebook, file cabinet, and storage container held paperwork for official town business. Dani and Shay noted anything they thought might lead to the fairy who would answer the whistle's song.
~~~~~~~~~~

The days turned into weeks and the weeks into months. I celebrated one year in the carriage house as the blacksmith of Bannock, and a few weeks later, Shay and I celebrated one year together, with the mystery of that alicorn whistle still haunting us.

~~~~~~~~~~

It was late one Thursday afternoon when the draft of the door opening forced a burst of air at the flame of the forge. Shay waited in my line of sight until I finished hammering the curve on a blade and returned it for reheating.

"Hello, love," she said, dropping her gear bag on the chair.

I turned around and waited for her arms to wrap around me. "Good day?" I asked, as she stepped back.

Her smile was an answer. "It was pretty good. D and I torched the tunnels near Brigid's cave and collected as much embryo material as possible."

"Why would you do that?"

Since Andrea's demise, the unhatched demon spawn had lain dormant on the tunnel walls. We'd wandered the mine back and forth, searching for clues about the mysterious fairy who would answer the whistle's call. If the creature remained trapped all this time, how could it still be alive?

"Dani and I wanted to clear out anything Andrea left behind."

"Any sign of our lost fairy?" I asked.

"Still nothing. The only place we have left is the loft the Mayor leased to Andrea."

"That's got to be it, right?" I walked around the back of the forge to cut the gas feeding the flame. "I'm surprised it's taken this long for you to check there."

"She had no next of kin, for obvious reasons, so the Mayor finally gave us full access to the building," Shay
~~~~~~~~~~

explained as she popped the top buttons on her shirt and slipped it over her head.

Dexter circled the two of us before flopping down in the scorched circle on the workshop floor.

"Are you going tonight?" I asked.

Shay tossed the shirt on top of her bag, ripped the velcro from the bulletproof vest, and set it on the table. Her uniform, every damn part of it, was appealing. She had my attention whether she was putting it on or taking it off.

"We aren't going tonight, no. We're both off duty tomorrow. Want to celebrate our anniversary in the dungeon of a demon?" She reached around my hip to tug my leather apron.

"Are you trying to woo me?"

Tiny lines formed in the corner of her eyes as she smiled with her entire face. "Is it working?" She pinched the clips on my shoulder and behind my back, releasing my apron, which fell to the floor.

"Darlin', you could woo me with cheddar cheese on a toothpick." I tugged her body closer.

"You're so easy."

We step-walked toward the apartment stairs. "We can spend our anniversary anywhere you want as long as we're together." I kissed her, and she hooked her arms under mine and carried me to the bottom step. "Do you think the answers are in the loft?"

"If they're not," Shay said with a sigh before setting me down so we could race up the stairs, "I don't know where we're going to look next."

~~~~~~~~~~~

"Stupid Andrea Peters," I mumbled.

Andrea's loft space was humorous in a frustrating way. For the property of a four-hundred-year-old half-demon, half-
~~~~~~~~~~~

human, the space was sparse. We'd expected to find thousands of books and journals, something–anything–that would explain how she'd kept her half-lives hidden for centuries. Instead, we found a space smaller than Dani's one-room cabin. The walls were bare, just like the tiny round table with a solitary chair. It was depressing even to me, and I had a *lot* of experience with confined living spaces.

"What the actual hell!" Dani pushed her hands against the wall.

She and Shay were in full uniform, as this was technically a BPD investigation, and I wondered when that expandable baton would come out to make a swing at the plastered wall. She'd spent most of the last few minutes pushing and pulling on anything that appeared anchored or not anchored to the walls.

"Where is the secret room?" She kicked the corner of the bathroom doorway. "Can't your dragon sniff it out?" She pointed at Dexter, who'd flopped himself in front of the balcony door.

"My dragon could, if there was something to sniff." The tone of Shay's voice was cool. I didn't understand why Dani's frustration continued to grow.

"Maybe she kept everything in the tunnels, and we can't find it," I said as I closed the cabinet door. The kitchen space– if you could call it that, with the tiny bar sink, a single electric cooktop element, and a dorm-sized refrigerator–was less than ideal, even for a half-human being.

"We've been in that mine for months. There's nothing." Dani's eyes focused on something out the glass-framed patio door.

"There's less than nothing now that we've destroyed the embryos." Shay kicked at the rug under the table.

We were standing in the second-story loft which prevented hidden staircases below us. And the lack of access to the ceiling left us trapped between vacant and empty.

"Where do we go from here?" I asked, watching Shay hold out her arms and close her eyes.

She was reading the energy of the space. Her fingers trembled, and I felt the pull of the Magick's ability to feel the interrupting presence of Andrea's power.

"It's a portal screen," Shay whispered, and I knew what that meant. The doorway in this loft was concealed. The wave of magick woke her senses, just as it had for me.

"*Secreta voca, ianuam, detege,*" Shay said.

The Latin tumbled in my head, and I stretched the limits of my knowledge to translate. She was summoning the hidden and unmasking a gateway, but a gateway to where? I stepped beside Shay and placed my right hand on the small of her back. If the Magick couldn't summon the path, perhaps the Magick and the Maker together could.

"Do you really think after all this time all you have to do is ask the door to open?" Dani's question was sarcastic, and the words fell hard against the weight of the room when an oval of dust and iridescent flakes spiraled in front of the glass panel doors.

"This is unbelievable." Shay held her hands toward the portal. "She had some serious power, and for years, she lived right under our noses."

"Don't." I grabbed Shay's wrist, clutching the protective cuff encircling it. I clenched tight enough to make her pause.

"We're going in there."

"You don't even know where *there* is!" I scolded.

"We do this for a living." Dani waved her hands in front of the portal, poking a finger into the swirling debris.

"I call bullshit," I said. "The two of you don't walk through spiraling portals for a living."

My arms snapped into a tight criss-cross in front of my chest. Yes, they were cops. They wore cop uniforms with belts that carried guns and tasers and normal crime-fighting gear.

They most definitely did *not* travel through mysterious circles of dirt for a living.

"Well, we kinda do," Shay said. "You've walked through Brigid's cave. That was like this. And we've traveled through space with the Rasavatam."

"Don't forget Dexter shifts us from place to place, kinda all the time, and he's really getting better at it," Dani reminded me.

I waved my hands in front of them, hoping they would stop talking. Standing in this room was not the time to relive the last twelve months of life in Bannock. Yes, we'd magicked our way around our tiny ghost town, Dexter could move each of us from places we'd been in the blink of an eye, and I had in fact moved through a flaming cave entrance to find the Hammer of Brigid, but this was different.

"Andrea Peters was something evil." I tried to persuade them that their view of the situation was horribly skewed. "She was—"

"We do evil," Dani interrupted.

"Well, we don't do, do it." Shay joked, swatting Dani on the shoulder with the back of her hand.

"Hey, I don't judge," Dani joked back.

"Stop it you two. This is serious. We're about to walk into…I don't even *know* what we're about to walk into!" My voice pitched higher as I realized just exactly how unknown the next few minutes would be.

"It's gonna be fine," Shay assured me.

She took a short step forward, and her leg disappeared through the gateway. Before I could say another word, her entire body faded from view. Dexter barked twice before leaping forward to follow Shay and Dani, going through behind them without hesitation.

The silence of the room was overwhelming.

"You going in?" Stout's voice broke my stunned stillness.

"Hell no, I'm not going in!" I yelled.

"The Magick will probably need the Maker in there." His wings snapped and flittered as he darted into the portal.

I stood alone, staring at the tiny shimmering debris spinning round and round in front of me. I reached forward, hesitant to touch it, when a hand jutted out, grabbed my wrist, and yanked my body through.

The way in was not quick. It felt like a tunnel in the mine, but this excursion tickled my skin as I drifted through. Tiny bursts of heat tapped my arms like baby bird beaks pecking at the earth. It was magick like no other, searching my body on a cellular level, determining if I had the right to enter.

My eyes stretched wide as I fell into the open space. Strong hands hooked beneath my arms, keeping me from falling to the floor.

"I've got you," Shay said, as my feet fumbled for a stronghold.

"That was weird," I admitted, surveying my body.

"Weird is right." Stout shimmied his wings. "That wasn't evil." His fairy hands slapped together as he knocked the dust from his body.

"What do you mean?" I asked, my hands clinging to Shay.

"You felt the magick; I know you did," Shay whispered against my head as she hugged me.

"I felt a lot of things. Most of all, you yanking me inside."

I took a moment to survey the space we were in. It was a cellar, much like the one that Benton created in the bar's basement, but this wasn't stone and brick. This was a single room built from rough-hewn timbers. Dexter was sniffing, side to side, back and forth, as he shuffled around the space. The floor was knotty pine, aged and stained from years of footfalls. I closed my eyes when I saw Dani standing beside the pile of boxes and books strewn haphazardly in the space.

"No more books!" I said with a laugh.

"So many books and files." Dani held up a pile of papers bound between two pieces of cardboard with twine bundling it all together.

"Are you demon fighters or librarians?" I joked because the seriousness was more than I could handle.

"Librarians are hot," Dani said just above a whisper.

"They sure are, especially when they have those dual points on their ears," Stout added, and the three of us stopped to stare at the hovering fairy.

"Wait, what?" I asked.

"Oh, did I say that out loud?"

"You sure did. Explain. And please do it without sharing your fairy kink." I was afraid to hear what he was about to share, but we knew so little about our friend who'd been on this planet for hundreds of years.

"It's not a kink," he said defensively. "I just find ears attractive. Especially the ears most librarians have in the fairy realm."

"That's sweet," Shay said as she stepped beside Dani. The two of them were about to untie the bundled pages.

"It's not a sex thing, though. Not like the two of you." He waved his hand pointing at Shay and me. "It's just…a thing. I can appreciate a gorgeous split ear when I see one, but I only want to see them."

I shook my head. I was pretty sure that my fairy companion was trying to explain more than I needed to know at this moment. "So, librarians not of the fairy kind, what are we looking at?" I asked as the twine fell from the bundled pages in Shay's hands to the table.

"This looks–"

"STOP!" I yelled.

"What?" Dani and Shay said at the same time and with the same tone of startled irritation in their voices.

"You're not just going to read that, are you?"

"Not since you've given the two of us heart attacks," Dani barked back. "Damn, Wildwood. Do we have to keep reminding you we do this every day?"

"Yes, yes, you do because I have to keep reminding you about the funny things that happen when Shay reads incantations and magickal history without researching it first!"

Shay sighed in annoyance. "If the two of you would stop. I was about to say that this is in Sanskrit, so I can't do anything with it now." She set the pile on the table and took two slow steps toward me. "Wil, hon. We've been looking for this place for months. We know a fair bit about Andrea and a tiny bit about Kai. This place is going to answer a lot of questions, and maybe it'll help us understand the dreams we've been having."

"Nightmares, really," Stout added. "You mean our nightmare demon in the box."

"Fine, but no reading without a proper circle and setup," I insisted.

"Circle and setup," Shay agreed, and she released my hand to return to the stack of papers.

"What about that?" Dani pointed to the split panel doors where the portal had been.

"It's the backside of the patio doors, right?" I asked. The sensation of passing through from the loft to this cellar seemed to split time and space. Was this a cellar in the loft? Or was the loft a part of this cellar?

"It could be. I've never passed through a portal. Have you, D?" Shay asked as she stepped closer to the split panel wall. She was about to open the doors. I just knew it. And as curious as I was to see what came next, I was also waiting for that other magickal shoe to drop.

"No, nothing like this," Dani said. "Andrea was something else."

"Understatement of the century," Stout grumbled, flittering to Shay's shoulder. "Can you feel magick behind there?"

"Can you?" Shay asked him.

"I can feel a lot of things rolling out of there, and not all of it is good."

"Is any of it?" I asked as I placed myself between Shay and Dani.

Stout flew to the pocket of Shay's uniform shirt and plucked at the alicorn whistle. "You should play that."

"Is there a fairy behind this wall?" Shay asked.

"There's only one way to find out," he said, landing on Shay's shoulder. "But yes, I'm almost certain there is."

Shay removed the tiny whistle from her pocket, and for the first time since finding it in the scorched remains of Andrea Peters' demon body, she held it to her lips. Shay hesitated, then puffed her cheeks.

"Blow it," Stout rasped.

I closed my eyes as the sound floated in the space between us.

"Open the wall, Shay," Stout said.

He flew to the cupped cutouts that looked like handles. I knew they weren't there before. Shay slipped the whistle back in her pocket and prepared to pull back the paneled doors. I was as excited as the rest of the beings in the room, but no one as much as Dexter, who was pawing and scratching at the floor in front of us.

"He says it's in there," Stout said, though he didn't need to.

Shay pulled hard but was met with resistance. The hinges rattled, and Dani stepped in to give it a tug. The doors didn't open. Dexter barked twice and sat, a clear sign we were exactly where we were meant to be.

"Let me try something." I tugged the fingerless glove from my sigil hand. "*Ignis*," I whispered, and the orange flame burst from my palm.

I waved it over the hinges, and the panel slid opposite to the direction the handles would pull. It was counterintuitive and a clever mask for whatever we were about to see. The energy of the Magick and the Maker rolled out like a wave, pulsing against my skin. There was so much goodness mixed in with the bitter taste of something evil.

"It's Kai," Shay said as she traced her finger over the first Maker's mark. The three primitive slashed lines formed the letter K, encompassed by a simple circle. It was definitely Kai's magickal space.

"I can feel her in here," I said, using my entire body to push the panel away.

Stout flew inside, behind the sliding panel, his wings battering against the glass. "Open it!" he yelled louder than I'd ever heard him before.

I stared, struck silent at the six-foot-wide glass enclosure. Stout was pushing against the grated top, anchored with a steel hook and eye fasteners. Forged by the Maker's hands, nothing could move them.

Nothing but the Maker herself.

Fasteners rusted with age held tight. Even as my thumb pushed against the eyelet, I couldn't help but pause and stare at the miniature ecosystem inside the flourishing terrarium. The front corner held a rounded piece of stone, covered in green moss. The floor of the glass enclosure was a patchwork of pebbles and green, with a tiny pool of water inches from an overturned clay dome. A frail fairy stood in the fractured archway, frozen in place, eyes wide with surprise.

Stout's face was smooshed against the glass as he yelled again, "Hurry! Open it!"

I worked the latches free, and seconds later, Dani and Shay lifted the heavy mesh cover. Stout darted beneath their hands and wrapped his arms and wings around the tiny creature. It collapsed against Stout's embrace.

"What the hell did we just do?" Dani asked as she tipped the metal cover to the floor.

"I think we found the lost fairy," Shay said.

Stout struggled to fly with the delicate creature in his arms, so Shay cupped the two of them in her palm. Stout fussed over the prone body, delicate compared to his stubby self. He spit in his palms and rubbed the mess across the fairy's face and wings.

We watched, stunned to silence by the two creatures in front of us. Stout was the third fairy I'd ever encountered and where I'd gained all of my limited knowledge of the fairy world. I was clueless about the mini ritual taking place before us.

"Any clue what's happening here?" Dani asked, and I sighed, glad that I wasn't the only one lost.

"Best guess, that fairy fainted at the sight of all of us after months alone?" Shay suggested.

Stout raised his eyes to us. "Do you have demon sift?"

Shay nodded and ripped the velcro on the pouch of her pants. "It's enough for a human wound, so this should be plenty for our new friend."

Dexter pushed his face through the gap between Shay and Dani, snorting and puffing his nose at Stout.

"Calm down, Dex," Stout said. "We just need the sift. The fairy is weak but alive."

I watched Stout kick the cap off the bottle and dig an arm inside until his hand gripped large flakes of demon anvil dust. He broke it into bits, like crumbling crackers into a bowl of soup. Then he hacked up two lumps of spit, stirred the ingredients into a paste, and, without taking a breath between, smeared it over the frail body beside him.

"I know!" Stout yelled at the huffing sounds coming from Dexter.

"What are you doing?" I kneeled closer to the fairies.

"This fairy is in shock," he explained. "Maybe a little magick deprived to boot. And Dexter thinks we need more magick than I'm capable of."

"What kind of Magick?" Shay asked, and I felt her hand close around my own.

"Yours," Stout whispered.

A heartbeat later, Shay's sigil hand burst with flame, and Latin words I didn't understand fell from her lips. Dexter's snout touched our clasped palms, and the three of us released a delicate trail of earth energy that cycled through the loft and tangled around the prone fairy. Stout jumped to his feet and hovered beside the fairy as it floated from the terrarium table's surface.

I've lived in Bannock for one year, and in that time, I've found my childhood crush and wooed her into becoming my partner for life, turned my welding and blacksmith talents into a thriving business, and found a family with Dani and Amelia. We've even added a dragon-dog and a beer-loving fairy to our happy–if unconventional–life. I've experienced the unbelievable, but watching the lace-thin eyes of our fairy prisoner flick open was just about the purest, most life-affirming moment I'd experienced to date. The pale hue of their skin darkened into a rich green, and the slow, almost absent breaths began to raise and lower the miniature chest.

The fairy jerked upright, and Stout was there, tiny hands closing around even tinier ones.

"It's okay," he said. "You're safe with me. With us."

The fairy made squeaking sounds, and Dexter pushed his nose close enough for the fairy to touch.

"Dexter. His name is Dexter."

The fairy's eyes widened with surprise, and I wondered what exchange of information was happening before us.

Stout looked up at Shay. "Her name is Clia. It's short for something, but she won't say."

"Why is she here?" Shay asked.

The sound of fairy language passed between them, and we watched the animated story rise from her strengthening body. Stout waved his hands, gesturing for her to slow down so he could relay the story.

"She belonged to Kai." Stout's tone was sharp. "And when the demon took the Legacy, Clia was enslaved by Andrea Peters and the demon that scarred her soul."

CHAPTER III

HEREDITAMENT

"She's been a prisoner for hundreds of years?" I asked.

Clia's eyes widened before welling with tears and Stout's head snapped toward me. "She—"

Our new fairy friend interrupted Stout, sharing scrambled sounds and animated expressions with him. Her delicate hands and arms flailed with fantastic storytelling as Dani, Shay, and I stared in awe. Dexter's butt dropped, and his paws held his upper body in place so he was as close to the conversation as anyone could be.

"She says Kai was her mother. Her human life-light," Stout explained. "She was not a prisoner to the Magick, but she was a vassal to the keeper."

Without warning, Clia pushed off the tabletop and darted toward the terrarium. Her wing flutter was nothing like the spoke-flicking sound of Stout's. Hers sounded like a whistle through the leaves of trees on a warm summer night, delicate and melodic.

She disappeared behind a sizable, feathered fern and reappeared with a tattered piece of fabric and a round bundle tied in a knot. My immediate guess was she was packing to fly away with us, but when the bundle dropped to the tabletop, it sounded rock hard. Her fairy hands moved over the bundle, and the knots were old, as was the object inside. She whispered words still foreign to my ears, and when the cloth corners fell away, a blinding light flashed, filling the room.

I felt the sigil fire burn in my palm, and Shay grabbed hold to connect her flame with mine. There was no heat, just a hypnotic voice.

"*Elot-too-igot ee, elot-too-igot ee.*" It was like a song, the voice of magick releasing a barrier long held.

"Can you feel it?" Shay whispered in my ear.

I could feel it, the power of the earth trembling beneath my feet and rising through my body to vibrate in my palm, the same palm Shay was clenching.

"What is she doing, Stout?" Shay asked, standing protectively in front of me and tugging Dexter's collar.

"She's telling you a story."

It happened, the flash of light and the shift of beings into a space so much like the safe bubble created by the spell workings of the Rasavatam. Our new fairy must also have been some form of a witch. I thought about it, wondering, was that even possible? My one year of experience with all things magickal did not include extensive knowledge about the inner world of fairies.

Clia's voice broke through the wave of magick. "Sister witch." She was looking at Shay, waving her to come closer. "My soul aches with joy. Blessed be."

"Can you hear her?" I whispered to Shay through clenched teeth.

"Can you?" She whispered back, never taking her eyes off the fairy in front of us.

"Did you cast the Rasavatam?" I lifted my sigil hand to reveal the flame, and the petite fairy flittered close to my fingertips, her eyes opening wide like bright white saucers.

"You can not be," she told me.

She dropped to my middle finger and stepped through the orange flame, stopping on the origin point of my sigil. Her wings disappeared in the flame, and for a moment, I thought she was ending her fairy life. My flame flashed, and Clia rubbed the surface of her body, bathing in the fire.

"Is this weird?" I asked Shay.

"You've got a four-hundred-year-old fairy taking a fire shower in your hand," Shay said. "It's odd, at the very least."

Clia's naked feet walked the sigil lines in my hand. "What are you?" she asked.

The fairy flicked into the air as I swiped my hand to point at my chest. "What am I? What the heck are you?"

"And how are you talking to us?" Shay asked.

Dexter snorted, and a puff of smoke floated from his nose. Clia put her hands on her hips and yelled at our K-9, "I'm getting to it. Give me a second. I've been alone for a long time, dragon."

"You belonged to Kai?" Shay asked, ignoring the argument between Dexter and the fairy.

"I didn't belong to her. We belonged to each other." Clia flew to Shay's hand, guiding it up so that the two of us were holding our sigil palms side by side. "You have a flame too?"

"*Ignis*," Shay spoke, and the blue flame sparked to life.

"Two become one?" The fairy hovered beside the flames. "You cannot be?"

"Heard that before," I said. "And yet here we are."

"You mixed the blood of the Magick with the Maker… and lived." Clia walked through Shay's ignis flame, lingering long enough to absorb the magic inside. Her feet clenched a knife wound scar, and the flame disappeared as Shay's arm recoiled to her chest. "Don't."

"But my dear one, they make your existence a thousand times more beautiful," the fairy explained. Her delicate eyelids closed, and I could feel the energy exchange between my lover and Clia. The fairy recoiled over and over, like strikes to her own body, until I lost count of the jerking motion. "Fourteen?"

Shay's eyes widened. "How could you know?"

Shay had fourteen scars on her body from a knife attack when she was in foster care. Magick she couldn't control went wrong, the consequences of which were the jagged marks on her arms and torso. She hid them from me for weeks, until one night when I walked in on her getting ready to shower. Our lives changed that moment, her trust in me and mine in her, and we rarely spoke about it now. Her body was beautiful, scars and all, but how could this creature know?

"They're connected," Clia explained. "Every mark on your skin is touched by the Magick's power. It's like a web. But this one..." She flew to Shay's torso and hovered her hands over the abdominal scar. The wound that my lover had protected with ferocity before we met lay beneath. "This wound is something special."

Shay jumped back, breaking the bubble created by the Rasavatam magick. The fairy's voice returned to the dialect that we didn't understand.

"Damn it!" Shay yelled, swiping nervously at the marks on her arm.

"What the hell was all of that?" I asked.

Stout buzzed around me. "What did you say to her?"

Clia collapsed, slumped over her knees, resting on the table with her hands tight over her face.

"I didn't say anything!" Shay yelled. "My scars fascinated her."

"Yes, they would. Because they're beautiful." I said.

Shay shook her head. "They've never been that to me. No matter how many times you say they're beautiful, I see the mistakes. I see what I did out of desperation."

"We do a lot of things for survival." Stout dropped in front of the glass terrarium wall. "Clia has lived in this cage for hundreds of years. I can't imagine what she's done, and yet she saw your beautiful magick first, not your scars. Listen to me, Shay. Clia has the answers we need to figure out the dreams."

"How are we going to get those answers when the only time we understand her is inside the Tome of Trouble bubble?" I asked.

Shay's hand covered my mouth. "No, love, we're not referring to that spell as the 'trouble bubble.'"

"Bu– –at'so muh– be'er!" I said through the muffle of her hand.

Shay was correct. I enjoyed quirky names to reference our magick creations and adventures, like my punch dagger, which once had an identical blade made for Shay. Forged from the demon steel of my first demon encounter, the Dagger of Doom held the power to flame and destroy just about everything. It also scared the crap out of me before I understood my magick and Shay's. I enjoyed calling the Rasavatam the Tome of Trouble, but in my defense, every time we used the book of legacy spells, shit got real, and sometimes our world tilted toward chaos.

I turned my mouth away from Shay's hand. "Baby, what's our next move?"

"Stout?" Shay asked our fairy who'd disappeared with Clia inside the glass walls of the terrarium.

Seconds later, we watched the two of them roll around in the moss-covered rocks and spit into the curved surface of a stone positioned in the center of the terrarium. Stout spit first, and Clia spit next. Her fairy spit didn't amount to much at first, so Stout spit again. I thought about the months Stout had survived trapped in limbo after Benton's death. Clia must need a beer or two.

The fairies slapped their hands together like children acting out games on a playground. Clia rolled over and over in the evaporating spit combination, and with the force of a bottle rocket, she sprang from the tank and flew to Shay. Her petite fairy body twirled in front of us, and one by one, she touched our foreheads. I felt the magick move through my face, tickling my ears. She stopped to hover in front of Shay.

"You wish to speak with the fairies?" Clia asked.

A jaw-dropping silence followed as each of us waited for more words to come. The sound was like a miracle, if miracles had audible expressions.

"Yes," Shay said.

It was all I could do to nod and stay present as the creature spoke. "It has been a very long time since I've been in the presence of the Magick. What would you ask of me?"

I looked at Dani and wondered if she was under the same euphoric spell as I.

"Tell us how you are here?" Shay asked.

"Perhaps you should sit." Before we could reach for furniture, Clia waved her hands; a wall panel opened, and two chairs slid across the floor. The first knocked Dani against her calves and popped her in the seat. The second stopped short of touching Shay. "Powerful," Clia said.

"Very powerful," Stout confirmed.

Shay pulled the chair between us and sat, slapping her lap to invite me to sit in the circle of her arms. It didn't feel like a power play between the fairy and the Magick, but maybe it was.

"Tell us," Shay said as her hand rested on my hip.

"It has been so very many years since I lived this tale, and every day between has been suffering like nothing else."

She hovered in front of us. "My life and my magicks were bound to the hybrid. Kai was my human life-light."

"What does that mean?" Shay asked.

"Show me your flame, Magick?" Clia asked.

Shay raised her palm. "*Ignis*," she whispered, and the blue flame burst through.

"Your life-light is not accidental. It comes from deep-rooted power. It is the bloodline of your ancestors." Clia stood in the burst of fire, letting it flow over her. "Kai's life-light was blue as well. I can feel her inside of you."

Shay hefted her palm, knocking the fairy away. It had been months since our fight with Andrea and the demon that took what remained of Kai. Shay still struggled, even though she thought she'd kept it hidden; her dreams woke me in the middle of the night. I wouldn't call them nightmares because Shay never left the dream world, but something happened to her the day her punch dagger disappeared inside the Gatekeeper of the mine.

"Kai was the first Magick," Shay said.

"And the first Maker," I added.

"The power was strong, and so was she," Clia explained. "But the demon inside the goddess is stronger."

My brain processed one word in that sentence, and it was the present tense use of the word "is." The delicate green fairy didn't say it *was* strong; she said it *is*. And that sent a wake-up call on a cellular level.

"You're talking about the hammer, aren't you?" Stout asked as he flew to hover beside Shay.

Clia nodded. "He's seductive. I watched him change her, and there was nothing I could do."

Dani spoke up, then. "Maybe we should finish going through this cabin. I don't like the energies I feel in here."

Shay turned her hand and placed it in mine before clutching the scruff of fur around Dexter's collar. Her eyes closed, and I felt the vibration moving through the two of us.

"What do you feel?" I thought.

Her voice was in my head as we communicated through the Rasavatam magicks. *"I feel a lot of things, and some of them aren't very good."*

"I feel that too," I thought.

"It's not safe to bring any of this magick, as it is, to the carriage house," Shay said, and I agreed. Her hand fell away, and the magick separated.

"What was that all about?" Dani asked. "You two just checked out."

"It's a Magick and Maker thing we've been working on," Shay explained. "Here's what I'm thinking. We should spread out and each take a pile and sort through it. If you think we need to take something, I'll put a bind on it and wipe away any magicks Andrea might have left behind."

"You think it'll be that easy?" Dani asked.

"We're connected, and Andrea has been gone for so long, I'm almost certain any barrier she had inside this space will be easier to undo."

"If that's the case, how do you explain the portal and the mask that exists between the loft and the cabin?" Dani asked.

I'd been wondering about that myself. If the power of Andrea and the Keeper was truly gone, how was her cabin still hidden?

"I don't have that answer," Shay said as she picked up a stack of papers. "I'm hoping something in here will tell us."

<center>~~~~~~~~~~</center>

"I can't read any more of this," I said as I tied the loose pages back into their bundle.

There was one difference between sorting through Andrea's loft and Benton's cellar, and it wasn't an extraordinary sense of organization. It was having a second fairy translator to decipher the pages and folders stuffed with cryptic papers. Our former Assistant Mayor kept records of everything that happened in Bannock from the moment they stole the land from the Indigenous people. Kai was bound to Bannock by the power of the hammer, and year after year of her long life, she watched the people come and the grasses of the prairies disappear.

"If I was her, I'd be pissed, too." I slapped the bundle of paper.

"I wish we could undo it," Dani said.

"The past is our present," Shay said as she dropped her notebook on top of a storage box. "Kai knew she was losing control."

"She was alone with her magicks," Clia said with the most reverent tone. I could feel the adoration. "When she struck her mark to Brigid's Hammer, that collision of good and evil changed everything."

"The demon took hold?" I asked.

"It lured her, dragged her into an evil place, and she never came back to me." The fairy flew to the glass panel of the terrarium. "That hateful thing extinguished my human life-light and locked me inside. Without a care for the trap that was set, I flew right in there, and she never let me out."

My finger traveled across the top of the enclosure, and I stopped to take in the space that had held our new friend for so long. There was a stripe of water that I'd call a river if four pieces of glass did not contain it. The log she called home was no bigger than a loaf of bread. I couldn't see what was inside, but I hoped there was some kind of fairy bed for her to rest her head. What mystified me more, though, was the plant life thriving inside. It was like a miniature rainforest that had somehow kept Clia fed and watered for hundreds of years.

"A lot has changed," I said to her as she kicked over rocks and pieces of bark.

"Not for me," she whispered, and the hollow tone broke my heart.

"Especially for you." Shay held her palm to the fairy, inviting her to leave the terrarium prison. "You can come with us."

"Just like that?" Stout interrupted with his hands planted on his hips.

Shay stared at him. "Yes, just like that."

"You're not going to make her take an oath or swear fealty?"

"He's got a point," I whispered. "What if she's bound to the demon in Andrea?"

I heard the snap of wings before I felt the silent whip of them fluttering. Clia ripped a wave of magick as her voice tumbled Stout across the room. "I'm bound to the Maker and to the Magick. The only way to break that connection is with the song of Monoceros."

Shay reached in her pocket and held out the alicorn whistle. "This?"

Clia's eyes went wide, practically disappearing into her face, just before the fairy fell to the pebbled floor of her greenery-filled prison.

CHAPTER IV

DISPLACED

"That's always going to be gross." I whispered to Shay as Stout smeared his clumpy spit beneath Clia's nose.

As nasty as that was, though, another thought was preoccupying my mind: what trauma had the tiny unicorn whistle dredged up for our new friend?

"She's waking up," Stout said.

"Pierce, we need to get out of here," Dani urged as she dropped her files inside the box. "Elemental energies are out of whack in this cabin, and they're growing."

"I'm pretty sure it's the presence of the Magick and the Maker," I said.

"I'm positive that it is," Shay confirmed. "If you think about what Andrea was doing here–how long she was festering with that Keeper inside of her–there's no telling what kind of evil we're standing amongst."

"And what she's had to endure." I pointed to the glass enclosure where Stout held his new friend.

"Should we contain her?" Dani asked, slipping the lid onto the file storage box.

"I'll talk to her when she's awake."

We finished sorting through the loft space. It was no surprise that Shay wanted to take every tome in the room, but there were more than we could carry, so she settled on the Sanskrit texts and cast protections on each book before taking them from the loft. By the time Shay completed her spell work, Stout had Clia bundled in a scrap of fabric, and we decided this wrap would keep her contained until we returned to the carriage house. As much as Shay hated to bind the fairy, she wasn't willing to risk the safety of this family.

Dani grasped the door handle. "Do you think we can just walk out this door?" She twisted the knob.

"Maybe we should go back through the portal," I suggested, holding a hand out to Stout so he could set our new fairy onto my palm.

Shay being Shay, she stood beside Dani with Dexter tight to her hip. Dani released the handle, and Shay's fingertips passed over the worn brushed copper knob.

"Feels like magick." Before I could reiterate what a terrible idea it was to use that door, Shay twisted the handle and pulled it open. We were no longer standing in the space of Andrea's cellar lair but in the second-story loft.

"Well, that's kinda cool." Dani waved her fingers in front of her face, checking that all of her had made it back in solid form.

"Very cool," Shay whispered as her hand reached through the disorienting loft space stitched together with the cellar. "Hand us the boxes, Wil." My mouth was wide from more than shock, and she smiled at my hesitation. "Wil?"

"Yeah, I just...What the hell is this magick?"

"It's the transcript'd power of the Ra-sa-va-tam," Clia explained, with a heavy accent on each syllable. "It's clear that you have the ancient text and know its power."

I looked at Shay, and she stared at the fairy bundled tight in Stout's arms, the two resting in my palm.

"We're learning," Shay explained.

"You're learning fast," the fairy said as she relaxed against Stout. "I can help you understand the magicks inside those boxes."

Shay didn't say a word as I set the fairies on the table and passed Andrea's archives to Dani. We were making a lot of promises at the moment and trusting a creature that we had every reason to suspect would bury us in the evil that had possessed the former hybrid, Kai.

Our exit through the door didn't have the stimulating pecks and pinches against my skin I'd experience upon entry, and I was happy about the change. If we had to return to this cabin in the future, I hoped Shay would alter the portal passageways.

I carried our fairies like precious cargo as we passed from Clia's prison cage in the cellar into the modern space of the loft. Her fairy eyes dilated as they swiveled to take in the surroundings. Her excitement made me dizzy, and there was no way to make what she was seeing make sense after four hundred years of terrarium life. We had a lot to explain.

As we exited the building, Shay activated the side door of her K-9 unit vehicle, and Dexter leaped inside. I set Stout on the pass-through ledge, and he held tight to Clia.

"You got her?" I asked.

"We'll fit here as long as Red takes it easy on the drive."

"Stout!" I yelled at him. He knew Shay didn't like the nickname. "One of these days she's going to slap the shit out of you."

"Not today, though." He laughed.

"Probably not," I said as the door on the rear of the patrol car slammed.

"Everyone ready to go?" Shay asked as she stretched the belt across her shoulder and locked it into place.

"So far, so good," I said and stared at our fairy to keep silent. "Clia is going to need a lot of help," I whispered as I reached to hold Shay's hand. I felt the life-force rush of energy pass between us when her fingers tightened on my own. "She missed everything. This land wasn't colonized when Kai was her Magick and Maker self."

"I can't imagine what it was like for her this entire time, trapped inside a glass cage with no one to care about her." Shay raised her shoulder to shrug away a tear. She was silent for a long moment, thinking I'm sure, like I was, about what to do with everything that had happened in the last few hours. "Before we work on Andrea's archive, we have to be certain our new fairy feels safe and free."

I turned to stare at the group in the gated space of the K-9 SUV. Stout and Clia were whispering back and forth. Her wide-eyed gaze as she pointed at the flickering dashboard and the modern elements of the car's interior was charming.

"I'm not sure that'll be easy," I said.

"Baby, we can do easy. I know we haven't had many opportunities in this last year, but maybe, just this once, we can ease Clia into the modern world."

I was skeptical of Shay's optimism because complicated seemed to be how everything happened for the Magick and the Maker. But I wanted to believe. I honestly did.

The drive was typical winding back roads, and as we hit the city limits, our new fairy friend perked up.

"Take it easy," Stout grumbled as Clia struggled to escape the fabric wrapped around her.

"Where are we?" she asked, her tiny fingers threaded through the patrol car's dividing grate so she could look out the windshield.

"This is where we live," Shay said, and I smiled at the word "we."

This was our home, our carriage house, where the two of us lived and thrived and were making a life together for however long the Magick and Maker legacy kept us alive.

"Soft feet on hallowed ground," Clia whispered, and I turned my head to look at her.

"What did you just say?" I asked.

"Your house is built on hallowed ground." She closed her eyes, and I felt the pulsing sensation of the Rasavatam unite us. "The book of books is inside your home. It isn't wise to leave it."

Shay's hand wrapped around my own. "We are tied to the magick," she said. "No one can touch it."

"Kai thought that, too," Clia said with a sigh. "And yet here we are, lost in the wake of the evil that understood how to manipulate that tome."

"Is it all fairies?" I asked. Stout and Clia had a way of sharing facts about our past that scared the magick right out of my soul.

Clia tilted her head at me, confusion and, perhaps, curiosity written over her mini green face. "Is it all fairies, what?"

"She's wondering if every fairy shares the past in fractured little pieces." Stout helped Clia to her feet as Shay whispered words in Latin to release the binding wrap from her.

"It's not my intention to do that." Her wings spread from her body as the fabric wrap fell away.

"How does the Rasavatam and our carriage house create a sacred space?" Shay asked.

"That's the easiest question you've asked." Clia slipped through the diamond-shaped dividing grate that separated the kennel partition of the K-9 patrol car from the front seat. She floated between Shay and me to land on the control panel mounted to the dashboard. "Your magick is life. The Rasavatam roots your living magick to the elements and connects you to everything."

"Everything?" I asked.

How was that even possible? Innocence connected Shay and me to each other, sure, but magick that we didn't understand when we were fifteen years old, and now somehow connected us on an infinite level? My eyes closed, and in my head, it sounded like two doors slamming shut.

"Baby." Shay cupped my cheek, and my head relaxed into the touch. "It's just a word. You know you've felt what that book can do, and we understand the Tome of Trouble more than we ever have. We've got this."

"We've got this" had become the catchphrase of catchphrases for the Magick and the Maker. Shay and I didn't stumble through ignorance towards magick darkness very much anymore. We were better able to see it coming now.

"The Tome of Trouble will always make me nervous," I admitted. "It's like a loaded gun, and you know how I feel about those."

Shay adjusted the duty belt around her waist, placing her palm against her holstered service weapon. "I know exactly how you feel, but we've—"

I placed a finger against her lips. "We've got this, I know. But we've also got a traumatized fairy that knows that book better than you and me, and that might be the unknown that's freaking me out."

"You don't need to worry about Clia," Stout piped up. "She's bound the same way I am. We couldn't hurt you even if Andrea came back and demanded it."

My head whipped around to glare at the fairy. "That's not funny." My voice, fueled by his casual remark and triggered by fear, came out louder than I wanted.

"I didn't mean it to be funny. I was trying to prove a point," Stout said.

"We have a rule, Clia," Shay said. "The same rule we gave Stout when we brought him into the carriage house. If you want to be a member of this family, you must swear to protect us, just as Stout did."

The frail fairy rested on the dashboard, her prehensile feet tipping the switch that controlled the hazard lights. Stout had the same ability to use his toes, and I wondered if this was a trait every fairy possessed. It seemed useful either way.

"I am tasked to serve the Magick and the Maker," Clia said. "There is no duty I would rather hold, but the demon that trapped me has lingering magick that I cannot release on my own." She smiled sadly. "I can serve only one, and as long as the alicorn sings the old song, I cannot swear fealty to another."

I reached for the whistle in Shay's front pocket. Until this moment, we hadn't played it. I held it to my lips, placed my fingertips over each hole, and blew a quick puff of air into the tapered mouthpiece. The sound was impossible to my ears and a gorgeous vision to my eyes. Music wasn't something I paid attention to. It was background noise to keep me company most days at the forge, but the joyous sound flying from this carved horn of a unicorn was pure, unencumbered, delicately inspiring magick.

Clia froze in her seated position, and I couldn't tell what effect the sound had. She didn't cover her ears or hide from the music. I wondered if she was happy or sad.

"It has been so long," Clia said as her body hovered above the dashboard and floated close to my hand. She stepped across my fingers. "Play it again, will you please?" Her smile was so wide it filled her face.

I held the whistle to my lips again, and this time I played a song. It was more like a kazoo style humming than a flute's tremble, but the fairy danced in the air for as long as I played.

"Is that what you wanted?" Shay asked.

Clia's smile was the perfect response. "Oh, yes. It has been so long since the song made me dance. Evil lips cannot make melodies for a fairy to dance to."

"We should go inside," Shay said, her head darting back and forth. She was probably checking to see if anyone was watching the fairy dance on the front dashboard of a Bannock Police car. She was right. It would be difficult to explain to a tourist.

"Are you ready to see the inside of our home?" I held a hand out to Clia, and she walked into my gloved palm.

"You cover your mark. Is it still dangerous to be a witch?" she asked.

I looked at Shay, and she replied, "It isn't like the old days. Not like you'd remember them. No one hunts us because of our religion."

"But they hunt you?"

"Not as such. We live together, we love together, and as far as we know, the only thing hunting us comes from the demon Andrea answered to," Shay explained. "But it wasn't always like that."

I didn't like the word "hunt," or the idea of being hunted, but I guess as far as history goes, society hadn't been kind to practitioners like Shay and me.

As I exited the patrol car and approached the bright orange door of the carriage house, Clia began, "That is how the Rasavatam came to–" She paused mid-sentence when her eyes took in the space of my workshop. Clia's wings spread open as she flew to land on the anvil. Her tiny toes trampled across the top, and she kneeled to press her hands against the cold metal. "Your Maker powers are like an elixir."

I stood in the workshop, Shay close to my side as Stout and Dexter approached the fairy who was now prone on the anvil's face.

"When I came to live with Kai, she understood my fear of iron ore. It kills the fairy soul from the outside in," Clia explained. "The book of books has the Spell of Aversiveness. So Kai blessed me with an affection for a smith's work. This is the closest I've been to her in hundreds of years." Her body trembled, and her tears pooled on the cold metal.

"That magick was part of Benton's arsenal, too," Stout said as he buzzed to sit beside Clia. "It is most uncommon for our kind to be near the ore, and yet we are bound to the Maker. The Rasavatam cuts the 'irony' out of our situation."

The fairies laughed at their shared experience, and I stopped to think about what they'd said. I'd filled the workshop with every kind of metal you could think of. It was my job to fuse it, mold it, shape it, and make it into something we could use to change the world. But Kai, in her solitude, was so much more than the simple metalsmith of Bannock, forging tools in a small mining village. She was my sister in creation, single-handedly scripting powers and holding her own. My first and possibly my only connection to an unknown magickaly seeped past.

Clia pushed away from Stout and continued to survey the carriage house workshop. She hovered over the grinder and the casting cart. Her wings flittered as she dangled near my hammers and tongs. "You work here." She pointed at me.

"Every day, yes," I said, not hiding my pride.

"It is excellent work." She followed Dexter with her eyes and gasped when the massive German Shepherd dropped inside the sacred circle. "*Monstroum!*" she screamed in a pitch so high I had to cover my ears.

Shay was confused. "Dexter is not a monster."

"Not the dragon," Clia clarified, flying over to Dexter. "The circle he occupies."

The ring in concrete was a sacred space for Shay, Dexter, and me. We cast our most powerful Magick's in that circle, always aware that there was one massive Gatekeeper demon buried beneath.

Through clenched teeth, I whispered, "She's referring to the Gate—"

"I know what she's referring to," Shay interrupted. "But I also know the monster is gone. I made it go, and it's never coming back."

"You should not have buried it here," Clia said solemnly.

I walked to the candleholder on the pedestal and handed it to Shay. She whispered the flame to life, then held my hand, and together, we stood inside the ring. The walls of the carriage house came to life with the scrawling runes and maps painted by our beer loving fairy. Clia hovered, spinning slowly as she took in the brilliant sight. There was nothing left of the evil that the Gatekeeper had brought to our home over a year ago.

"By the goddess," the fairy said as she laid her hands against the brick-and-mortar wall. "The book of books. Who put this here?"

"I did." Stout landed on the empty candle stand. "My Magick was losing her, and..." He paused to clear his throat, fighting his emotions. "Kai was fading, and she needed to pass the legacy on to the next."

"A warrior," Clia whispered, not as a question but as an affirmation.

Shay swiped her tears with the back of her hand. "She was so much more than that."

"So your Magick was also a friend to this Magick." She pointed to Shay.

"Yes," Stout and Shay replied together.

"How many have there been?" Clia asked.

I answered her question with another question. "Magick and Maker practitioners?"

"Yes."

I left the center of the circle, and the illumination faded as I climbed the stairs to the apartment to retrieve the ancestry scroll. The aged parchment was attached tightly to the weathered bone, and I took the stairs two steps at a time to return to the workshop. Shay was clearing my project from the tabletop when I set the scroll on the table.

"She won't be able to read that," Stout grumbled as I anchored the end of the scroll with a piece of scrap steel.

"Right, it's masked." I tapped my fingers against my forehead.

"She also knows the Rasavatam." Shay's fingers tripped the tumbling bone across the tabletop.

"What do you see, Clia?" I asked.

The silence was heartbreaking as she crumbled on the primitively slashed Maker's mark. This belonged to Kai, and it was clear from Clia's reaction that she could read the history of our ancestors.

"She was more than you will ever understand. More than one human had any right to be," Clia said.

I nodded in agreement. "I've seen her."

"She came to you?" Clia asked.

"Not like she was in person, but I had visions of her and the earth energies she possessed."

"She was of the motherland, like you," the fairy explained, pointing at me.

I shook my head and looked at Shay, questioning. "What does that mean?"

"Indigenous," Stout explained.

"Wait, what?" I stumbled. Shay was quick to find a chair and help me into it. I was a child from nowhere. Abandoned at birth with no place to call home and no people to call my own.

"What are you saying, Clia?" Shay asked, her hand still tight on my shoulder.

"You must have known." The fairy spoke without accusation.

"I'm an orphan, a child of no-one," I said in a whisper.

The fairy flew to my sigil hand. "You are of the legacy. You are an ancient soul that came before all that is."

I didn't know what she was saying. Every word that came after "Indigenous" was a white noise hum to my ears. I could sense the conversation around me, but I was lost in the feeling of belonging for the first time in almost thirty years of not knowing.

I stared at my hands–the hands of a working woman, the hands that loved Shay with the most intimate of touches. My skin color had meant nothing to me. My history wasn't even a faded memory, and yet this sprite of a stranger had just turned a blank page to reveal something I once could only dream of being: part of something.

I felt hands rub against the seams of my jeans as Shay called my name. "Wildwood, love."

"The earth really is my mother," I whispered as tears dripped from my chin.

CHAPTER V

AUTOCHTHONOUS

"It's a lot," Shay whispered as my body trembled in her arms.

We lay together in the warmth of our bed. It was well after sunset, and although my hair was wet, I remember little after kicking out of my jeans and stepping into the shower. Shay was my guide, my North star, and as she held me, nothing felt more true.

"Something has always connected me to Kai," I said, still pressing tight against Shay's body.

"You are connected to Kai in ways that we never knew, and I'm so happy that you have that answer after all of this time."

"What do you think it means?" I asked, twirling my finger in the sweep of Shay's hair.

"I'm not sure," she admitted. "It doesn't change much. Without a name or a place to start, it's just an explanation for your gorgeous eyes, this magnificent hair, and the contrast of your skin against mine when I lay beside you."

"You're really talented at helping me see that life can be an adventure."

Her arms squeezed tight. "I have wanted for little, ya know." She cleared her throat, and I felt the tremble of seriousness in her body language. "Foster care left more than physical scars for me, and it's always been comforting that you and I had similar origins. But now…"

She paused, and I pushed back so I could look into her eyes. "But now, what?" I asked.

"Now you have a chance to find your family."

I crawled to my knees to straddle Shay's legs and rest on her thighs. "You are my family." I touched her chin. "You are the only family that I'll ever need."

"But you've looked."

I shook my head. "I looked a long time ago. Then I found the only answer that I will ever need, and that's you. You, Shay Pierce, are my family. You have always been my family, and you will always be."

"But you should find out."

I took hold of her hands. "Why?" I asked but didn't let her answer. "They let me go. Whoever brought me into this world didn't want me, and I've let that go."

"Can you honestly do that?" Shay asked, and the tears that followed were the first signs of insecurity I'd seen in my lover since the night I saw her scars for the first time.

"It's just you and me," I said with complete confidence and honesty. "However I got here, I'm grateful, but there is no love out there."

"But what if we could—"

"Waste our happiness on a dream from childhood instead of living for the now?" I interrupted.

She smiled. "When you put it that way it sounds different."

I kissed her chastely, then pulled back. "We have always been different, you and I. Long before the Legacy of the Maker, long before this mark." I held my palm to her and whispered, "*Ignis.*" She did the same, and I pressed my fire against hers. The powerful flame that surged between us was more than magick. "It's you and me, baby."

"You and me," she repeated. "I like that."

"And Dexter," I added.

"And Stout." She smiled. "And I guess Clia, too, now."

"You see." I reached for the hem of her shirt. "I already have a family."

Her chin tipped, revealing the pale skin of her throat as the collar of her shirt lifted over her head. "You have some thoughts, my love?"

"I have many thoughts," I said against the softness of her lips.

~~~~~~~~~~

"No," I mumbled against the warmth of her tight belly as the synthesized beeping of the alarm clock woke me from a night of dreamless sleep.

"Yes, baby."

I used what little weight advantage I had to keep her beneath me, but she was stronger and motivated to arrive at work on time. "No fair." I pouted as my head flopped to the mattress.

"You had me all night and into the morning, and if you want, you can have me tonight when I get home."

"*If* I want?" I propped my head up on my palm as I watched her pull a bra over her head. Aside from the unclothed Shay, I was particularly fond of superhero Shay. As she kicked into her pressed uniform pants, I wasn't shy about adoring her. "Oh, I most definitely want."
~~~~~~~~~~

"Good." She ripped the velcro of her vest apart and slipped it over her t-shirt. "You want to have some coffee with me?"

"Does it involve me getting out of bed?" I asked and didn't hide my tongue traveling across my lips as she snugged the buttons on her shirt.

"Yes, and it also involves you putting on a shirt." She tossed the wad of clothes at me as she sat down to lace her boots.

"Right, we have a family of fairies out there."

She looked up, smiling at me. "Thank you for last night." Her head tipped down, focusing a little too much on shoe tying. "I'm not sure where that came from."

"We're together, Shay. You and me, baby." I kicked my feet up, still laying on my belly but revealing my completely naked body. When she looked at me, I saw temptation, and even as she stood to leave, that look was enough, for now.

When I came into the kitchen, she was checking the charge on her taser and locking it into her duty belt. Then she tucked a compact knife into her boot. The absence of her punch dagger was obvious, and I wondered if it weighed on her.

"You miss the dagger?" I asked.

Her head bobbed. "It feels weird, putting this around my ankle."

I left the kitchen to retrieve my latest creation for her. The blade was lighter than the original, made from a combination of demon steel and forged with the hammer of the goddess.

"It's not blessed yet, but I made you a new one. It's just like the old blade, and maybe you could try not to punch this one clean through a demon's throat."

"It's beautiful." Shay gripped the handle, adjusting it to fit in her fist. "Gosh, Wil, this is a wonderful surprise!"

"Happy anniversary," I said, pushing the dagger away with two fingers so I could move into her arms and kiss her cheek.

"It seems appropriate for the two of us." She removed the original sheath from her gear bag and secured it to replace the cheap one she'd just put on. "I have something for you, too, but…" She twisted her wrist to check her watch. "I don't have time to give it to you this morning."

"I guess I'll have to wait."

"Patience isn't your strong suit." She laughed.

"I'll do my best to make it through. You working a regular seven to three today?"

"I should be. D and I have to write up what we found yesterday and catalog the boxes we packed." Shay ripped the velcro for Dexter's vest, and he bounded to her side to gear up. They made the most adorable crime fighting team.

"All of it?" I asked, wondering why they would document the magick-filled texts and tools we'd boxed.

"There'll be two reports. Dani will write up the civilian list, and I'll write a non-civilian one." She smiled as the timer on the coffee pot chimed. "You want?" She held up a cup.

"Please." As I sipped my coffee, I asked, "Do you always write two reports?"

"I've only had to do something like this a few times. Massive magickal archives don't just pop up in the department."

"Is it going to be a big deal?" I was ignorant of the procedures and requirements for demon investigations.

"Andrea's death was deemed undetermined by the department. No relatives, no questions. I guess that's one benefit of being a four-hundred-year-old demon."

Her tone was sarcastic, but I knew she meant every word. "What about the books and tools over there?" I asked, pointing to the boxes next to the bookshelf.

"I'll talk to the chief, explain that they need translation, and he'll give me all the time I need to sort through it."

"That's a hefty job," I said.

"Not for the Magick of Bannock." She winked as she snapped the top on her travel mug.

"So cheesy, Pierce." I snagged the loop of her pants as she walked by. "Be safe out there."

"I've got this amazing family to come home to. Safe is all I'm going to be."

I listened to her feet on the stairs and the padding of clawed paws against the solid floor of the workshop. The door opened and closed and then they were gone. It was my least favorite moment of the day.

I took a sip of my coffee and waited for the sound of fairy wings to come down and Stout to request his morning beer. The more that I thought about it, the more I realized that he hadn't interrupted my conversation with Shay, which was absolutely odd.

I kicked the step stool over to the bookcase and climbed up to find my flying friend. He wasn't fast asleep or diving into a box of crackers. He was buried deep in a magazine, reading the words to his new friend, Clia.

"What'cha reading?" I asked as I sipped a bit of my coffee. The slurp was intentional.

Stout's head whipped around. "Geez, firebug, you nearly stopped my heart."

"I guess I should say good morning." I laughed, and Stout stood from the page.

"It's a delightful morning," he proclaimed, and Clia followed him to the edge of the top shelf. "We've been brushing up on modern times."

I reached behind them to flip the magazine to the cover page. *"The Cauldron's Fire,"* I read aloud. "Where did this come from?"

"It was in Andrea's box of goodies," he explained. "It's got some shocking truths about the realm. Clia and I are on the thirty-third issue."

I took a long look at the living room space and the stack of magazines strewn between the couch, the dog bed, and the bookcase. "So, what have we learned?"

"Not much that's new for me, but Clia? I think she's in overload." Stout closed the magazine.

Clia nodded. "Yes, although the author lacks humor, and his voice is a bit…" She paused, staring back at the cover art. "…hostile."

"I guess that would fit Andrea's style." I held a hand out to my fairy friends, and they stepped into it. "Shay just left for work, so the two of you have me for the day."

"We've been up all night." Stout smacked his lips and arched his back to push out his stomach. "I could use a belly warming."

"I guessed as much. You usually come running when the coffee pot chimes." I laughed as I set them on the table.

"That's my fault," Clia said. "I just wanted Omata—I mean, Stout to keep talking and then the sun came up."

"Don't you worry, Wildwood. We are solid to help with research today." He flew to the door of the refrigerator. "How's about a cold one this morning?"

Tugging the handle to open the fridge, I dug around on the shelf. "What about you, Clia? What makes your dust shine?"

I held the beer out to Stout as I popped the cap off the bottle. He didn't wait for a glass and speared the bamboo straw in the drink.

"It's been a very long time since I fueled my dust," Clia said. "I'm not sure you can access what I need." Her eyes widened from Stout's enthusiastic beer consumption.

"What is it called?" I asked.

"Would you have catswort?" she asked in the daintiest voice. It didn't match what I'd heard. Stout drank beer, but Clia ate the warts off a cat? I tried to hide my displeasure.

"Cat warts?" I asked for clarification, hoping that I'd heard wrong. Out of all the jars and bottles in the apothecary, I couldn't remember warts of any kind collected or contained.

"That's right." She smiled and didn't hide her excitement.

I shook my head. "We definitely don't have warts. Also it feels a little edgy considering we're witches, what with all the negative stereotypes associated with us and warts."

I heard the slurp of an empty bottle and watched Stout draw his sleeve across his lips. "It's not the warts from a cat. Geez, Wildwood, it's catswort."

He said it like he'd explained everything, but I still had images of a cat wrangler plucking enormous growths from the fur of a feral cat.

"Thanks for clearing that up. Maybe we can check the magick room?" I suggested and led them down the hallway.

The elemental workings of magick had surrounded Clia as she'd survived in that six-foot terrarium wall. The mini ecosystem was clearly enchanted, but without Andrea as a source, it's impossible to guess how long our new fairy friend would have survived. It was clear as we rounded the doorway that somehow Clia was a witch. It was also clear that she connected to the apothecary space the same way Stout connected to the top of the living room bookcase.

"This feels so wonderful." Clia hovered in the doorframe. "May I enter?"

"Of course. This is your home."

She spent the next few minutes admiring the books on the shelves and the jars in the cabinet cubbies. Her wings flittered and rested as she hovered and fell, over and over, until she found exactly what she needed.

"This is the one." She scrunched her tiny hands with anticipation.

"Catnip?" I read the bottle and laughed. It was so obvious now that I could smack myself. "So what do we do?" I knew how to pour a beer for Stout but didn't know how Clia would consume these crumbly leaves.

"Tea would be lovely." She floated to sit on the cork in the bottle and accompanied me back to the kitchen.

"Tea is almost as easy as a beer," I said with more relief in my tone than was probably appropriate.

The simplicity was a comfort. I put on the kettle to boil water and poured a handful of leaves in the pot. Clia was at my wrist, sniffing and savoring the tiny flakes that drifted as I crumbled the leaves.

"Might I have just a few tiny pieces?" she asked, and I sprinkled some on the counter.

The delicate creature tumbled and rolled across the plant, sniffing and taking deep breaths of the aroma and rubbing the oils on her body. She was like a kitty, and it was adorable, and I wondered if Andrea had ever given this much of the herb to Clia in the four hundred years she was held captive.

Our tea kettle whistled, and both fairies stood on the countertop watching the color bleed into the water from the leaves like children watching new cartoons. The tint was light, but Clia knew when it was ready, and she scooped a portion in her little hand. The heat had no effect on her fairy skin, which I found curious. She'd bathed in my *ignis* flame earlier, too. Perhaps she had magickal abilities that protected her from heat?

"This is the most wonderful thing." She squealed as her hand dipped in for another scoop.

"Catnip is going to be interesting." I sent a quick message to Shay, giving her the rundown on this catnip situation. I thought about the garden in the greenhouse on the roof. "If Shay had some growing, could you show me which plant it is?"

Clia nodded her head before diving face first into the steaming liquid. As I thought about her need for the plant, I remembered Stout had been extremely enthusiastic to have a beer after coming to us, and he'd only suffered a two-month dry spell.

I slid the roof access panel open to reveal the glass-framed structure which drew from the morning's full sunlight. Shay had dozens of plants growing and twice as many plants drying from her foraging adventures with Amelia. In this moment, I was envious of their knowledge.

"When you've finished, come look and see if she has any growing," I said, plopping myself on the stepladder.

"I think your woman is just about the most perfect human," Stout said, followed by a hearty whistle. "She sure knows how to care for things."

I thought about Shay and how she moved through the world. It was difficult not to be in love with someone so selfless. The garden she grew in this space that I built perfectly combined our strengths. "She sure the heck does."

Clia flew in and swooped across the tops of the plants, her tiny feet tipping and tilting the greenery as she surveyed the space. "This one." Clia dropped to rub herself against the leaves. "Oh, yes, this is divine."

"When was the last time you had catswort?" I asked. It was obvious it had been a while, but if Andrea needed fairy magick, she must have kept Clia fed.

"I would get a single leaf on every full moon." She pulled at the plant to show the portion. One strawberry-sized leaf each month seemed like a terrible way to torture the small being.

"I'm so sorry."

"I have survived, Wildwood. I can thank you and your love for that."

"It was all of us. We work together as a team," Stout grumbled as he sniffed around the plants. "You're part of our team now, too." He held a hand to her. "Right now I think we should dive into the Sanskrit papers to give our fearless leader a break."

"That's really cute," I laughed. "But you know that she's going to want to go over every single word."

"Don't you worry," he said. "There's plenty of research for all of us."

I left the fairies in the kitchen to pour over the boxes of files. I had plans to finish a project right after informing Shay that I'd underestimated how much catnip we were going to need. It was a perfect day to get lost in the rhythm of the forge. A tourist shop was opening in town, and I'd planned to make a few art pieces to put on display that would draw people to my demonstrations.

I also had a surprise for Amelia that was close to complete. Material from Benton's demon steel stash helped make the project lightweight. The work was relaxing; get the metal white hot and hammer the shape. The movement was so steady that I didn't hear the door or feel anyone's presence until a hand touched my shoulder. I moved the steel back into the forge and dropped the door to keep the heat inside.

"Hello, beautiful." I set Brigid's hammer on the anvil and held my glowing sigil hand to Shay.

"It still does that. It's so beautiful." She grabbed my hand to admire the pattern.

"Yep, still does that, and it feels kinda good as I work. Like it's always been there." I pulled her close for a kiss. My hands touched the back of her neck, and it felt different. "What's this?"

"I thought I'd lighten up a bit."

A tingly sensation hit my heart. "With an undercut?"

Shay frowned. "You don't like—"

"Oh, I like. I like very, very much." I kissed her hard, my hands dancing against the fuzzy sensation of her short hair on my fingertips. "Very hot."

"I'm glad you approve."

When she leaned back I asked, "How was report writing day?"

"Probably not as fun as this." She took a quick peek in the forge. "What's cooking in there?"

"A little enchanted surprise for our barkeep." I noticed the paper bag tucked on top of her work duffle. "What's in there?"

"A little something for our new family member." She patted the paper, and it made a satisfying crinkly sound. "Want to come up and see?" Her smile was intoxicating, as was the enticing gleam in her eyes. She had me, and she knew it.

"Let me shut this down. I'll be right behind you."

Shay pecked my cheek before climbing the apartment stairs. I shut off the gas for the forge and placed Amelia's surprise on the anvil to cool. The last step was to polish the surface, and once that was done, our friend could try out her new magick-infused prosthetic.

I hooked my apron on the wall, and as I reached the top of the stairs, I saw Stout and Clia in a serious conversation with Dexter. The K-9 was puffing and grunting with excitement, and both fairies listened with such intensity that I didn't want to interrupt. I heard Shay's velcro tear away and knew she was close to my favorite part of uniform removal.

"Hey, there," I whispered as I pivoted in the bedroom doorway.

"Heard me, didn't you?" She was wearing a BPD t-shirt drawn tight across her breasts. As she slid the uniform pants down her thighs, they dropped to the floor in a crumple. Shay had a short table beside her chair, and I admired the way she laid out the contents of her pockets. "Did you see our dog?" she asked, stepping into jeans.

"I did. What's that all about?" I asked as I sat on the bed.

"I don't know. He's been hyper all day, and I swear he was talking to himself." The fly of her pants lay open as she flipped her t-shirt off and unclipped her bra. I didn't move. I watched with a smile as she tugged the clean shirt over her bare skin. "He was grunting and snorting and making such a ruckus that I had to take a long edge-of-town drive to settle him. That's when I stopped for this."

She was saying words as she rubbed that stubble hair, and I had to admit that most of them went in one ear and out the other. I was more focused on her zipping up those tight jeans and buttoning the waistband.

Snapping her fingers to get my attention, she said, "Hey, eyes up here!"

I licked my lips, which were suddenly and uncomfortably dry. "Drive to where?" I asked, but I was pretty sure I already knew the answer.

She stepped in between my knees and draped her forearms over my shoulders. "Don't get upset, but we ended up at the mine. I think he was looking for embryos."

"You shouldn't go there alone."

Her forehead crunched with a frown. "I'm hardly alone with Dex."

"You know what I mean." My thumbs hooked into the loops of her pants, and I tugged her close.

"It was safe." She kissed my forehead. "But it kinda feels like he's going through withdrawal."

"You think our boy is hooked on demon embryos?"

Her shoulders tensed, and she pulled out of my arms. "Maybe. I don't know how else to explain it."

"Have you asked Stout to talk to Dexter? Maybe he can just tell you why he gets so riled up."

"Huh, that's a good idea." Her smile was adorable. "So, remember this morning when you 'happy anniversary'd' me?"

"Stabby thing made with love." I ran my toes from her ankle to her knee. "You love it, right?"

"I adore it." She opened her work duffle and removed a small velvet bag. "There was a moment, not so long ago, when you said something to me that really stuck."

"I did?"

She pulled on the strings to open the pouch. "You did."

"Look at me being the great life partner," I joked.

"You call me a superhero." She played with the strings on the bag. "But I'd say that you're one, too. You build me up and make me feel invincible because your love for me is so solid."

I fidgeted on the bed, drawing designs in the sheets. It felt like the entire world was fading around us. Her steady fingers reached for my shaking ones.

"But that's not all." Her voice broke as she tried to contain her emotions. "When we talked about family, about commitment, about the future, you never wavered. I didn't feel like much of a superhero next to you."

"I love you, Shay, and I always want you to feel invincible in my arms." Aching to hold her, I started to stand up.

"Wait, just stay there." She kneeled in front of me, and my heart pounded in my chest.

"You're not?"

She glanced down at herself, realizing exactly how it looked to me. "Oh, no. This isn't that. You'd know."

"Whew." I faked wiping sweat from my brow.

"Whew is right. We don't need that to be committed, but what we do need is this." She opened her hand and held up a stone the size of a quail's egg.

"Not the rock I was expecting."

Her nervous half-laugh was endearing. "It's a piece of meteorite."

"Interesting lure to get me to love you."

"There's more." She kissed my nose and continued explaining, "This stone has been outside of this world. It existed beyond our means to travel, and yet here it is, somehow. Just like you and me."

Her message was becoming clear, and suddenly I loved this jagged piece of rock more than I thought possible. My heart hammered in my chest, and I was certain Shay could hear it. She took my hand, raising it just enough so I could hold it in my sigil palm.

"*Ignis*," she whispered, and our individual flames burned through the stone.

My voice hitched as I said, "It's...stunning."

"We're like this stone, Wil, because we've been so far apart that it seemed impossible, but then somehow..." She swallowed hard. "Somehow we made it here. We made it to us. I know this year's been terribly hard, but it's also been what I dreamed love would be."

"This is perfect." I cradled the stone to my heart, still holding her hand in mine.

"I love you, Wildwood Blackstone, more than yesterday but probably not as much as tomorrow."

"I love you, too, Shay Pierce."

She kissed me then, light touches to my lips at first, until my mouth opened to hers.

"We have fairies and a dog waiting for us out there," she whispered against my lips.

"No, don't break this spell."

I pulled her into the V of my legs and squeezed her to me. We stayed like that for a quiet eternity, balanced as the Magick and the Maker of Bannock, and everything felt right with the world.

"We should go check on our family," Shay said over the top of my head.

"We should."

She held her hands out and helped me to my feet. "Wait, I have something for Clia."

The zipper on her duffle was open enough for her to grab a paper bag. It was a curious little parcel, and I followed her with interest into the living room.

"What the hell!" Shay yelled, and I bumped into her where she stopped.

I'll admit it was not a common sight, and it definitely reeked of magick. Dexter was in full dragon form but remained the size of a dog. I didn't understand how he could be the size of a house in the wild and reduced to the size of his canine form and everything in between. That wasn't the oddest thing I noticed though. It was the delicate green fairy stroking his beak and scaly face. No words were spoken, but communication of an otherworldly kind was happening between them.

"Dex, why are you in dra—"

"Shh, he's telling us." Stout flew at Shay. "He said he could hear the Gatekeepers."

The paper bag fell from Shay's hand, spilling the leafy contents all over the floor. "They're back?"

CHAPTER VI

SILHOUETTE

"Shay, baby." I called her over and over, but she stood frozen in place. The seconds felt like hours. "Honey, you've got to come back to me." I looked at Stout. "Why did you have to just blurt that out!" My voice was more like a yell, and he didn't deserve that adrenalin-fueled reaction, but my lover rarely lost her shit.

"I didn't mean—"

I held up a hand. "Not now. Help me."

Shay's fingers clamped around mine as I closed my eyes, calling her with rooted earth magicks. *Shay Pierce, you better come back to me right now.* I thought the words, and in the same moment, I felt a furry nose rest on our joined hands. That was what we needed, the closed circuit of magick energies completed by our dog.

"Wil, no. They can't *be back,"* Shay pleaded in my head. *"We killed them."*

When I opened my eyes, I saw the cascade of tears trailing through the creases at the corner of her eyes. We had killed them all *and* their monstrous spawn *and* anything that moved in every inch of that mine.

Or so we thought.

"I'm so sorry, Red." Stout hovered behind me. "We were just so caught up in Dexter's story that I wasn't thinking."

Shay wiped her tears with the heel of her palm. "What was Dex telling you?"

"Is this for me?" Clia squealed.

She was already rolling around in the leaves on the floor, crunching them against her nose like fresh flowers in the spring. It was possibly the quirkiest scenario that'd ever taken place in our home: partially catatonic Shay, doe-eyed Dexter, meek Stout, and a not-so-delicate euphoric green fairy rolling around on a pile of catnip.

Shay dropped to one knee and picked up the bag to scoop the contents back inside. "Yes, catswort just for you. Freshly foraged, and there's plenty more where that came from."

"It's a wildflower?" I asked.

Shay nodded. "More like a weed to some, but there's a patch behind the bar, and I'm thinking maybe Benton planted it."

"For the fairies?" I asked.

"Or for the cats," Stout joked as he flew toward Dexter. "So your animal here, he's hyped up because the dream we shared was more fact than fiction."

"But that was months ago," Shay kneeled in front of her dog. "Why now?"

"Clia's magick," Stout said as he landed on the tabletop. "And traveling through that portal. We shouldn't have taken him to that bitch's lair."

"Lair?" I questioned. "Dramatic, don't you think?"

"What else would you call it?" He shrugged. "She had a stockpile of elementals, notes, and books. It was creepy and hidden by a magick portal. And she kept a fairy in a terrarium for over four hundred years. It was a lair for sure. One hundred percent, no doubt!"

Shay shook her head. "So what happened to Dexter in the *lair*?" Shay laughed at my eyes rolling so hard they could have fallen right out of my face.

"He ate something."

"An embryo?" Shay asked, more calmly than I would've expected.

"He's not sure. That's what we were trying to figure out when you walked in," Stout explained. "Clia was reading him."

"And?" Shay walked to the table in the kitchen. It was her first full glimpse of the research materials the fairies had spread out everywhere. "What did you find?" She looked to Stout, who sat captivated by the green fairy still rolling around.

"Um, we…" He held his hand up.

"A little smitten?" I joked, and he didn't respond.

"Or maybe the weed is influencing him, too?" Shay smiled.

"It's not that," Stout insisted, but his cheeks were slightly redder. "Clia thinks that Dexter might have linked to the demons like Andrea and Kai."

"That bitch!" Shay hugged Dexter around the neck. "We should have—"

"Stopped investigating what we didn't know?" I said. "That would mean you'd need clairvoyance or ESP."

"Or just common sense." Shay kicked the stool next the table and sat down to survey their work, shifting pages from side to side, making grumbling sounds that didn't match the curiosity in her eyes.

"What is it?" I leaned in close enough to whisper in her ear, and her arm came around to pull me against her backside.

"From the looks of this," she said, picking up the Tome of Trouble, "they're Rasatavam incantations, is my guess. Maybe half written spells that Kai didn't finish."

"Or something Andrea was planning?" I said and almost wished that I hadn't when Shay turned the pages over.

"*Iscateran,*" she whispered.

I was clueless about the word. "What?"

She turned to look at me. "It's clearing the magick."

"What do you mean, clearing?" I scooted her forward so the two of us could occupy the same bar sized stool. My cheek rubbed the back of her neck, and she tilted into me as I enjoyed the feeling of her buzzed hair on my skin.

"There's not room for two on here." She tugged me tighter to her back, keeping her hand splayed just above my hip.

"Your body is telling me something completely different, lady." I kissed the base of her neck, just below her ear. "Tell me what you meant by clearing?" I whispered and her hand came up to wipe at the spot where my lips just touched.

"You make it impossible sometimes."

"Glad to hear I've still got it."

"Oh, you've got it, alright." She flipped the paper over and took a calming breath. "Whoever wrote this half-spell invoked safeguards to prevent reckless recitations like the way we released the Magick and Maker powers. I used the *Iscateran* to bind it to itself."

"And that worked?" I asked, mostly surprised that a portal hadn't opened or a giant hadn't appeared. I was also thinking about fairies. With two of them living in the house already, the last thing we needed was to have more of them flying around.

"It worked, but this is a curious half-written document."

"It isn't *half* written," Clia said as she flew up to land on the table near the page. The fairy seemed aware, not high or even affected by her recent aggressive tumble with catnip. "Andrea was translating it." She flew to the Tome of Trouble and forced the book open. "She was trying to recreate it without using this." The spell on the page was written in Sanskrit, and although I didn't know what it said, I'd seen enough to identify the language.

"Do you know what she was trying to do?" Shay asked as her eyes scanned the page. Her talent for speed reading was one of the most fascinating gifts Shay had and was handy when examining magick and spell work.

"It's powerful transference gateway magick," Clia explained.

"Like the spell cast in the loft?" I asked, and for the first time, I thought about the power of that spell and that it was still alive months after Andrea's death.

"No, not that spell." Clia sat on the pages. "She was looking for the way out of Bannock, and that could only be through the land of my people."

"Fairy land?" The words burst from my mouth unfiltered, and all heads turned to me. "What?"

Clia spoke first. "The land of the Fairies is protected. The magick required to break through could only come from pure goodness. Anything else would cause eternal chaos and destruction, unless..." She walked across the papers, shuffling one over the other as she disappeared into the abundant information.

"Unless what?"

"She was trying to bleed me of my magick. This spell would never work like that."

Shay held up the tome. "This reads..." She paused, analyzing the writing in her head as she translated, "'Divine is the way; split edge of humanity can't travel the heaviness.'" Shay's forehead scrunched as she thought about what she'd just said. "That doesn't really make sense does it?" She pulled out a piece of paper and began writing.

"Well, not the way you transcribed it, but you are very close," Clia said as she landed on the text. She stepped across the words, hopping back and forth as she translated into perfect English. "This first part: *'the right of way is for the divine.'* You had that bit, but the second half is about Brigid's purity in the hammer. *'The Maker's bind weighs heavy on the path.'*"

"So I'm the problem?" I asked

"On the contrary. Wildwood Blackstone, you are the solution." Stout hovered close to my face. "The bind that the Maker carries is not to the hammer; it's to the enchanted partnership with the Magick."

My mouth fell open, the explanation rendering me speechless. *What if,* I thought, *I'd been a complete bitch all those years ago and hidden from Shay in that prairie grass? What if my attraction to her had faltered for just a moment, and we'd never made that oath? What if I'd never drawn that knife blade across her palm and bound us to one another forever?*

It felt otherworldly to put all of those decisions together to form a perfect line from my heart to Shay's, and yet here we were: the Magick and the Maker, bound eternally by love and by a power so strong that it might just end a four-hundred-year-old quest to possess all of humanity.

"Wil?" Shay rested her hands on my shoulders, ducking her head to look into my eyes. I was thunderstruck. Who wouldn't be?

"Will it be over when we understand the spell?"

"No, love." Shay shook her head. "It'll never be over, at least not how you hope."

"Because of this?" My hand fell open to reveal the sigil marked in my flesh.

"*Ignis,*" she whispered, and her palm flashed a gorgeous blue. "Because of what happens when you and I come together." The flame met my palm and the combination of hers meeting my own flashed a brilliant green. "We can do this." Her forehead rested against mine.

I heard the whisper behind me; Stout and Clia stood with their heads together, and I overheard Stout explain, "They do this a lot."

"They're so precious." Clia folded her hands to her chest.

"Kinda irritating sometimes to watch that kind of love." Stout flew to the top of the bookcase. "Get a room!"

"Deal with it," I yelled back, never losing the connection with Shay.

Her eyes said everything as she turned me in her arms to whisper, "Would you like to open a portal to the fairy world with me?" She asked it like she was inviting me to take a simple trip for iced coffee.

The muscles in my shoulders flexed, and she held tight as I tried to pull away. "You really know how to kill a mood."

"That's not all I know how to kill."

Her half-laugh wasn't funny to me. Her life as a police officer in the human world was enough to fear, but the other life she lived, the one filled with nightmarish monsters and inexplicable realities, was one I hated.

"Fairies aren't always nice, you know."

But I was mostly guessing. In my entire experience as a witch, I'd met four fairies: one didn't seem real for the most part, another was a fleeting glance at my new reality, the third spent hundreds of years in a glass box, and the last was Stout, a foul-mouthed, beer-guzzling, mysterious secretkeeper sworn to help us in the least helpful ways. All I knew for certain was that I didn't know a damn thing about fairies.

"How would you know?" She called my bluff.

"I'm just weighing the odds against all the magick I've experienced and the history of life in Bannock."

Shay held my hand. "You and I are the Magick and Maker. The powers in that book are forged, not bestowed, and they belong to you and me. And we aren't going to doom this mission before we've determined what it is."

"What is it then?" I asked, noting how petulant I sounded. "I mean, we open a portal to the fairy world, they get pissed at us and poison us with wads of spit or something, and then we disappear from the world as we know it?"

"Come on, Wil!" Shay's huff was part laugh and part frustration. "The magick is connected to the fairy world so there had to be a fairy involved in its creation."

"There was also a person named Andrea, and I trust nothing that monster did. And now you want–"

"I'm sorry," Clia interrupted. "She never possessed the Ra-sa-va-tam."

"How do you know that?" I asked.

"Because if she had, the two of you would not be here." The tone in her voice left no room for doubt.

"See what I mean?" I shook my head. "Ultimate evil, death, and destruction. They follow us. I'm telling you we should just stay home and leave the portals to the professionals."

"Wildwood, we *are* the professionals," Stout grumbled. "We may be new at it, but we're all there is."

The room was silent except for the dreadful flutter of his wings. Andrea's cruelty replayed in my mind, and I shuddered at the memory of the wings being torn from Stout's back.

"And that should make me feel better?" I snapped.

"No, not better. Just a little less frightened," Clia said.

"A little less." My sarcasm was not lost on the room. but it was Dexter who pushed against my hip.

"He says you have to trust us," Stout told me. "He says he won't let us down this time."

Shay dropped to her knees to fluff the dog's face. "You didn't let us down buddy. Not ever."

Dexter gave a soft bark as the two of them nuzzled into each other.

<div align="center">~~~~~~~~~~~~</div>

With practiced ease, Shay poured over the pages of the Rasavatam with Clia at my workshop table. I'd taken up the flame of the forge, reinforcing my confidence in the hammer's magick. It was a group decision to leave Dani and Amelia out of this research quest just in case the spell translations were a sinister trap to move us out of Bannock in some unexpected– though now sort of expected–portal passageway plot twist.

"I'm not sure we have access to 'sunshine in a bottle.'" Shay half suppressed a laugh as her pencil stopped on the paper.

My hammer rested on the anvil as I waited for the steel to heat, but I wondered, with all the apothecary supplies we had access to, how we didn't have a bottle of everything a witch might need to open a portal to the fairy realm.

Clia's wings curled around her back, a response we'd learned was equivalent to side-splitting laughter in the terrarium. "It's a fairy thing. Trust me, between Stout and myself, you've got access."

I shook my head. There were many things I'd learned in the year I'd spent with Shay, wonder-filled first-time experiences that some people could only dream of, and I was certain that no part of me wanted to know how two fairies made sunshine in a bottle.

"Makes sense, I guess." Shay shrugged, obviously not thinking too deeply about it as she returned to her writing.

I was the only one thinking–perhaps *over*-thinking–and it irked me so much that I couldn't fight the distraction. No matter what I'd said about not wanting to know, my curiosity was getting the better of me. "I'm sorry." Then I stopped. "Okay, I'm not sorry. I have to know, please."

"Know?" Shay's eyebrow raised, and the adorable lines of curiosity formed. "Know what, love?"

"You're an adorable tease. Just spill. Tell me how *sunshine* is made."

It was obvious what I meant, but she was feeling playful and empowered by the magick energies swirling around the workshop. With a grin, she said, "I think there was a big bang. And then there was a supernova and a collision of outer space-y things! Then, BOOM! Sunshine."

The delivery was entertaining, a perfect execution of delightful humor, and I was having none of it. I tossed my gloves on the anvil, and the raging illumination of my palms was in full glow as I cupped her face and smashed a shameless kiss on her lips.

"The Magick of Bannock is quite the smart ass today," I chided.

Our bodies separated just enough so I could see the playful gleam in her eyes.

"Every day, baby." She kissed me.

I pushed the table out of my way so I could sit in her lap. If I had to live with the mystery of fairy magick, she would get nothing accomplished until I was satisfied that my mystery was solved.

"How about you and I take a break so your smart ass can feed me a burger. Then maybe we can talk some more about that big bang?" My hands curled tight to contain the hammer energies, and Shay touched her fingers to the glow of my palms.

"The power feels so good, doesn't it?" Her eyes were closed, and her euphoric smile was just about the sexiest expression I'd ever seen on her face.

"It feels wonderful." My stomach picked that moment to gurgle and rumble.

"Are you hungry, baby?"

"So very." The reply came out throaty and demure.

Clia made herself known with a cough. "'Sunshine in a bottle' has nothing on the Magick and the Maker." Her wings curled and uncurled before she launched from the tabletop. "Are we going on an excursion?"

I got up off of Shay's lap and extinguished the flame of the forge. "Burgers at the bar and maybe some catnip for you?" I suggested.

"It's not like that," the fairy explained as I hung my apron on the wall. "You must understand that rationing catswort has been a strain on my ability to do just about everything. Andrea knew that much."

"We're sorry you had to endure so many years with her," Shay said, stacking the pages into a pile.

"I will adjust." That was all she said before disappearing up the staircase.

"I can't imagine living like that for hundreds of years." The words came out as a whisper although I wasn't trying to hide my sadness.

"Alone except for the torture. We should keep an eye out for her to break. No one is that strong." Shay pushed her papers inside a messenger bag.

"Should we be worried?"

"Nope, just aware," she assured me. "We've seen enough trauma responses to recognize when it comes."

"How do you think a fairy will manifest trauma?"

"I don't have a clue." Shay's shoulders lifted with a shrug.

"Rolling around on a pile of catnip seems pretty tame," I joked as I stretched a hand out to her. "Maybe we should talk with Stout? He has more experience."

"You mean with trauma?" she asked.

"Well, *that*," I said, "but mostly with being a fairy."

Shay didn't say anything, but she still looked pensive when we left, her leading me out the door, then shutting it behind us.

~~~~~~~~~~

The dinner crowd was in full swing at the bar, so we opted for the back-room service door entry. Shay carried the supplies, and just before I unlocked the door, Clia made a curious observation.

"A noble warrior fell on these grounds." Her hands pressed to the trunk of the tree along the line of the property. Shortly after Benton's death, we'd noticed the disappearance of its leaves but never gave it a thought when the surge of demons came. Apparently, Clia had an explanation.

"How did you know?" Shay asked.

"No leaves. It's obvious my people came and took them to the grave."

"Wait, what?" I asked.

"We use leaves for protection," Clia said. "Oak, maple, walnut, any, really. But this tree was planted long before your warrior's death." Clia's hands cupped the deep lines in the aged tree's bark. The ripples swooped and hitched in a monotonous pattern from the earth to the sky.

I looked at Shay, who was staring at the green fairy loving on the ancient tree.

"Did you notice the blanket over the warrior's grave?" Clia asked. "It's an eternal embrace for a fallen warrior protected until the end of time."
~~~~~~~~~~

"I wonder if Benton knew that?" Shay whispered, mostly to herself, but I took hold of her hand to give it a comforting squeeze.

"She was like you." Clia rested on the spindly twig. "She made a lot of magick inside this building. There are strong boundaries rooted here."

Not knowing what to say, I turned the handle to open the service door, and the five of us made our way into the cellar beneath the bar. Shay and I stood at the top of the spiraling stairs, watching Clia explore the space.

"Powerful, indeed!" she exclaimed.

She hovered over the coal forge, sniffing her way up the vent pipe and returning to fly around the pile of weapons and the shelves of books. She flittered and floated in and out of the apothecary wall and used her agile feet to move bottles until she found what she was looking for.

"Hypericum Perforatum," she read the label.

"St John's Wort," Shay said.

I couldn't resist poking a little fun. "What's with all the warts?" I joked, but not one being in the cellar laughed. "Come on, first there's catswort and now St. John's. How many worts can there be?"

"As far as I'm concerned," Stout grunted, "the best wort comes from a good brewery."

"Beer?" I laughed. "What a surprise."

"Can't have beer without a solid wort." Stout slowly licked his lips. Standing in the basement of a bar that had a long list of microbrews was the perfect place for our incorrigible friend.

"St. John's Wort is a plant," Shay explained as she took the bottle from the shelf. "The summer solstice plant." Shay held it to the light, and I could see the bright yellow flower petals perfectly preserved inside. "Sunshine in a bottle. So smart. What else do we need Clia?"

"An empty vessel." She hovered over the mismatched pile of jars beneath the forge. "You'll need Stout. And you'll need me, too. Together we can prepare a tincture that will carry the sunshine magick."

"Are you gonna spit in that bottle?" I asked, but I was almost certain that they would.

It wasn't so long ago that Stout had used his spit-based fairy dust to intoxicate Shay. That experience led to one pissed off witch and one extremely misunderstood fairy.

Clia's bright smile was the only answer.

"So what happens once we blend up some sunshine?" I asked.

Shay put her arm around my waist. "We open a portal?" I could tell she was guessing by the tone of her voice.

"We have to meet the Giants of the Crater," Clia said.

Shay's hand squeezed mine. "Did you say giants?"

My mind flashed back to the day the Maker powers came to me. There was a dark basement, a runic spell, and illuminated incantations that left me seeing fairies, a dragon dog, and one hairy faced giant. That last one had been so fantastically unbelievable that I'd almost forgotten about it.

"Yes, giants," Clia said matter-of-factly. "But don't worry; they'll welcome me."

Shay and I just stared at her, neither of us sure how to explain to our pint-sized new friend that *that* was the least of our worries. Eventually, though, Shay recovered and started doing what she did best: research.

~~~~~~~~~~~

"How do we get off this crazy ride?" I asked as I fell into a nearby chair. I stared at Shay who was standing in front of the shelf of books, her fingers tapping against the spines as she searched through. "Giants? Really?"

"There's a reference here." She sidestepped to the next shelves. "I remember the text, but I'd honestly filed it under 'highly unlikely.'"

"Because who sees giants, right?" I knew I was babbling and redundant, and after a year with my girlfriend, nothing should surprise me. And yet, something always did.

"No, just unlikely to still be present in Bannock." Her index finger hooked over a tome, and she flipped it into her hand. "I've been here a long time. Never had a face to face."

"I saw one," I said, drumming my fingers nervously on the arm of the chair. "Just that one time. And I thought it was because of my Maker power infusion."

"Ha, infusion." Shay laughed.

"The infusion wasn't so funny at the time, if you recall."

"I recall all of it." She turned to look at me, clutching the book to her chest. "Incredible memory." She tapped the side of her head.
~~~~~~~~~~~

"Giants don't reveal their presence unless it's necessary," Clia explained. "To pass through from this realm, you must present yourself to them."

"We are going to see giants." I said it out loud and gave my arm a pinch. The test never failed. Or maybe it did. Because every time I did it, that smidge of pain in my arm always told me, "Yep, this is all real!"

Shay opened the book in front of me, smiling as she turned through the pages. "We're going to see giants."

~~~~~~~~~~~

"Is this the right shade of denim to wear to an introductory meeting in Giantville?" I was only half joking as I pulled on a pair of jeans.

I wondered about the world outside this small town. Magick was everywhere I went, but had it always been? How had I existed so blind to the ways of magick and witchcraft?

Shay's arms came around my hips as she pulled me close. "This is just perfect," she whispered in my ear, tickling the sensitive flesh.

I giggled and gently pushed her lips away. "Do you ever stop and think about living in Bannock?"

She gave me a squeeze, then let me go so I could finish getting dressed. "What do you mean?"

Pulling a t-shirt over my head, I said, "I've been here just over a year, and I've spent a huge chunk of that time fighting some fantastic things."

"I've been here twelve years, and I only understand about half of what's anchoring Bannock to the world," she
~~~~~~~~~~~

admitted. "This town has grown in more ways than I thought possible."

"It goes back hundreds of years, and sometimes that history feels like more fiction than fact."

"It really does," Shay agreed, leaning up against the dresser to watch me. "The demons, and that mine; the powers of Brigid and the earth. Everything's connected."

"Yeah, but fairies and unicorns? And now Giantville?" My hands punched through the sleeves of my flannel shirt.

Her smile was charming and wrinkled the corners of her eyes. "Aren't you just a tiny bit excited about meeting giants? Curious at least?"

"No, I'm not." I threaded my punch dagger through the loop of my belt.

"I don't know if you should carry that?" Shay reached for the sheathed blade.

My hands stilled. "Why not?" I shuffled away from Shay, and it was then that I noticed something that struck me as odd: the way we were dressed was similar "You're not going to gear up?" The unbuckled belt on my waist flopped against my thigh.

"I'm not sure if I should."

Shay was a lot of things, but first and foremost, she was cautious, sometimes to the point of carrying every weapon she could, earthen and not. We were about to go into unfamiliar territory with no armor and not a thing hammered by the Maker of Bannock. I felt the flush of fear warm my face.

"What if Andrea's been there?" I asked. "What if we meet these giants, and they crush us like an empty can of beer?" It felt dramatic, but I dealt with 'what ifs' most of the time.

"According to my research," Shay said, "the giants hold the portal as protectors. If Andrea had a way to them, she wouldn't have stayed in Bannock. She needed the Magick and the Maker, and she needed the Tome of Trouble."

"You trust people and creatures that could let us down."

Shay reached for the buckle of my belt. With slow movements, she threaded it tight. "I trust you, and I trust myself." Her hand slipped into mine. "*Ignis*," she whispered, adding as our flames flared together, "And I trust this."

CHAPTER VII

QUEST

"How do we know where to go?" I asked, strapping the seatbelt across my body in the passenger's seat of Shay's patrol car.

It didn't seem like a dumb question because we lived in Bannock, which did *not* have giants roaming around on the streets.

"I'm going to rely on Clia and a bit of simple deduction for that." Shay tilted her head toward the back of her patrol vehicle. The department had outfitted this SUV to carry Dexter as a

working K-9 unit, and our fairy companions sat beside him immersed in secret conversations.

"Are you nervous?" I asked, my eyes locked on the backpack slumped near my feet.

After much conversation, I'd convinced Shay that the giants would either welcome or reject our magick, but it would be better if we weren't left without something with which to defend ourselves. So we'd brought a few things I'd created. Three handles poked a tented formation inside the bag. Our two magickal axes and Brigid's hammer gave me a sense of comfort.

"I'm not nervous, mostly excited." She gave me a quick glance. "You?"

"My demon fighting skills have plummeted since Andrea's—"

Shay gripped my arm. "You were amazing then, and you're amazing now."

"Yes, I got knocked unconscious in an amazing fashion."

Shay paused for a moment, and I wished I knew what she was thinking. "You're here; she's not." Her eyes remained fixed on the road. "You might not think you're amazing, but we needed everything the Maker created to save us." Her thumb hitched to point at the fur ball behind us. "All of us."

My eyes closed as I remembered the lifeless Dexter spread out on the carriage house floor, the pain and desperation in Shay's voice as she begged the universe to save him.

"I really hate what that vile woman did," I said, resting my head against the window. "She almost destroyed us all."

"I don't think giants are like demons."

"You think they're big fluffy cuddlers like Dex?" I asked.

"Probably not like Dexter, but if they had plans for this mountainside, they would have made their presence known by now."

"Giants," I whispered, noting the awe in my voice. "Do you think our Magick and Maker abilities will matter to them?"

"I wish I knew," she said as her dashboard monitor activated with a call from Dani. Shay's thumb swiped the answer button on her steering wheel. "Pierce."

Dani's voice filled the front of the SUV. "Hey, Pierce. You headed to Grant's Pass?"

"About twenty miles out. You going to meet us?"

Amelia's voice came over the speakerphone. "We are, but there's a problem at the bar, so we're still here."

This was the team. All of us coming together to save a small town mostly in the dark.

"Wildwood's never been to Grant's Pass, so let's meet at the State Park and hike from there," Shay suggested, then ended the call.

"They almost sound excited," I said. "I hope the bar issue isn't serious."

"Probably just a paperwork thing." Shay smiled. She was silent for a long moment, then she said, "Dani got the answers she always wanted about her mother's death. It was such a gut-punch that she wants the cursed nightmares to be over for us. She'll help us figure out the dreams. There's still evil at work here, and Grant's Pass is the only clue we have."

The name of the town clung to my memories. I'd traveled little in the last year, the carriage house keeping me busy, but the isolated mountain town had come up a few times: once, when Dani suggested a special doctor for Shay, and another time, when we questioned the origin of our dragon-dog. "Grant's Pass is where you got Dexter, isn't it?" I asked.

"Benton got him from a puppy mill seizure, yep."

"Were there giants involved?"

My question wasn't meant to be funny, but Shay laughed. "Not that I recall. Why, what are you thinking?"

"I was thinking how much you don't enjoy a pleasant coincidence."

Her smirk crinkled the lines in the corner of her eyes. "True."

"And if Dexter came from Giantville, do you think Benton had knowledge of their existence?"

"I'd bet my retirement that she knew."

I stared out the window, taking a moment to think about the secrets that never stopped. Benton set us up to succeed by planting Stout in our lives, but Stout had limited knowledge, except to understand that the answers were somewhere in the thousands of books hidden in multiple locations. All the secrets kept us in the dark, one that put us in danger, despite being meant to protect us. The concept was complex and ridiculously dizzying.

"I just wanted a simple life as a welder," I whispered.

The words were out of my mouth before I could stop them. Hell, before I even realized I'd said them. At Shay's sharp intake of breath, my hands came up to cover my mouth.

After she pulled her vehicle to the side of the road, she draped her arms over the steering wheel and turned to ask, "You have regrets?"

My eyes squeezed tight, tears falling from the corners. My palms were sweaty; my heart rapidly pounded in my ears. What a colossal screw-up...

Long before coming to Bannock, I'd dreamed about Shay. My nights were solitary, clinging to the memory of a pale, scrawny, redheaded fifteen-year-old who owned my soul. Sure, I dated people after her, but it was Shay that my spirit held out for.

Now we sat, idling alongside a winding mountain road, and she doubted fifteen years of pining.

I shook my head. "My only regret is that it took so long to find my way back to you."

Shay's head fell against her arms as she looked at me. "I was ready when you got here, but yeah, sooner would have been better." She stretched across the armrest to grasp my hand. "I wish it was easier."

"The simple life?" I joked.

"Being this."

She turned my hand over to trace the sigil seared into my palm. The half-moons joined by ancient symbols was the origin point of my bond to Brigid's flame and the power connecting me to my blacksmithing hammer.

"Having you makes living as the Maker easier, not harder." Her hand moved back and forth over my mark, and the connection grounded the anxious energies inside me. "Someday the evil that's chasing us will be gone and then we can be an old, boring couple." There was confidence in the way she spoke.

"Old and boring?" I asked. "We're ageless, baby, so we'll have to settle for tired and boring."

"Maybe we can just live happily ever after." She squeezed my hand before she shifted the SUV into drive and pulled onto the highway.

"I think I like that idea, even though it's for fairy tales."

"Stick with me, sweetheart," she said, grinning, "and I'll give you a life better than any tale you've ever read."

My smile was impossible to hide, and her own smile set my mind at ease. "Promise?"

"Cross my heart." Her finger drew a criss-cross pattern over the demon-plate vest she wore.

"I'll take a superhero promise over a white knight any day," I told her.

"I guess that works out perfectly," she said.

We were building a life together, as complex as it was. We'd made a home, found fulfillment in work, and even managed to pull together a rag-tag group of chosen family. The sinister remnants of Andrea's evil loomed, but after today, we might have the tools to end her scourge forever.

Shay's phone rang again, and she activated the hands-free feature with her thumb. "Pierce," she answered.

"Yeah, Pierce, you're on your own in the mountains." Dani's voice crackled through the poor reception. "Amelia needs—bar—leaving." The call ended, and Shay sighed, looking at the map on the GPS. "Well, that's the last of the cell reception while we're up here in the mountains."

"Sounds like something is broken at the bar," I said.

"Amelia's there, and I've no doubt she can handle it." Shay's hands shuffled around the steering wheel as she turned off the main highway onto a rough paved road.

"It's just you and me and the trio in the back."

"You going to be okay with a long hike?" She didn't take her eyes off the road as it narrowed to a single lane passing through a covered bridge.

"I thought maybe not having Dani and Amelia here would change that plan, but it's not going to, is it?"

Her smile was wide and mischievous. "I guess I'm giving all the piggy-back rides." She flexed her bicep for me, and I reached across to give it a gentle squeeze.

"Oh, goddess, superhero. That's hot!"

"Behave, the kids are in the car." Her head tipped toward the occupants in the kennel.

"Hardly kids," Stout grumbled. "Collectively, we're older than everything but the Indigenous cultures on this continent. Kids! Tsk, tsk."

I attempted the mental math. Clia was at least four hundred years old and Stout was more than a hundred. Dexter was the X factor in the equation because I could sum neither dragon nor dog years up.

"My sincere apologies," Shay said as she stretched to see the occupants in the back seat.

The silence that followed was comfortable, and I stared out at the green hills where rugged and ripped stone pushed through. There was no rhyme or reason to the direction of the road; Shay would pick up momentum on one straight away and then a sharp turn would switch us back in the direction we'd just come. It was nauseating. But then the trees would clear, and the breathtaking heights would come into view as we climbed further from Bannock and closer to the unknown.

"Are you as excited as I am to spend a few nights out here?" Shay asked as the Grant's Pass mile marker came into view. Three miles of winding and then we'd be at our destination.

"Still not sure about camping," I admitted.

"You've camped before, haven't you?"

That was a great question. What is camping? I've lived in my car, but that was for survival. I've consumed cold soup right out of the can, but that was for the same reason. There was nothing about homelessness that was equal to planned tenting and cuddly campfires.

"No, I've never camped before."

My scrunched nose and the light blush on my cheeks didn't go unnoticed because Shay asked, "Tough subject?"

"Being homeless was hard, but asking for help was harder. So, yeah, I've never camped."

Shay didn't say another word as she turned into the state park entrance. The road zigged and looped until we came to a stop in a restricted area, a perk of being in a law enforcement vehicle. Shay turned off the ignition and shifted so she could face me.

"The past is the past," she began, "but it's also part of you, love. And I don't care what you had to do to get here. I'm just so glad you are."

"Me, too."

"We're glad that you're here even when you forget we are also present." Stout's laugh was grumbly and rough, but I felt the honesty in his words.

"Did you bring enough gear for camping?" It seemed like an obvious thing to ask since I didn't even have a second pair of socks.

"I unloaded most of my tactical gear, and Dani gave me a second two-person tent for them. It'll be a little less cozy without them, but yes, I brought what I thought we might need." Shay opened her door. "Come see."

I grabbed the backpack by my feet and followed her around the SUV, watching as she opened the drawers to reveal equipment I wasn't familiar with. "What's this?" I asked as I poked the rubbery pouch.

"Hydration bladder." She picked it up and opened a flap in the backpack beside it, slipping them together. "This hose will come through this." She pinched a pocket open. "And we can drink while we walk."

I threw my bag beside hers, and our Maker creations clanked together. "Will one of those fit in here?"

"Not the same way. You can have this bag, and I'll carry yours."

"What will you drink?" I asked with immediate concern for her hydration. Adulting really is strange. I spent most of my foster care life without ever thinking about a glass of water, and here I was thinking about a bladder full of it.

"There's a canteen." She held up the stainless-steel container and hooked it on her belt.

"We're really going camping," I said, more to soothe my overstimulated brain and convince myself that sleeping in the thick of the forest would be safe.

"Under the starry night." Her hip bumped against mine. "Everything we need is in here." She patted the overstuffed bag after hitting the release button on the pocket of her shirt. Before Shay could call him, Dexter was pushing his nose inside the SUV. "Hey, buddy. You ready for a hike?"

He barked once and flipped around to perform the most acrobatic zoomies across the grassy area of the parking lot. It was adorable, and a little odd, when he behaved like a true-to-life dog.

"I guess he likes it here," I joked.

"He was born on this side of the mountain," Stout said, landing on top of the Maker backpack.

"Did he tell you that?" Shay turned around, resting her lower back against the vehicle.

"He wouldn't *stop* telling us," Clia explained. "He pointed out every place he'd been while training, and he told us that his dragon was born just over that ridge." She pointed to the snow-covered peak.

Shay flipped through the pages of her trail map. "That's more than a five-mile hike through some pretty tough terrain."

"Closer to six, and I'll bet you wish our wing-ed friend could fly right about now?" Stout's short half-laugh shared no sign of humor.

"It'd be even better if you could carry one bisexual and her lesbian girlfriend," I joked as I poked my finger toward his motionless wings.

"No can do, Wildwood. You're going to have to use that old-fashioned heel and toe method." He flipped his fingers in the air to imitate the walking motion.

"Don't worry, we've got this, Wil," Shay assured me. "We can handle a six-mile hike."

My boot kicked against the ground. "I guess I'm mostly dressed for it."

Shay held open the straps of my backpack, and I slipped them over my shoulders. Even with the added gear, it was almost weightless. "Did you enchant this?"

Her smile was the only answer I needed.

"Damn that magick is so cool." It was less than a year ago when Benton willed her demon steel to the two of us, and along with that came a backpack we could overstuff with gear and still maintain weightlessness. Weeks later the spell wore off, and I wondered now when Shay had learned to recreate it. "How? When?"

"The Rasavatam is how. And as for when? The other day when Clia and I were talking about the fairy steel in your workshop." Shay hopped in place to put a backpack on, but hers was twice as big as mine, stretching almost a foot over her head.

"We *are* only camping overnight, right?" I asked. She looked ready for a week in the wild.

"At least one night, but I've got the next four days off, so I flipped the carriage house sign to "back in a few" and scratched out hours and wrote days on a piece of paper." Wrapping an arm around me, she declared, "It's date week in the woods on a quest to find Giantville, baby." Then she whistled. "Dex, come here buddy."

The dog complied, and Shay's smile was sweet and almost enough to make me forget how much I didn't want to go rough-it camping. She handed me a pair of trekking poles and clipped a tube on Dexter's vest.

"What's the dragon-dog carrying?"

Shay closed the doors and clicked the locks on her truck. "With any luck, that's how we're catching dinner." She tucked a plastic card under the wiper blade. "I'm going to text Dani and give her the location of our parking spot."

I was only half listening as I stared at the tube bouncing on Dexter's side. What could it be? It was less than three feet long, so it couldn't be a gun. There was a padded bag attached along with two zippered pouches. Maybe the takedown bow was in the backpack and Dex was carrying the arrows? If Shay was hunting for our dinner, I was beyond excited to watch her shoot. It could only be my crafted bow that never missed, since of all things that could maim or kill, Shay was terrible with a standard recurve.

"I can't stand it," I said as I noticed Shay was already ten yards away from me.

"Can't stand what?" she yelled over her shoulder.

"What's in the tube?"

"In the what?" she asked, confused.

"What's for dinner?"

"Oh, that." She pointed to the dog, who was prancing toward the trailhead. "Fish. With any luck, we're having fish." She didn't say another word as she kicked at her trekking poles and followed Dexter toward the trail.

"Fish," I whispered, thinking about the one time I'd been fishing and actually caught a fish that you could use as bait, not as a meal. I hoped she was as skilled at fishing as she was at almost everything else.

~~~~~~~~~~

"Just turn the rock over so I can see." Shay held the long piece of line with one hand as she opened the plastic case. "What do the bugs look like?"

She was asking a lot of me as she connected the pieces of her pole into something close to ten feet long. What did the insects crawling on this rock have to do with fishing?

"What, are you an entomologist?" I joked.

"Right now, yes. Wings or no wings?" she persisted.

"Wings," I said, holding the dead bug up so she could see it.

"Perfect."

She picked a fuzzy hook from the case, and within seconds, she had it tied to the end. We had one pole, and I was content to watch her as she pulled her arm back and forth, whipping the line with elegant arcs. Shay swished and swiped over and over until the line landed in a twirly pool of water caught in the rocks of the stream. Seconds later, she tugged the line, and a fish wriggled and writhed in the air until it flipped off the end and plopped back into the river.

"Oh, nice try, baby!" I called to her, "Maybe you'll catch the next one."

Blushing from my encouragement, she waved the hand not holding the fishing rod, looking adorable as she stood knee-deep in the water.

Shay played the fly-fishing game for almost an hour with the same level of luck. They were biting and dancing in
~~~~~~~~~~

the air, but she just couldn't get one to shore. She turned away from the water, sloshing one foot after the other until she was in front of me.

"Maybe we need some better luck," she said. "Want to try?"

I didn't want to get in the water, not with my boots on. "Maybe next time?" I held my hands up in protest.

"I guess we could eat the freeze-dried noodles with meat." She hitched her thumb at our backpack laying a few yards from the river's edge.

"Does the label really only call it 'meat'?"

"Yep, but I'm not sure it's actually meat. It might be that chewy vegetable protein imitation stuff you love." She laughed as she tugged me to my feet.

"I don't want meat noodles." I wiped my hands on my pants. "How does this work?" The grip of the rod was covered in cork, which looked well worn. "Since when do you go fishing?" We sidestepped to the sandbank where my toes touched the water edge.

"It's a solitary thing I used to escape. It's been a while since I needed to fill my free time." She winked at me.

"About twelve months?" I blew a puff of air at the reel, pretending to remove imaginary dust.

"Yep, that'd be a good estimate." She positioned herself behind me, her breasts pushed against my back. Her next words were breathy against my ear. "Someone showed up to fill a space or two."

"I'm glad you found time for me between fishing, target practice, and all those superhero duties."

Her laugh was warm on my neck as she guided my fingers with hers to grip the rod. "Fly-fishing is as close to therapy as you can get, and there's no co-pay." She pulled the bright orange string from the spool and clumped it onto the ground near our feet. It looked like a tangled mess.

"That pile of string makes me want to go to therapy," I joked.

"I'll show you how this works. Be patient."

The fingers of the left hand pinched the string as her right arm, synced with my own, moved in slow, rhythmic swings. There were only a few yards of fishing line as we began, but little by little, the motion sucked my tiny fly lure out toward the river's flow. I wanted to fall into her body and rest in the motion. Back and forth, line inch by line inch. It felt absolutely perfect to be in her arms.

"Is this fishing or foreplay?" I teased.

Our wrists flicked forward with a snap, and the spool of line on the ground sucked up like magick, the tiny fly lure hitting the far side of the river upstream.

"That, my darling, is the most erotic fly cast of my life." She kissed my neck and stepped back, leaving me alone with a drifting hook in the water.

"Foreplay it is." The smile on my face faded instantly when I felt the tug on my pole. "Oh, shit!" I yelled. "Oh, shit! Oh, shit!"

"Don't panic. This is fishing."

"I'm panicking because I don't know how to do fishing."

Shay laughed. "I don't think the fish know that." She grabbed the bright orange line and tugged it. "Baby, you're catching a fish. Hold the orange line and start pulling it in. Don't let the fish get too much room to wiggle away."

Just as she said it, my fingers fumbled the string, and the fish flipped out of the water and off of my hook.

"I guess he got away."

Shay pulled the line back into a pile in front of us. "They're fighters today."

"Does this mean noodles and meat?" I asked.

"Giving up so fast?" She pulled her hair away from her face.

The river water rushed against the toes of my boots. "I'm not excited about getting my boots wet. You remember that part, right?"

"Do you want fish or noodles?"

Before I could answer, Dexter jumped from the grass and launched into the water. His entire fur-covered body submerged in a wrecked plunge.

"We are *so* having noodles," I said as the animal moved through our fishing zone. "He's going to scare them off."

Shay wound the fishing line in and tossed the pole on shore. "Dexter!" The commanding tone of her voice made me pause, but the animal didn't stop. I saw his tail flip once with fur, and seconds later, he resurfaced with a spike-ended dragon tail.

"What is he doing?" I asked, but Shay didn't answer.

"He doesn't want noodles and meat either," Stout said. "We all kinda took a quick survey, and Dexter decided he was going to put you out of your misery."

We didn't get to ask anything else before the dragon head popped up and launched to shore. Dexter opened his mouth, and four gorgeous fish dropped out onto the sand. Shay jumped to catch them before they wriggled and squirmed their way back into the water.

"He caught us fish!" I yelled a little louder and more enthusiastically than I'd intended.

"He sure the hell did." Shay tossed one up near our campsite. "Help me, love."

The two of us stumbled to grab and flip the wriggling fish away from the water.

"Good job, Dexter!" I cheered. "We're eating fish tonight!"

Shay spent the next twenty minutes cleaning and spearing roasting sticks through Dexter's catch. With the help of two strong fairies and my Maker skills, we built a fire for cooking, and we feasted on our river trout.

"I have no idea what noodles and meat would have tasted like, but that fish was just about the best diner I've ever eaten," I confessed, rubbing my full, soft belly.

"Don't let Diana hear that. She'll burn your burgers."

"If your bar princess made fish like this, I'd let her burn all of my burgers." I poked the simmering fire.

"I guess Dexter gets the gold star for fishing." Shay clipped the fly from her line and rolled the spool tight. "As long as we have him, I don't need to stand knee deep in an icy cold river."

"Double gold star on dry feet." I clapped my hands together. "What's next on the hike to Giantville?" I asked, well aware that the sun would set in a few hours.

"Have you ever set up a tent?" Shay asked as she scraped the remnants of her tiny camp plate into the fire.

I swished my hands in the wash basin. "Nope, but I'm guessing that I'm about to learn."

"Stout, you and Clia are on dish duty." She pointed to the collapsible bucket by the river as she dropped a drawstring bag on the ground at my feet. "There are two tents in here: one for us and one for the family."

"Just because you have your own tent doesn't mean we won't hear the two of you," Stout grumbled.

"We're not having sex in a tent!" I yelled at him and looked up to see the blush on Shay's cheeks. "Are we having sex in the tent tonight?"

"You already said that you're not." I heard the clash of metal plates and utensils.

Shay raked away the sticks and stones from the campsite with her foot and rolled out the smaller of the two tents. "Dexter, Clia, and Stout can sleep over here away from us."

"Holy Brigid, you are truly my champion, superhero." I released the cord that tied my tent in a bundle. Mimicking

Shay's actions, I cleared a space to roll out our tent. "I'm not sure how this goes."

I dumped out the tangle of bungee-connected poles and looked up to see Shay threading hers through the loops on the outside of her tent. Seconds later, a dome appeared, and she was hammering stakes in the corners.

"Give me a second, and I'll help you." When she said, "a second," this time she meant it because I stood back and watched her assemble ours with no hesitation.

Stout and Clia carried the dishes and set them on the bolder to dry. "It feels like rain." He sniffed the air.

"We can put everything inside the tents now, and they should be safe through the night," Shay said.

"What about the things that live in this forest?" I asked. It was the suggestion of storms that conjured thoughts of additional dangers. Monsters lived in the wild, not just in Bannock.

"We've got our weapons." Shay picked up my backpack and put it inside the tent. "We also brought along a fur-faced dragon." She ruffled the hair around Dexter's ears.

"He is good in a fight," I said.

I sat down against a fallen tree in front of the fire, letting the rise and fall of the flames comfort me. Fire was the source of my Maker power, but it was so much more. It influenced every part of my life. I got lost in the moment, thinking about Brigid's gifts and my hammer. It would be a few days until I returned to the forge, and it felt strange to need it so much.

"What are you thinking?" Shay asked as she lowered herself to sit behind me.

My back rested against her as her hands came around to rest on my thighs. "I was thinking about blacksmithing."

"Makes sense." She rested her chin on my shoulder. "What else?"

"Nothing else." We were camping in the middle of a massive national forest, and I felt perfect trust that she would protect us. "I don't know how to explain it, but I feel safe here."

"In the forest?" she asked.

I nodded. "Does that seem weird?"

"Not really. You've always had a connection to earth magick. It makes sense that the farther you move from civilization, the safer you feel." Soft hands moved under the hem of my shirt and rested on the soft of my belly.

"Your body so close to mine might have something to do with it, too."

"Hmm, maybe."

We sat in silence for a long time, basking in the heat of the dancing flames. Dexter curled on the ground beside us, and Stout and Clia set off on an exploratory flight. It took little to imagine what it must be like for Clia to be able to roam freely after so many years locked inside a terrarium cage. I'm sure some part of me would disappear and never return. I felt the weight of my mind fade as my body relaxed into Shay's embrace.

"Are you falling asleep, love?" Her whispered words tickled just enough to wake me.

"Just a little," I admitted.

She stood up and held her hand out to me. "Come on, let's go get some sleep."

Letting her pull me to my feet, I patted the butt of my jeans to wipe away the grass and dirt. "Why haven't we gone camping before? I kinda like this."

"Probably the demons and power transfers and maybe inheriting a dragon and a fairy or two. They've kept us a little busy." She led me toward our tent. "Dexter." His furry head popped up, and his ears flicked to capture the sound of Shay's voice. "Get in your tent, buddy."

His body flexed as he stood, hesitating for a moment before shaking to shed the sticks and dirt from his fur. It was cuter than my butt swipe, and I knelt for a second to hug him around the neck.

"Goodnight, dragon-dog." I booped his nose with my fingertip and he trotted to the tent we'd set up a few feet from our own. "Are you tired at all?" I asked as Shay zipped the door of our tent.

It was spacious for a two-person setup, and I'd be able to stretch my full five-foot-five-inch length. Even Shay's nearly six-foot height still left room for our shoes to nestle in the covered entryway.

"I'm not tired at all, but you are."

As we settled down, I got my first taste of what sleeping in this tent would be like. The foam-covered floor didn't feel like our mattress at home, but I was sure I could sleep.

"It's been a while since I've hiked." The excuse was lame at best because I'd been in the city most of our years apart.

She crouched near the doorway taking the time to unlace her boots and settle them, opening the tongue so she could put them on quickly. It was a charming habit.

She crawled across me until her face hovered over mine. "Baby, when was the last time you hiked?"

"Like further than getting supplies for the forge?"

Her laugh was slight and knowing. "That is *so* not a hike." Her lips touched mine before she rolled onto her back and opened her arm so I could cuddle up against her.

"I've never been on a real hike," I confessed.

"Hmm..." The sound vibrated against my ear, and I propped myself up on my elbow so I could see her face.

"What's that mean?" I asked, struggling to read her face in the dark.

"It means that the two of us need to do more of this. I like hiking with you."

"The walking part kinda sucks, but this is very nice." I hitched a leg over her hip as my fingers slid beneath the hem of her shirt to rest on the taught skin on her abs. I knew my hands were cold but she didn't flinch.

"You know the kids can hear us?" She chuckled.

"Pay attention, superhero. I'm still fully dressed."

Shay rolled to her side, pushing up to hover over my body. My fingers traveled along the muscles of her forearms, sneaking inside the loose fit of her shirt sleeves. Her body was a delight, something she'd kept hidden for so long that was now the most breathtaking part of my life. With one hand on the tent floor, she used her other hand to pop open the buttons on my flannel shirt.

"I can fix that, you know?" Her smile was mesmerizing as I lay there, gasping, heart pounding with lust as she held her body above mine

"With just one hand?"

My fingers tightened on her biceps as I tried to pull her on top of me, but she pushed to straddle my thighs. Resting on her knees, she pulled both of her shirts over her head and yanked my collar to lift my body from the ground.

"Two very capable hands." The thickness of her voice was enough to command a white flag of sexual surrender. "We're about to wreck the solitude of this forest."

There was no hesitation as I tossed my shirt off. "Damn, Shay. What's gotten into you?"

She didn't say a word as the buttons on her pants popped one by one and she kicked out of her jeans. I licked my lips as the light of the moon peeking through the canopy illuminated her chest. My hand raised toward the muscles of her abdomen, but she caught them just before I could touch.

"Uh, uhh," She pointed to my pants. "Off with those."

Would it always be like this? I thought as I fumbled with the zipper of my fly. Would we always want each other so much and need to touch each other so much that all sense faded around us? My fingers trembled as her hand tangled in mine.

"The first time I ever wanted to kiss you was outside in the wild," Shay purred. Our lips were inches apart as we knelt face to face. "You were so free-spirited, and I wanted to be like you."

"You were kinda skinny and so little back then." There was nothing reserved about the way my eyes traveled from her lips to the hollow of her throat, down along the curve of her breasts, to the plane of her flexed abdomen. "You're not so skinny anymore." My fingers caressed the scars on her skin. "So damn beautiful."

Her hand cupped my breast. "Goddess, Wil. You take my breath away."

And she took mine away as the two of us made love in our tent, crashing into each other and wrecking the solitude of the forest long into the night.

CHAPTER VIII

BASE

"**D**amn," I whispered into the stillness of the morning.

The throbbing numbness crippling my arm was from the silent woman beside me. Shay's body mass was already greater than my own, but this morning it felt like the entire forest had slept on top of me. I tipped my shoulders, attempting to relieve the pressure to no avail. It was a tough decision to wake her, but there was no moving this woman.

"Shay," I whispered her name, and she didn't move. "Honey?" I shook my hips to jostle her torso.

"Mmm."

The noise reminded me of the morning Stout had misused magick in the carriage house. I panicked at the memory, threw my girlfriend off my arm, and watched her eyes pop open.

"What's wrong?" Shay had a remarkable ability to go from deeply asleep to fully awake in a snap, and right now her huge wide eyes were cutting through the silent darkness around us.

"You were asleep." If I'd had it in me, I would have smacked myself for the comment. Of *course,* she was asleep; that was hardly an explanation.

"I do that a lot at night." She wiped sleep from her eyes.

"But my arm...and then you made a noise, and I panicked."

"You panicked because your arm made noise?" She raised her palm to silence me before I could say another word. "No, wait." To my disappointment she turned to find her shirt and pulled it over her head. Shay wiggled into fresh boxers and yesterday's jeans. "What's wrong with your arm?"

Always the cop, she was on top of the situation. "It fell asleep under you." I clenched my fist open and closed to help increase circulation.

She rubbed my bicep, then tickled my skin all the way to my hands, stimulating more than my arm. "How's it feel now?"

"Better." The sound of me swallowing echoed in my ears.

She smiled as she surveyed the rest of my naked body. "And the noise?"

"That came from you, and I thought you were poisoned or drunk on fairy and anvil dust."

Her hands moved from my shoulder to my palm, caressing the heavy sensation of numbness away. "I'm not poisoned. I'm completely alert and thinking as straight as my queer little heart can be." Her lips pressed to the palm of my hand. "How's that feel now?"

I took a slow, deep breath. "Better," was the only word I could form as I closed my eyes to her touch.

"Would you like to get dressed and maybe finish the last few miles of the hike?" Her smile felt like waking from a dream as she cast her love through the space between us.

"You know, if you keep it up with all of that happiness, I just might go anywhere you lead me."

Maybe it was the lovemaking from the night before, or perhaps it was the mountain air, but with the touch of her hand and that smile on her face, I felt a lightness that I hadn't for most of my life.

"Well, today I'm leading you to Giantville, and maybe if we're lucky, that will lead to a demon-free future." She reached toward the opening of the tent and picked up my shirt.

"I would like to vote for next level luck, please." The t-shirt came flying toward me, and I caught it. "That's harsh for a superhero. I thought you were supposed to be all chivalrous and noble." I flipped the cotton material until I found the neck and sleeves.

"You were singing a different tune last night." Her finger hooked my discarded underwear. "I'm pretty sure the thoughts going through your mind right now have nothing to do with chivalrous acts."

Shay was absolutely correct; I was, in fact, thinking about begging her to touch me last night and into the morning, remembering how I sank my teeth into the muscle of her shoulder as she hurried her fingers inside me. Oh, yes, her touch was, by my definition, undoubtedly righteous. I swallowed hard and looked into her dazzling eyes.

"Wildwood Blackstone, you're being very naughty right now."

I scooted in front of her, the length of my t-shirt barely touching my curvy hips. "I can't help it. You bring out the naughty in me."

"How noble," she joked and handed me fresh panties from her backpack.

"Exactly my thought." I finished dressing as she laced her boots, unzipped the door of the tent, and crawled out.

"What the…" She stopped mid-sentence.

"What the what?"

My head popped out of the open netting, and I gasped. The sight in front of us was stunning. A thin haze of pink fog surrounded the second tent, where a dragon-dog and two fairies slept.

"Who's magick is it?" I asked, kicking into my untied boots.

"Well, it isn't mine, and it's obviously not yours, so it has to be theirs." She crept closer, and without hesitation, Shay's hand swiped through the fog.

"What's it feel like?" I asked.

She chuckled. "Feels like…"

"It feels like we didn't want to listen to the two of you go at it all night." Stout's grumble penetrated the haze. "I swear it'd make a Bliation blush."

"Make a Bli-a-what?" Shay asked.

"A Bliation blush." He unzipped the door of his tent and flew out. "A Bliation. You never heard of them?"

"Not a whisper," Shay replied, and I confirmed I hadn't either with a silent headshake.

"From the sound of things, you know about tops and bottoms." He cleared his throat, and I could almost hear the hard blink of surprise Shay's eyes made.

"Oh, goddess, Stout please don't tell us about fairy sex or compare us to porn," I begged. "It's too early."

Clia exited the tent, followed by our prancing dragon-dog. "It's not sexual at all," she explained. "It's more about vulgarity and thoughtlessness."

"You're losing me." Shay sat on the fallen tree.

"The Bliation are our fiercest warriors," Stout explained. "What they lack in chivalry and manners, they make up for in ferocity and bloodlust."

"Basically, you're saying that me making love to my lady would take out an army of menacing fairies?" I huffed my breath over my knuckles and rubbed them across my chest with pride.

"Yeah, something like that," Stout mumbled as he flew toward the flameless fire pit.

"And what does that have to do with the pink fog?" Shay asked.

"We put up a noise barrier," he explained.

I felt the heat of a blush warm my cheeks. "Oh."

"'Oh' is right. Geez, you were 'oh-ing' for hours." He wasn't holding back, but in our defense we're in love, and who wouldn't want to make love under the moonlight of the forest.

"Tell me about the barrier." Shay disregarded the intimacy conversation and went right for the magick.

"That's nothing, really," Clia said. "Fairy magick with a dash of dragon enchantment to boost."

"Why would you need a spell like that?" I asked.

"Barriers are shields," Clia said. "Easy magick to allow the practitioner to move through a space. The Rasavatam is loaded with barriers for many situations."

"Sex barriers, though?" I *almost* said it without giggling.

"Sometimes silence is necessary," Clia replied.

"Sometimes it keeps a fairy from screaming into the void of the forest," Stout grumbled.

"Is-te vide, glo-este," the fairy whispered as Dexter crept around us to create a circle in the dirt. "You've used this spell before, Shay. As the Magick."

"Yes, in the tunnels after the attack." Shay took hold of my hand, grounding the two of us with earth energy.

"It's powerful and simple and should be kept at the ready."

"Are you expecting trouble?" I asked, feeling the muscles of my body constrict with anxiety.

"Always." The three responded almost in sync, and I should have known. Everything we did came with a sprinkle of trouble.

"I thought the giants were good," I said with a childlike innocence that startled me. Shay disappeared inside the tent.

"They are," Stout assured me. "It's all the other wild things out here that we need to be aware of, remember."

I thought about our night in the woods, the ease with which we'd set up camp and cuddled in front of the fire. Last night, I'd felt safe in Shay's arms, but now Stout was making me wonder if my approach to camping had been too casual.

"Like what?" I asked, watching bundled bedrolls fly from the tent to the tarp on the ground.

"Bears." Shay's head poked out of the mesh door. "Mountain lions, wolves, coyotes. Maybe a lynx." The list grew longer, and I was glad we were discussing this in the daylight. I could identify a bear and maybe a wolf, but the rest were a mystery.

"You could also encounter shape shifters that can manifest into any and all of those things," Stout added. "They're harder to fight."

"Shape shifters?" I said with a squeak.

Shay stepped out of the tent and kicked a corner stake. "Don't panic, love. You've forged excellent weapons, and even when you're sleeping, I've got you."

"What about when *you're* sleeping?"

She smiled as she pulled up the final stake and the dome of the tent collapsed. "This." She held up her wrist to show me the polished cuff. "This." She knocked her knuckles against the demon kevlar covering her chest. "And this." She tugged the snap on her handgun.

"Don't forget about him." Stout pointed at the dog, who lay licking in between the pads of his paws.

"And especially Dexter," Shay chortled as she flipped the tent poles to collapse them into the storage bag.

"I think I liked it better in the carriage house," I joked as I held the compression bag for our sleeping blankets. "And that barrier we put up? I like that even more." The barrier wasn't perfect, since Andrea had planted a bit of herself inside a file we'd carried into the carriage house, but once that was removed, we'd been safe inside Shay's Magick protections.

"As long as we travel together, we're all safe," Shay promised me.

"Until we find the thing in our dreams," I reminded her.

"Giantville first." She cinched the drawstring on her backpack.

"Right," I agreed and poked at the fire pit. "Do we have a plan for food?"

Stout flew beside me. "Did you bring a six-pack?" We looked at Shay for an answer.

"I have two cans in the bottom of that bag." She tipped her thumb toward the backpack I'd carried. "One for today and one for tomorrow."

"Just one?"

"Had to keep things light, my friend." Shay unzipped the bottom of my bag and removed a foil wrapped can. My eyes locked on the wrinkled aluminum wrapping that Mama Pierce taught us when we'd lived in her home. My smile must have been unusual because Shay paused before opening the can. "Thinking of Mama Pierce?"

"Yes, and of you."

She peeled the foil away and crumpled the ball in the backpack. "You know we didn't have much, but we had her."

She popped the tab on the can of beer and set it on the fallen tree. Stout rummaged through the backpack for a straw, which Shay had also remembered to pack.

"She's probably the only reason I have you." My arm circled around her waist, and my head fell against her shoulder.

"Before we get too sentimental," Stout said, slurping from the can, "what's the plan for today?"

Shay opened the side pouch of the backpack and dropped a few leaves beside the can of beer. From the way Clia zipped toward the plant, I was certain it was catnip.

"According to Clia, we head south into that mountain." Shay turned with her hand in the air, looking like a rotating weathervane as she pointed south. It was adorable.

"Perfect, so what did you bring for human breakfast?" I stared at her backpack, then glanced at mine. "Please don't say noodles and meat."

She removed a plastic bag filled with pellets. "I'm not a complete wilding. Dexter gets his regular kibble and we get..." She reached in for an iridescent pouch. "Eggs and meat." She whispered through smiling teeth. "Just add water."

"Is this any better than the noodle and meat combo?" I asked.

"Not by much, but it's loaded with protein, and today, we're gonna need it." Shay set the warming canister on the rock beside the fire pit. "*Ignis.*" Her palm flame flickered to ignite yesterday's coals. "It'll only take a few minutes, and your tummy will be full."

"Yay," I said, but it lacked enthusiasm.

While Dexter and our fairies finished their breakfast, I took a moment to relieve myself in the woods. It was a stunning landscape of wildflowers and tall trees. The thick brush prevented me from wandering too far, which was probably keeping me within a safe distance of my favorite people. This forest called to me, and I felt at home standing inside it.

Today had promise; everything around me suggested we were correct in our choice to be here. *You're Indigenous.* The thought ran through me, though if felt impossible to understand the meaning of that without guidance from someone like me. "Like me" had meant nothing before now. There had been no one to compare *me* to.

I wandered back into camp to find a brown speckled pile of rehydrated eggs. Shay was dashing her plate with so much pepper that I was certain this would not be a delicious experience.

"Can Dexter go fishing?" I plunged my hands into the wash water before picking up my plate.

"I thought about it." Shay took a reserved spoonful.

"We could put your thoughts into action." I sat on the log beside her.

"You're going to want to put pepper on it." She handed me the paper packets.

The eggs looked like rubber, and when I pressed my fork into them, they felt like it, too. The first bite wasn't as bad as I expected, and I just reminded myself that it was better than being hungry. I had way too much experience with being hungry.

"Full of protein," I said, feigning enthusiasm. "Yum."

We finished our food in comfortable silence, and in the end, it was the perfect fuel to carry us to our next meal, which made me think of noodles and meat.

"Please tell me Dexter is going to fish for our lunch."

Shay laughed as she poured water over her plate to rinse it clean. "First, I'll try it, then you get a chance, and as a last resort, Dexter can get dinner for us."

"More fishing?"

"We're following the river. It makes sense." She took the empty plate from my hand, rinsed it, and put it into the backpack. In a few minutes, no one would know we'd camped in this spot.

The hike was not as complicated as I'd expected. We had two fairy guides as full-on compasses and a rambunctious dog that would transform to clear a path when the brush grew too thick. Shay was razor focused on finding the portal entrance and had also planned a perfect overnight hiking adventure. Despite all that, though, I was just this side of terrified. Giants might be nice to fairies but would they instantly trust the Magick and the Maker?

And, I wondered grimly as we trudged through the forest, *what would they do to us if they didn't?*

CHAPTER IX

GOLIATH

"Are you sure we're still traveling south?" Stout muttered beside my ear.

It felt like we'd hiked for hours as we walked Dexter's path. Although I could hear the river, I could no longer see it, and that went against Shay's plan.

"We are definitely headed south." She held up her compass.

"We should be there already," Stout said as he flew toward Dexter, who had flopped at the edge of the forest. "It's been over two miles."

I felt something, like a heartbeat, then everything around me disappeared. The tall grasses circling Dexter swayed in the breeze. It was warm against my face, like my lover's caress, but it wasn't Shay's. She was beside me, aghast from the same sensation.

"Take my hand." Her voice was hushed, not guarded, more sentimental.

The sigil in my palm burned, and the Maker's mark soldered to my protective wrist cuff sent a vibration that traveled through my hand and into Shay's.

"I think we've arrived," I said, awestruck.

My eyes closed as the breeze traveled across the grassy space. The earth was singing her song, and I fell to my knees, overwhelmed by the energy. Shay didn't let go, and I felt her magick move to balance this unknown force of nature.

"It couldn't be anything else," Shay said, dropping beside me. "Can you carry this?" she asked, and I understood that *this* was the powerful surge making my body tremble.

"I can. I just need a minute." It took almost five for me to stand on my own and another for me to balance without the anchor of Shay's arm around my waist.

"What do you think it is?" I asked.

"It's a barrier," Clia said. "Much like the one surrounding the carriage house. But this one is giant." She realized what she said and smiled sheepishly. "For lack of better terminology."

"We found it," I whispered.

The ground shook. I've never experienced an earthquake, but as the trees swayed behind us and bark and twigs popped on the ground at my feet, I knew something big was here.

"We did, and it feels like they found us, too." Shay's arm came around to push me behind her. Wearing demon kevlar protected her from everything...at least until now.

My wild thoughts about meeting the giants of Grant's Pass fell a little short because the creature that materialized in front of us appeared to be just over seven feet tall and mostly human.

"Are you lost?" The voice was deep and perhaps meant to intimidate, but we'd conquered demons, fought massive spider creatures, and destroyed the evil inside Andrea Peters. This person was not a threat.

"We aren't lost. We're looking for a place to plant this sunshine in a bottle." Shay pulled the small glass container from the zipper pocket of her pants and held it up. Dexter crawled through the tall grass, camouflaging himself from the stranger.

"What makes you think you should plant it here?" They delivered the question with a tight smirk.

Shay whispered, "*Ignis,*" and her hand burst with flame.

"The Magick lives again." Then they looked at me. "Do you, too, bring the power of the goddess?"

I raised my hand, and before I could whisper the word, our mini giant swelled to nearly twenty feet and dropped to one knee.

"Forgive my rudeness."

I looked at Shay, and she looked at me. I didn't know what to say, so I waited.

"I am Helms," the giant said. "Keeper of this pathway."

"So this is the portal?" Shay asked.

Helms nodded. "This is the way to my people, but we didn't expect your presence."

Shay dropped the bottle at the giant's feet. "We're looking for passage to the fairy world."

Helms picked up the container, and it looked like a grain of rice in his massive fingers. "That way is not open any longer, not for hundreds of years."

Stout flew to the giant's face. "That's not possible. I'm here, and so are many from the fairy realm."

"You're only here because you've been here," Helms told him. "Not one soul has passed between, not since the fall."

"The fall?" I asked.

Helms leaned closer to me. "A great evil passed by my predecessor. They were like me, the keeper of the passage, but trickery came to pass, and their death led to the collapse of the passages between all the realms."

"All?" I asked. "How many are there?"

"More than the mortal world can count. And that truth is what the great evil came to destroy."

"What great evil?" Shay asked. "Was this an army?"

Helms shook his head slowly and seriously. "It was just one. The evil of evil and the fractured form of what you hold there." A giant finger pointed to my hand.

"The sigil of Brigid." A warm sensation moved through me as I spoke her name.

"Yes, the Magick and the Maker, I feel the power is strong with you."

My hand rested on Shay's hip as she positioned her body between us. Without a whisper of a word, Dexter appeared at Shay's hip, his ears perked and his body ready to pounce. Helms laid a palm on the ground, and our dog growled.

"Dexter." Shay's voice broke the silence, and I jumped at the sound.

Helms looked surprised. "The Magick and the Maker possess a shapeshifter."

It was a statement more than a question as Helms stood to full height and spoke a command in an unknown language. The tall grasses spiraled round and round, much like the portal in Andrea's loft. With a wave of a hand, the giant escorted us to the passage.

"Your fairies may join us," he said. And then the massive giant stepped into the portal, leaving us to stare at one another.

"I'll go through first," Shay said as she knuckle-bumped the demon kevlar over her chest. "If it's evil, it'll probably send me right back out, so be prepared to catch me."

I tried not to laugh at the absurdity of the situation, but this was the kind of crazy unknown that followed us all the time. "Catch you?"

"Just widen your stance." She turned around to kick my back foot out a few inches before kissing me, then Shay stepped into the spiraling pathway and disappeared.

"Shay!" I yelled her name, and Dexter leapt forward before I could grab hold of his collar.

I waited, frozen in place, like a boxer expecting the hit to come. Everything in the field was silent, including the portal. The absence of sound outside of my body was a powerful contrast to the pounding of my heartbeat in my head. My pulse was racing, and my hands held a position like a catcher primed for a fastball pitch. Where had they gone? I felt a tap on my shoulder and turned to see Shay standing behind me.

"What the hell?" It squeaked out of my mouth. Shay's eyebrow raised at the sound, and her giggle was the embodiment of mischief. "Where'd you come from?"

"Take my hand, and I'll show you."

The passage between our world and the giant's was a fantastical dance of light and sound, *nothing* like the pecks and probes of Andrea's portal. I felt Shay's fingers tighten around mine.

"It's like I'm swimming in happiness," I said.

I heard rather than saw Shay's smile. "I know."

We could have been traveling for minutes or seconds. I lost track of time as we stepped through every color of the spectrum. If glitter was an emotion, that's how it felt to leave our reality and enter this new one. I didn't have to wonder why it was guarded by a giant.

Our feet landed on a crumble of loose rocks and sand. It looked earthly, but it couldn't be, could it?

"What is this place?" I asked.

"This is the pathway home," Clia said as she flew down a grass and gravel footpath.

The ground trembled as Helms stepped over us, covering twenty-five yards with each stride. We'd have to hurry to keep up with two enthusiastic fairies and one giant.

I felt a pinch on the back of my arm. "Ouch."

"Just making sure this is real." Shay smiled as she reached for my hand, which was rubbing the burning pinch site.

"Woman, you need to pinch your own arm. That hurts."

"That's why I pinched you instead." Her smile grew.

"Uh huh." My tone was biting. "I can attest that this is, in fact, real."

Shay stopped fast, and I bumped into her as we reached the top of a hill. Giantville was a spectacular sight. The walking path met with a stone roadway twice the width of any superhighway I'd ever seen. What looked like a mile was merely a few hundred steps for our new friend as Helms waited for us to catch up.

I rubbed my arm where Shay had pinched it and rejoiced in this new realm.

"We're really in the land of giants," I said, feeling detached from reality.

"And it's better than I imagined," Shay marveled.

"Wait until we get to the fairy world," Clia whispered. "You'll feel like Helms there."

I wondered what that would be like and what else was ahead of us. I felt a little like Gulliver, going on an adventure of extremes–not taller than everyone around him, but smaller.

Shay's hand tightened in my own as we stepped onto the roadway. The buildings ahead of us were massive works of stone and mortar, like castles found in medieval worlds. I reached back to feel for my hammer, comforted by the balance Brigid's power gave.

"You good, baby?" Shay asked as she stopped to watch a group of giant beings cross the road ahead.

"About as good as I can be under the circumstances," I admitted.

"It's a lot to take in, even for me."

"Yeah."

I was just as captivated by the fantastical sights around us as Shay was. My eyes darted everywhere, trying to take everything in. The trees were twice our earthly size; the plants and flowers were massive. Everything in the realm of giants was bigger than in the human world, and I didn't have broad enough sight to absorb it all.

"I think Helms is waving us to move faster," Shay said as she raised our joined hands to point.

Stout zipped around our heads excitedly. "This place is amazing. There's a fruit tree over there. I think they're like grapes, but they're not on vines, and when I tasted them it was like drinking a beer! In what universe does beer grow on trees?"

I had to laugh. Only Stout would taste unknown fruit and believe it was beer just for him. Then my mirth was replaced with concern. "Why would you do that? Eat an unknown fruit?" I didn't mean to treat him like a child, but we were dealing with a ridiculous level of unknowns.

"It's called blamberry," Clia said.

She held one up as we continued to walk, and I was shocked she could even lift it. It was like she was defying the laws of physics. It looked ridiculously huge in her hands, and when I took the basketball-sized fruit from her, the rind rubbed off on my skin.

"Is it magick?" Shay asked, touching her fingertip to the juice.

"It is whatever you desire," Clia said with a smile.

"Naturally Stout would desire beer." I thought for a moment about what I most desired, about the passion of life and longing. In short, I thought of loving Shay. As I thought about taking a bite, I was sure my face was burning a bright red.

"You're not thinking about noodles and meat, are you?" Shay's whisper tripped the hairs on the back of my neck, sending tiny flesh bumps to high alert on my arms.

"Definitely not noodles and meat."

"You going to give it a taste?" she asked.

I shook my head, "Not in public."

Her laugh was loud enough to draw the attention of some of the giants who were congregating nearby. Our small statures were inviting a crowd, and Helms returned to where we'd stopped.

"I see you found a blamberry." He pinched the fruit between his fingers. "They're not quite in season, so your mouth might not be as excited as you might like." The juice squirted before Helms popped it through giant lips. "Nope, not quite ready," Helms' expression was much like eating a lemon when expecting an orange. "Although, with the size of your taste buds, it might hit differently."

"It tasted real to me." Stout flew closer to the giant's ear, and the two chatted as we walked into the town. Helms led us through the streets, and as we traveled the city, it was clear someone had informed the citizens of our presence.

"I'm taking you to see the town leader," Helms said. "Your desire to pass through to the fairy realm will meet with much resistance."

Shay jogged to keep up with his huge strides, but I was happy to linger behind and take in the gawking citizens, many of whom looked like they might be children. Giant children, obviously, but children nonetheless.

"Hello." I said to a young looking giant.

"Hello," they squeaked and turned to run inside.

The building looked like a bakery or perhaps an inn. It was hard to tell because the windows were double my height and it was impossible to see inside without stopping and climbing a wall, but the smell of freshly baked bread was unmistakable.

"This place is fantastic!" I exclaimed, staring at the buildings and envying the scrolling ironwork on the structures.

Shay continued to walk, and I felt the pull against our tangled fingers as she encouraged me to follow.

"We live a simple life," Helms said humbly.

"It feels a little medieval," Stout said, not unkindly. "Not much for modern things?"

Helms shrugged his huge shoulders. "We consider ancient ways more practical."

"No motor vehicles?" I asked.

"You mean like in your Earth cities?"

Hiding my smile was impossible, and I hoped he wasn't insulted. "Yes, like Earth cities."

"We used to be able to borrow from alternate worlds," he said, "but that has been long prevented. The realm delivers everything we need for the people here, but we've had to become accustomed to what you might consider the old ways."

"A simple life indeed," Shay whispered.

I caught a glimpse of her out of the corner of my eye, and it was then that I noticed something. Until this moment, I hadn't seen the shadows beneath her eyes or the way the gorgeous lines didn't wrinkle as much when her cheeks pinched with a smile.

Before I could mention it to her, Helms said, "The children of the town have run ahead to tell our leader of your presence."

"They'll welcome us in peace, won't they, Helms?" Shay asked.

He smiled. "You'll be pleasantly surprised."

Helms reached for the iron ring handle on the massive door in front of us. The tug seemed effortless, but I could tell by the squealing of the hinges that this was a barrier against invasion. Something or someone important was behind it. Helms held a hand up for us to wait.

My eyes traveled through the marvelous chamber. The vaulted ceilings were an architectural triumph of stone and steel. The frameless windows meshed with twisted iron created a sense of safety from whatever could manage to reach the twenty-foot height from the floor. The stonemasons of Giantville were obviously exceptional artists.

Helms' steps were slow and calculated as he approached the line of weaponed guards. He looked petite among the serious faces. Whispered conversations were held, and moments later, a voice echoed through the chamber.

"You may approach."

Shay stepped forward, blatantly keeping her entire body between me and potential danger. My hand fell to the small of her back, touching the weaved nylon holding her demon kevlar in place. There was comfort in the weight of my hammer in the backpack and the magickal axe on my hip.

One of the guards stepped forward. "Our wise leader requires all approach unarmed."

"This request is not possible," Shay informed him, her voice echoing between the chamber walls.

The guard lowered a spear head, pointing it at Shay. "Our wise leader—"

The demand was cut short by a voice breaking through the armed line of giants. "The Maker of Bannock is a weapon," it said. "There will be no fight here; Brigid is her hand."

My palm opened, and I stared at the mark of the goddess burned into my skin. "Brigid is my hand?" I asked mostly to myself before the voice of their leader rang out once more.

"Only the Maker of Bannock wears the sigil of our goddess." The leader's head tipped. "We are one with her."

The chamber space vibrated with the simultaneous echo of every creature repeating their leader's praise. "We are one with her."

Brigid was their goddess, too. My feet shifted to move forward, but Shay's hand stopped fast over my heart, holding me in position. "Wait."

I didn't question her about it because she knew the magickal world better than me.

"Do not be afraid for your safety in this chamber, Magick of Bannock," their leader said.

"It is true, then," one guard whispered to another.

"Leave us." Their leader waved a hand, and the echo of marching feet faded behind the oversized wooden doors. "Approach."

Shay squeezed my hand, and together we stepped closer to the leader of the giants.

"And your shape-shifter."

"Dexter, *ante*," Shay called, and the dog was against her hip, matching us stride for stride.

The giant stepped down from the elevated platform, sitting on the bottom of a set of steps so that we were closer, almost face to face.

"You have come to the Passofgrant, the land of giants. I am lord of this realm, Kharle the third."

"Do we call you lord?" I asked.

"You call me family. Brigid is the mother of us, and so we are flesh kin."

"But you are the leader of the giants?" Shay asked.

"Today I am."

Shay's brow pinched with confusion. "I don't understand."

"There is no importance in labels. Our world changes, and we adapt." Kharle rubbed their hands together in excitement. "The Maker and the Magick of Bannock have arrived in Passofgrant. We have waited hundreds of years for this to be true."

"You have?" I asked.

"There is much to share, and I'm certain the Earthen hourglass limits your visit with us."

"Yes, but we have not traveled so far in distance, just in space," I said. "Well, at least that's how it felt moving through the portal."

"Ah, yes. It feels strange to move between worlds. I remember it so well. With good fortune, you'll come to understand that soon." Kharle stood and walked toward the chamber doors. "Come, and I will take you to the realm keeper."

"More giants." My eyes scanned the room for Clia and Stout, but they were nowhere to be found. "Where have our fairies gone?"

Shay called to them. "Stout, Clia?"

"Your friends are safe. Helms has taken them on ahead," Kharle explained.

"To meet the realm keeper?" I hurried my pace to keep up with my speed-walking girlfriend and her K-9.

"Yes, I suppose that is what you would call it."

The vague explanation was confusing, though *most* of what was happening around us was confusing. We were walking down another stone path leading out into the tall grasses. It felt familiar, and for a moment, I froze when the swaying blades tickled my hand.

The flash of memory was like a real time experience, but in my 30 years, I'd never stepped foot in this realm. The smell of the grass was sweet, and wildflowers I couldn't identify speckled the field with color. My feet were weighted to the soil, and the grab around my ankle–those spindly, taloned fingers–felt real.

"Wildwood!" Shay's voice was loud, but the gravity of my illusion kept me trapped between reality and whatever was the current opposite. "Wil." Her mouth was inches from my ear, and I could feel her arms around my shoulders, holding me tight to her demon kevlar.

"I've been here before," I whispered.

I heard Dexter barking, and seconds later, his howl turned into a ferocious roar that felt somehow connected to my experience. A dragon beak nudged my sigil hand, and the three of us disappeared into a circle of safety.

"Wildwood?" Shay held me.

"The field from our dreams. This is the field from our dreams." My heart hammered in my chest as I felt for the backpack on my shoulders.

"How can that be? Honey, you've never been here before."

"Maybe not, but the Maker of Bannock has."

~~~~~~~~~~

There have only been a few moments in my life when I've felt like a situation was twice lived, experiences I was connected to beyond my choosing. The most memorable had left me bound to the love of my life after an innocent slice of a knife. The most recent was right now, standing in the tall, swaying grasses of the Passofgrant fields.

Without hesitation Shay had placed a Rasavatam bubble of protection around us, and as we stood inside the circle, I wondered about the last hour of our time here in the land of giants.

Shay grasped my hands. "Tell me."

"It was the field." My body trembled, thinking about how absolute an invasion the memory was. "I was in the grass, just like in the dream, but you weren't dancing. Something grabbed hold of my leg, and I couldn't move."

I was hyperventilating, mostly because every bit of it triggered the memory of demon Andrea and the assault in the
~~~~~~~~~~

tunnels of the mine. Her evil, that monstrous violation, inched through the carefully bundled memory.

"Breathe, love," Shay urged as Dexter's head poked up through the loop of our arms to rest on my elbow. "I think he wants to help."

When I closed my eyes I saw the shadowed hand. Gulping for air, I choked on the vision. "I shouldn't close my eyes."

"Where are you Wil?"

"I'm in the field." My focus was on the rocks beneath my feet and the warm touch in my palms.

"You're in Giantville." She raised her eyebrow, encouraging me to ground myself with our shared earth energy, waiting for my reaction.

"Giantville," I repeated.

"You're not in a dream, love. You're right here with us."

When Dexter's nose puffed a spiraling swirl of smoke in my face, I said, "Our dragon is here."

Shay smiled. "That's right."

Her voice, the unending devotion in the way she pulled me back to her, was the anchor I needed. I wasn't alone. I could do this.

"The demon is here, Shay."

"Let's talk to the giants," she said before whispering the words to break our barrier spell.

"Your magick is powerful, Maker of Bannock," Kharle said.

"Will you please call me Wildwood? And I didn't make that magick on my own."

Ignoring that, they said, "Let us continue so we can see to the Keeper."

My steps were cautious, like everywhere my feet hit might be more dangerous than lava. As the giant led us onward, the pebbled path turned to dirt and then disappeared into lightly trampled grass. Apparently few ventured this far from the town.

"We are close to our destination," Kharle announced, but they stopped just before a wall of stone. "This way is not desirable for any of my people, so you must go on ahead alone."

"Wait, what do you mean?" Shay asked, but before an answer came, the leader of the giants was gone.

"What the hell is going on around here?" I threw my arms up in defeat, Shay by my side, was hesitant to step around the stone barrier.

"It's over here!" Stout yelled, and before we could take a step, the fairy was fluttering in front of us.

"It?" I questioned.

"You'll understand when you see."

Shay held her hand out, and I grabbed hold. We took the last few steps together as Dexter ran full sprint toward the unknown.

"Dex!" she called, but he continued. "*Reditus.*"

It was a command to return to us, but he ignored it, and seconds later, his barking once again turned into a roar. It was like nothing I'd ever heard from him before. It wasn't rage or fear or defensiveness. It was the kind of sound you make when you understand ultimate sacrifice.

Dexter was mourning.

Our dragon stood in the grass, a sorrowful stare in his eyes as he looked upon the reflection of his kind. Before us was a strange and heartbreaking sight: a dragon and a small giant frozen in crystalized stone.

"Dexter." Shay said his name, but the animal refused her call.

"This is the portal to the fairy realm," Clia said. We couldn't see where she was as she was somewhere behind the beings petrified in stone.

It took me a moment to find my voice. "What...what is...who are they?"

Stout walked through the grass, stopping where Dexter's taloned claw sunk deep into the earth. "He says that they would be family."

"There can't be many dragons in the world," I said.

"Not in this one, but I guess with the gateway frozen in stone, Dex could be the only one." Stout rested his hand on Dexter's talon. "Can you come back to them, Dexter?"

The dragon's head tilted toward Shay, who stood still, waiting for her animal partner to return, but he did not transform.

"He says that they've been waiting for us," Stout continued to translate.

"Impossible," I said.

There was heat in my palm. The fire radiated up my arm and through my shoulder, and when it reached my neck and face, the images came. The goddess was sending a message, and although unspoken, it was loud and clear. I saw the Maker, Kai. She'd been here with her hammer. They'd welcomed her much like they'd welcomed us, but she didn't come in peace. The face of the first Maker morphed between human and demon, and I watched as their combination of evil summoned spider demons that smothered the gateway keepers in a solid tomb of living death. My heart raced with the revelation.

"Wil!" Shay called me back to her, and I felt two powerful hands grasp my arm. "What did you see?"

"It was Andrea, wearing the mask of Kai." I raised my sigil palm toward the frozen guardians. "She did this to them the same way she tried to do it to me." My body collapsed to the ground as my knees buckled. The vision was more than I could carry.

"What do you mean?"

I pressed my hands to the ground, hoping that whatever world I was in would vibrate the same way my earth did. The power was intoxicating as the magicks of Giantville moved inside me.

"Wildwood."

"Put your hands down, Shay." I tugged her wrists until she kneeled beside me and her palms lay beneath mine. "Do you feel it?"

"Goddess, yes." Her breath hitched as she drew in the full energy of this land. "What—"

"It's coming from the portal," Stout explained. "Dexter says it's how we help them."

"If Andrea did that…" Shay shuddered as she pointed to the keeper and their dragon.

"The demon inside her did." I pushed up from the ground.

"How do we undo it?" Shay asked as I helped her to her feet.

The vision was clear, as if instructions had played out in front of me. I saw the attack of the demon spiders and remembered the hardening glaze of their splattered corpses. The weight of Brigid's hammer thumped against my back and I whipped the bag off and removed Brigid's hammer.

"I'm pretty sure we need this." I held it up, and the energies of my sigil flame surged through the handle, lighting each runic mark one at a time, bringing every etched strike to life.

"Impressive," Stout croaked.

Shay's cheeks flushed. "Isn't she just?"

Our dragon scooted back toward us and planted his nose on my forearm. His snorted puff of smoke was confirmation that we were on the right path.

"Can it be that easy?" I whispered. "They've been trapped for hundreds of years, and just one whack of my hammer, and it ends?"

"All we can do is try," Shay said, angling herself between me and the keepers frozen in time.

"What happens if you're wrong?" Stout's question was sobering, and a flutter of doubt snuck into my body.

Pretending that I wasn't nervous, I shrugged. "What's the worst that could happen?"

Stout held up his fingers, counting things off on them one by one. "Death, dismemberment, destruction."

Shay's hand came up to silence him. "Destiny," she whispered as her eyes froze on my own. "Destiny, my love, and everything that the Magick and the Maker have existed for."

Stout snorted. "That's all very romantic, but do you really believe that your magick hammer is gonna clunk on them and *bam*, they're free?"

I took a deep breath before I said, "We won't know until we try."

My fingers clenched the hammer's handle, and the stones of the path crunched beneath my feet. I approached the stone figures, and everything around me felt weightless as I raised it to strike.

"Stop!" Clia flew in front of my arm. Her delicate body should've been no match for me, but she was using fairy magick to halt my swing. Her wings flittered so fast that I felt the magick rolling from her miniature body.

"What the hell?!" I exclaimed.

Clia tone was sharp. "The explosive power of the hammer will decimate this entire valley."

My palm opened, and Shay caught the hammer before it hit the ground.

"*Ex-plo-sive?*" The word trembled from my lips.

"You strike them without guidance," she warned, sending a shiver up my spine, "and they will disintegrate along with the portal to our world."

CHAPTER X

FRACTIONATION

"It couldn't be easy, could it?" I complained. My shoulder scratched against the boulder as we sat on the ground. The sensation reminded me that, although we were here looking for resolution, we didn't have enough details.

"The Rasavatam is a bust." Shay patted the book as she set it on the ground. "There's nothing in my notes, nothing in this archive." Her finger swiped through the electronic file she'd compiled on her phone. "Tell me why you think Brigid's hammer will shatter it all, Clia?"

"The Goddess is light and good. She brings all things, but evil is also a part of it." She stood close to the hammer that lay on the ground beside me. "This isn't just a representation." She pointed to the etched artwork on the backside of the hammer. "This is the heart of the demon. The truest evil to exist and the unfortunate legacy of the first Maker and Magick of Bannock."

"Is it connected to the creature in our dreams?" I asked, but I already knew the answer.

"It has to be," Shay said. "This thing..." She picked up the hammer and flicked her finger against the chiseled image. "It's trapped here, and Kai–or Andrea or whatever–they listened to that monster and wanted to get to the fairy world so much that they would destroy access before letting anyone go through again."

Clia nodded.

"To what end?" I asked.

"What does evil ever want?" Stout grumbled. "They want us all to be lost in despair with them."

"I won't do that," Shay said defiantly.

My hand touched hers. "Neither will I."

"What's the answer, then?" Shay asked as she drew our bodies closer.

I attempted to understand the countless feelings flowing through me, but what troubled me the most was Shay's inability to solve this puzzle. Her magicks were the backbone of our lives. She was the research woman who found the answers. If she didn't know, who would?

"The legacy of the Maker is the answer," Clia said.

My head fell back against the boulder, which had been warmed by the sun, and I stared up at the sky. A deep, solid blue was all I could see for miles. The weight of my Maker abilities was heavy, a burden as never before because what's the point of this magick and the power of Brigid when it can't be used for good?

"What does that mean, the legacy of the Maker?" My eyes stayed fixed on the sky.

"It means you create," Clia explained. "It means you forge what you can fix, and you use the power of creation to make something better."

The idea that I could forge us out of this situation seemed improbable. The blue of the sky was no longer soothing as my palm fell on the handle of my hammer. This magick from the goddess was the foundation of the Maker power. Me, a simple welder and blacksmith, was somehow going to fix hundreds of years of hardened demon guts? Seemed unlikely to me.

My eyes closed, shutting out the world. Beyond my sense of vision was the sight of magicks so old that wisdom from the origin of the Maker filled my mind. I returned to the cave of the mother, where the hammer I held lay trapped for hundreds of years, just like the keepers in front of us.

It was me who'd released Brigid's magicks, but it was Shay who had the answer. "Holy shit!" I squealed, sitting up straighter and blinking hard to adjust to my eyes being open again. "I know what to do." The force of my excited twist knocked Shay sideways as I jumped to my feet. "I know what to do!"

She looked up at me. "What?"

"Dexter." The animal looked at me. "Come here, buddy."

"Talk to me, baby." Shay's arm rested on my shoulder.

"It's the fire that doesn't get hot." I blurted out the words, set free from the memory of the hammer's head once hidden beneath the crust of demon death.

"Wait, the fire that what?" Shay's eyebrows pinched with confusion.

It was so simple it was laughable. "It's the same thing that was on the hammer. The dried guts of those spidery demons but on a giant level." I reached for my hammer and held it out to Shay. "Remember?"

She nodded, then she lit her fire and held her hand to mine. "I remember." Her wink was adorable. "What about Dex, though?"

"His flame might just tip us in the right direction. Our dragon-dog releases a dragon trapped by demons for hundreds of years. It's almost poetic." I chuckled as we stepped closer to the Keeper's portal.

"Flame, duh" Stout said. "It makes sense that the three of you would use fire."

"So how do you think we should do it?" I asked. "We can't pass them through our *Ignis* fire like we did with the hammer head."

"What about Dexter?" She looked at Stout. "Can he create flame without heat?"

Our fairy hovered close to Dexter's face, waiting as our dragon answered. "He says why would he ever need flame without the heat, but he's willing to try."

Moments later we were standing in a field with a dragon and giant, frozen in what we believed were the crystalized remains of demon guts. We were about to direct our goddess given gifts of flame toward them with dragon fire as the surprise ingredient. What could go wrong?

"How are we going to test the flames without melting the keepers?" I hesitated to ask.

Shay walked through the tall grass toward the forested area farther from the center of Passofgrant. Standing on my tiptoes, it was a challenge to see what she was doing as she collected sticks and branches. Her voice grew louder as the distance stretched.

"You and I know we can make a flame without heat," she said. "I suppose Dexter just needs us to help with the suggestion."

"Do you think he understands intuitive reflection?" I asked.

"Stout?" Shay returned with a pile of sticks. "What's he say?"

We watched as Dexter's head tilted toward Stout. "He says he will try."

We stacked the pile of sticks into a tower, intending to catch it on fire, but hoping that we would not. Shay's palm hovered above the wood. *"Ignis,"* she said, and blue flame flickered toward the earth. I repeated the incantation, and my orange flame escaped from the sigil in my palm. The colors mingled, flashing and crackling as we waited for Dexter to open his mouth.

"Keep it low, Dex." Shay coaxed him closer to us. "You can do it."

His dragon nose inched in between our hands, and when he opened his mouth, the flame burst forth wildly, disintegrating the sticks to ash.

"Maybe try a little lower next time," I said with a laugh.

Shay looked at the fairies. "We're gonna need more sticks."

Stout and Clia darted toward the forest as Dexter's chin dropped to the ground.

"Don't get discouraged." Shay rubbed the scales on his head and whispered in his ear, "Wildwood had a hard time at first, too."

"Hey!" I yelled.

"Well, you did."

"Yeah, but I was new to the whole magick thing and so very not a dragon." I crossed my legs in front of me, getting comfortable for our unhot fire-building experience.

Clia and Stout collected sticks and branches for the next hour. The sun was fading in the distance, and Dexter was still turning everything to cinder and ash. We attempted water baths and anvil dust combinations. Our fairies offered spit, and we even mixed all the magicks into a fantastic slurry, but Dexter still couldn't make a heatless flame.

"Okay," I said, pacing, "what's the trick?" It wasn't a question as much as a statement made in frustration.

"Maybe we can do a binding spell, reduce the flame he makes?" Shay was thinking out loud, very much like I was.

"Should we camp out here tonight?" I asked, and I felt the pull of my grumbling stomach.

Shay looked up to track the sun. "It'll be dark soon. I'm not sure about going back into town."

"Since Dexter made us a fire, how about something to eat?" I hitched my thumb toward the sound of moving water. "Fishing with a dragon?" I waggled my eyebrows.

"Baby, no. Don't do that. I will go catch you a dozen fish if you don't do that with your eyes.".

"What, this?" I waggled them again.

She jumped at me, wrapping her arms around my waist and spinning me in circles. "No, no way." Her kisses peppered my face as I felt the dizzying sensation of her love and the rings we were leaving in the dirt.

"Feed me, woman."

"I'd be happy too." Shay stopped twirling me, and my feet touched the ground. "Dexter." The dragon leaped from the ground and bounced through the grass toward the river. "We'll be right back." She winked and ran after her dragon, followed by two zipping fairies.

They were gone long enough for the fire to fade into a perfect bed of hot coals for charring fish. Dex broke through the tall grass first, and by the excitement in his bounding leaps, I was sure their expedition had been successful.

"I hope you're hungry." Shay raised her arms to reveal two large fish hooked on each hand. "I have no idea what these are, but Dexter's devoured about a dozen already." She laid them on the boulder. "I had time in between to clean them."

"He ate a dozen?" I marveled, watching as, still in dragon form, he lay curled in a ball, licking in between the talons on his feet.

"I had to remind him there were other mouths to feed." Shay walked away, and a few minutes later she returned with pointed limbs to stake the fish, a handful of rubbery plants, and a huge smile on her face. "Fire looks good."

"Dex started it; I just had to keep it going." I pointed at the pile in Shay's hand. "What you got there?"

She dropped them in my lap. "Chicken of the woods."

"Chicken of the what?" I know my face said twice as much as my words because Stout guffawed, pointing at me and clutching his stomach.

"It's a mushroom," Clia explained. "They grow wild in just about every realm."

"Why are they called 'chicken,' and are they safe to eat? I mean, mushrooms don't have the best reputation."

"You'll love them." Shay skewered the mushrooms and added a dash of pepper from the mess kit.

"I guess I'm about to find out," I said, crossing my fingers that they'd be good *and* wouldn't make us sick.

We sat against the boulder and watched the sunset. The sky faded from a brilliant blue to a hazy, foggy gray. Shay's hand rested on my thigh, and I couldn't stop wondering if our life could be like this in the future. We would figure out how to free the keeper and their dragon. We would gain access to the fairy world, but what then? The evil trapped in my hammer called us, just as the purity of the goddess had done not so long ago.

The outcome could be so very different. The Magick and the Maker of Bannock, Shay and I wore those titles not just in name. She had abilities we had yet to reveal, and so did the dragon laying beside us. We needed him now. The three of us made a powerful triangle, so much like the end points on the triquetra symbol long faded from Shay's body. Those symbols and signs from the goddess were once on our bodies, and it made me wonder about our boy.

"Where are you, Wildwood Blackstone?" Shay's question fell against my ear, and the tickle of it sent a shiver to my cheek.

My hand instinctively rubbed at my prickling skin. "Just thinking."

"About?" She leaned forward to rotate the fish and pinch the mushrooms.

"Our magickal abilities."

"Hmm." The sound vibrated between us.

"Just hmm?" I joked.

"Well, I was waiting for you to share more." Her fingers tangled in mine. "Talk to me."

"You remember when our powers transferred?"

"Impossible to forget." She squeezed my hand, reassuring me of our continued connection.

"I was thinking that Dexter never had that. Not like we did, and I wondered if he has hidden powers like us?"

Shay didn't say a word as she reached to move the roasting sticks. Her eyes drifted between our dinner and the dragon curled in a ball, talking to the fairies.

"Honey, did you hear me?" I asked.

Her smile, lit by the glow of embers, was not the answer I was hoping to see. "He's a dragon."

I wasn't sure what she was getting at. Her proclamation was pretty obvious, especially now when he wasn't in dog form. "Yeah, sweetie, he's a dragon. And?"

"No, I mean what more should there be?" The frustration in the furrow of her brow was adorable and also a clear sign I might be onto something. "Isn't transforming into a dragon his power?"

"Maybe it's not. Maybe he's meant to be a dragon, and the dog is his disguise?"

"I suppose that's better than a pair of black spectacles with a big nose attached," she joked, then removed a fish and a skewer of mushrooms from the fire. "You're thinking there's another spell?"

My face hovered over the food as I took in the perfect aroma, trying to curb my hunger and ignore my grumbling stomach. "I can't believe you're *not* thinking that. There has to be a bigger legacy bond because he has magick beyond his dragon form, and right now we need him to find it."

"Maybe I should have—"

I interrupted her. "No, there's no 'maybe I should haves.'" I tossed scraps of fish at the flames. "You can't know everything." I pointed at the backpack filled with books and tools. "We've muddled through so far." The skewer of roasted mushroom lingered near my lips, and with hopeful anticipation, I nipped a bit with my teeth.

"You like it?" Shay asked as she sandwiched fish between her piece of chicken of the woods.

"It's pretty good. I'm kinda surprised."

"Trust the fairies," Stout said as he grabbed a slice of mushroom to share with Clia.

My girlfriend was silent for the longest time before she asked, "Do you think Benton struggled in the beginning?" I wasn't certain the question was directed at me as she stared at the fire. "I mean, she worked with Jacob and they fought against and eliminated an entire class of demons. She had to know, didn't she?"

Shay turned to look at me, and the childlike stare nearly broke my heart. I loved her for the incredible strength she had, for the ability to overcome the wounds of our past. But every once in a while, when doubt crept in, that fifteen-year-old girl was still tucked inside her.

"Do you remember the first time you and I worked magick together?" I asked, but I knew the answer to my question already. There was no way she didn't.

That first spell was intense and incredibly intimate. Her hands, scarred yet still delicate, moved over the table with perfect intentions. The smell of incense, so much a sense memory now, brought magick to my heart for the very first time.

"I'll never forget," Shay said.

"We followed our instincts."

She smiled. "You followed mine, that's for sure."

"It got us here, that's my point," I said.

"What does that mean for Dexter?" She threw the bones of her fish in the fire. "We're in the middle of nowhere, in the land of giants, and now we have to figure out a spell to release a dragon's inner magick?"

"Yes."

Shay held her hand over the fire, activating her blue flame. "How, Wil?"

"What if we use my spell from the mill and your spell from the old courthouse?" I suggested.

"On him?" She pointed at the dragon who was now snapping for pieces of the mushroom Stout was eating.

"My lips are kinda tingly," I said in lieu of an answer.

"Tingly?" Shay repeated.

"That's the mushroom," Stout yelled. "It ain't gonna kill ya, but some people get that sensation."

Shay's finger touched my lips. "Are they numb?"

I shook my head. "Not numb, tingly."

"You're sure it won't hurt her?" Shay asked the fairies.

"Stout's right," Clia said. "It's just her body reacting to the 'shroom. It'll fade in a little while. Eat more of the fish, maybe rub something on your lips."

"Glory be, never tell the two of them to put their lips together or we'll be under that sound bubble again tonight." Stout tore a chunk of mushroom from the skewer. "Like horny teenagers, I swear."

Shay did kiss me, mostly to protest Stout's last comment, and I was pleased to invite her lips to mine. "Can you feel that?" she asked as she pulled away from me.

"Oh yea, I feel you." My eyelids were heavy, and I truly felt nothing but the thumping of my heart and my pulse raging to southern parts of my body.

<center>~~~~~~~~~~</center>

"Please don't move." The boney hand pressed down on my chest, and the weight felt like an anvil crushing my body. "They're here."

I tried to respond, to force out the questions racing through my brain. Why? How? But I couldn't take air into my lungs to speak.

"They've come." The voice beside my head wasn't Shay. It wasn't anyone I could identify in the dark, and yet, it was here beside me, snugged into my backside, suffocating me with fear.

"If you move, it'll be free," the voice warned.

Trauma responses are real, living things. My heart raced in my chest, pumping blood, pounding intensely as every moment of fear triggered the fight response I've had since my childhood. New homes in foster care meant new people; some were nice, but many were not. If you didn't charge ahead, there was no chance to survive, and right now I wanted to survive.

The glove-taut skin of the hand smothered my mouth, preventing me from asking questions as I struggled against the force holding me still. Sweat dripped from my forehead as whispers tangled in my hair.

"Struggling will get us all killed," the voice hissed.

This can't be real. The space was all wrong. I should be inside a tent, wrapped in Shay's arms, feeling the cool discomfort of the ground at every point my body rested against it.

"Fight is what kills." The hand slipped around my throat, a slow, tight grip, squeezing until my fingers came up to pull at it, my lungs struggling to recover as I gasped for air. "It's not broken."

Ignis, I thought. My eyes opened and the blaze of orange flashed before me. I'd never summoned Brigid's power behind closed eyes and never in my sleep. Reality blurred as

Shay pressed up beside me. Her hand touched mine while I strained to take a breath. Our flames mingled together into a glow of hallowed green, and I felt her magick soothing my own.

"Wil, what is it?"

I knew her body. After all the days we'd spent together tangled in the world of demons and magick, my soul knew when she was near. "Dream," I gasped through hitched breaths.

"I'm here," she said over the top of my head as she held me to her chest.

"Whatever it was, it wants us to go." There was no heat as my flame hand gripped Shay's, but the glow lit the space of the tent.

"Demon?" she asked.

The most I could do was whimper as I shrugged. Turning to look into her eyes, I asked, "Did you dream?"

"No, baby I didn't."

The dream had felt so real just moments before. I ran through every emotion, every sensation, trying to uncover the message behind the visit. "The dream told me not to move."

She paused before asking, "Move how?"

"I don't know. Just that something is here, and if I move, it'll be free." The fabric of Shay's shirt muffled my voice.

"Wait, if you move, or if you make a move?" Her legs opened, and she pulled me into the V of her thighs.

"I don't know." My voice was small and full of fear and uncertainty.

We sat in silence for a long moment. In the last year—more specifically, since the powers of Brigid shifted to me—my dreams had become so real that it was often too much. Thankfully this one, although dark and suffocating, was not one that would haunt me in the daylight.

With my head pressed to Shay's chest, I could hear the rhythmic beat of her heart. It was steady and slow, and it went a long way towards calming me down. I know she was dissecting what little I could remember, but the ease at which she could control our energies was more than magick.

"This is the first prescient dream we haven't shared in a long time." She spoke against the top of my head, and I felt the vibration of her throat. "That has to mean something." Her arms released as I leaned into her.

"You think that's relevant?" I asked.

"What do you do when parts come together and are so strong they're impossible to break?" Her question was spoken aloud, but I was certain she meant to think it because she didn't wait for my reaction. "You find a way to weaken one of those parts."

"So, I'm the weak part," I said.

"Not necessarily you. But if we are the whole, one of us needs to fall. And since you're the power behind Brigid's hammer, I think they'll come for you."

"So the dream is about that evil, that thing that possessed Kai?"

"I don't think it is. I think your dream is a warning from the keeper of the realms."

This hung heavy in the air between us, the only sounds were the crackling of the coals and Dexter snuffling contentedly as Clia pet his scales. This was all too much for me to handle.

Holding back tears, I said, "I just wish I knew what it meant."

"Me, too, love," Shay said, holding me close. "Me, too."

CHAPTER XI

ALCHEMIC

"Just leave it up," I said as we poured water over the fire pit. We were currently debating whether or not to pack up our gear. "Do you really think we're going to free the keepers today?" The dream still lingered in my thoughts, and I couldn't shake the idea that I was the weakest part of our whole.

"Not with an attitude like that." Stout sipped at the last drops of his beer. "We got to keep trying."

Clia nodded from where she was sitting cross-legged beside him. Her consumption of catnip was delicate and dainty compared to Stout's slurping of his frothy beer, and the contrast was amusing.

"He's right," she added between nipping on the stems. "I think your flames are the answer."

"Wildwood's dream, although vague, seems to point in that direction." Shay stirred the embers until the smolder was gone. "Dexter needs to find the softer side of his fire."

"He needs your magick," Clia told her.

"That's what I think too." Shay sat beside me as I wiped the last of our dishes

"So if that's what you think," I said, watching her cautiously, "the smile on your face must mean you also have a plan?"

Shay's eyes glistened with excitement as she said, "We're going to combine the two summoning spells: my Magick incantation and your Maker incantation."

"So you like my idea?" I asked.

"I absolutely do."

~~~~~~~~~~

"This could be dangerous," Stout said as he scribbled the translations with Shay's pencil. "I've changed this word so it'll include your dragon-dog over there." He tipped the eraser at Dexter.

"Perfect!" Shay beamed. "And I've done the same for this spell."

Shay sat with her back against the boulder, notes on the ground all around her, as she converted the incantation. Between Shay and Stout, they knew dozens of languages, and with Clia as the secret fairy decoder, they'd spent less than an hour putting the written components together.

I was on the prowl for herbal elements growing wild, and in the land of giants, I was having disappointing luck. "Do you think Helms could help us with the horehound and bay?"

"We might not need them if we've got a lodestone. Is there one in the kit?"

I rolled the canvas out on the ground; Shay's travel altar lay tucked into precisely stitched pockets. I opened the velcro flap to remove the stones inside. "Crystal, agate, rose quartz, a black one I don't know, and your conjuring stone."

"Black tourmaline," she said.
~~~~~~~~~~

"This one?" I held it up for her to see.

Without taking her eyes from the papers in front of her, Shay said, "Wait."

I froze in place. "What?"

"Your anniversary present?"

"My meteorite?"

Her head shake was adorably self-deprecating. "Why can't I just know everything?" She was saying it mostly to herself, but Shay's expectations of herself were sometimes beyond reality.

"No one can know everything, but how about you let me in on what you're thinking?"

"Something not of this world connecting us in this world." She moved closer to me. "You have the stone, right?"

The smile on my face was the answer she needed. "I do."

"Brilliant!" She smashed a kiss on my cheek, excitedly. "My girlfriend is so brilliant."

"I am," I said, opening the side pocket of my backpack and removing the egg-sized stone. "What do I do next?"

"We'll need to do a salt wash on it and all the tools." Shay stopped reading her notes to look at me. "Can you set up the altar and do that part?"

Nodding, I made quick work of setting things in place. I unfolded the cloth, trimmed with silver Celtic knots. One by one, I removed the athame, a tiny white taper candle, and the jar of salt. Our breakfast plate would have to work as a basin for the water.

Thoughts raced in my mind as I tried to remember the words I needed. I drew a pentagram with the salt, preparing to call the elements to me.

"Fire, light from the darkness, be in my circle." I set the white taper candle on one point of the star.

"Water, wash away the past and summon the new." I poured water from our canteen onto the plate and set it on the second point of the star. The placements moved clockwise as I continued.

"Air, source of life, breathe into this stone unity with those before us." My fingers flipped the feather as I placed it on the star's third point.

"Earth, the place we call home, mountain to cave, the rock in our solid foundation, I call you to this circle to cleanse this connecting stone." I held the meteorite in my palm, raising it high before setting it on the star's fourth point.

"Spirit of the Maker, I call to you." My wrist gauntlet held the mark of the Maker. I removed it and placed it on the fifth star point.

"Goddess of goodness and kindness, be in this circle. Cleanse this stone, and guide our magick with purposeful intention," I said without hesitation as I poured salt and water over the stone on the plate. "So mote it be."

"So mote it be," I heard Shay say, followed by Stout and, finally, Clia.

"The stone is ready," I said.

"I'm about ready, too." Stout dropped his pencil to peek over Shay's shoulder. "You about done, Red?"

Shay closed her eyes and pinched her nose in frustration.

"You know, she's going to pop you one day for calling her that." The meteorite felt coarse in my hand as I rubbed the surface dry.

"Maybe, but since she's not *my* superhero, I'll stick with the feisty Red."

Shay's hand came up to silence the two of us. "Superhero is sweet. Red? Not so much. I have a name you know."

"I could call you the Magick of Bannock, like the leader of the giants." He stood on Shay's shoulder, touching a finger to his chin as he thought. "T-MOB for short."

The smile on my face was absolutely not how Shay wanted me to react. I opened my mouth to make a joke, but she cut me off. "No! Please, just…no."

"But baby," I said, giving a fake pout, "T-MOB is so cute. I mean, ten out of ten on the adorable scale."

"Wil! If either of you start calling me T-MOB, I will magick you right out of this realm." The pencil in her hand slapped against her notes. "I'm serious."

"She's serious," Stout repeated as he pretended to walk off the ledge of her shoulder. "T-MOB has spoken."

Shay swished her hand at the fairy, missing him by an inch. "You know I have one super-secret reserve beer left. It might just fall and spill all over this campfire." Her eyebrow raised as she waited for his reaction.

"You wouldn't!"

I couldn't hold my laughter. "From the look on her face, Stout, she just might."

Shay turned to glare at me, but from her position on the ground, it was less intimidating. "And *you!* You like getting in these pants." She ran her finger up and down from her waist to her ankles. "That name better not cross your lips if you want to *keep* getting into them!"

My palms came up in surrender. "Got it, Shay! That's your name, and I should wear it out." I took an enormous step backward. "Got…it!"

"You better both get it." She pushed up from the ground. "Now that the comedy routine is over, do you think you and Stout could hit the river, grab some thistle, and fill the cook-pot with water?"

"Yes, Shay," Stout said, giving her a salute. "We can do that."

Stout grabbed hold of the pot handle and flew beside me. Our walk to the river was short, and I wondered where the thistle grew. Shay would know we could find it.

"T-MOB!" I cackled when we were out of hearing range. "Dude, that was so great."

I held my knuckles up for a fist bump. His knuckles tickled my own when they hit.

"So good."

~~~~~~~~~~

"Water and thistle." I set them on the boulder. "It's a good thing fairy hands are too small for those prickly things."

"Prickly wings," Stout corrected. "Thistle is the plant of plants in our realm. It's easy to find."

"Taking a bath in thistle twigs helps young fairies with their first flights," Clia explained.

"Really?" I asked, thinking about Dexter's aversion to using his wings. "What does it do?"

"It makes the body lighter," she said.

"Fireface says he isn't going to fly," Stout said.

The dragon lay curled on the ground, but his head came up at the mention of his name.

"He's about to do something." Shay crouched in front of the animal. "You're about to come into full dragon magick, and maybe that confidence will help you soar."

"He said–" Stout paused as Dexter interrupted. "He says he wants to help, but flying isn't his way."

"Fair enough," Shay said as she shuffled the pages together. "Rage a fire for us Dex!"

She pointed to the bundle of boughs and sticks, and our dragon opened his mouth to flash a streaming yellow flame at the pile. Fire raged as it crackled to life, and Dex's butt hit the ground to sit beside Shay. Dragon-dog pride was alive and well in the wilds of Giantville.

"What's next?" I asked.

"We do some spell work, and we help our dragon reach his full potential."
~~~~~~~~~~

Shay, as the Magick of Bannock, had gained confidence beyond that which I'd experienced a year ago. She was physically strong; it was impossible to miss as the muscles in her forearms flexed, but she was more than that. She was magically powerful in a way that I cherished and did not envy. We looked to her, all of us, as the keeper of answers. And as we assembled around the ring of salt, our complete trust in her abilities gave me confidence that we would succeed.

"Wil, you stand beside me. Dex–" She called the dragon. "Here." She slapped her thigh, and the dog dropped to the ground beside her.

"Where do you want us?" Stout asked, hovering over to Dexter.

"Stay close. I'm going to need some fairy dust to mix with the demon sift."

Stout rubbed his hands together, excited to add his magick to the spell. "Got it."

Time seemed to stand still as Shay read the words on the first page. Stout's translations worked instantly, and we watched runes and other symbols appear on the scales covering Dexter's back.

"Are you writing them down?" Shay asked as she poured moon water along Dexter's neck and shoulders.

"These are beautiful," I said as I sketched the spiraling triskeles glowing a golden yellow on his shoulder.

"Water, fire, earth, pentacle." Shay started listing everything she saw. "All the same." She placed her palm flat on the scales between Dexter's eyes.

The spells that activated our Magick and Maker powers manifested massive images on our backs. I didn't see one forming on the K-9.

"Remember your dragon image?" I asked Shay.

"Yes, and your goddess." She nodded. "He doesn't have one."

"Not yet." I raised his taloned foot. "Maybe on his belly?"

"Let me read the second incantation."

Shay tossed the first page into the fire and began chanting the second. Her voice was hypnotic, and Dexter must've felt it, too, because his head fell to the ground, eyelids drifting open and closed as he succumbed to a magick-induced sleep.

"He's out like an enchanted light." The ground beside him was cold as I sat. "Come here." I waved Shay over. "The grass is freezing." Before Shay could take a step, ice formed all around us. Anywhere moisture rested, droplets of ice formed.

"It's working." Stout's hands and face were purply blue as he chattered to fight the cold sucking through the air. "Keep reading, Shay."

She continued to recite her translations, fighting through the shiver as, inch by inch, the world around us froze.

"It isn't fire," I said, awestruck. We were trying to fight fire with flame, but in a glorious bit of irony, it seemed our dragon-dog held a fierce penchant for ice.

"It isn't fire," Shay repeated, taking both of my hands and placing them over Dexter's eyes. "Dragon of elements. Fire, Earth, Air and Water. You are the dragon of Bannock." Shay's *ignis* flame forced through me, igniting my own as we channeled the powers of Brigid to wake the sleeping dragon.

"I am the light, she is the light, he is the light," Shay chanted, and soon, I was joining in.

Together we said the words over and over. Our dragon remained in his place, so still that he was almost frozen. There were elements of transferring power that were still needed and I reached for the meteorite.

"Fairy and demon?" I set the rock in front of Dexter's nose and tipped the cork out of the bottle of anvil dust. The flutter of fairy wings hit my ears before I felt Stout land.

"I'm ready." His throat made a gurgling sound as he hacked his spit onto the plate holding moon water. "Clia."

He waved her over to us, and they took turns spitting on the pile of demon sift I'd dumped. Shay used our athame to mix the elements into a slurry, and with the blade's tip, she drew two ancient symbols, one on each side of the stone, before placing it on the long plane of Dexter's nose.

"What's next?" Clia whispered to Stout.

"Now we wait for him to wake," Shay said.

She sat on the ground, her arm slung over the shoulder of her K-9, the other palm pressed to the soil. Whatever magicks existed in the land of the giants, Shay was calling upon all of them. The flesh of her arms, freckled and scarred, looked pale beside the sleeping animal, but their bond was never more clear. She would will his magick into existence and save us all.

The temperature of the surrounding space made me shiver. "Are you cold, baby?" Shay asked and motioned for me to sit beside her.

"It's him. He's throwing off so much freezing energy right now."

"Come here." Shay opened the buttons of her shirt and wrapped me against her chest. Shay wasn't wearing her vest, and when my arm swooped behind to rest on her hip, she wasn't wearing any of her usual weapons.

My head settled on her shoulder. "You're a bit underdressed."

"Magick like this..." She paused, thinking. "I didn't want any barriers. We don't know enough about demon steel or his shape-shifting abilities. I just wanted to be careful."

"That leaves you unprotected, though."

I felt her body tremor with a short laugh. "Don't be anxious, love. Magick protects us, too."

"You're not worried, are you?" I asked.

She held me a little tighter. "About my safety, you mean?"

"That, and about him." My hand rested on Shay's where she was touching Dexter's shoulder.

She drew a circle around her face. "I'm wearing my brave face."

I looked into Shay's eyes. "Honey?"

"It's a superhero thing." She kissed me. "It'll be okay."

It felt like hours as we sat beside the sleeping animal, waiting for some explosion of power to seep from his dragon body. There was no resounding boom or cosmic crash, just a half-hearted whimper as our dragon rolled to his side, turning his tummy to Shay like a happy pup.

"Hey, there, my guy." Shay's hand rubbed back and forth across the pebbled skin of Dexter's belly.

Our dragon's body was tough, impenetrable by kevlar standards, but he curled into the touch. Stout was there, hovering above us, listening to whatever Dexter was sharing.

"What's he saying?" I asked.

"Hold on." Stout raised a halting palm to me. "There's a lot going on that he can't explain."

Shay stood, and the action made Dex flip and roll to his feet. The yellow glowing images were no longer on his torso scales, but I could see one circle still burning around his shoulder. It wasn't difficult to interpret the letter K as it appeared, and before I could say anything else, the legacy of the maker scrolled through the circle–from Kai to Gorath, then Sabine and Jacob, stopping finally at my mark, the one perfectly cast and soldered to my wrist gauntlet. There was no recognition of the Magick's lineage, just the permanent branded style mark of this Maker.

"What does it mean?" I said as my fingertip traced the symbol.

"It's like your sigil." Shay turned my hand over. "You are both marked by the magicks that tie you to Bannock."

"But what about you, Shay?"

She hesitated for a long moment, turning some thoughts around and around. Her hands stretched out to me, palms up, revealing the wounds she'd received all those years ago when magick took hold of her soul. "I think I've worn mine for a very long time."

"Blessed be," Clia squeaked as she flew back and forth between us.

"Blessed be, indeed," Stout said solemnly.

"What do we do now?" I asked, a little disappointed to break the intimacy of this moment.

"Let's go back to the portal and try to free the keeper." Shay swiped at the leg of her pants, sending dust and dirt into the air.

"Shouldn't we test his magick?" I asked as the dog sprinted off through the tall grass.

"On what?" Stout asked. "It's not like we have some spare hardened demon guts lying around."

"I know that." I rolled my eyes as Shay and I collected the altar tools and placed them into the storage bag. "It's just, what if we hurt them?"

"You've got a point." Shay turned to Stout. "Fly on to the town and find Helms. Tell him what we're about to do."

"And then what?"

"See if they can offer any advice."

Without reservation the fairy zipped away. Clia watched him go, then turned back to Dex and said, "His magick is tied to the Maker and Magick powers."

"Yes, we see that," I said a little miffed at the idea that we'd have missed that fact.

"The two of you," she continued, not noticing my tone, "your intuitive nature will regulate his newfound strength."

"So you think we won't fry the keepers?" Shay asked, and I couldn't stop the doubtful huff that escaped my lips.

"You could try it out on the mass resting on the ground by their feet," Clia suggested.

Her wings flittered as we approached the portal where the keeper and their dragon stood frozen in time. Dexter sniffed around the ground before his dragon tongue flipped against the solidified demon remains.

"Dexter! Stop!" Shay yelled at him.

The animal froze in place. This was another case of what we don't know *can* hurt us, and as much as Dex liked the flavor of crunchy demons, alive or dead, the last time he devoured unhatched embryos, it nearly killed him. We didn't know what creature was the source of this blackened material.

"He says it tastes like the *Huic Ostiarus*," Clia said.

"A Gatekeeper keeping the keepers of the portal locked in limbo forever," I thought out loud.

"The evil of Bannock summoned them. Dex says there were hundreds."

Just as Clia finished her sentence, I felt the rush of earth energy pull me to my knees. Shay's hand rested on my shoulder, and her heartbeat pounded with mine as we saw the past. Kai, possessed by the hammer's evil, stood in this very spot, yelling at the giant who kept tight to their post. They didn't move and one by one, spider demons the size of a herder's goats crept from snaking cracks in the ground. Kai's demon called them, squealing a sound that forced the keeper's dragon into a trance. The two of them never had a chance; the demons exploded, one after the other, sacrificed by the monster taking root in Kai's body.

The scene was tragic as Kai punched and kicked, trying to break the glasslike solid form. She'd outsmarted herself by forming a bond she couldn't break. Days of magick and demon summoning could not undo the barrier she'd mistakenly made.

As quickly as the vision appeared, it faded, and I felt Shay's hand on my shoulder. "You saw it, right?" I asked.

"Yeah, as if it happened today. The first Magick Maker was doomed from the start."

"The hammer broke her. Brigid's hammer broke her!" The backpack dropped from my shoulder as I felt the weight of carrying my hammer.

"It wasn't the hammer, love." Shay opened the bag and removed it. "This has an enormous ability to create, both good and evil. Kai couldn't carry all of it alone. No one could." She held the hammer out to me, and I took hold of it.

"We do it together."

Shay nodded. "You, me, and Dexter. We do it together."

We stood, side by side, the three of us touching one another with a connection that demons had feared through the ages. Dexter stared at the base of the frozen keeper and their companion. Perhaps he was trying to communicate with the creature; it was impossible to know.

Before we focused our combined flames, Stout returned, followed by the buzzing thrum of dozens of fairy folk and a stream of giants. The gathering was beyond overwhelming, and Shay positioned herself between me and the new strangers. Or she attempted to, at least. But when the mass of creatures, big and small, became a crowd, she surrendered to the gathering.

"Word kinda got out that you were here," Stout explained.

"I see that." Shay's head turned to take in everyone. "Are they all here to watch?"

"The giants have given fairies space in their realm," Helms said. "But nothing is like being with your own."

For all the months we'd spent searching and translating, not one time did I ever consider what it meant for the creatures of other realms. The fairy world was trapped, locked in a tragic bubble, because nothing from the realms of the universe could enter and nothing could leave this way. There were more fairies hovering around us than I'd ever imagined, and it was clear why. They wanted to see home.

"You have the support of Passofgrant, and you have the magick of the fairies, too." Helms nodded at Shay. "We wish you victory, Magick of Bannock."

What were we about to do? The weight of countless realms was literally in the palms–or flames–of our hands.

"Mother goddess, Brigid," Shay said, raising her hands toward the encased keepers. "We call upon your fire."

Shay didn't whisper the command, but her palms still flashed with flames. I gripped the hammer of the goddess as my own palms flared with an orange glow. The gasp of the surrounding crowd was loud, oddly synchronized, and their energies charged the air with hope. It was at that exact moment I felt it. I knew without a doubt that on this day, we would free them from their frozen place.

Our dragon drew himself into a ring, expanding so that his tail wrapped around to his front claws. This was our sacred circle, held together by the three of us. Dexter's mouth opened. It wasn't fierce; it was so gentle that he might pluck a stemmed flower from the grass with his lips. The yellow flame that snaked from him mingled with Shay's and then my own.

The action was intuitive, just as Shay had taught, and I stepped toward the feet of our encapsulated keepers and gave their prison a quick blow with my hammer. I kicked the piece that broke free, and it flew at Dexter's talon. It wriggled like a fish out of water. Dex focused his flame at the mass, flashing, turning it to ice, then swallowing it whole. The gleam in his eyes was one of complete satisfaction. Somehow he knew he could devour the remnants while in his dragon form.

"Dex," Shay whispered, awed and a little nervous.

With one success under my belt, I found that I wanted to jack-hammer away at the statued beings, but we couldn't end hundreds of years of imprisonment with reckless impatience. Back and forth we went, Shay holding our flames as I chipped away slowly enough for Dex to eliminate the demon debris. *Chip, chomp, chip, chomp.* We had a steady rhythm until the first bit of flesh was revealed. We worked from head to toe, believing that if they came alive, they would need to take a first breath. This was the strangest womb ever conceived.

The giant's eyes opened, blinked a few times, and went wide with wild awareness. I hammered faster now to unmask the nose and mouth, getting ahead of Dexter.

"Wil," Shay called my name. "Slow your pace."

Dexter continued to flame and gobble what wriggled at my feet. The dragon had a bottomless pit of a stomach, so I didn't stop tapping away with my hammer. Shay held the magick for the three of us, and when the remnants broke free from the face of the trapped giant, their gasp for air was almost as loud as that of the gathered crowd. This giant would be free today after hundreds of years frozen in this cocoon.

"It's going to be alright," I said as the giant struggled to break free. Helms stepped closer, and the look of relief and recognition on their face needed no explanation.

"Belos, my love." Their foreheads touched, and Helms' giant arms came around the still solid forms as tears fell from both their eyes.

"Helms, my love."

My hammer stopped as I took in the sight of two lovers separated by hundreds of years in this demon crust. The moment wasn't lost on Shay, either, and her hand fell to my shoulder. I couldn't imagine the pain of life without her for hundreds of years. How did they ever survive?

"Perhaps you should continue?" Stout urged. "Once they're free, so is every fairy in all the realms."

I moved to hammer out the face of the dragon, still frozen in the time capsule. I shut out the sound of happy tears as best I could, trying to avoid hearing their expressions of love. The handle of my hammer felt weightless as adrenaline and magick flowed through me. The three of us chipped and scraped until the animal's head was free.

Being aware without the ability to speak must be terrifying, and I felt for this poor creature and its master. The animal's eyes blinked rapidly, then it took a deep breath before crying out. I didn't know how to translate, but Dexter did, and his scaled torso turned, his wings spread wide to move in front of Shay and me just before a stream of fire spewed from the imprisoned creature's mouth.

"Be well, Hermes," Belos said soothingly. "All is new with us. This is freedom, not capture."

The captive dragon turned toward the voice, and the animal's attack waned as their keeper companion brought comfort. There was so much more of their prison to break away, and it felt impossible, but I didn't tire. The more I chipped away at the demon remains binding them, the more I wanted to continue.

Hours passed, and one by one, more fairies gathered around. Maybe it was excitement over their own impending freedom, but I was certain they could sense the portal releasing from the confines of the barrier Kai's demon had created so very long ago.

"How are you holding up?" Shay asked, the smile she wore warming my soul.

"I could do this all—"

Hermes broke free from the ground and, without hesitation, sprang into the air, swooping and stretching its long-restricted wings. The flight was like something out of a childhood dream–and even some I'd had as an adult. There was nothing that compared to a flying dragon.

"Stunning," I breathed as Shay's arms slinked around me and her chin dropped to my shoulder.

"We did that," she whispered.

The moment of awe broke as two massive giants kneeled in front of us. It was too much, being present in this moment, surrounded by cheering fairies, jubilant giants, and a dragon circling overhead. Shay pinched the back of my arm, and for the very first time, I didn't cry out in surprise.

"Yes, love," I told her, beaming from ear to ear. "This is all very real."

~~~~~~~~~~

"He looks satiated," I said as I watched Dex nibble at the beans of his paws.

Shay's body shook as she snickered. "He ate all of that demon sludge, so he's probably high as a kite." For reasons we didn't know, our dragon had transformed back into the German Shepherd we adored.

"Maybe. Do you think he should rest before we talk about what comes next?"

She held me, arms hooked around my hips, her chest snugged tight against my back as we sat in the dirt. The celebration continued as the giants of Passofgrant held up Belos as a hero.

"Look at them." Her head tipped toward the crowd of fairies waiting for the keeper to return to open the portal. "They've waited hundreds of years. They're done waiting."

The lovers' reunion was hard on my heart. I didn't want to imagine a world where Shay stood frozen and I couldn't rescue her from her bindings. But a reunion such as the one we were witnessing would be unimaginable, would transcend everything that kept me tied to her. I would never leave her side.
~~~~~~~~~~

"You think Belos will want to be apart from Helms ever again?" I asked, rubbing my fingertip against the scars in her palm.

"I know I wouldn't." She squeezed me tight. "I'd have stood there for hundreds of years. I'd have used every source of magick to free you."

"I don't want to think about it."

She kissed my cheek. "We don't have to think about anything but finding the fairy realm and getting answers to the dreams we've been having."

Shay tried to stand, but I wanted more time in her arms. I needed a short escape from whatever was coming next.

"It's inevitable, love." Her voice was warm against my ear, and if we were anywhere else, I'd let her touch me everywhere just to affirm that we were *us*.

Brigid's hammer lay on the ground, close to Dexter's nose. Me being the Maker of Bannock had benefited us today, but I wondered if the next phase would be as easy.

"The fairy realm awaits you," a voice said over our shoulders, and Dexter popped up on his feet.

From the deep tone, I'd have guessed a giant, but it was the most road weary fairy I'd ever seen. Their delicate features were gaunt, almost to starvation, and the soot-covered rags on their body were held together with rough-tied thread. Whoever this fairy was, their journey to this place had been a very long and arduous one.

"We were resting for a bit," I said. "Letting the keeper of the realm have some time."

"There is no more time," the fairy replied as it flew toward the spot where Belos and Hermes had stood frozen just hours before. "We have waited hundreds of years to return to our brethren. The time is now."

Shay stumbled to her feet and held a hand out to help me up. "What do we need?"

"You hold the alicorn," the fairy said.

Shay stepped around the crowd to find our backpack. She unzipped the side pouch and held the whistle up. The alicorn whistle, barely the size of Shay's finger was almost as big as the tattered fairy.

"There can be no blessing larger than the one that brought you here." He hesitated to take it, his hands lingering over it like a long-lost friend. Clearly, he treasured the alicorn bone. "We can go home."

"And you'll allow us to come with you?" Shay asked.

"There is no other way. There is a debt now, a debt so large it will never be repaid. From this side of the realm, you may pass." The fairy flew away, laying the whistle in Shay's hand as if it was a treasure.

"Are we packing to go?" I asked.

Shay twisted her wrist, looking at her watch. "This is so weird."

"Baby, you're going to have to narrow that statement down because, from where I'm standing, it's all pretty weird."

"Time." She pushed her arm toward me. "My watch says it's still Wednesday. That can't be. Can it?"

"It has to be Friday, at least. We camped for two nights."

"Time is kinda funny like that," Stout said. "Age, time, they don't really matter outside your realm. Beings just move with the light and the dark."

"What happens when we go back?" I asked.

It seemed like the obvious question. What was going to happen? Would we have aged? Would Dani and Amelia have aged? Would the world that we knew be gone?

Shay patted my hand. "You're overthinking."

"Stop being so calm."

"Baby, that's what I do." She chortled as she moved closer to hold me. "We'll go back to Bannock, check in, then come back ready for whatever's next."

"Can we do that?" I asked, awash with a sense of relief at going home, of feeling the safety of our protected walls.

"We need to do it," she said. "And I'm going to take a few weeks of leave from work."

Shay, as always, had a plan before I'd even taken time to digest the situation.

We didn't leave Passofgrant alone; the giants and their fairy friends accompanied us to the portal, and when we said our farewells, Clia asked to remain in this realm. I'm certain her newfound freedom was a struggle, and being with more fairies was helping her come to terms with her time held captive. All of those existing in Giantville had been affected on a visceral level by the demon inside of Kai.

"We'll return as soon as we can," Shay said just before we stepped through the portal home.

The world in which Bannock existed seemed so small as we stood in the field. A new keeper, smaller and slighter than some of the other giants, stood waiting by the gate, replacing Helms, who was still with Belos.

"You served us well, Magick and Maker of Bannock," they said. "There is much cause for celebration."

"Thank you," Shay and I said at the same time.

"Will you return?"

Shay smiled. "We will be back soon to journey on to the fairy realm."

"Then we will meet again." They stepped backward through the portal. "Soon." The gateway closed and access to the world of giants disappeared with it.

"This is really our life?" I said.

Shay held her open palm to me. "It really is." We walked toward the path. "You doing okay?" she asked.

"I'm better than okay now. That felt like something out of a fantasy novel."

Shay adjusted the pack on her back and glanced at her watch. "Friday."

"So your watch works, just not in Passofgrant." I hooked my arm through hers, and we shared the hiking path back to our car.

"Yep, and we've got a couple of hours until sunset. Hike fast or camp out?"

It was a tough question to answer because as much as I enjoyed cuddling up in that tent, our bed was calling me home. "Hike fast sounds pretty good. Maybe a warm shower tonight and comfy cuddles."

"And no tent sex!" Stout grumbled as he flew beside Dexter. They exchanged words, and Stout laughed. "Peace and quiet is right."

CHAPTER XII

FLETCHING

"That's unbelievable," Amelia said, sliding another beer to Stout.

We'd gone home to change and clean up only to discover that we were out of beer and the food in the refrigerator was less than edible.

"It was insane." My arms flailed with excitement as I explained Helms and the leader of the giants, and that it

wasn't Grant's Pass like everyone in the human world believed. I talked non-stop until Shay's arm snugged around my shoulder.

"Slow down, honey. You're going to make Amelia's head explode." The two women laughed as Dani carried food to us at the bar. "Thanks chef," Shay joked.

"Yeah, blow it out your a—" Amelia's hand flew over Dani's mouth.

"It's been hell in the bar for the last two days," Amelia said as Dani stepped back behind the bar. "While you were saving giants, we were inundated with strangeness here."

"What do you mean, *strangeness*?" Shay asked before taking a bite of her hamburger.

"Stuff gone missing; switches flipped when I know I shut them down. I had to come here at three in the morning when Pete called me on patrol." Dani's hands clenched the bar as she spoke. "This place is haunted, I swear."

"I'd say Danielle was exaggerating," Amelia said, "but all of that and more has been happening over the last few days."

"It's my folk," Stout said, stopping with his lips hovering over his straw. "Word is out that the portal is open. They're closing up their spaces so they can travel through."

"Wait, what?" Dani leaned closer to our fairy.

"The barrier between the human world and the fairy world is gone and so is their inability to go to that realm."

"So, what are they doing messing around with the bar?" I asked, wondering what a fairy could need with turned on lights and stuff gone missing.

"My guess is that anything that can carry belongings has been hard to find, and since the fairies of Bannock were welcomed here by Benton, they took most of her stuff: cups, mugs, dish towels. We can carry a *lot* of goods in dishtowels, especially those tea ones." He didn't miss a beat as he slurped another sip of beer.

"Are all of them leaving for good?" My tone was, to my mind, innocent enough, but it was pointedly directed at him..

"For now, not forever." He kicked back against the ridge of the bar.

"What about you?" Shay asked, apparently deciding to cut to the chase. "Will you leave us to return to your realm?"

"That's not for me to say, Red." He avoided eye contact, but it wasn't because of the use of the terrible nickname. He was answering the question while also asking one. Stout had taken an oath to serve the Magick of Bannock, and the only one who could release him from that vow was Shay.

"Let me ask differently." She reached out a finger to touch his foot. "Would you like to return to the fairy realm?"

"Yes, I really would."

It was an answer that didn't shock me, and yet my heart sank. In the months since our fairy came to be in our lives–in our family, really–I'd grown fond of him and his beer drinking ways. I wasn't ready for our home without him in it.

"I understand, and I release you from your oath, Stout." She said it, just like that. No preamble or anything.

Amelia froze in her place behind the bar, and I felt a tightening in my heart. This couldn't be.

"But you don't have to leave," I said, closing my eyes to mask the glaze of tears.

"There's time." He stood and walked across the bar to me. "I knew you liked me."

There was no way to hide my emotions. "I don't just like you, you jerk."

"That's even better to almost hear." He looked up at me. "I don't even dare guess what's in the realm now. A lot can change, you know."

"That's why the fairy exodus is happening," Dani said as she slid in beside Shay. "You know the cook? That guy was a goddamn fairy. I just thought he was a small dude, but he just transformed. Wings appeared out of his shirt, and the ass said, 'Gotta go,' and that was it."

"Wait, the cook was a fairy?" It shouldn't have been such a surprise. I had come to understand magick, transmogrification, and hiding in plain sight. But it still floored me. "Does that mean half of Bannock is leaving?" I asked.

"Mostly just the fairy folk," Dani said.

"We'll adjust." Shay smiled as she sipped her beer.

"That means you're up next as fry cook." Dani punched Shay's shoulder.

"Or we could just put up a 'help wanted' sign and close the kitchen until we hire someone new."

Dani shook her head and laughed. Shay could cook but there was more skill required to make food for people, even in a place like Slammed.

"Enough about the bar; when are we going back?" Dani turned to rest her shoulders against the solid wood of the bar.

We'd discussed returning to Passofgrant on our hike home. Shay needed to take leave, though a two-week vacation wouldn't put a dent in the months she'd accumulated. We would repack our gear, including my forged candle, and prepare to meet the evil chasing us in our dreams.

"I'm meeting with the chief tomorrow morning," Shay said. "I'm taking two weeks off so Wildwood and I can really solve this."

"Wildwood? You're going to take *just* Wildwood?"

Dani's tone was harsh, and if I was being honest, it hurt my feelings. I was the Maker of Bannock, sworn to arm the Magick of this town. This wasn't my first day on the job, even if I wasn't as experienced as Dani or Amelia. But then I started thinking about it more, turning everything over in my head. Now that I'd heard it said out loud, maybe taking just me *wasn't* such a great idea.

"Maybe we should talk more?" I suggested.

My voice broke with a mixture of hesitation and a tremble of fear. We would find welcoming arms in the land of Giants, and I could only guess the fairy realm would allow us passage to wherever we are meant to go. But we were hunting a nightmare, the evil that had haunted our dreams. If we were going to find the Gatekeeper to end all humanity, maybe another cop and her ridiculously skilled archer wife should come with?

My bravado as the Maker all but evaporated. "They've fought more otherworldly creatures than I have. What if we need them?"

"That's what I'm saying, Pierce. Listen to your woman." Dani hitched her thumb to point at me just as Amelia came around to the bar.

"I didn't just hear you refer to Wildwood as 'her woman,' did I?" she asked incredulously. There was an edge to her voice, too.

"I did, and I stand by it. Pierce wants to cut us out of the fairy realm. That's some bullshit!"

Amelia gave her wife the kind of look that only twenty years of commitment could decipher, but it didn't deter Dani. "Don't give me that glare." Dani pointed at her best friend, staring her in the eyes. "We're going if I have to magick my way down the trail."

"And when there's trouble?" Amelia asked.

"We kick its ass." Dani punched the air.

"And when someone gets hurt?" Amelia covered her wife's fist with her hand. "I'm not trained like the two of you."

"You're the best of us with a bow." Dani took Amelia's hand in her own. "There's safety in numbers. Didn't we learn that in the mine?"

"We did," Shay said. "But we also learned that any of us might not return."

"No one would write that story, Shay," Dani countered. "A trans woman, her one-legged wife, their lesbian best friend, and her bisexual girlfriend? No one in this world would write that death."

"Your faith in our storyteller is larger than mine, D." Shay pounded her fist on Dani's shoulder as she took the last bite of her burger.

"I'm going." Dani moved to take a sip of her beer.

"Where she goes, I go too." Amelia grabbed the beer from her wife and finished the glass.

"I guess that's settled," Stout said as he tapped the side of his empty beer. "Another please?"

"If all of you are going, I guess we better stock up on fairy dust and demon sift." Shay looked at me as she reached over to open the tap and pour our fairy another beer. "Drink up Stout. We're going after trouble."

And so it was decided, against Shay's best judgment, that our team would head back to Passofgrant to gain passage to the fairy realm. Dani and Shay would get the gear in order, Amelia would see to the bar, and I would make sure I armed us for every demon known by the superhero I cherished.

~~~~~~~~~~

"Two weeks," Shay said when she and Dani walked into the carriage house. They were in full uniform followed by the perkiest, prancingest Dexter I'd seen in days.

"Time off all set?" I asked as I placed the steel back inside the forge.

"Yes!" Shay did a little victory dance. "The department is good without us. Believe it or not, demon activity is so low they were talking about forced time off, so here we are."

She stopped on the opposite side of the anvil as I swept the demon sift into a collection jar. I'd spent the last few hours forging arrowheads from demon steel so we'd have plenty of sift for whatever was to come.

Dani counted the jars, pointing to each one in turn. "You think that's enough?" she asked with a cheeky, crooked half-smile.

"There's six," I said as I filled the jar in my hand to the top.

"Who's carrying all of that?"
~~~~~~~~~~

I laughed as I handed the container to her. "That would be you and her." I tipped the jar to point at Shay and then at Dani. "You'll each get some. Cops are pack mules, too."

One of the arrow points had reached tempering temperature, so I removed it and set it down on the floor to cool beside the dozens of others I'd made.

"Stubborn and pack are completely different. You can ask my wife about that." Dani laughed as she stopped at the staircase to the apartment.

"You almost done?" Shay waited for a kiss, and I was happy to give her a quick one before turning off the gas line to the forge.

"I'm officially finished, and I've also got something for Amelia," I said. "Is she on her way?"

"She'll be here soon," Dani promised. "The bar clan is getting their assignments for the next two weeks."

"The bar is covered?" I hung my apron on the hook and followed them up the stairs, joking, "Diana to the rescue again."

"She's a princess and a rockstar at the bar," Dani said as she stopped at the top step.

"What are you doing?" Shay asked, voice raised, and I jumped the last treads to see the ridiculous stacks of paper and books strewn all over the floor.

Stout was frantically flying about, ticking notes on a piece of paper as he moved pages one after the other. "Clia had so many memories that I'm trying to put down for us, for you, just in case I don't return."

"Stout!" Shay called him out of his manic state.

"I must do this before we go," he insisted, his wings ripping through the quiet of the apartment. "In case something happens to—"

Shay cut him off with a hand in front of his body. "Stout."

"What?" His voice was louder than expected.

"You don't have to stay away." She held her hand to him, palm up, and the fairy hovered slightly above the largest scar on her skin. "Bound or unbound, you will always be welcome in this carriage house."

"I appreciate that, but we haven't confronted the demon god, and my last fight was—" He couldn't say it out loud, couldn't relive his torture and near-death at the hands of Andrea's evil.

"Just know." That's all Shay said, and Stout returned to the piles in the room.

"So we leave in the morning?" Dani asked.

"That's the plan." Shay walked over to the refrigerator, then stared into it incredulously. "Well, this is a joke."

"You said to empty the fridge, so we emptied it." I sat at the table.

"Amelia is bringing dinner," Dani said. "I already called, and she should be here soon."

"At least there's beer." Shay grabbed some bottles and opened one for each of us. She flipped the caps into the recycle bin and speared a straw into Stout's bottle with one smooth motion.

"You've got those bartender moves, honey." I winked and pretended to leave a tip on the table.

"You can repay me later." She winked back, and I made a swooning move.

"You two are cute," Dani said.

Stout snorted, still rifling through the stuff in front of him. "Wait until you camp with them." He looked up from shuffling pages. "Loud, out, and proud. Emphasis on 'loud.' Gay, gay, gay!"

"I guess I got here at the right time." Amelia climbed the last two steps. "It appears something is very gay?"

"Super gay, and it's the two horny gals over there." Stout blew a raspberry and disappeared to the top of his bookcase.

"Hello," Dani greeted her wife with a kiss.

"Hi, love," Amelia said and pointed to the workshop. "Food is in the car. Could you grab it?" Dani didn't say a word, just left to retrieve dinner. "It has been a day," Amelia huffed as she sat at the table.

"Bar?" Shay asked, then raised a bottle of beer. "You want one?"

"Maybe something a little stronger?"

Shay reached for the bottle on top of the fridge. "Scotch?"

"Hit me hard!" Amelia laughed as she double tapped the table in front of her.

"Hit her hard? You better not." Dani set the glass dish of food on the table.

"You are adorably protective." Amelia patted her wife's cheek, then took a sip of her drink. "Good." She surveyed the room. "So catch me up. What did I miss?"

"They approved our leave." Dani counted on her fingers. "Gear is packed." Her finger bent back. "Bar is set?" The last count ended as a question to Amelia.

"Bar is set," she confirmed.

Shay clapped her hands. "So we're doing it?"

"We're doing it." Dani took a sip of her beer.

"There's just one more thing I want to do." I got up from the table and went into the magick room. The contoured poles and a pile of arrow tips were sitting on the altar table where I'd done the blessing. I carried them into the kitchen. "So I took a few measurements at the bar, and I forged these for you." I leaned the walking sticks on the table beside Amelia. "And these." I opened the bundled square of fabric to reveal the arrow tips.

"For me?" Her eyes were wide with surprise.

"I know we're about to hit the trails, and I thought some magick-infused walking sticks would keep you steady. And since who knows what we'll meet along the way, the arrowheads are demon steel, too."

Amelia stood and took a pole in each hand. "These are very light."

"It's the same combination I used for the takedown bow, so they'll share energy."

Shay stood beside me. "The Maker of Bannock has badass magick skills."

"Sure as hell does," Dani said as she picked up the arrowhead and gently pushed the point against her fingertip. "These are gorgeous."

"Thanks." Heat rushed to my cheeks, and I hoped that I wasn't outwardly blushing. "I wanted to make a hiking attachment for your leg, but the more research I did, the more it seemed like a bad idea to hike on an untested prosthetic."

"It's a terrible idea, but the thought of a demon steel blade is intriguing."

"Maybe when we get back, then?"

I hadn't expected Amelia's comment to have such a sobering effect, but as silence fell around the table, I realized what everyone must be thinking.

"When we get back." Dani raised her beer, and we each did the same as we touched them together in unity.

~~~~~~~~~~

"How's it going back there?" Amelia yelled over her shoulder.

She'd taken second position on the hike, following Shay's lead. I was content to stare at my girlfriend's backside for the first few miles. We'd settled on making the entire five-mile trip to Passofgrant in one day so that we could rest for the night before traveling to the fairy realm.

"Looks *very* good from here," I said, grinning.
~~~~~~~~~~

Shay caught me surveying her body. "You're terrible." She pointed at me, and I pretended to be offended that I'd been caught.

"Hey, 'Melia," Dani said, "is there a dentist on the trail? Because the sappiness of these two is giving me a cavity."

I laughed, and Shay threw her best friend the middle finger.

"Nice, Pierce. Really nice." Still smiling, Dani said, "Hey, if you can put that finger down for a minute, what's our ETA?"

We'd been hiking for a few hours, stopping twice for water and to have a light snack of trail mix and jerky.

Shay checked the map tucked into the waist of her backpack. "Not far. About ten minutes, and we'll be at the clearing where we met Helms."

We continued on our way, and, just as Shay had predicted, nearly ten minutes later, the friendly giant greeted us. "The Magick of Bannock, we receive you well."

Shay stepped forward with her hand stretched out to the giant. "Thank you for the welcome."

Their bodies met in a strong forearm shake. Helms turned to me with the other arm in my direction.

"And the Maker of Bannock, we receive you well."

I repeated Shay's greeting. "Thank you for the welcome." We gripped forearms, and the giant held us as if it were a blessing.

"And the beast of Bannock, we receive your fire well." He tipped his head to Dexter, and there had to be an exchange of some sort between them because the animal moved close enough that his nose pressed against the giant's forearm.

The greeting made us feel welcomed back to Passofgrant. It was a surprise to see the giant standing at the entrance to their realm.

"It is wonderful to see you. I didn't expect you to leave the side of your beloved," I said, stealing a glance at Shay.

"We have duties, but our reunion was blessed." Helms looked over Shay's shoulder at the unfamiliar faces. "You come with friends." It was a statement more than a question as Dani and Amelia walked closer.

"Danielle and Amelia Forrest," Shay explained. "They're not just friends; they're our family. We hope to bring them into the fairy realm with us."

Helms squeezed our arms once more, then released us to examine the worthiness of our companions. "For what purpose will you enter this most protected realm?"

"They have come at my request," Shay said before Amelia or Dani could answer. "Dani is my second after the Maker of Bannock, and her wife Amelia is truest with a bow."

"You'll need no battle readiness in the fairy realm but know that the noble warriors of Passofgrant will be at your side when you confront the evil that trapped my love." Helms' hand stretched out to Dani and Amelia and when they touched it, the giant fell to his knee. "Family of the Magick, we receive you well."

"Thank you for the welcome," they said and waited for the giant to release them.

"You are called wives as we are called sacred-hearted. Many gifts upon your union." Helms released their arms and stood before us.

"How is Belos?" Shay asked.

I was wondering the same, but I also wanted to know something else. "How is Hermes?"

At the mention of the dragon's name Dexter's ears perked up.

"All are well," Helms assured us. "Back at their posts, too."

The realm of Giants had a wild way of dealing with years of separation. "How can you stand to be apart after being separated for so long?" I asked.

"It is what the sacred-hearted do," Helms said, as if that explained anything.

We continued our walk toward town, and more of the townspeople stepped out, welcoming us warmly. This time, there were bows of gratitude and offerings that Helms waved away.

"I don't think I'd leave Shay's side if we'd been apart for hundreds of years." I reached for her hand and held tight.

"I'm with Wildwood on that," Dani said. "No way Amelia's leaving me, either."

"There are things larger than life pairings." Helms stopped to look at us all. "I miss him no longer when the door to our home opens and Belos is there."

"The love between giants is mirrored in their size," Shay said.

"I will take you to my love, as the fairy portal has been active with reunions on both sides of the realm. You will enjoy many rewards when you pass through, Magick of Bannock. And your skills, Maker, will be requested for demonstration."

"So they know what we did here?" I asked.

We were moving from the town to the tall grass where the portal existed. It was then that I saw the dragon circling high in the air.

"Clia has shared the tale of the Magick and the Maker. You will be welcome, and they are eager to end their struggle with the great evil."

"The demon from our dreams?" Shay looked at me nervously.

My arm went limp at the thought of confronting this terrible evil. I wanted to be fierce when the fight came, but I wasn't confident that all the weapons I'd created would be enough.

"Brigid's broken half," Helms said. "The opposing force bound to the Maker's power."

"I'm bound to that monster?" We stopped in front of Belos, who'd heard most of our conversation as we approached.

"Every realm is bound to good and evil," Helms replied, though it didn't do anything to settle the anxiety clawing at my chest. "There is no way to survive, one without the other."

"That sounds rather defeatist," Dani whispered under her breath.

Helms shrugged. "It is the truth of existence. We will always fight the battles because there will always be battles to fight."

This was not the conversation I wanted to have as we entered the next phase of this quest to end our nightmares. There would always be evil. Part of me knew that. But would it always be the kind that wanted Shay and me dead? Did happily ever after include demon-forged weapons even after all the sacrifices we'd made? I stood, frozen in place as Dexter transformed into his dragon self and Hermes circled us one time before massive talons opened to clench the ground as it landed beside Belos.

"I can't believe what I'm seeing," Dani said, and Shay laughed.

"Ridiculous, I know," Shay said.

Dexter moved closer to the nearly mirror image of himself, and the two laid side by side. When Dexter had transformed for the first time all those months ago, I thought I'd seen nothing so unbelievable. But today, as we stood in this field, something transcending magick was taking hold of us all.

"He's a little smitten." Stout hovered over Shay's shoulder.

"Wouldn't you be?" I asked. "They're freaking dragons!"

"Hermes is no longer bound, and she wants him to fly with her," Stout explained as he listened to the dragons talk.

"But he's afraid to fly," I said. "Isn't he?"

"We do a lot of things to make people happy," Stout smiled.

"Welcome to the realm, Maker of Bannock," Belos said, and the dragons raised their heads toward them. "The fairies are waiting to greet you."

"Thank you, Belos," I said, bowing my head.

"You have the hammer of the goddess?" they asked.

I felt the weight of her hammer more than ever as it hung over my shoulder. "I have."

"Keep your Magick close as you work for the fairies."

"Hey!" Stout flew toward the keeper of the portal. "I'll protect the Magick and the Maker. My loyalty will always fall to them."

"Be well, as you pass through," Belos said and stepped aside to reveal the spiraling wall of purple debris.

"Is it just like that?" Dani asked.

Shay raised her hand to touch the gateway point. "Just like—" Her fingers disappeared through the mist as her voice broke.

"What does it feel like?" I stood beside her, my hand on her hip.

Shay stepped back, holding my sigil hand in hers to pass it through the portal. "What does it feel like?" Her whispered question moved through me, and the sensation of her passionate touch was the only feeling I had as our hands disappeared into the gateway to the fairy realm.

"Are you touching me?" I asked.

"Oh, yes, that's exactly what I feel, too." Shay's voice echoed.

At first touch, the portal debris–whatever it was spiraling before us–stripped away self-control and all the inhibitions protecting us. It was seductive, and every cell of my body wanted more.

"This feels like it should happen behind closed doors." I said it louder than I'd meant to, and I heard the laughter of the giant guarding the portal.

"Your Maker and Magick bond intensifies the right to pass." He waved us to move forward. "The fairy realm is quite seductive. Be aware."

It was the last thing Belos said before Shay called Dexter to our side. The three of us moved through the wave of sensations, and the fairy realm came into view. Neither Shay nor I considered what it might be like for Dani or Amelia, those not blessed by the goddess to move into the fairy realm. We were too focused on the feelings flooding through us and the sights our eyes were feasting on.

We weren't walking, nor were we floating; it was some kind of motion in between. This would be a place to escape, and I wondered if this was how it felt to use drugs. It was something I'd avoided as a child and into adulthood purely for the absence of control. Once you've had it control stripped away, it's difficult to choose to let it go.

Shay's feet hit the ground first, and she quickly snatched at me to keep me from falling.

"I've got you," Shay said, and every part of me felt gotten.

"I hope we're going home like that."

The smile on her face was confirmation that we'd been thinking similar thoughts. Dexter was beside us, along with Stout, who hovered near our dragon. Dani and Amelia hadn't passed through.

"Where's Dani?"

"They aren't coming," a voice said. Whoever it was appeared to be hidden.

"What do you mean, they aren't coming?" Shay made a move to step back through the portal, and I tugged her to me.

"Honey, don't move through that portal alone." My voice was loud, not quite a yell, but Shay's eyes were wide. She heard me.

"We need them, Wil."

"What we need is the Magick of Bannock to stay focused on what's ahead. Whatever is holding Dani and Amelia in the realm of giants, they aren't in danger there." My hands wrapped around the shoulders of Shay's vest as I gave her a shake. "Look at me."

"What if they're stuck?"

"They aren't stuck anywhere," the voice said again, but this time the fairy made themselves known.

Stout was loud but fast as he zoomed toward the realm keeper. "Ari, is that you?"

"Omatarius, is that you my brother?"

"It is, my sister."

I had never seen a hug quite like it before. They were touching each other, but that wasn't the only connection between them. They were flying in sync, hovering together in some beautiful, choreographed dance. It was a sight to behold.

"It has been so many lifetimes," Ari said.

"You keep the portal? What an honor," Stout said, and the three of us watched in silence as their reunion continued.

"Your Magick and Maker, along with the shapeshifter, have opened the gateway." Ari gave Stout a huge smile. "Clia told us the tale, and the king moved me to the gateway as soon as passage resumed."

"So you joined the Bliation?"

She nodded in confirmation. "Even though we could not move outside the realm, we still trained; we still understood that it will come. We–"

"It?" Shay interrupted.

"The evil you seek," Ari said, releasing her hold on Stout.

"See, that's not how we interpreted it," Stout said. "Evil is seeking *us*. Seeking *them*, to be more specific." He pointed at Shay and me.

"We will give you passage to the place you seek, Magick of Bannock," Ari promised. "But know that the fight is in a realm that is open because Belos and Hermes are free."

Stout sighed. "The price for freedom must be paid."

"And the rest of my family, where are they?" Shay held her palm out to the spiraling portal, and the fairy flew in front of it to stop us from passing back through.

"Your family is safe," Ari said. "The giants have taken them for their own protection."

"Protection from us or from you?" Shay said, eyes full of suspicion.

In the few minutes since passing through the portal we'd experienced just one solitary fairy who we knew was part of the new world. The problem was this Bliation, this warrior of their realm would not let us move beyond the isolated rocky ledge.

"Your family has not earned the right to pass through," the fairy said, her tone too snippy for my liking. "There is no free movement between the lands of the giants and the fairies."

Shay grabbed my arm and pulled the two of us away from Stout and Ari. Our plan to confront evil with an enchanted archer like Amelia and a trained fighter like Dani, was being side-tracked by this pocket-sized warrior.

"We're going back for Amelia and D." Shay made a move toward the portal. "Dexter!" Her call alerted Ari, and before we could go back through, the passageway disappeared.

"The Bliation will escort you to the King."

Ari's wings twitched, and if we weren't already on guard, we might have let it slide. But we were beyond uneasy, and Shay and I both reached for our weapons. Before we could draw them, though, a swarm of fairies surrounded us, and we had no choice but to accompany the warriors of the realm to their king.

"You realize we opened the portal allowing freedom to move again after hundreds of years?" I said, but it fell on deaf ears. None of the fairies even turned to look at me.

Stout appeared between Shay and me. "They will no longer listen to you. Remember how I said they were the badasses of the realm?"

"I do."

Shay grabbed hold of my hand to tug me into her circle of protection. "They're just following orders, it would seem. If we have any hope of getting Dani and Amelia through, we'll need to take it up with their king."

Our feet barely touched the ground as we made our way to wherever they were taking us. It wasn't that we were flying so much as the hundreds of Bliation forces carried us in the direction they chose. It was infuriating. Given what we'd done for them, the freedom these beings now had because of us, I'd expected a little more kindness.

"What should we do?" The question came out as a whisper between my tight lips.

"Exactly what they ask of us for now," Shay said out of the corner of her mouth as she watched Dexter transform into dog shape to frolic with the less aggressive forces of the Fairy realm.

There are probably hundreds of books and oral traditions about fairies. Before moving to Bannock, I'd have believed all of them were tales told to keep children amused. But now I knew the truth. I wasn't a child, and this ride from the portal to the fairy kingdom was certainly *not* amusing.

"Place them here," a voice said, and the three of us landed hard on the pebbled ground.

For a land filled with seven-inch beings, the buildings were enormous. The walls in Passofgrant had been built with massive boulders, while these were made from millions of stones, but the final products were the same. Castles seemed to rise from the ground, stitched together with the greens of sod and moors. It was fantastical, and if I wasn't afraid of what came next, I'd want to study their architecture more closely.

"Who are you?" Shay asked, finding her balance once more.

I gasped and cried out as Shay fell to her knees.

"Speak only when you are told to," Ari ordered.

As Ari's magick forced my girlfriend to the ground, Dexter's carefree attitude changed. His fluff of fur feathered into flickering scales as his face morphed from German Shepherd to the fiercest of dragons. His bark hissed with fire–not the cooling flame connected to the Magick and the Maker, but the unapproachable heat of a deadly blaze. Dexter's tail curled around us, creating a ring impenetrable by any outside force. He was in control of the Bannock dragon power.

"Calm your beast!" the leader demanded.

Shay fought to get to her feet, defiantly disregarding the king's order. Instead of trying to soothe Dexter, she yelled, "We have come here to pass through this realm and confront the evil that trapped *you* here for hundreds of years, and yet you attack us."

"Calm your beast, or we will grant nothing to you."

In response, Shay whispered words in Latin, and the ground beneath our feet trembled. She raised her palm enough for her *ignis* flame to burst through, and before I could take a breath, our hands came together, the power of the Bannock three creating an incredible dome of protection around us.

"They control the Ra-sa-vat-am," Clia hurriedly explained, flying in front of their leader. "They are the Magick and the Maker, there is no doubt, and they have come to end this, not to betray us. This is not like before."

It was then that I noticed something that angered me beyond the rage already building inside of me. Stout had been bound to a post in the ground, his wings tethered. For a moment I flashed back to the day Andrea had taken me and tortured our loyal fairy. I remembered his wings being torn mercilessly, and the damage his body endured. As I looked at our friend, I could see the same terror in his eyes now as I had then.

"Set him free!" I yelled, my voice shrill, choked with emotion.

Stout turned to look at me, and I saw it, the fracture in his always sharp demeanor. "They won't hurt me, Wildwood."

"They are here to help," Clia pleaded. "They are bound to the goddess."

"Our betrayer was bound to the goddess, too," the king reminded her. "And where did that lead? Three hundred years trapped inside this world."

"I was trapped, too, and they set me free." She flew to the edge of our shield, and as she approached the barrier, Shay allowed her through. "See? They have come to end this."

"There is no end to evil," the king said.

"If we have any say," Shay called out, "this will end. We will find and destroy the evil that has trapped and tortured our realms for ages."

"Those are bold promises," the king said, speeding from the protective line of the Bliation forces to hover just outside our bubble. "We heard promises from the Magick-Maker all those years ago. How are you any different?"

"It isn't power that we seek," Shay said. "It's never been about power. We only want peace and an opportunity to live free." The barrier around us faded as the flame of our *ignis* fires cooled.

"We released the giant and their dragon at the portal," I reminded them. "That should prove our intentions."

Before we'd left Bannock this morning, we thought the fairies would welcome us as heroes, but this confrontation, this rejection of our help, was a shocking surprise.

I looked at Stout. "What can we do to convince them?"

"Wait," he said. "They will either hear what your heart says and let you through, or they will not, and there will be no passage to the place that you seek."

"Maybe that's the answer," Shay mused aloud. "Evil *will* come in some form we can't see. We want to fight with you."

"That's just it, Magick of Bannock," the king said, his voice cold and unyielding. "We do not welcome another fight. The last one left us locked in this realm for hundreds of years."

Shay and I exchanged a glance, and I could tell she was feeling just as hopeless as I was. No words passed between us, but the question in her eyes was clear.

Oh, love, what are we going to do now?

CHAPTER XIII

CAPTIVE

The rest of the day went as it began, we hiked out of the fairy castle, led by the Bliation forces. Stout was correct about their attitude toward humans, and although we'd presented ourselves as the Magick and the Maker, with Dexter as the third, they did not trust that we'd come to find the evil that had started this seemingly timeless battle.

Brigid's hammer–and my connection to it–was what they feared. From their experience, the bond between myself and

the goddess brought with it the unexpected presence of evil. As I stared at this tool, felt the energy of my power flow between us, I had an overwhelming sense of sorrow that merging with it had led to Kai's unavoidable demise.

"What's going on in there?" Shay tapped my temple.

"Thinking about this." I set the hammer on the sleeping bag in front of us.

Shay picked it up and traced the runes with her fingertip "Tell me what you're thinking."

I picked at the lines in the handle. "There's a lot of history in this chunk of metal."

Shay rotated the head to look at the other side. "Understatement of the year, love."

"Yeah, so, remember last year when destiny 'led' us to it?" I said, making little quotation marks with my fingers. Shay snickered. "The power transfer that happened would've been something Andrea felt because of her link to Kai, so that power surge had to have called to her like it did to me."

"What are you saying?" Shay twisted the hammer again, this time landing on the pixelated outline of the demon's face.

"Power is corruptible." I laid my sigil palm over the outline. "But this power, it's linking us all, and without balance, it's not safe to be carried, for *any* creature from *any* realm."

Her hand remained on the hammer's handle, and as my sigil flame flared, so did hers. In between, the brightest shade of green flared up to blast through the demon outline.

"You feel it?" I asked.

Her knee moved closer to mine as we sat cross-legged. "Oh, I feel it alright."

"Kai was alone, and it hurts my heart so much to know she never had a chance."

Shay's mouth turned down. "But *we* have a chance, and we'll get through to the fairy king. We'll explain that we're balanced by the goddess, and that thing…" She pointed to the image on the hammer. "That thing will not win."

~~~~~~~~~~

I didn't mind sleeping outside in the wild, not with Shay beside me, but in the realm of fairies, there was a hell of a light show that kept me awake. I'd read about the aurora
~~~~~~~~~~

borealis, seen pictures of the ribbons of green and gold streaming across the night sky. Fairy lights were something completely different, and I wondered if they were so bright because of the two of us and our human presence.

"Can't sleep?" Shay's hand dipped beneath my shirt to rest on my belly.

"Oh, icy hands, woman!" I grabbed her fingers and tucked them to my chest.

"See, that's so much better," she whispered against the nape of my neck. "I should have started here." She wiggled her fingers to cup my breast.

My breath hitched, and I rolled over to face her. "You and those cold hands are not getting in here tonight." I pecked a kiss on her nose.

"Just a little hand warming?" Her fingers traveled over my ribs, and back to the hem of my shirt. Her touch was gentle, but she knew that my head was somewhere else when I closed my eyes. "Hey, what is it?" She tapped my chin.

"I want to get out of here. This place doesn't feel right."

Shay sat up in the tent. "It's realm travel and new energies. We're surrounded by them, and our Magick and Maker powers are untested here."

"How many realms are there?" I asked. A question that seemed innocent. I'd met giants and fairies so far, but what other other-worldly creatures were there?

Shay rolled to her knees and unzipped the tent door. "Come with me."

Her fingers wriggled in the space between us. I was hardly dressed in a t-shirt and light thermal leggings with nothing on my feet. Shay was similarly outfitted, but she slipped her shoes on. I tucked my sockless feet into my boots and followed her.

Shay helped me to my feet. and as her arms came around to hold us together, she pointed to the night sky. In this realm, in the land of fairies, the night sky looked very different.

"Are those stars?" I asked as the back of my head nestled against her shoulder.

"No, baby." Her hand clenched my own, and she raised it toward the sky. "Each of those lights? They're realms of this universe."

"Like stars in the earthly sky?" I asked. For the first time in hours, I felt the grounding power that was simply Shay.

"Exactly like that, but each of those hold creatures from places you've never dreamed."

I turned in her arms. "Like our Gatekeepers?"

Her arms squeezed around me. "Unfortunately, they aren't all peaceful."

Shay went back to the tent and returned with our sleeping bag liner. She opened it into a single blanket and wrapped the two of us together.

"So the realms are vast. What does that mean for us?" I asked.

When her arms tightened, I knew what she was going to say. I could feel her uncertainty like it was my own.

"I'm not sure what it means, yet, but we have to convince the fairy king that we've come to make things right. And not just for us, for everyone who's been trapped all these years."

"Sounds easy."

Her body shook, her laugh filling the surrounding quiet. "Simple as can be."

We stood there for the longest time, her arms wrapped around me, the two of us bundled tight in our blanket cocoon. We knew nothing was easy about moving through realms, and we also knew that conquering the stranglehold of evil would require more than just the Magick and the Maker.

~~~~~~~~~~
~~~~~~~~~~

"Do you think we should worry that Stout and Dexter didn't come to our campsite last night?" I poked the coals, watching the eggs and meat rehydrating in the pan.

"I hope it's a sign that they're working on convincing the fairy leaders." She poured the last of her canteen water over the mushy pile of food.

"Do you think Stout can convince them?"

She stirred the food. "He's been with us for months. He knows who we are, but he's also been under our influence."

"Clia hasn't, and she's been very silent."

"That's not fair to her," Shay scolded. "She tried to talk sense into the king yesterday."

Shay worked the food in the pan, scraping back and forth. It wasn't hard to miss her overly focused concentration, and I wondered what she was thinking. My wait was brief because she wasn't thinking at all; she was reading the energy that was coming at us.

"Get down." Shay dropped the spoon in the pan and dove at me, the two of us hitting the ground hard, as a force of energy came around like a massive dome to protect us.

The force of her body knocked the air from my lungs. Coughing into the dirt, I found my voice again. "What the hell?"

"They're coming for us." The green in her eyes darkened to near black. She pushed off the ground, ready for what or whoever was coming.

"They, who?"

I crawled across the dirt to stand beside her, but the surrounding energy was a distraction. I poked my finger at it and felt her. Shay was the force, and touching it made every cell of my body come alive in ways I didn't understand.

"Holy goddess, Shay. What are you doing?" I pressed my palms toward the energy field, and it was frighteningly erotic. "Honey, what is this?"

She looked back at me, catching the blush on my face. "Maybe don't touch it so much."

It was ridiculous, this exchange, the completely bare energy of my lover. How was I supposed to stand inside of her and not touch it?

"Come here, next to me, Wil." She stood solid, feet planted to the ground. "Bring your magick closer."

There was something in the way she'd asked that made me think–really slow down to think–about what might come next. We were demon fighters, not giant fighters or fairy fighters, and yet here we stood, poised to face the tiniest creatures known to us.

I put my hand on her shoulder, and the reaction was instant. The energy popped and crackled with a static charge, and unless we let it, nothing was touching us today. I heard the dense flutter of wings and the rustling sound of hundreds of fairies approaching. Stout appeared first, and the look on his face said everything.

"Your shield isn't necessary," he said. "You should put it down."

"Stout, we don't know who to trust out here!" Shay yelled.

"Trust me when I say, put the shield down."

But the volume of Bliation forces that followed made Shay double down on our protective barrier.

"I trust you, Stout. I really do. But this doesn't feel like the welcome wagon."

She stepped back, moving closer to me, and the surge of energy cycling between us doubled the strength of our wall. I heard the barking before I saw Dexter running full force toward us. He was no longer the cuddly furball but had transformed into his dragon self.

"Dexter!" Shay yelled, seconds before the animal leapt at us.

Time stood still. His hooked talons extended from his feet, and his shell-like scales shimmered in the daylight. He looked fierce, feral, but he was also coming at us in a way that made me question whose side he was actually on. So many things could have happened in those few seconds as his beak of a nose pierced the barrier, and my first thought was injury or, worse, death.

But it was Dexter, *our* Dexter, and when the full size of his dragon form passed through the field of protection, he phased back into the German Shepherd we'd first cuddled on Shay's cottage couch.

"Dex," Shay said, visibly relieved.

Her hand fell to her hip, and as his wet nose pushed into her palm, the barrier doubled in size, knocking all the Bliation fairy forces back. This display of power, although impressive from the inside, only reinforced their stance against us.

"Put your barrier down!" Stout yelled again, but I couldn't believe this fairy army was approaching us peacefully.

"The barrier stays," Shay said, her voice loud and commanding.

Dexter barked twice, and his head twitched to the side as some form of communication took place between him and Stout. Dexter transformed into the dragon, thus expanding the protective ring and forcing the fairies further from us.

"You stupid–" Stout began to scold, but the dragon's fierce screech made everyone pause, even Shay.

"What is it?" Her eyes narrowed as she asked Stout, "What is he trying to say?"

"He says there's no threat from the three of you unless the fairy army doesn't stand down."

In all the chaos, I hadn't noticed the fairy king. He stood watching the exchange with his entourage. I scanned the crowd that had formed, filled with hovering fairies of every color, shape, and size.

"This show of force is what we feared," the king said to the crowd.

"There is no force here. We're just protecting ourselves." Shay's voice was calm, so calm that it made the pounding of my pulse settle.

"You come here expecting cheers when you bring *that?*" He stepped toward my hammer.

Perhaps I thought it–or maybe not–but for some reason, my hammer spun on its head and dredged a shallow channel in the ground as it moved toward me. Bliation forces attempted to fan a wall to stop it, but the shield Shay commanded protected Brigid's creation, too.

"There is evil here!" one fairy yelled as the hammer whirred by her face.

"I have sworn an oath to you, my king, but also to the Magick and the Maker of Bannock." Stout moved himself in front of the barrier. "Their presence here is peaceful. I swear this on my life." His wings made a fierce and loud clipping flutter as he hovered above our shield. "They've come to finish what evil started."

Stout's wings stopped. His body didn't hover but fell like a stone toward the ground. Shay's hand reached out, almost directly in the path of the falling fairy, and just as it seemed the barrier would devour our loyal friend, he passed through to land in Shay's palm.

The crowd let out a collective echoing gasp. It had been a tumble toward death, true and clear, to penetrate the Magick and Maker barrier, but here was Stout, alive and well.

"You idiot!" Shay yelled at him.

I leaned over her shoulder and stared as he laid in her palm, gasping and clenching over his chest. "It was a leap of faith," he said through choking gulps for air.

"Not a wise one," she whispered, and he rolled over to stand.

"Okay, but I–"

"You have made a choice, Stout of Bannock," the king interrupted.

"We are here in peace," Stout said. "And if you let us, we will prove it."

"Wait, what?" Shay flipped her hand, and Stout hovered near her face. "What are you doing?"

"I'm getting us out of this mess." He fluttered to the barrier's edge.

"It feels like you got us into it," I muttered.

Stout waved me away and said, "There is nothing evil in the way the Magick and the Maker move in the realms."

"So you have said, but we do not know how this could be true," the king replied.

"How about a challenge?" Stout suggested.

Shay snatched him from the air and whispered, *"Ish fa lia dua."* All sound was now locked inside the barrier with us. "No, there will be no challenge!"

His voice met hers in size and volume. "You don't get it! They can't see past what happened to them before, and that means they will not let you go at all!"

"What do you mean?" I asked.

"That's what I've been trying to tell you." He stomped his foot against the air, and if I wasn't currently worried that we were about to die, I would've found it funny. "I was up all night, trying to convince someone–*anyone*–that peace is your way." He paused, then added, "When you aren't slaughtering monsters."

"We only slaughter monsters," Shay shot back.

"Ah, but what does the Magick of Bannock define as a monster?" he asked.

Her gasp was sharp and telling. "So that's the game. They believe we kill everything that isn't like us?"

"You are holding a powerful barrier up against them," Stout reminded her.

"While they're charging at us with fairy green berets!" I yelled. It echoed off the barrier like I was screaming into a hollow tunnel.

"This isn't the answer, Shay." Stout was near her face, staring into her eyes. "I have trusted the power of the Magick and the Maker since my first day with you. I trust you now to make the right decision here."

Shay stared out at the assembled crowd for a long moment. Then, finally, she appeared to make a choice. "Dexter." She called to him, and his furry form pressed to her left hip. "Wil, love, come stand at my right."

We stood together, the three of us, and before I could ask what we would do next, the barrier fell away.

"We will meet your challenge." She stepped toward the Bliation soldiers hovering near the king.

The forces advanced on us, and for a second, I thought we would end up in the tiniest of dungeons, but the king nodded at us, turning to the crowd.

"The Magick of Bannock takes our challenge!" he announced. "There is but one true and certain measure of good."

"You cannot—" Stout began, but the hand of the king came up to silence him.

"The purest test of goodness is the ability to command the alicorn." He raised his arm, and an image appeared over his head. Fairy magicks filled the surrounding air. "Evil tries to tame the power, claim what is pure in love and goodness." The holographic unicorn horn twisted in the air, displaying what looked very similar to the whistle Andrea once possessed.

"Is that the whistle?" I whispered to Shay, and she gave me a slight confirming nod.

"The challenge is this," the king said, unknown magicks making the sound echo around us as if he spoke through a megaphone. "The Magick and Maker of Bannock have two sunsets to accomplish the task." He turned to us, and the smile on his face was anything but friendly. "You must bring us the Unicorns of the Glade."

Silence followed his proclamation, and when I looked to Stout for answers, his head fell in defeat.

"You say you are good, then you bring that abomination into our realm." The king pointed at the hammer. "I promise you this: if you can both wield that monstrosity *and* bring us the Unicorns, we'll know that what you proclaim is truth."

"How?" I asked.

"That is the question, isn't it?" He turned and waved a hand, and moments later the field in front of us was empty.

"What the hell just happened here?" I asked, grasping at Shay's outstretched hand.

"An impossible task," Clia said. "There is no way we can proceed in the realm of fairies. The unicorns have been gone for hundreds of years."

"Because of this?" I held the hammer toward her.

"No. It is because of this." Clia held the whistle in her hands. "At least...we *think* so. We have no real idea how or why they disappeared. Nor do we know where they went. We've never been able to find any evidence, written or otherwise."

"What about in the Rasavatam?" Shay asked.

Clia shrugged. "It could be."

"So we are looking for what, exactly?" I asked as I walked toward our tent.

"Unicorns," the others said in unison.

I smiled and shook my head at the impossibility of our situation. Then I pinched my forearm as a reality check and said, "Of course we're looking for unicorns. We already have fairies and giants; why not throw in some actual living unicorns?"

I sat beside the smoldering fire, wrinkling my nose at the slop of our breakfast shriveled in the scalded pan. "What are the odds we can eat and research at the same time?" I asked.

"Fireface and I will get on that." Stout waved at the dog, and they ran off toward the sound of the river.

"I'll come too," Clia followed.

Shay activated her *ignis* flame, removed the pan from the heat, and scorched it clean.

"That's kinda cool." I said as she scraped the burned food into the ash of the fire.

"It really is. I love holding flame." Shay set the pan aside. "Let's build the fire up so we can cook when they come back."

We wandered away from camp, picking up sticks and pieces of trees I couldn't identify.

"Now that we're alone, tell me what you think about this unicorn thing?" I asked as I snapped a branch across my thigh.

"Well, that whistle is from one, so they have to exist."

"And the king really wants them, so that must mean something." I handed my sticks to her, and she tucked them into the backpack. "Any idea how to find them?"

She stopped, turned around, and looked at me. "I was hoping Clia could help. She spent a lot of time with Andrea and that whistle."

"Damn that horrible creature." I shook my head. "I don't know how Clia survived her torture."

"I can't let myself think about it," Shay said as she turned back toward camp. "I did have an idea when the king posed the challenge, though."

"Oh?"

She stopped, and I walked into her. "Hi." She said as she turned to hold me in her arms. She kissed me.

"Hi yourself." I kissed her back and we stood there for a long moment. "So you were thinking?"

"Mm hmm." She adjusted the bag on her shoulder and continued walking toward camp. "What if there's hidden text in the Rasavatam?"

"You think there is?" I asked.

She nodded as she stepped through the trees and into our campsite. "I think we should give your candleholder a light and go through the book."

"You think that the secret path to the unicorns is written in Sanquis' blood on the pages of the Tome of Trouble?"

"When you say it like that, it's too much like X marks the spot." She smiled as she crossed her legs to sit on the ground.

"But you're going to try it anyway, aren't you, superhero?"

She thumped the book in her lap. "We need answers, and at least this is a start."

Her *ignis* flame flashed bright against the candle wick, and she placed it on the ground between us. The alicorn whistle lay on the stone beside me, and I picked it up.

"Unicorns are supposed to be the stuff of dreams," I mused, mostly to myself, but Shay chuckled.

"Dreams, fantasies, all of that is real, and if the consequences of not finding them wasn't so scary, it would be exciting." She held the flame and trailed it over the open pages of the book.

I fell back in the grass and held the white bit of horn above me, rotating it around to study the single finger hole and the window for airflow. The bore was the width of my pinky, and as I scrutinized it closer, the size made sense. This was the instrument of a fairy.

I rolled to my side, watching Shay swipe the candle's illumination over the pages. "What do you see?" I wiggled toward her for a closer look, dropping the whistle on the ground between us.

"I don't see anything yet," she said, turning another page.

"I don't mean to bring you down, but who would've written anything about unicorns in the Tome of Trouble?"

Her hand stopped, and she set the candle on the ground. "I don't know, but what else can we do?"

I heard Stout before I saw him. "I think you could have left us four, you big old pig of a dog."

The tall grasses nearby wriggled as Dexter walked towards us. It was almost as adorable to hear the single side of the conversation as the animal frolicked with a tangle of fish hanging from his mouth.

"Breakfast," I said gratefully. Even though we were surviving on mostly fish, I was happy to put off consuming the mysterious meat and egg combination a little longer.

Shay set the pan on the flames, and as it warmed, she scaled and cleaned our food. "I'll admit I'm about ready for a burger from the bar."

"Anyone snag a few of those blamberries?" Stout asked as he hovered beside Clia and Dexter. "They would hit the spot right now."

"How would it look if the Magick and the Maker stole blamberries?" I asked, almost wishing we'd tried them because the mention of a burger made my mouth water.

"Sorry, it's fish and fish only," Stout said.

It would have been amazing to drink a cold beer along with the steaming fish, but we opened the canteen and sipped water as we ate. The meal satisfied our hunger, and that was all, but it wouldn't be long before our fairy would need a boost, and I wondered what we might have to try.

"Do the fairies make beer?" I asked, and I glimpsed Clia playing in the flame of our candle.

"They make this strange concoction that passes," Stout grumbled, "but it's not like the bar."

"Not much is." Shay said, and she rotated the skewer over the embers.

Stout grinned. "Dani and Amelia must be spittin' mad they got sent home."

He pushed off the ground and flew beside Clia, conversing with her in their fairy language as she flitted over the book. The two of them were so captivating that I laid across the grass to watch them.

"I'm sure I'll get an earful when we return," Shay joked, but when we didn't laugh with her, she turned her attention to the three of us, staring at the light show taking place on the open pages of the Tome of Trouble.

"You better come look at this, Red," Stout said. "I think we found our way out of this mess."

CHAPTER XIV

LEMONADE

"You've got to be kidding me," I said, resting my chin in my palms.

Clia's dexterous feet rolled the alicorn whistle back and forth, revealing the tiniest of symbols squeezed on the surface. Text, the text we were searching for in the Tome of Trouble appeared on the alicorn whistle, lit by the flicker of the candle's flame.

"Goddess, it's unreal," Shay said as she sat beside me, fidgeting with my fingers.

"Can you read it?" Stout asked, and when Dexter barked at him, he relayed the animal's thoughts. "He says he can feel them."

"Feel them?" I blurted the words out and looked over my shoulder, certain I'd see the army of fairies returning. "What does he feel?"

"The Monoceros," Stout said, and he dropped beside Clia. "He says he understands now, and that Shay must play the flute."

"Flute?" I rolled back onto my calves, hunching over the symbols glowing on the alicorn's surface. "Can we just pause for a second and catch me up on what the heck that is?" I pointed to the symbols on the alicorn whistle and started to say something else, but I realized just then that Shay was whispering. "Are you reading that?" I asked.

Her voice grew louder as she chanted, *"This is the song we sing. This is the path we bring. This is the way back home. This will be what is known."*

"Play it. It's a flute, Shay." Stout flew closer, and I noticed the appearance of two more holes on the alicorn. He pushed the flute closer to Shay, and she picked it up.

"Are you sure this is right?" My hand touched hers, stopping the flute inches from her lips. "The odds don't always tip in our favor when we jump in."

"Sometimes they do." She held my hand in her lap, then with a shrug, she added, "Eventually."

"Dexter says it's right," Stout said.

Shay's lips parted as she took a quick breath. I could feel my heart hammering, and when the music played, the sound was beyond anything I'd ever heard, even in my dreams. It was unimaginable, drippy and sweet, the notes making my soul dance and calling me, sending me in a direction I couldn't deny.

Dexter's eyes went wide, and he barked loud enough for us to see him scratch at the ground before following the music away from camp.

"It's pulling me, too. What do we do?" I asked. The rest of our circle seemed just as mesmerized by the music and the dazzling light show it created.

"We follow." Shay picked up her backpack and snuffed out our candle, pushing it inside the bag along with all the notes she'd scribbled in the last few hours. "This is for you."

She held Brigid's hammer out to me, and without missing a beat, we followed Dexter. His dog body phased into its dragon form, and as he moved through the brush and tall grasses, his girth cleared a path for us to follow.

"Isn't this a little too trusting?" I asked.

Shay laughed. "For any other animal, maybe, but he speaks to the creature world, and I definitely think he's onto a scent."

"More like he's onto a sound," Clia said. "That whistle-flute, I mean. That flute never sounded like music in the hundreds of years Andrea forced its magick on me."

We followed Dexter for what felt like hours. The sun was high in the sky, and the heat of the day left a sheen of sweat on my face. It did the same to Shay, and it was clear that we'd need a rest if we planned to push ahead.

"How many hours of daylight do we have left?" I asked her.

"Six, maybe seven." Shay took hold of my hand. "Don't worry too much. I can feel the magick rising. We're almost there."

"Almost where?" I asked, but I knew the answer. Dexter could hear the unicorns, and somehow, they were waiting for him.

"Shh."

Stout put a finger to his lips, and we watched Dexter shift into his dog form again before crawling on his belly toward a wall of stone. The structure hadn't been built or assembled but formed by the forces of nature. We were as far from civilization as we'd ever been.

"There is a portal here." Clia floated between Shay and me. "Play the flute again."

Shay's hands were steady as she raised it to her lips, and the song was just as sweet as it had been the first time she'd played. Dexter pushed his nose to the stone, and his dog face disappeared through it.

"He found it!" Clia exclaimed as she darted to follow the dog. But she slammed into the wall and fell to the ground with a surprised "oof!" A force we couldn't see was stopping the fairy from passing through.

"We can't go with them," Stout said, and he waved Shay and me forward. "This is Magick and Maker powered spell work. Fairies have no business here."

"You ready?" I watched Dexter's tail disappear as he stepped into the stone.

"Not really," I said, but the force of the portal's energy tugged me through.

The journey was quick, almost immediate, in fact. As we stepped through to the other side, Shay's hand came up to cover my mouth.

"*Don't say anything out loud,*" she urged me. "*Speak through the Rasavatam. Something is here and until we understand what it is, we stay silent.*"

Her thoughts filled my head, and as I centered myself in this new realm, I noticed the crumbling structure in front of us. It looked like the carriage house, but hundreds of years older and built from translucent stones that reflected the light of day.

"*The energy here is almost painful,*" I thought as we continued forward through the camouflage of tall grasses.

I wished our fairies were here, mostly to understand what Dexter was doing as he crawled toward the building. Shay crept beside him, and as the instincts of investigation kicked in, the two of them moved in perfect harmony to sneak a look inside.

I heard grumbling voices before I saw the creatures they belonged to, and all three of us hit the dirt. I could see through the crack between the slatted wall and counted seven creatures side-by-side, standing in thick layers of dry grass. The contrast of the brown straw and the silvery animals was like sunrise and sunset, and I couldn't deny the draw of magick moving from them through the ground and into me.

"*Monoceros*?" I thought, but how could they all be if only one had an alicorn on their head?

"*They are,*" Shay confirmed.

As we watched them, something else moved into view, something that made my heart clench and my stomach twist. There was a demon in their midst, stalking through the herd of creatures with malice oozing out of every pore. Its body was so much like the Gatekeepers we'd conquered that I had to close my eyes to block out the visions of the attack in the mine. It clung to my memories and invaded my very being. I reached for Shay's hand, and the force of our Magick and Maker energies reminded me that we'd been through worse and we were still here.

The demon's voice shocked me out of my thoughts. "You've got one full rotation of light," it said as it stopped in front of the smallest unicorn. "I'm coming back, and if you don't drop it, I'll kill this one."

The reflection of a blade swiped through the air, hovering near the throat of the largest animal. The demon spun toward the barn exit and walked away. We watched it disappear though an invisible doorway, perhaps a portal to another realm.

When I turned back, Dexter and Shay were crawling through the fence wall and approaching the animals. It was obvious Dexter was speaking to the largest animal; the two were communicating with head tilts and scratches in the dirt. Dexter growled loudly, and the smallest of the unicorns stood up and walked over to him.

"What are they doing?" I asked.

"I have no idea, but the magick is intoxicating," Shay whispered.

Dex transformed into his dragon self, and the other six unicorns leapt to their feet. It was then that I noticed the chains tethering them to the ground. I stepped out from the shadows, and as I approached, all seven animals turned to stare at me. It would have been flattering, the adoration in their eyes, but the weight of their chains was a burden. They returned to a resting position as I kneeled to touch their bindings.

Then I caught sight of the rest of the barn. It was a blacksmith's workshop, and I wanted to investigate further.

The sigil in my palm burned, aching like never before, and one unicorn moved closer to push their nose against it. Our magick was incredible, the animal drawing strength from my Maker powers. The exchange was like touching pure joy.

We didn't speak, but I knew what they wanted. These chains needed to be broken, and the power inside Brigid's hammer was just the thing to do it. But before I could, the smallest animal tipped its head, and the alicorn on top dropped to the ground. Dexter scooped it in his mouth, and before we could do anything else, he switched to his dog self and ran to Shay's side.

As the two of them began running towards the portal, I said, "Wait, we need to help these creatures!"

"Not yet," Shay said, gesturing at me to follow her.

Our exit was almost as abrupt as the slide through the portal back into the realm of the fairies. Shay and Dexter disappeared, and seconds later, I felt the rise and fall of shifting from the portal entrance back into the camp we'd set up just outside of the fairy kingdom. The trip left me dizzy and sick to my stomach.

"Damn, Dex. Maybe a brief pause between would help." I dropped to my hands and knees, rolling to my side until the swirling disorientation ended.

"Give it a few seconds, it'll pass." Clia hovered near my face, and as my stomach continued to churn, I curled into a nauseous ball.

Shay crawled beside me. "That was maybe a little too much." She spooned in behind me, and I was content to lay there until the spinning and irritation stopped, but the fairies and the dragon dog had other plans.

"While the two of you are cuddling, you might want to come and listen to Dexter's plan," Stout said.

Shay sat up and, despite the rumbling in my stomach, I pushed myself against her body and relaxed into her arms. Dex had deposited the alicorn on the rock beside the fire. Clia examined it by climbing inside the hollow of its base, spreading her arms and legs to her full three inch height.

"It shed a horn for you?" Stout asked, and Dexter growled and barked. "There were seven!"

It was almost humorous to listen to the one-sided conversation, but the information that Dexter collected from the captive animals was essential to what came next, so we needed to know now.

"What did he learn?" Shay asked, apparently reading my mind.

"He's kinda still going, but Wildwood needs to forge a chain breaker," Stout said before going back to talking with Dexter and Clia.

Shay leaned back to look at me as I asked, "How am I supposed to forge anything here? The carriage house is days away."

Stout called over to us, "He says you have to go back to the forge where the unicorns are kept."

And there it was, the most impossible of impossibilities. "Is he going to go back through the portal to get it? And I have no idea how to make something to break magickal chains."

The reality of our situation was wearing on me, no matter how much it might resemble a fantasy. Fancy tools aren't the most essential things, but the right tools get the job done. The idea of passing through to that demon's barn and leaving again without the magickal creatures was too much even for me.

"Dexter and I will go."

Shay started to stand up, but I pushed her back down, asking, "Do you know what tongs I need?"

She and Dexter exchanged a look before she admitted, "We don't."

"How about coke? How much, if any, will you bring back here"

"Coke? Are you thirsty?"

Grinning, I stood up and helped her to her feet. "Oh, baby. If you go without me, I'm not sure what I'll be forging with." She scooped me up and walked toward Dexter, carrying me the entire way. "So...not a drink?"

I looped my arms around her neck. "Definitely not a drink. I need to burn it."

"I thought it was coal in a forge?"

As she set me back down, we watched Clia roll the alicorn closer to the fire. "Coal is dirtier," I explained. "Coke burns hot, and I think if we have a choice, hot is what we'll need if I'm going to forge something strong enough to break those chains."

The plan felt risky at best, especially since we hadn't discussed it so much as went along with a plan a sometimes-German Shepherd had come up with. But it seemed solid enough: go through the portal, have Dexter shift us in, grab what we'd need, and shift us out. Easy as could be in a perfect realm, but that wasn't where we were, so we made plans to escape in stages if necessary.

With a clear route in mind, our shifting journey back to the demon barn was quick, and while my stomach settled,

Shay watched for the demon. Then I hurried over to the forge and surveyed the available blacksmith tools. From the arrangement of the space, it was clear a human-sized creature had worked here a long time ago. It was impossible to guess just how far in the past that had been, but from the thick layer of dust on everything, it had been a few lifetimes, at least.

While Shay kept a lookout, I gathered long and short handled tongs, a honing stone, and as much fuel for the forge as our backpack could hold.

"We kinda have a problem," I whispered, pointing at the anvil. "We need this."

"So take it," Shay whispered back.

I squatted in front of the oddly shaped steel, pulling it to my chest and cradling it with my forearms. It was more than a hundred and fifty pounds, and as much as I wanted to flee fast, the best I could do was a squatty, shifting waddle. Shay quickly understood the dilemma. We needed Dexter's help to make our retreat, but he was tangled in conversation with two of the largest animals.

"He needs to shift me to the portal, or this will take a week," I said.

Shay flopped the backpack over her shoulders, picked up the tools, and hissed at Dex, "Let's go, buddy."

I heard the crunching of feet on gravel and turned toward the closed barn door. It was now or never. The hinges creaked, but before the door opened, I felt the wrenching draw of shifting out of the barn and back to the portal entrance. Before I could call her name, Dex disappeared and reappeared with Shay, carrying all the supplies we'd need.

"That was a little too close," I said.

Dexter watched over our shoulders as Shay entered the portal, and I followed behind her. "Way too close," she said, dropping the bag on the ground by our campfire.

"Should we go back?" My heart was heavy from the thought that the demon might hurt the animals. It had to have noticed by now that the alicorn had dropped, and when it couldn't find it, there would probably be hell to pay for those poor creatures.

"It's too risky without a way to free them," Stout said sadly. Then he jerked his thumb at Dexter. "He says they can trick the demon with magick and hold him off for a short time, but the clock started ticking when they gave us that." He pointed at the alicorn.

"What do you need from us?" Shay asked me as she opened the backpack.

"I need a basin for the coal, a stand for the anvil, and time to figure out how the alicorn behaves in the forge."

I was doing my best to make it all seem possible even though I didn't believe it was. Forging demon steel had happened by accident, but the horn of a mythical creature could do any number of things.

"Oh, and a tree stump," I said. "Can you get me a fresh cut about this high?" I made a fist and held it eight inches from my hip, about the working height for the top of this found anvil.

"We're on it," Stout said, saluting me.

Dexter gave a loud bark, then the dog sprinted into the forest followed by two fairies.

Shay had started unloading our backpack. "What are you thinking?"

I opened the handles of the tongs to loosen their pivot point, saying, "Honey, I have no thoughts about this thing." I pointed at the alicorn. "I'm going to make a forge pot and set it on fire. That's the best I've got."

"So, aside from a tree stump, what else do you need?"

I sat on the rock. "I need a forge. Something that can handle two thousand degrees."

"Something besides Dexter's face?" She laughed.

I thought about our dragon and his flames and then I considered the unpredictable temperatures he would produce. "Not going to work. I wish it could."

"So what can we use?"

"In a perfect world, we would use my forge in the carriage house."

Shay stared at me, her eyes scrunching as her brow knotted together. "What about in an imperfect world?"

"The flattest rocks you can find to stack around this." I slapped the enormous boulder I was sitting on. "There's just enough surface to hold the coke, and we can make a tunnel to blow air to feed it." The science of fires was simple: air and fuel. The complexity of managing forging temperature was going to be the truest test of my Maker abilities.

It took less than an hour to collect stones and stack them into a rugged yet usable place to burn coke. Dexter returned with a bit more than a stump in his dragon teeth and proceeded to gnaw until the stump was the correct height to hold the anvil. I stacked coke and whispered, "*Ignis,*" to ignite the flame. It wasn't pretty–in fact, it was the least beautiful thing I'd ever assembled–but it held tight enough to make the coal a blazing orange-white glow.

"So what do you think breaks demon chains?" Stout asked as he hovered over my shoulder.

"Hammer?" Shay suggested, and I held Brigid's hammer up to her.

"If this won't do it, what else will?" I felt the glow of magick fill my palm as I tucked the alicorn into the embers. "We need to feed the fire." I made a pumping motion with my hands. "The forge in the carriage house is fed with gas, but this needs an air supply, so get over here, all of you, and fan this fire for me."

It was charming to see fairy wings flap over and over, stoking the embers. I used the tongs to push the alicorn into the center of the heat, and we watched the science of a unicorn horn cooking at over a thousand degrees unfolding in front of our eyes.

"Do you think it'll melt?" Stout asked as he took a rest from flapping.

"I wish I knew," I replied. "Obviously, that demon was doing something with the alicorns, so, Clia, maybe pause on that heat for a minute."

I raked the coals over and pushed them back, moving the heat against my one and only chance with this material.

"It's glowing." Shay squatted for a closer look.

When I fished the alicorn from the heat, it *was* glowing. And more than that, it looked like glass, so I was hesitant to strike it with my hammer.

"It looks fragile," Stout said but Clia shook her head.

"You should strike while it's hot," she said.

"How do you know that?" I asked.

She pushed at my hammer hand. "I'm guessing."

In the last twelve months, I'd guessed at a lot of things when it came to magick and being the Maker. There was something in the sincerity of her words that made me lay the alicorn on the anvil and strike it. My eyes were only partially closed, as I expected an explosion or some type of mystical burst of energy, but instead, the alicorn flattened like every piece of human made steel I'd forged before.

My sigil lit, and that energy moved through the handle and into the head of Brigid's hammer. Strike after strike, the metal moved, until the silhouette of a blade appeared. I passed the material back into the coals, and our fairies blasted it with the force of their wings. Back and forth we went, hammer strikes and heat, one then the other, until that alicorn was transformed into a blade that I hoped would break mystical chains.

"It's beautiful," Shay said when I laid it on the anvil.

"Do you think it'll break the chains?" I looked at the wide-eyed fairies.

Stout shrugged. "Never had to break demon chains." He looked to Clia for an answer.

"Don't ask me. I've been in a terrarium for the last four hundred years."

Shay stood beside me, her hand on my hip as we watched the weapon cool.

"In a perfect world, this sucker will break the chains, and we'll prove to the fairy king that we are here to end the evil that's holding the realms in fear."

"I applaud your enthusiasm," I told her. "And I also think we should do a little Magick and Maker spell to give it a boost."

"How long 'til it's cool?" Shay asked.

"It'll be awhile, but I'm going to wrap the handle with leather and cord, so we can bless it as soon as you set up an altar."

This part we knew, the magick of being the keepers of goodness in the earthen world. Elemental blessings in the fairy realm made me wonder.

"Can we call on our magicks here like we do in Bannock?" I asked.

Shay shrugged. "We won't know until we try."

She opened the zipper pouch on the backpack and removed the canvas roll. I remembered the first time she blessed our athame, the blade made from fairy steel, and how exquisitely her words took hold of me.

"Oh, goody, more experiments in the fairy realm."

"You know what they say about lemons, don't you?" she said as she snapped the altar cloth in the air before guiding the drifting fabric to the ground.

"That they are tart, right?" Clia replied with the most serious of tones.

"Nah." Stout laughed, "When life gives you lemons, you gotta make lemonade, Clia. It's a human reaction to the abundance of a useless and otherwise inedible fruit."

"And the ade helps?" She hovered over the athame as Shay laid it on the cloth.

Stout landed. "Maybe it does, but not like you think. Lemons are gross. Humans think that when life gives you a big bucket of gross, you transform it into something tasty by making it sweet."

"So we are going to make the demons sweet?" she asked with an innocence so pure it hurt my heart.

I picked up the alicorn blade and laid it on the rock Shay placed in the middle of the altar cloth. "If this alicorn works, we'll make lemonade out of all of those chains."

CHAPTER XV

UMBILICAL

"**I**t's so beautiful," Shay whispered over my shoulder.

I was weaving with a single strip of cord scavenged from the tie down of our tent. We were taking a gamble that the tarp we'd use to shelter us from rain wouldn't be required because I needed every inch to create a covering that Shay could hold to break the chains.

"I've never done a handle wrap like this," I said nervously. "I've seen them on survival gear, but until today, I didn't know

I'd make a weapon on a demon anvil stolen from a unicorn forge."

"And yet, your ability to adapt is impressive." She kissed my cheek and I felt the tremble of her giggle against my skin.

"Thank you, love." I singed the end of the cord with my *ignis* flame and handed it to her. "Are you ready to take on those chains?" I wasn't sure *I* was ready, but if she was, I would follow her.

"That demon said he'd be back." She paused, her brow furrowing. I could tell she had something on her mind, something she worried would frighten me. "When we get there, we'll have a fight on our hands. I'd be happier confronting evil with the full force of our family if the demon is there."

I knew she meant Dani and Amelia, and I had to admit I wished they were with us, too. "It'll be the three of us."

She swiped at her cheek with the back of her hand, and my head snapped up to look at her.

"Hey, what's going on?" My thumb brushed at the tear on her cheek.

"I'm still processing that this realm exists. *And* the realm of the giants. And now I'm having to deal with the fact that there's a world where unicorns are forced to give up their horns. And we don't even know what for!" Her head rested in my palm, and she closed her eyes.

"We've got this," I said, but it was obvious by the tremble in my voice that I wasn't convinced either.

"You, me, and Dex. That's the power of us and this." Her hand was steady as she clenched the alicorn weapon. "We don't have a choice because failure brings an end to the legacy of the Maker."

I thought about the possibility of failure while we packed the blessing tools inside the backpack. It's nothing we haven't experienced before. The earliest parts of our lives were marked by failure. We were fortunate to have Mama Pierce, and after that separation at fifteen years old, fate or destiny led me back to Shay. But otherwise, life had been pretty cruel to us. It was sobering to think about, and as I studied her folding the altar cloth and tucking everything we'd used for blessing into the bag, I hoped that, just this once, life would be kind.

Shay was standing in what I liked to call her superhero posture–clenched jaw, tight ponytail, and flexed shoulders that carried the weight of our future while stoically preparing to fight this unknown. "This is packed and set." She patted the bag.

"But you're not." My voice was a whisper. "I think we should take a minute."

I pulled her into my arms, the racing of my heart betraying my brave attempt at keeping calm in this storm. My heart was pounding in my chest, and she could feel it.

"Maybe we should."

~~~~~~~~~~~

"Do you think someday we'll get to complain about being bored?"

Her laugh jostled my head where it rested against her chest. We lay tucked together on the sleeping bag, her arms holding me tight to the length of her body. "The first time either of us complain about boredom, we'll open a portal and remind ourselves about today."

"Do you ever doubt this?" I raised my sigil hand.

Shay's finger traced through the scorched markings in my palm. "I have never felt more powerful or more protected than when this hand is at my side."

"Just this hand?"

Her palm slid against mine, and her fingers tightened until our connection felt impossible to break. "It's a good place to start." She kissed the back of my hand. "I thank every deity in every realm that helped you find your way back to me." Her arm tightened around my hip.

"It wasn't a deity, baby. It was the Magick of Bannock."

"Benton," Shay whispered, and I could only imagine the memories and emotions that saying that name invoked.

"She's kinda to blame for the last year of our lives."
~~~~~~~~~~~

"It's so crazy to think about what she did." Shay pulled away from me to sit up.

"Do you have regrets?" I asked.

She shook her head as she turned to look at me. Tiny wrinkle lines crinkled around Shay's eyes. "Only the lies and secrets."

"Yeah, they did *not* help."

She slapped her thighs. "We should get going."

As we exited the tent, we could see the fairies speaking with Dexter, the three of them so engaged in their conversation that they didn't hear us approach.

"Making plans?" Shay asked.

"Your dragon is telling us about the unicorns," Stout explained.

It was sweet, the way they'd tucked themselves into the dog's tail, a cozy circle holding them tight. Dexter's attention turned to Shay, and I wished more than anything that he could share what his eyes were trying to relay.

"What's he got?" Shay's fingers scrunched through the lengths of fur around his neck.

"He wants to take them all out at the same time."

Shay nodded. "That's my plan. If we leave one behind, it won't be alive when we return." She tossed the backpack over her shoulder. "Let's head out," she said, and seconds later, she and Dexter disappeared from the campsite.

"I guess he's in charge, now." I laughed, and the dog reappeared to take me to Shay. As the dizziness knocked me to the ground, I wondered if I'd ever get used to shifting.

"I've got you," Shay said as she helped me to my feet.

"Damn, that's rough." I left my arm around her waist. Dexter barked a few times before nudging us toward the portal stone.

"Dexter," Shay told him, "I want you to take us into the woods by the barn. It'll give us more time to settle from the shift before we make a move to free them."

As Shay disappeared through the portal, his nose tipped into the air, and he barked, which had to be an acknowledgment of what she'd said. I followed close behind. There was no time to catch my footing or even take a full breath as my body moved from one location to the other. The smoke pouring from the barn was unexpected, and Shay pulled me down to the ground, the two of us staring wide-eyed as the building was engulfed in flame.

"Stay low," she whispered, and before I could respond, her voice was inside my head. *"Let's go in silent mode, okay?"*

I nodded, and the three of us crawled through the grass. *"Do you think they're gone?"* I thought as I watched the wall of the barn collapse.

"I hope not." We turned toward Dexter to find that he'd disappeared. *"I hope he's just going closer for a look."*

I was just thinking the same thing when he reappeared with a mouthful of straw from the unicorns' stable. The smoldering ends were a good sign that we needed to move and do it now.

Shay vanished, and I waited longer than I thought was normal for him to move us as a team. Dexter didn't return, and the sound of screeching spilled out of the burning walls of the barn. I clutched Brigid's hammer in my hand, the only weapon I had since Shay still wore the backpack. The ground crackled with every step I took across the stones and scattered debris.

"Shay!" The call from my mind to hers went unanswered, and I stepped inside to see her twisting my alicorn blade into the unyielding binding chains.

"I've tried everything," she thought.

Dexter's dragon wings stretched around to shield her and the seven animals from the heat of the fire.

"Let me!" I said it out loud instead of thinking it, sure that if the demon was here, it would have revealed itself by now.

Brigid's hammer fell at my knee. The alicorn blade was warm from Shay's touch, and as I leveraged the tool, it didn't break the chain free. I tucked the knife edge against the loop of the chain, the sizes so different that this task felt impossible. Brigid's hammer called to me, and without pause, I raised it above my head and struck hard against the blade.

Nothing.

"Hit it again!" Shay cried.

Dexter growled, announcing that something evil had come. He remained wrapped around us, but his body expanded in size, and he let out a roar of flame as he held the demon off.

"Filthy dragons," the demon sneered. "Your fire cannot break the chains."

The laugh that followed was reminiscent of the sound Andrea had made during my attack, and the tools dropped from my hands, the memory leaving me dizzy and nauseous.

Shay took hold of the blade and hammer but when the handle touched her hand, the blade of Brigid blasted through the hammer's head. I knew what it meant, and so did Shay. She stood at her full height, hefted that sword, and hammered the alicorn blade against the braided chains. The strike was brilliant, and when the two parts clashed, sparks flew in every direction, blasting the chain to pieces.

The unicorn stood tall and leaped from the bindings toward the demon, the collision breaking through the heat of the flames, through the barrier of Dexter's wings, and through the power of the Magick and the Maker. Shay raised the sword again and again until all seven of the creatures were free.

With the alicorn blade in one hand and Brigid's magickal steel in the other, Shay leapt over Dexter's wing until the two were shoulder to shoulder, advancing on the monster.

"It cannot be," it said. "Your lineage is dead."

Dexter leaped forward, but the demon raised its hands, deflecting the advance. This was no earthen Gatekeeper demon.

"Your dog is just a beast." The demon waved a hand, and the unicorns blew backward, flying toward the flames. "Beasts are my specialty." It waved again, and the broken chains reassembled link by link, threading together to retake the animals into the flames.

"I see the fear in your eyes," Shay said as she stepped toward the demon. "Is it this?" She held the alicorn knife. "Or is it this?" She twirled the blade around as her wrist tipped Brigid's weapon.

The demon moved; it was subtle, but it was enough to confirm that Shay had scared it.

"The Magick has returned," the creature said, mostly to himself. Or perhaps it was a call to the power that ruled him.

"I have, and your dominion over the unicorns ends now." Shay's ability with the blade was distracting as she sliced through the air, moving closer to the demon, step by step.

"The enemy of my friend!" he screamed as he lunged toward Shay.

I'm not sure what the creature expected from the Magick, but it was clear it wasn't a battle style that included sword and dagger. Honestly, *I* didn't expect it either, and I watched in awe as she advanced. The demon had a weapon up his arm, a spire of sorts, and when it pierced through the back of his fist, Shay hesitated.

That hesitation came with a price, as the demon lunged out and lanced her shoulder.

"Bitch!" she yelled, and with the force of Brigid's steel, she struck the creature.

Nothing.

The collision of blade against spire was silently deafening, and both froze at the impact. Dexter stopped advancing on the demon; the unicorns stopped running for safety. It took me a moment to figure out what was going on, but then I realized. The demon had struck out at the cuff on Shay's wrist, and that was the lucky break she needed. Brigid's blade held the demon in place as the alicorn dagger pierced the demon's heart.

The joints in its skeletal legs buckled as the monster fell to the ground. Shay pulled her arm back, and she staggered away until she was close enough to stumble against me. Her shoulder wound was deep.

"Dexter!" I yelled.

He reacted on instinct, and a moment later, the two of them disappeared.

"Shit!"

I watched the demon wriggle and writhe on the ground. Before I could make a move–which would've been completely stupid, as I was holding no weapons–the largest unicorn started trampling the creature. One after the other they joined in, each taking turns crushing the demon that had kept them chained for years. Pulp and gore lay strewn across the ground as the last unicorn retreated.

I didn't notice him at first, but Dexter had returned, standing behind me, watching the carnage as I had. "Hey, buddy, we should—"

I felt my body move from the burning barn to the portal stone and back through until I was standing beside Shay's prone body.

"Hey." She waved her arm, still clenching the weapons that were dripping with bright red blood–*her* bright red blood.

"Oh, goddess." I dropped to my knees and began stripping away the layers covering her skin. The backpack was on the ground, and I rummaged through it in search of the demon sift. "Where's the anvil dust?"

"Side," she winced through clenched teeth.

I wasn't calm; I was barely thinking as I turned the backpack over and shook everything to the ground. "It's not here, honey."

The blood pooled around her shoulder. "Side." Her voice was a whisper this time, and I looked at her eyes. They were glassy just before they shut.

"Damn it!" I screamed and pushed the altar cloth aside. The contents were there, scattered across the dirt, but the one ingredient I needed to keep her from death was nowhere to be found.

Dexter appeared with the first of the unicorns, which was covered in the remains of the trampled demon. Dex transformed into his dog self as I yelled, "Find the anvil dust, Dex!"

As he sniffed through the grass, I hooked my arms beneath Shay's and dragged her to a more comfortable position. Her shirt was off, and she lay naked from the waist up. There was a water bottle near my feet, and I didn't waste a second before pouring it on her wound. The gash was over eight inches long, from her neck across her breast and toward her ribs. Without the anvil dust, I wasn't sure she would make it back to camp.

"Dexter!" I yelled again, but he was gone.

I knew I was panicking, but for so long we'd relied on the instant reaction of anvil dust to heal the wounds inflicted during a demon fight. Now that we didn't seem to have any, I couldn't think of anything else that could help her. Taking deep breaths, I thought back to what I knew of first aid.

Shay's shirt lay on the ground. Snatching it up, I wadded it tight and pressed it to the wound. Her body jolted, but she didn't wake. *What do I do?* I wondered helplessly, closing my eyes as tears pricked at them.

I felt her chest rise and fall, which was a good sign. As long as she was breathing she was still with me.

"Shay, I don't know what else to do." My voice was pitched with fear and sadness.

The unicorn stood nearby, seemingly guarding the two of us, though I didn't know what from. There couldn't be a threat in the middle of a field in the fairy realm, could there? I heard the thrumming flip of Stout's and Clia's wings before I saw them, and I hoped that meant there was demon sift in their hands.

"Do you have it?" I asked before they had a chance to react to Shay's prone position and the blood pooled around us. I didn't dare move my hands.

"It's not at the camp," Stout said sadly. "Not in the tent. Not in the bags. We can't find it anywhere."

Clia sniffed at the pooling blood in the dirt. "She doesn't have a lot of time."

"What else can I do?"

"Shift her back to camp," Stout said, looking for Dexter but the dog was still gone. When Dex appeared a few seconds later with two more unicorns, Stout flew at him. "I don't care what Shay's mission is. Get her help. She's going to die."

"What the hell is he doing?" I took off my shirt and twisted it so I could tie the cloth over Shay's wound. Normally, I wouldn't move her with her being so gravely injured, but Dexter was able to shift her, so it would be safe. I hoped.

"The unicorns. He says they need to be here."

It was all I could do to contain my fear as I watched the color drain from Shay's face. The animals behind me stomped and snorted, and I wondered if there was another way to get Shay to help. But Dexter was the safest way. The only way.

He shifted back with the last of the animals, and I grabbed him by the collar. My eyes locked with his as I yelled, "She's dying, Dex! We need demon sift, and we need it now. No more unicorns. Shay needs you."

To my dismay and frustration, he disappeared again.

"What the hell is he doing?" I yelled. "Dexter!"

"He's going back to the carriage house," Stout explained as he landed on my hands. I was holding tight to Shay's shoulder. "He'll be back."

To the carriage house? How long would it take to travel from realm to realm, through portals and countryside?

"Her heart is slowing," Clia said as she fell against Shay's bare skin.

"NO!" I yelled, and the flame of my sigil burst through my palm and into the open wound of her shoulder. "Don't you leave me. Not like this."

There was nothing we could do as we watched the poison move through her body. Her normally pale skin was so white that the light of day made it shine in the sun.

"Dexter!" I yelled for him because I didn't know what else to do. His return with the anvil dust was the only hope we had.

"The Maker of Bannock has magick," Clia said. "Move her heart with your own." She made a motion for me to lay my hands on Shay, but that meant letting go of the pressure on her wound.

"If I don't hold this, she'll bleed."

"Without a heartbeat, there is no blood moving."

Her words shifted something inside of me as the idea of Shay's heart stopping sent a wave of grief through my body. Without another thought, I moved my hands to the center of her chest. "One. Two. Three," I counted, trying to remember the class from the eleventh grade that taught us how to do CPR. I'm sure I was supposed to breathe into her mouth, but it was all I could do to pump my arms against her chest. "Don't you leave me," I chanted over and over and felt the first pop of her rib. "I don't want to do this without you."

Magick moved from me into her, the fine lines of Brigid's power tethering the two of us like never before. She was going to stay, and I would will it to be because nothing would be the same without her. It felt like I was at it for hours as the fatigue set in, but Stout and Clia were there to keep me going. I wasn't sure how long I could last as the crack of a second rib split through the silent air.

When Dexter returned, he had just one thing clamped in his jaw: the entire canister of demon sift that I kept on the floor of the workshop. It was filthy with unsifted remnants from the forge, but it didn't matter. Pure or not, Shay needed all I could give her.

I ripped the cloth away from the bleeding wound, opened the canister, and scooped both hands inside, not caring how ridiculous the amount I was grabbing was. Blood stained me; her blood was like a sleeve on my arm. I pushed the demon dust into her wound, cramming the gap full, smearing it over her chest, and watching the coagulating effect pucker the texture of her skin. Nothing changed; her skin was still pale, and the rise of her chest was almost invisible.

I tugged Dexter to us, and before I could ask him to take Shay back to camp, the three of us shifted and landed in the dirt beside our tent. Dexter had never shifted the three of us together, and I wondered if that meant her life force was so low that she barely registered as a third person. I didn't want to linger on the thought as he disappeared again, probably to go grab the fairies and their unicorn friends.

"Shay?" I whispered in her ear as I leaned closer to listen to her heart. "Please come back."

In the past, she'd had painful reactions to demon sift until it took hold and cured whatever injury we were patching up. But today, she lay still, unconscious to the pain.

All I could do was wait.

Our camp was busy and full once Dexter finished shifting Stout, Clia, and the unicorns. I could tell they were trying to be quiet as I lay with Shay in my arms. It felt like a hopeless race to see what would take her first, the blood loss or whatever poison the demon had left behind.

"Wildwood?" I heard the worry in Stout's voice.

"Hmm?" It was the only sound I could make because I knew if I spoke, I'd lose what little control I had left of my emotions.

"We need to move the unicorns to the fairy castle," he said. "The king will want to know we've succeeded, and if it looks like we're hiding them, they might think there's some kind of trick."

"No, Stout."

"What do you mean, no?"

I pulled Shay up into the V of my legs so I could keep her close. "No, that's it. We don't move until she's awake."

"It could take days for her to recover," Clia said as she peeked over the stone ledge by the fire.

"It won't," I said and waved our dog to come lay beside us. "Give her some of your magick, Dex."

It was the last thing I could think of doing to try and help the woman I love. His dragon powers had to make a difference–they *had* to. He must've thought so, too, because his fur transformed to scales, and his entire body curled us into a cocoon.

I meant what I'd told Stout. No matter what, we would stay here, as long as necessary, to bring Shay back to us.

CHAPTER XVI

PERSPECTIVE

"It's been hours," I heard Clia whisper to Stout. "There's nothing we can do," he whispered back. "The animals won't leave without the Magick and the Maker. They set the unicorns free, and they must repay the debt."

"So we're just going to sit here?"

"You should be very good at that by now," he joked, but she didn't laugh.

"The longer we stay here, the more likely it is that the king will sense the unicorns' presence."

Despite their best efforts to keep their conversation to themselves, I could hear every word. Although Shay was no longer wounded–the anvil dust had finally done its job–we surmised that the poison from the demon was keeping her locked in a toxic slumber. We didn't know what was happening inside the body of the Magick of Bannock, but I wished more than anything that I did.

"I can hear you, ya know?" I said as I wriggled out from underneath Shay.

"Then you know our time is short." Stout waved at the unicorns grazing in the field. "The magick emanating from those animals is massive. Even if we could mask it, the king's forces will feel it when they patrol the site."

"What do you want me to do?" I asked, stepping closer to the fire to warm my arms.

"We should take them to the king," he said. "It'll prove who you are and what you've come to do."

"It'll be dark soon." I turned to look at Shay. "I'm going to take her inside the tent, and hopefully, when the sun rises, she'll be ready to finish this bullshit, and we can move on."

"Move on?" Stout yelled. "She's in some kind of demon sleep, and you think you're going to frolic off to confront this ultimate evil tomorrow?"

"I have no idea what we're going to do tomorrow because I can't ask her. I can't talk to her. We didn't have a plan after freeing them because we didn't know if we could." My arms flailed, pointing from Shay back to the grazing unicorns.

"I'm sure the plan didn't involve you camping out while waiting for her to wake up," Stout shot back.

Our voices grew loud, but we were in the middle of nowhere, so it didn't matter. "I'm not going anywhere until I know Shay's recovered. She'd do the same for me."

"She'd do what needed to be done!" Stout flew close to my face. "Don't let your love for her cloud your judgment."

I closed my eyes, trying with every bit of control I could gather not to smash Stout like a bug. I drew in a breath and let it out as I turned to face him. "It's because I love her that I'm going to ignore what you said. I need her. We all need her. And until she can confront whatever hell spawn Andrea answered to, we will wait," I circled my finger, pointing at everyone and everything at our campsite. "*All* of us. We don't go anywhere until she's ready."

I turned to look at Shay, but she wasn't lying on the rolled-up shirts. Her shoulders were resting against the boulder, her eyes blinking hard as she stared at me.

"Shay?"

"Uh, I think so." She groaned.

My shins hit the ground as I kneeled beside her. I brushed the dirt and bloodstains from her cheek as I moved her hair out of her eyes. "Baby, you're back."

"Back?" Her voice was scratchy as she rolled to adjust her position. "Where the hell are we?"

"Um…" There was so much to explain. "What do you remember?"

"I remember unicorns and Brigid's hammer sword, and I got…" She felt her shoulder, and the blanket draped around her fell, revealing her naked upper body. "And I'm naked." She scrunched her shoulder to gather the cloth near her throat. "Why am I laying outside naked?"

"You're not completely naked," I said, pointing to her jeans. "Kept your pants on."

"Baby, where's my shirt?"

I pointed to the blood-soaked clump of material behind her, then I took off my flannel. "Here." My hands trembled as I draped the shirt over her shoulder.

"Explain, please." Her hands punched through the sleeves, and I was suddenly aware that the two belligerent fairies had disappeared into the field with the grazing unicorns.

"When we freed them," I said, waving a hand at the animals, "the demon attacked, and it hit you with its spire."

Shay rubbed the back of her neck. "I kinda remember that."

"Yes, well, there was poison or venom or whatever in that thing, and I couldn't find the demon sift."

"It was in the side pocket of the backpack." She tucked her knees against her chest. "It's always there."

"But it wasn't," I told her.

"How long?"

I knew what she was asking, but I didn't want her to know it had been close to taking her life before Dexter returned. I didn't answer.

"How long, Wil?"

I fought to hide the tears as I shook my head.

"How long did the venom go untreated?"

My voice broke as I said, "Over thirty minutes."

"What happened to the bottle that was in the backpack?" She pushed her hands to the ground to steady her as she stood, stumbling a bit. I was there to steady her as Dexter nosed himself into the conversation.

"We don't know," I said. "I turned the backpack inside out looking for it, and Furball here had to shift to the carriage house to get more."

"That's why it took so long?"

I nodded, and before I could say anything more, Stout was there.

"Dexter moved pretty fast." His voice was grinding, hesitant, as he stumbled over his emotions. "It almost killed you, Red. You should probably go lie down."

"He's right." This whole day had been solid nightmare material. "How about your ribs?"

She patted her chest and rubbed over her torso. "They hurt a little. Why?"

"She...she p-pumped your heart." Stout stumbled over the words.

Shay's eyes were wide. "Did it stop? How am I—"

"Don't, Shay. Just tell me what your body feels like." I put my arms around her, and we sat near the fire.

"I'm tired. Shoulder feels tight." She rotated her arm, and I heard the snap of the injured shoulder joint. "I'm definitely not one hundred percent."

"We should rest here. Take a breather before we take them to the king." I hitched my thumb toward the animals stomping through the tall grasses.

"There isn't time to rest." Shay rubbed her hands over the fire. "Whatever was guarding the unicorns, that thing wasn't alone, and when the truth is discovered, they'll come looking for them."

I didn't know how Shay did this, keep her mind so clear, so totally focused on the task that she wouldn't take a breath to recover. I needed her. Even more than the power we shared, I needed what she could do with that brilliant mind.

"We understand everything you're saying, but less than two hours ago I was cracking ribs in your chest to keep you alive." I turned away to take a breath.

"Okay."

My head snapped around to look at her. "Okay?"

"I'll lay down, but only if everyone else stays alert. The unicorns' energy is powerful, and the king's Bliation forces will come." She turned to Clia and Stout. "You need to go see the king. Tell him we have a gift."

~~~~~~~~~~

"Your heart is so steady."

My hand lay pressed between Shay's breasts, the warmth of her skin almost as comforting as the vibration against my palm. Her back was tight to my front, and I wished we were back home where we belonged.

"I'm calling on our magicks," she whispered.

I pulled the zippered edge of the sleeping bag over our bodies. "Are you?"

"True confession?"
~~~~~~~~~~

My voice was breathy when I answered. "Always, please."

She cleared her throat, saying, "My chest is a little sore."

Every muscle in my body tensed. "You should see a doctor—"

She interrupted, gripping my hand where it stilled on her chest. "The Rasavatam saved me today. There isn't a medical professional who will understand what demon sift does to me internally."

"The Grant's Pass physician?" I suggested.

"No one, love."

I tugged her tighter. "So it wasn't luck?"

Her hitched laugh shook the two of us. "It was you and Dexter and the magicks of the Maker. You saved me." She relaxed in my arms. "You."

I didn't need to see her face to know that she'd drifted off to sleep. It was enough to feel her rest where my bicep was tucked beneath her. I closed my eyes, wishing for time to heal and time to center our magick for the fight to come. Her heartbeat lulled me to sleep.

~~~~~~~~~~

"Come out!" The nylon material of our tent ruffled from the impact.

"What the hell." My voice cracked as the yelling woke me.

"You should probably come and see this." Stout's face smashed against the open netting at the bubbled top of the tent.

"Shay?" I rubbed her shoulder.

"It's okay, I'm awake." She rolled out of my arms and onto her knees. "Where's my cuff?" Her fingers wrapped around her wrist where my demon forged piece usually fit.
~~~~~~~~~~

"It's here." I reached toward the pile behind me. "Maybe put all of this on."

Shay took the armor vest and dropped it over her head. She didn't secure the velcro, and as I considered the reason, I was certain the sound it made was important. She slipped on her cuff and felt for the strap on her ankle. "Punch dagger?"

"Under your boot."

It only took a minute or two for us to redress ourselves and leave the tent. It didn't surprise me to see two distinct assemblages of creatures in front of us.

A line of unicorns stood tall and strong, preventing anything from entering our campsite. Dexter was in their midst, dragon scales tipped in defense, with four unicorns on his left and three on his right. Nothing was getting to Shay or to me unless they had the strength to penetrate this line. Looking at them now, I was glad they were in front of us and not on the opposing side.

"The king summons you."

The voice was thunderous, and I laughed as the four-inch fairy hovered as close to the line as he could. He said nothing else as the platoon of fairies, nearly thirty by my count, hovered in their most threatening positions.

Shay held her hand out to me. "We've slept enough. It's time to prove who we are."

The trip to the town was short, and the fairies created a circle around us, the unicorns trotting by our side. As we entered the town, fairies of all shapes and sizes flocked to watch the parade of humans, a dragon, and seven stubby-alicorned unicorns marching to see the king.

Their excitement was palpable, and I was sure I would've felt it, too, if I wasn't part of the parade.

"How are you feeling, love?"

"Strong enough for this," Shay assured me, head held high.

Something happened as we approached the vast room where the king waited: the Bliation forces fanned out to cover the space between us and the king. To a fairy this room was vast, but to Shay and me, it felt no bigger than a high school gymnasium.

Stout took the lead, and when he was a few feet from the king, we understood why. His gravelly voice was louder than I'd ever heard it. "You claim to be fair, to be just, but you sent the Magick of Bannock to her death!"

Shay's hand dropped from my own and made its way to my hip. The tip of her finger looped through my belt. She only ever did this if she felt threatened.

"Stay here," Shay whispered through clenched teeth.

I had a sneaking suspicion as to why she looked so angry, one that was confirmed when Stout yelled at the king, "What did you think would happen to her without the demon sift?"

The Bliation forces swarmed around our fairy. Dexter's fur ridged straight up his back as the feral sound of our German Shepherd froze all the dragon scale plates in place. Stout was the norm in a room filled with fairies, but it was instantly clear that Dex was not.

"Wait, what?" I said as Shay's head tipped.

She knew. Somehow she'd figured out that the king's forces had stolen the lifesaving dust. Rage bubbled inside of me as the sound of Shay's cracking ribs echoed in my memory.

"You will be silent, or they will remove you from the realm." The king waved a hand at his special forces.

Dexter's body expanded, and the Bliation forces stopped in their tracks.

"We've played your game, king." Shay's hand held tighter to my hip as we stepped forward. "My life is not a toy for your pleasure."

"The Magick lives." The king's laugh was bitter, so much like the sound of evil we'd dreamed about all those months ago.

"To honor the challenge you demanded," Shay reminded him. "But you don't fight fair, do you, king?"

"Tests aren't meant to be fair, are they?"

I wanted to lash out at him, snatch him from his tiny little throne and strangle him. He could've killed Shay with his deadly little game. As it was, we still didn't know what the lingering effects of the venom could be.

"Now that we understand how the king of this realm rules," Shay said, "there can be no trust between us. But unlike you, we're honorable. We will fulfill our obligation and present the unicorns to you."

There was no snark or edge to Shay's voice, just cold honesty. The seven animals stepped forward, and although we couldn't hear it, some communication was taking place between the unicorns and the fairies.

"What are they saying?" I asked, my whole body taut with anxiety.

"The unicorns are telling the king what happened to them," Stout explained.

"And...?" I waved a frantic hand to encourage faster storytelling.

"The demon Shay fought?" Stout said. "He was one of many keeping unicorns for their alicorn magick. They said it works like fairy powder or like the magick dust that cured Shay."

"Why are they collecting the powder?" Shay asked.

"They, uh, didn't say." Stout hesitated long enough that Shay asked again, louder this time.

"Why was the demon that almost killed me collecting alicorn magick?"

"Calm down, Red." He hovered in front of us, waving at her to lower her voice.

"The same reason the dust from your anvil is so important," the king said. "It cures, and it sustains. The Maker has a great deal of magicks, and that creates freedom. To move between realms with such powders can make you invincible."

"It was you or one of them." Stout pointed at the line of Bliation fairies. "You almost killed the Magick of Bannock. Do you even understand that you sent her in there without—"

"It's done." Shay raised her hands to halt the conversation. "Permit us passage, and we will leave the realm and only return to pass through."

"Done!" the king yelled, and the Bliation forces pivoted in the air to make way for us.

"Your actions, king, they shame our realm!" Stout yelled.

Before we could stop him, he flew out of the castle. Clia was quick to follow. I knew very little about fairies and even less about the realm they disappeared into, but I hoped they would be safe.

Shay released her hold on my hip, and although the Bliation forces lagged behind us, they were still obviously acting as our escort out of the city.

"You think they'll help us break camp?" I joked.

Shay gave my hand a tight squeeze before releasing it. "I think they'll be happy to see us go. Apparently, rescuing magical creatures wasn't proof enough of our intentions. I thought this realm would be different."

"Fear has a tight hold on that king." I kicked at a stone as I walked.

She kicked the stone to keep it in motion as we made our way to the edge of our campsite. "Fear is no way to lead, even in the fairy realm."

Dexter nipped at the rock and played with it like a kitten with a ball of twine.

"Safe passage to and through," one of our fairy escorts said. "We will sense your magick, so don't try anything funny."

"We have no intention of staying in this realm," Shay said, and the fairies turned with military precision and disappeared from sight.

"I guess anyone who thought fairies were cute never actually met them," I muttered as I kicked at the tent stake to free it from the dirt.

"Guess not."

We turned when we heard a crunching sound. "Did he just eat that rock?" I asked, staring at Dexter with a mixture of horror and amusement.

Shay opened the tent. "Sounds like it." She shook her head and disappeared inside.

"We need to get out of this realm," I said as a sleeping bag launched out of the tent at me. "Dial it back, superhero."

The compression bag fell at my feet. I had hoped that Shay would agree with me, but from the way she emptied the tent, it was clear what her plan was.

"We're going back to that barn, aren't we?" I mashed the sleeping bag into the bag and cinched it into a tiny bundle.

"There's no option to do anything else." Her arms were full with the gear from the tent.

I tossed the bundle to the ground. "We have no way to heal a wound. It doesn't make sense to go anywhere but home."

"We go back, investigate, and then we can go home. There has to be a trail to follow, and I need to know before it disappears."

"I'm going to fight you on this." I closed my eyes, trying to force the memory of her slashed chest from my mind. "You should be in a hospital, Shay."

"I don't want to fight about it. I just want–"

"Maybe you don't have to," Stout's gruff voice interrupted.

"Oh, Goddess, not now, Stout," I mumbled, and it occurred to me I hadn't heard the sound of his wings.

"But Clia and I went on a mission."

"What kind of mission?" Shay tossed the backpack on the ground to fill it with the gear at our feet.

Clia flew close to us, carrying a drawstring pouch in her toes. "A mission to protect the Magick and the Maker of Bannock."

The bag dropped to the ground with a thud, and I picked it up. "What is it?" I asked as I felt the weight and drew the leather cording apart.

"Every bit of your demon sift." I heard his wings fluttering with some of his old bravado.

I looked at Shay. "I guess we don't have to fight, after all. At least not about this." I cinched the drawstrings and tossed it to her.

"How did you get it?" Shay asked.

"I might have asked a Bliation fairy if they knew how the king stole it," Clia explained. "And that fairy might have led me to the secret hiding place."

"Might have? Why?" I asked. "Why would one of them betray the king?"

"Not everyone in the realm believes you're here to hurt them," she said.

"When they discover the sift is missing, it's going to make returning through this realm difficult." Shay was mostly talking to herself as she squeezed the pouch.

"Probably, but we can't go forward without it." I put my arm around her. "We can go back to that barn and look for traces of the evil that was fractured by Brigid's hammer."

"Let's bury the fire pit and get going." Shay knelt and began rolling the tent, squeezing out all the air to condense it. "Dexter!"

When he didn't immediately make his way over, we looked behind us to see where he'd gotten to. It was adorable watching him frolic through the tall grass.

"He's acting a little goofy," I said. "Almost like a puppy."

"I think he enjoys spending time in the realms. Makes him feel at home," Clia suggested. "I can relate a bit to that."

"Dexter!" Shay's voice was different this time, commanding in a way that snapped the animal to attention. It was time to work, and he knew it. He stopped, spun in the dirt, and leapt to Shay's side. As cute as it was, it was also, as always, a little intimidating.

"Site looks good," I said as I threw the bag over my shoulder.

"No trace, no scent," Clia said.

She spit in her hands and rubbed them together, chanting something that sounded mostly like fairy gibberish. But the look on her face told me it was a serious spell. Dexter transformed into his dragon form flashing flame everywhere Clia's dust hovered over.

"What are they doing?" Shay asked.

"Erasing us from the realm," Stout explained.

"Erasing?" I asked. "What's that mean, exactly?"

"When the king learns what we've done, the Bliation forces loyal to him will seek us out."

"Us?" I twirled my finger to make an encompassing circle in the air to include everyone standing in this campsite.

"Mostly the traces of fairy magick. We're easy to follow." Stout hovered between Shay and me. "To be honest, we should go separate ways."

"No." Shay held her sigil hand out to him. "We go together, or we don't go at all."

"Wait, is that last one an option?" I joked.

"Absolutely not." Shay laughed as Stout launched himself in the direction of the barn's portal.

"Doesn't hurt to ask," I said. "Perhaps we'll get there, and the demon will shudder with fear and surrender."

"Unlikely," Stout snorted.

I laughed as Shay took the first steps toward this new unknown. "Always worth a try."

As Shay grabbed hold of my hand, I hoped that our next stop wouldn't be the end of us all.

CHAPTER XVII

BOLTHOLE

"I'm going in for a look," Shay whispered. We were standing less than fifteen yards from the scorched remains of the barn we'd raided to save the unicorns. I couldn't see any movement inside, and from our location, the building appeared empty.

"Not without me," I insisted.

"Can you just—"

"What?" I interrupted her. "Forget that you almost died less than twenty-four hours ago?" She looked back at me. "No, I can't. So we're going together."

Shay closed her eyes and lowered her head. She obviously didn't want to concede, but she was going to. It felt like a victory, even if it was a small one. This argument was nothing compared to the fight that might be waiting on the other side of the barn wall.

She rubbed her face. "Okay, we all go." She waved her flattened palm toward the ground. "Low and slow."

Dexter crouched down on his belly, and I admired the two of them in action. It was more common, recently, for me to see them in this mode, but as I stood watching them, I couldn't help but fall in love with Shay all over again. She was alive, her hair tucked in a ball cap, ponytail limp against the under-cut above her collar. In dog form, Dex was at her hip, the two of them moving together in perfect synchronization.

I was probably doe-eyed, which is why Stout tapped my cheek and joked, "Maybe get your head out of her pants."

"They aren't in her—"

He clamped his hand over my mouth. "Shh."

I was smart enough to stay quiet as I kept close to the ground and followed my superhero and her K-9 partner.

Shay peeked through the same hole in the wall through which we'd seen the unicorns yesterday. The tense silence was broken by the snap of bone beneath my feet. Looking down at what I'd stepped in, I grimaced at the disgusting tar-like sludge of what was left of the demon the unicorns had pounded to the ground. Crouching in full tactical gear, Shay didn't make a sound, just held up a thumb and turned it up and down, asking me a silent question. I gave a thumbs up, and she and Dexter crept through the doorway.

The chains lay exactly as we'd left them, along with whatever was still inside when we'd escaped. There was no sign of demons, in fact, no signs of life aside from our own.

"Nothing's here." Shay broke the silence.

"Dex says he can only smell the guts outside," Stout said as Dexter continued to sniff the corners of the barn. "Nothing else has been here since us."

Then Dexter barked twice, turned in a circle, and dropped to a straw-covered pile on the floor.

"Whatcha got there, buddy?" Shay knelt beside him, feeling beneath the animal's fur and pulling out a fractured piece of demon, hardened almost to stone.

"I think he was going to eat it" Stout said.

"It is from the…" I didn't need to finish that question because we all knew it was.

Shay picked it up, and Dexter snapped to grab it. "No!"

"It's the snack of dragons," Clia joked.

"He likes the buzz," Stout added.

"No, Dex!" Shay dropped the remains behind her, squatting to look in the dog's eyes. "No buzzing when we're working." His nose let loose a disapproving puff of smoke. "Ante!" Shay waved her hand, and the command sent him back to sniffing around. Then she asked Stout, "Do you think that's going to be a long-term issue?"

"What? His taste for demon guts?"

She wiped her hands through the soot and dirt. "Yes, when all is said and done, will he need that?"

"Maybe we should start weaning him." I laughed as I suggested it.

But Shay just nodded solemnly. "Maybe we should. I just…" Shay's words drifted as something in the corner caught her eye. She kicked at the panel in the wall.

"What is it?" My hand fell to the small of her back.

"The next realm." Shay's fingers clenched the slatted wood, and her foot kicked up on the frame. But even after two powerful tugs, the structure didn't budge.

"Maybe a little less superhero and a bit more Magick of Bannock?" I whispered in her ear.

"Good call." Her hands fell to her side, and as I took hold of one, Dexter slipped against Shay's hip to touch the other. "*Secreta voca, ianuam, detege,*" Shay said, and we watched as the mirage of a wall disappeared into a familiar spiraling cloud.

I grabbed Shay's wrist. "Slow down."

She didn't listen, just cinched the backpack to her waist and checked our surroundings. "We can't do slow today, love.

We either do this now or whatever is coming gets the upper hand."

Touching her cheek, I said, "I don't like it."

She kissed me. "Duly noted."

Her hand tangled in my own, and the five of us passed through the swirling cloud and into the unknown. The sensation was like Andrea's portal access, and I wondered if we'd exit inside her secret room. For the seconds it took us to travel, I hoped it would be–we'd be on familiar ground in our own realm, at least–but it wasn't.

Shay landed first, boots on the ground like a trained professional. I flopped like a beginner gymnast on my first day, very proud to land on my feet…almost.

Wherever we were was so quiet that it was almost oppressive. We didn't dare say anything; we hardly dared to breathe. We were in a void of some sort, and we stood shoulder to shoulder, back-to-back, each of us scanning in different directions.

Shay's voice sounded in my head. *"It's so quiet. I'm hesitant to move."*

"Are we between realms?" I thought, watching as Stout and Clia tangled in the fur around Dexter's collar. That he'd remained in dog form was always a good sign. Threats usually puffed him into dragon mode.

"It feels solid under our feet," Shay said. *"We…we need to press on."*

I wasn't about to let go of her hand, my own hand slick with sweat and trembling, as we moved through the void and into what I'd expected since the first time I'd seen it all those months ago in my nightmare.

The grass was the brightest shade of green I'd ever seen, mixed in with splintered amber reeds. I closed my eyes as the wind salted the air and mingled with the scent of the flowery tips. I was so lost in the feeling of bliss that radiated from all around us that I didn't want to move.

The sigil in my palm burned, and I felt the vibration of Shay's flame where our hands met. Our dog was gone, replaced by the largest manifestation of his dragon form I'd ever seen. *How can there be such danger in a place that feels like home?* I thought, before Shay tugged me until I was safely behind her.

"*Rigescunt indutae,*" she said as she drew the alicorn knife from her belt. I was content to stand behind her, but she was talking to the growling dragon beside her. "Don't move," she whispered, and I froze like she'd commanded me and not him.

I felt it, as they both must have, the tremble of evil confronting everything that was good in us. We'd arrived at the place where the demon collecting alicorns was feeding its lord. If we were going by what'd happened in the nightmare, the truest danger was at our feet, so I looked down, unsurprised to see the slatted pathway there.

"Is this a dream?" I whispered, and Shay pinched my arm, causing me to cry out, "Ow! No."

"Shhh." Stout hovered near my head. "It was here."

He pointed at the dragon crouched down to track a scent, and we followed him through the grass and along the winding slatted walkway to its end near a massive fieldstone building. It was an ancient structure, built from hammered steel with rustic mortared walls.

"He says we should put up the barrier and all go together," Stout said.

Shay whispered the spell, and the protective bubble surrounded us. As we moved, so did it, until the oversized doors blocked our way.

"I have to leave the barrier to open it," she said.

Before I could protest, she stepped through our bubble, grabbed the hand-forged steel ring, and wrenched the door open. Today, Shay was wearing every piece of armor I'd made to protect her, and when a blast of power blew out from the doorway, her body went flying with it.

"Shay!" I yelled, but she was already tumbling and, without pause, rolling to her feet.

"I'm fine." She thumped the armor on her chest with the cuff on her wrist. "I'm fine."

And all of us were, thankfully. The door hung open, and we were able to get our first look inside.

"It's dark," I said, stating the obvious.

Shay returned to our protective bubble, and together, we advanced toward the unknown. We both summoned our flames, the light flickering across the walls, leaving ominous shadows as we progressed through the building. Dexter growled before returning to his furry self.

"He says there's no*thing* here," Stout translated, and I noted his emphasis on the "thing" part of that word.

The shield dropped, releasing Dexter to sniff through the building. The stone walls made the space feel cold and damp, reminding me of the cellar in the old courthouse.

"Can you feel the magick in this place?" Shay asked. The fact that we all said yes at the same time was a clear sign that whatever resided here was powerful.

"What's the plan?" Stout asked.

"Look around I guess." Shay held her flame waist high and stepped forward with caution. I stayed close by her side. "Looks like someone slept over there."

In the corner of the room, there was a primitive frame of rough-cut limbs thatched together to hold makeshift padding that served as a mattress.

"So cozy. I want to just move right in," I joked, and Shay laughed. The sound was reassurance that, although the building was creepy, it was also vacant.

"Winter cottage?" Shay poked at the table beside the bed.

"Or summer. Would be nice with this natural draft." I raised my flame to show the movement of air in the room.

"That's quite a breeze." She followed the flow of air coming down a stone staircase.

"Notice anything about this?" Stout asked as Dexter took the lead up to the second floor.

"It's old?" I answered.

His wing flutter went silent as he settled down onto the sill of the slotted window. "Yes, but—"

"It's designed for defense," Shay cut in. "The spiral gives whoever guards this place the tactical advantage." She turned around to show us how she'd win in the fight.

"Like castles." It was a statement more than a question.

"Something important is at the top of this staircase." Shay hooked her thumb into the velcro above her hip as she adjusted her vest. "*Custodire*," she said to Dexter, the command to protect us, locking him in place. "Wait here for just a second." Shay touched my shoulder, then slid gloves over her hands and unholstered a weapon. "I'm going to check the blinds." She pushed her taser into the palm of my hand. "Just in case."

I didn't know what it meant to check the blinds, but I knew I could tase whatever evil came at me. She took a few more steps until she was out of my sight, her K-9 and our fairies waiting at my side.

"She's quite fearless," Clia said.

"Red's like no human I've known," Stout bragged.

I didn't respond to their admiration of my lover, too distracted by the taser in my hand. But I snapped out of it as soon as I heard a loud noise and something crashing to the floor.

"Damn it!" I murmured, rushing forward.

There was another thump, maybe the sound of a person hitting the floor. I ran as fast as I could, finding Shay standing in front of a table, a knife sticking out from the surface and a board on the floor.

"What is it?" I asked.

Shay wasn't holding her flame anymore; she'd switched to the high beam of a tactical light clipped to her service firearm.

"It isn't here, but it was." The light shone on the surface of the table. It traveled over crude images carved in the wood. "Kai," Shay said, followed by, "Gorath." Her flashlight moved on to the next. "Sabine." She was silent when the light stopped.

"Jacob," I said.

Her hand trembled as it rested on a mark we both knew well.

"Me," I gasped.

There it was, a symbol that should not exist in this wicked realm, but it was there, gouged into the splintered surface.

"What does it mean?" I asked, never so afraid to hear an answer to a question.

The look Shay gave me rocked me to my core, as did the words that fell from her frowning lips.

"It knows who you are."

CHAPTER XVIII

CHASE

"**S**top moving!" I yelled as Shay scoured the room. Her reaction to the Maker's marks on the tabletop was to go into extreme search mode. She found the candle holders in the room and lit them all until she could see into every corner. She tipped every shelf, turned over every piece of furniture, until she was satisfied she'd found every trace of what lived here.

"That's alicorn powder," Stout pointed out as Shay tore the cover from a crate. "We shouldn't leave that behind."

"I want to burn this place to the ground!" she screamed. "They're hunting the Maker of Bannock."

My knees buckled a little, and I rested my back against the wall to steady myself. "Hunting?" I squeezed the taser in my hand before setting it on the table. My finger traced Kai's mark where it was carved into the surface. "How did it know?"

"Andrea Peters and that thing inside of her," Stout said.

"But how?"

"I don't know, and right now, I don't care." Shay lifted the crate. "We need to get back to Bannock. If it knows about you, it has to know where to find you."

I stuttered. "But we aren't there."

"It probably doesn't know *that*," Stout said as he flew toward the staircase. "Can Fireface shift us home?"

Dexter was currently more concerned with sniffing at the crate in Shay's arms. But Shay gave him a command, and seconds later, Stout and Clia disappeared with the dog.

"You seem very uneasy," I said, once it was just Shay and me left.

"I want to get you out of here, just in case."

Dexter returned before I could say another word, and we shifted back to the fairy realm through the portal.

"Something isn't right!" Stout yelled, as we exited.

The fairy flew toward the town. I chased after him with Dexter following close behind.

"Why do you say that?" I asked.

"There should be Bliation forces waiting for us, but they aren't."

Then he let out a strangled cry and pointed to something that made my heart sink: a lifeless fairy body on the ground.

"They're being slaughtered." His voice was heavy with emotion.

"By whatever lived in that building?" I asked.

"No way to be sure yet, but it is a good guess," Clia said as she stared at the body.

"Where's Shay?" I asked, looking at Dexter for an answer.

The dog barked twice, and Stout translated for him. "She's coming through with the alicorn dust. He can't shift her with that."

"We need to wait for her." I heard the panic in my voice as Dexter barked again, and a relieved smile spread across my face when I saw what he was barking about.

"You don't need to wait." Shay set the crate on her hip, and I rushed to hug her. "We need to get this through the portal and back to Bannock."

Dexter was already gone, following the fairies toward the town. "We should go after them."

"This is too important to leave here." Shay walked in the opposite direction of the town, heading to the portal.

"We can't just leave them," I argued.

"Dex will get everyone home," Shay said. "I'm more worried about what might happen in Bannock."

"You think it's going after Dani and Amelia?"

She nodded, and I hurried to keep up as her walk turned into a slow run. "I think it might be, and I need to get back to warn them."

"But the barriers will keep them safe, won't they?" I asked.

She stopped to turn and look at me. "I can only hope."

Her answer made me curious and also panicked. "So are we hiking to the portal?"

"*I'm* going to. I want you to see what's happening in the town."

"Shay, no. I don't want you to be alone."

"We don't have a choice. We have to split apart to solve this."

She threw the crate on her shoulder, and without a kiss or a hug, she raced toward the portal and back to Bannock. I stood in disbelief, watching her disappear.

But I still did what she asked, even though it went against everything I wanted. I ran toward the edge of the town, where I found Dexter, Clia, and Stout.

"What's happening?" I asked, short of breath from the run.

"They overtook the forces loyal to the king. The king is dead, and the realm is in chaos," Stout explained in a hurried rush of words.

"What can I do?" I asked.

"The Maker and the Magick of Bannock are to blame," Clia said, shocking me until she added, "At least that is what I'm hearing."

"You need to get out of the realm." Stout pushed at my shoulder. "It's not safe for you here."

"According to Shay," I said, "nowhere is safe for us right now."

"Where is she?" Stout asked.

"She's returning through the portals with the alicorn powder."

"That's good," he said. "Go. Take Dexter, and stay with Shay in Bannock."

"What about the two of you?" I asked, worry for them rising in my chest.

"We will be safe among our own," Clia assured me as she took hold of Stout's hand. "We will return to Bannock with news when we can."

I didn't wait for additional instructions. "Take me home, Dex."

I placed my hand on the scruff of his neck, and seconds later, we landed at the portal for the Giant realm. We passed through and shifted again. At no point in the journey did Dexter stop for directions or commands. We were going back to Bannock the fastest way he knew to get us there.

When my feet hit the ground just outside of the Grant's Pass portal, I fell to my knees. My hands pressed into solid ground, and I was certain I would lose what little was in my stomach. The earth energy rising through my palms was comforting.

Dexter circled me, and I held up a finger. "Give me a min—" Before I could finish my sentence, we were at the trailhead, only a few yards from where Shay's car had been parked.

It was gone. How could she be so far ahead of us? It didn't matter because the K-9 shifted us to Bannock, and I fell against the bright orange door of the carriage house before vomiting in the garbage can outside the building. It took me a few minutes to recover as I fought the straps of the backpack, dropping it and slumping beside the door frame.

Dexter paced the building, sniffing for his partner, then came to lay his head in my lap.

"Maybe you should find her," I said, covering my mouth to fight the nausea. His nose lifted, then he snorted a puff of smoke and vanished. "And then there was one," I whispered to myself.

I reached into the side pocket of the backpack for my cell phone. Not knowing what time it was—or even what *day it was*, I called the bar, grateful to hear Amelia's voice when she answered.

"Hello, Wildwood," she said. "You're home?"

"Yeah, I'm at the carriage house." I hesitated, wondering if I should blurt out that Shay was missing. "You haven't heard from Shay, have you?" My voice hitched, hanging on the hope that she'd gone straight to the bar.

I heard the intake of breath. "No. I haven't seen her since they separated us in Grant's Pass." She waited.

"Has Dani?" But I already knew the answer.

"Not that I know of, but Danielle's still at work."

The police station was the last place I wanted to go, but it was also probably the last place Shay would stop, today.

"I'm just going to call her, double check." My head fell back against the stone wall of the carriage house, the ground below me warm from the sun.

"You do that. I'll wait to hear from you."

My stomach was still gurgling, but I was pretty sure I'd already emptied the contents of it. Hoping I wouldn't throw up again, I stumbled to my feet and spun to brush the dirt from my ass.

"Hey there."

The voice made me jump, but it also made my heart soar.

"Shay?"

"It's me." She was covered from head to toe in what looked like dirt, holding the crate of alicorn powder.

"Goddess, love. Where have you been?" I looked around for Dexter, almost certain he'd found her and brought her home.

"It's a bit of a trip to get here."

I smiled, knowing that I was still dizzy, and nauseous from the shifting return to Bannock. "Yep, still trying to steady myself." I leaned in to kiss her, but she backed away.

"Let me get this off before you touch me."

She kept the crate between our bodies, and it was then that I realized there was no patrol car, there was no Dexter, and the person in front of me was giving off unrecognizable energy.

"What's going on?" I sidestepped until my back was against the bright orange door. The boundary of protection penetrated my skin.

"We've just come through quite a few realms, maybe you're feeling that?" she suggested, stepping closer to me.

She set the crate on the ground and brushed down the length of her sleeves. I stared at her, scrutinizing every motion. Taking her hat off, she slapped most of the powder from her body. It looked like ash or dirt.

And then it clicked.

"Are your hands cold?" I asked. Shay still wore gloves, something unusual for her off the job.

She looked down at them and tugged the fingertips one by one to remove them. "Not cold, just trying not to touch anything."

My hand fell to the doorknob, my back remaining tight against the protection barrier's edge. I looked at Shay's hands–really looked at them–and tried to hide all the emotions that raced through me.

There were no scars on her skin. This woman in front of me was *not* Shay. This wasn't my superhero.

Keeping my voice level, I said, "We should go in and get whatever that is off of you."

I didn't want to turn my back on this thing, and I tried to steady my hands as they fumbled through my bag to locate my keys. My heart raced until I could finally put my sigil hand back on the door. Whatever it was pretending to be Shay, it couldn't touch me now.

The key hit the lock, and the tumblers fell into place like resounding gongs. I pushed the door open, leaving the backpack on the ground, and stepped inside the carriage house.

"You want me to take the crate?" I asked.

"I've got it," Not-Shay assured me.

The keys in my hand dropped to the floor as this imitation of Shay attempted to step inside. "Are you sure?" My voice broke, and I fought to hide the tremble as the crate dropped to the floor.

Its head tipped back to sniff the air. "Such power from the Magick of Bannock." It breathed in again but didn't step forward. "But so very mortal."

"Where is she?" I yelled as I reached for the closest weapon I could find, a forge rake. I was suddenly aware that the hammer of the goddess was two feet away from this shapeshifting monster.

"Some place you'll never find her."

The creature's laugh was loud and sharp, like a knife to my heart. I had to believe that Dexter could locate Shay, but for now, this thing was my problem.

"Your weapon is laughable." It stepped closer. "So mortal of you to believe you can touch me in this realm."

"Where is she?" I screamed again, swinging the tool back and forth to protect my body. I knew I wasn't much of a threat, but I needed to get closer to my backpack.

A car pulled up, and Shay's doppelgänger and I turned to see who it was.

"Look, more human toys to play with." It laughed.

"Pierce!" Dani yelled from the window of the car.

"It's not Shay!" I screamed as loud as I could before lunging forward at the creature without hesitation.

My shoulder slammed into the immovable being, but I was an arm's length from the backpack and the hammer of the goddess. A cloud of dust puffed off the creature's body, covering my shirt.

How could I have thought this was a good idea?

The car door opened as I reached for the bag. I didn't mean to throw Dani into the fight, but I was almost certain Brigid's power would make a difference. The heat of magick filled my palm as I gripped the handle. My dirty shirt was tangled around the hammer's head, but at least I was armed.

"Where the hell is she?" The power of magick filled me, strengthened me, but it also activated the demon image on the head.

Dani came around the patrol car, taser drawn as she approached. "What do you mean, it's not Shay?"

In the seconds it took for her to ask, the creature punched the ground. Everything around us trembled. I steadied myself in the door frame as Dani dropped to one knee. The doppelgänger punched again, and the earth opened beneath its feet, a crack wide enough for dozens of people to fall through. The doppelgänger disappeared into the abyss.

"What the hell." Dani pointed her taser toward the ground before the crevasse closed, sealing the creature below.

"I have no idea."

She hooked the backpack with one hand while using her body to guide me into the carriage house, patting my shoulder. We'd be safe in here. No evil could enter.

"Where's Pierce?"

"I don't know. We got separated just after we found *that*." I pointed to the crate on the floor.

"What is it?" Dani kicked it with her foot to knock it out of the carriage house.

"No, don't." I grabbed the container and dragged it to the workshop table. "It's alicorn powder, and if it was evil, I couldn't bring it in."

"Right, the barrier." Dani holstered her taser and keyed the mic on her lapel. "Forest to base, I'm 10-6."

I heard the static-y reply, "10-4."

Then she turned to me. "Tell me what's going on. Amelia said Shay didn't come back with you."

I dropped the hammer on the table and turned toward the door. "It's a lot to tell, but right now we need to find her, and we need to do it fast."

"How fast?"

"As soon as possible." I pulled the drawstring on my backpack and removed the pouch. "Because I have our stash of anvil dust, and her body isn't strong enough to handle another injury without it."

CHAPTER XIX

SUCCESSION

"What are you going to do?" Dani asked as she gripped the edge of the table. I'd given her the briefest summary of the last few days, careful to add specific details about Shay's near-death experience. "You really going after her with just a hammer?"

"I also have an axe. And if I stop to see your wife, I'll have a bow." I cinched the buckle on my belt, double checking each weapon was within reach if I needed them to fight.

"Was Pierce wearing body armor?" she asked.

I took a slow breath and considered the question. "From head to toe, yes."

"So the protection magick in her demon armor isn't working anymore?"

"I don't know what's happening. Maybe it's losing strength because we've been moving through realms, or maybe it's that demon's powers." There was another possibility, one that was hard for me to say out loud. "Or...or maybe I'm just not the Maker I think I am."

Dani didn't say a word, and the silence brought an ache to my soul.

"You're an extraordinary Maker," someone said as the door hit the wall with a loud thud. I turned to see Shay staggering into the carriage house with a dragon keeping her upright.

"Holy goddess!" I yelled and dropped everything to help them.

"Holy? Maybe just a bit." She pointed at the cut on her temple and the scratches on her knuckles and her hands, those gorgeous, scarred hands. "But goddess? I'd have to argue against that at the moment. I'm not feeling much like anything but a punching bag."

Dani threw one arm around Shay, and I took the other side as we walked her to the chair. "What happened?" I asked.

"It was a nightmarish trap." She swiped at the cut on her face, her hand coming away with blood. "When I hit the top step in the cottage, the demon pulled me toward the center of the room. I hit something hard and then I was falling."

I listened as I tore the pouch of anvil dust open. The handful I grabbed left particles scattered in a path as I moved to work on her wounds. "Falling where?" I asked as I sprinkled the dust on her temple and pushed at her to open her hands. There were so many abrasions, as if she'd climbed through patches of briars.

"In that cottage." She gasped through clenched teeth as the anvil dust bubbled in the wound. Her sigil flame flashed, and as difficult as it was to see her in pain, it comforted me to know she was my Shay.

"That's where it must have switched her," Dani suggested.

Confusion furrowed my brow. "Switched her how?"

"Did anything touch you, Pierce?"

Shay closed her eyes, still riding the pain of the cure and trying to focus on whatever had taken place in that cottage. "Maybe?"

"Think."

I stepped in between them. "Give her a minute."

"With that thing somewhere in town. We don't have minutes to play with." Dani pulled her phone from her belt, hitting a speed dial number. "Hey, honey, you need to batten down the hatches." Then she hung up without any further explanation.

"Can someone please tell me what's going on?" Shay pushed off the chair to stand.

"A shapeshifter made its way to your front door," Dani explained, saying it as if things like that happened every day.

And that was it, the straw that broke the camel's back. And me, if I'm being honest. My whole life, I'd wondered about the universe and about the creatures that dwelled within its realms, thinking of fairies and giants and unicorns as myths, delightful stories humans told each other for entertainment or for good-natured scares. But I knew the truth now. None of them were charming myths. And neither, it seemed, were the things that go bump in the night.

A shapeshifter had somehow taken hold of Shay, and this doppelgänger could continue moving through town as her.

"So that's what happened..." Shay said, looking just as shaken as I was. "It touched me, but it also felt the sting of your armor, Wil, so I went down the trap while it must've hit the wall." Her hand covered the vanishing wound, and crumbles of crusted dust and blood fell to the floor. "I remember hearing a loud noise before I hit the ground below the cottage."

"That's the noise we heard before we found you in the other realm." I paused. "Well, not *you*, but the thing that looks like you. And we took the crate and got out of there. Dex shifted us one at a time, but he didn't bring you." I rubbed my temples, dizzy from the thought of the body swap.

"He found me," she said, giving him a loving pat. This whole time, Dexter hadn't left Shay's side.

"I sent him back." I smiled. "He kinda ditched me for his partner." I shuffled the fur around his neck.

"I'm not sure I could've dug my way out." She stared at her hands. "These aren't the best shovels." She stumbled to her feet. "I need to get something to drink." She was cautious on the stairs, taking one at a time with a tight grip on the handrail.

I stared at Dani. "She's going to need some rest."

Dani tipped her head toward the door. "I'm going to go check on Amelia and do a loop around town before my shift ends. That thing may have dropped into hell, but it won't stay there."

"Yeah," I closed my eyes, holding back the image of the monster with the stolen face. "I'll have Shay call you when she's feeling up to it."

Dani left without another word, and I raced up the stairs to find Shay standing at the kitchen sink.

"Where's Stout?" she asked as she turned on the water to fill her glass.

"Dexter shifted you back here, right?" When she nodded, I asked, "And you had to pass through the fairy realm?"

"We did."

My hand rested on the small of her back, as much to comfort her as to assure myself that she was here and she was herself. "I left Stout and Clia there."

"Do you know what's happening with the fairy king?" She twisted into my arms and slumped against my body.

"The king has lost his crown, and his head, too, I guess."

I wished I was strong enough to sweep her in my arms and carry her to bed, but I was not. The best I could do was hold her glass of water while she leaned on me as we walked. Dexter didn't leave her side as we entered the bedroom, and he flopped to the floor when Shay sat on the corner of the bed. Her hands were slow as she ripped at the velcro, and I stepped in to take charge of undressing her.

"Here, let me help you," I said gently.

It had been a few days since we'd slept in our bed, and the same since we'd had a bath or shower. We both needed to wash. She was half awake, close to incoherent, and all I wanted to do was touch every inch of her body to reassure myself that she was safe.

Her shirt dangled around her wrist as she leaned against my stomach, and I felt her fingertips dig into the curves of my hips. Perhaps she needed to touch me as much as I needed to touch her.

"I'm exhausted, Wil."

"I can see that, my love." I held her.

"We should go back to the realm and get them."

I laughed. Of *course*, all she would care about is saving our fairies. "We can go in the morning."

"In the morning," she mumbled.

I left her there and went to turn on the shower. She walked, with help from me, to the bathroom, her hands pressed against the curtained wall as I soaped her hair.

"This feels so good."

She moaned as she turned around to rinse her hair, and it was all I could do to focus on soap, water, and shampoo. I touched the scars on her chest, and when she turned to rinse her face, I kissed the one on her back. She had no idea that her scars saved me today.

It took two washes before her hair was clean, and balancing to keep her on her feet while I washed myself was a challenge. She crumbled like a tangled ball of fatigue to the tub floor, as the dirt of our realm missions washed away. This would have to be enough because if she fell asleep, I couldn't lift her from this footed bathtub.

I turned the water off. "Baby?"

"Hmm."

The sound was endearing. "You need to stand up."

"Mm-hmm."

That was the most I would get out of her, but she stood when I clasped her hands to help her out and towel her dry. We didn't bother with a nightshirt or briefs.

"Thank you," she whispered as I pulled back the covers and laid her down.

I knelt to pet Dexter. "Keep her safe, buddy."

Today was done, but we were not. As I slid beneath the covers and wrapped myself around her, I felt the ferocity of protection like never before. Whatever was coming, it was clever and had the experience of many lifetimes to refine its skills.

I had Shay and Dexter, Dani and Amelia, and two fairies tangled in a battle for a realm we didn't quite understand.

~~~~~~~~~~

"What day is it?" Shay shuffled across the kitchen floor, plunked a kiss on the top of my head, and went directly to the coffee pot.

"I have no idea." My elbows rested on the table, a steaming cup of coffee in my hands, inches from my lips.

"The place is so quiet." She opened the refrigerator, then whispered, "Beer."

I turned to look at her. "I know."
~~~~~~~~~~

We didn't need to say it out loud; Stout's absence was hitting both of us hard.

"We have to go get them." She closed the door and came to sit beside me. "There's no telling what the king's Bliation forces will do to him and to Clia, especially now that their king is dead."

"Their realm was in chaos long before we entered it." I reached across the table to hold her hand. "We opened a portal that allowed freedom for all of those trapped fairies to move home."

"Kinda reckless of us." She blew over the rim of her cup, and I saw the mischievous grin light her eyes.

"There you are," I whispered as I felt the return of my woman. "I missed you."

"Thank you for rescuing me."

That made me pause and consider the events of the last few days. "Did I?"

She put her cup on the table and stood up. Her delicate fingers plucked the mug from my hands and placed it on the table. The move seemed benign, but my heart hammered in anticipation as she helped me to my feet. Her arms came around to hold me, nothing and no one had ever felt as much like home.

"You did." She rested her forehead on mine. "I have no idea what's happened since the attack, Hell, I'm still reeling from the poison. I can feel something is different, but I don't know what."

"We can figure it out."

She kissed me, and I came under her spell. "There's a lot on our plate, isn't there?"

I was dizzy from her lips. "Yeah." I could barely form the word.

~~~~~~~~~~
~~~~~~~~~~

Nothing brings Shay to a halt. We drank our coffee cold, and before I could zip the fly of my jeans, she was already plotting to research the alicorn powder, return to the fairy realm, and find the doppelgänger. Not necessarily in that order and hopefully not all at once.

Shay turned the polished demon steel cuff on her wrist, lost in thought.

"Talk to me," I said as I lit the forge.

We agreed I needed to make anvil dust, and we also decided that each of us would always carry a container of it whenever we left the safety of the carriage house. My only task for the next few hours was to manufacture a hearty stockpile.

"I'm bothered by the strikes."

"That's a mighty vague statement, superhero." I waved my hand to encourage more information. "Care to elaborate?"

"The venom from the demon in the barn. The doppelgänger's touch in the realm cottage. What's the link?" She sat at the workshop table, making notes on everything she could remember, beginning with the demon attack during the unicorn rescue.

"Demons and unicorns?" It would always be weird to me that I was seeking a serious answer about creatures I had thought were fiction up until recently.

"An unencountered breed of demon and the alicorn powder, as well."

I pushed a billet of demon steel into the flame. "You think they're linked?"

She nodded. "I absolutely do." She stepped around me to get to the crate of powder. "The doppelgänger brought this here, so it has to be important."

"Do you have any idea how the demon could impersonate you?" I watched as she pried the lid off of the crate.

"I think this powder is a factor." She removed the earthenware container wrapped in burlap styled cloth. "That demon harvested the alicorns for a reason, and since we found its stash in the cottage, it must have collected them for the doppelgänger." Shay removed the stopper from the container.

"Are you sure we should open that?"

I felt the heat of the forge and closed the door as Shay walked into the office. She returned with two respirators, a pair of first aid kit gloves, and a tin can from our recycle bin.

"Your intuition is fierce," Shay said, snapping the gloves over her hands. "Mask up."

I fit the respirator over my mouth and nose. She plunged the can inside, scooping less than what would amount to a handful.

"I don't know what power this holds," Shay said inside my head, *"but if the doppelgänger carried it through to the Earth realm, it has to mean something."*

I heard her thoughts, but I was having a few of my own. *"I thought it would be white."*

Shay's head cocked to the side. *"What do you mean?"*

From my observations in the demon barn, the gift from the unicorn, and Andrea's flute, the alicorn material was always white. *"How do we know this is alicorn powder?"*

"We don't."

Shay set the container on the table, and we each took a step back, and then another. I twisted the valve to cut the gas to my forge and then we took another step back.

Shay removed her mask. "It's inside the carriage house, so it can't be evil."

She didn't say another word as she raced up the stairs two at a time. It was comforting to see her energy return, but as always, her prompt exits left me curious. She returned with a bundle in her hand. This was the test kit, worn and battered from use long before Shay became the Magick of Bannock.

Longer, even, than she'd been a law enforcement officer, now that I thought about it. This was Regina Benton's kit to test things for a magickal presence.

"Do you ever stop working a problem?" I asked.

She hooked her hand around my neck, smacking my lips with a kiss. "Once in a while." She winked, and my heart hammered.

I cleared my throat, trying my best to focus on alicorn magicks. "What are you testing for?"

She pointed at her mask, and I covered my face again. *"Demons and known mystical creatures. It's all I can honestly do. I don't have a baseline for unicorn."*

Reflecting on how truly odd my world was, I watched her sprinkle bits of alicorn dust into the tubes of the test kit. The rubber bottles holding the test dyes were next, and she dripped the liquid in all five sample containers. We watched and kept watching until the seconds felt like hours. I squatted to get a closer look.

"They aren't changing." I sent the thought to her, and we stepped away from the table.

The mask dangled near her chin. "There's no demon in there, but we kinda knew that. But there's no mystical presence, either." She scratched at the back of her neck, thinking.

"No mystical presence *that we know of.*"

I tossed my mask on the chair. We'd been here not so long ago, back before we uncovered Benton's secrets and her past. She'd left behind more texts and tools than I ever imagined, but the one I missed most was our pint-sized fairy.

"Stout and Clia's realm knowledge would be very useful right now."

"Are you thinking what I'm thinking?" she asked as she covered her mouth again.

"I can't imagine that I am." I laughed as I watched her put a sample of the powder into a small tube, poured the rest into the earthen jar, and sealed it.

Shay pulled the mask off. "We need to find our fairy."

I shrugged. "You know, I *was* actually thinking that."

~~~~~~~~~~

Amelia slid the plate in front of me, and I sighed. We'd spent a few hours in the workshop, me stockpiling demon sift and Shay trying to sketch her very brief glimpse of the demon's true form.

"Rare, fries, and another beer," Amelia said.

"Thank you, you're a saint." I took a bite of my hamburger. I was happy for the fish when we'd camped in the mountains, but darn, this burger was amazing.

"Hungry?" she said with a laugh as she tapped the bar.

"She's not a fan of dehydrated meal kits." Shay took a moment to dress her burger, tipping the bun top over and stacking the lettuce, tomato, and onion on the patty.

I stared at her method of assembly, and it made me think about the forge and blacksmithing and demon steel.

"What's going on in that brain of yours?" Shay asked, but her attention didn't leave her task.

I had a mouthful of burger, and she turned to look at me when she was met with silence. I held up a finger to finish chewing, and after swallowing and taking a sip of beer, I shared my potentially dangerous idea. "So your burger got me thinking."

She had reassembled it and was cutting it in half. "My burger?"

"Well, not exactly your burger, but the stacking of veggies."
~~~~~~~~~~

I wasn't explaining my idea well, and she raised an eyebrow with a question. "You are aware the same vegetables are on your plate, too. They're good for you."

I chuckled and turned my bar chair toward her. "Not the veggies in particular. I was thinking about stacking demon steel but maybe adding a bit of that alicorn powder."

"How can you forge powder?" she asked.

"It's kinda simple, really."

"Share," she said as she took a bite of her food.

"It's the coolest thing, and I can't believe it took a bloody burger to make me think of it." I stretched across the bar for a napkin and plucked the pen out of Shay's shirt pocket. I made a quick doodle of a cuboid. "This is a rectangular container."

She nodded, mouth full of food, encouraging me to continue.

"If I build a box like this with steel, I can fill it, weld it closed, and forge a combination of materials." Her nod made it clear she was following. "I could fill all the voids with alicorn powder."

Shay wiped her lips. "Like my vest?"

I smacked the sketch. "Exactly like your vest but with the magicks inside the alicorn powder."

"What do you think it will do?"

"I think it will kill that asshole." I slapped the pen on the paper, and we continued to eat.

After another bite, Shay set her food on the plate. "It punched a hole in the earth, though?"

"Uh huh," I mumbled through my mouthful of burger.

"Like Andrea opened in the mine?"

I swallowed hard and looked up at her reflection in the mirror behind the bar. "Don't say it." I shook my head.

"Where else would it go?"

"Wait, before you go off on the next misadventure, "I said, "there's something I haven't told you, and it's been bothering me."

"What about?"

"The doppelgänger." I paused.

"Okay, what about the doppelgänger?"

"It said something about mortal earth power, and I think adding elements from many realms will strengthen my weapon." She tilted her head, thinking about what I'd just said. "Aside from the materials Benton gave us, can you suggest anything else?"

"Do I have time to think about it?"

I looked at the food on my plate. "Enough for me to finish my burger."

~~~~~~~~~~

"Class one?" Shay said as she counted on her fingers. She'd already ticked off the other three classes.

"Right here." I had crayon-sized pieces of demon steel, cut into chunks and separated into piles on the table.

"What about fairy powder?" she suggested.

"I have that last bit of fairy steel in there, but I don't want to add too much." I opened the container of alicorn powder. "This will fill the voids."

I'd already built the vessel to hold the loose components and painted the inside to make it easier to remove once I forge-welded the bits into a whole. As much as I disliked damascus steel, to fight this evil, I'd gladly make it.

Shay was in the open space of the workshop, stepping in and out of the sacred circle on the floor. She carried my demon candle holder and lit the wick with her breath. Dexter lay inside, flopped over like a lump.

"Come here for a minute." She waved me beside her. "I have an idea."
~~~~~~~~~~

"You do?" When I stepped into the ring, the walls of the workshop lit with images and runic scribblings.

"I was thinking about non-mortal elements." She sat beside Dexter and placed the candle on the floor.

"Okay." I felt the mingling of our energies when I sat next to her. Even after a year of magick, this sacred ring made me a little breathless.

"Monoceros" she said and reached in her pocket.

"The unicorn."

She nodded as she held the fairy flute to me. "Also, the constellation."

I took the instrument and held it to my lips. The song it played without my fingers covering the holes was magick to my ears. Pinpointed lights flickered as one-by-one they appeared on the ceiling until we could trace imaginary lines to draw the image.

"Not of the earth," I whispered.

"Yes, and what else has been where Monoceros have?"

I knew the answer to this riddle, and I rolled to my knees to reach into my pocket. The stone that wasn't a stone was inside.

Shay picked up the candle to light my palm. "Meteorite."

"My anniversary gift to kill ultimate evil." My fingers clenched around it as I said, "I don't want to give this up."

"You don't have to," she promised.

She got to her feet and walked out of the ring. Dexter rolled over, following Shay up the stairs. I was there, kneeling in my spot on the floor, staring at a flickering flame, holding my anniversary stone.

Shay returned, fully armed and armored with Dex on her heels. "You coming?"

I cupped the candle with my sigil hand, snuffing the flame as she tugged me to my feet. "Where are we going?"

She grabbed the ready bag from the wall, "Oh, it's a surprise."

~~~~~~~~~~

"Delora's Rocks," I read the sign over the parking lot entrance.

The white outline of paint around each letter was peeling from age. Delora had clearly been selling rocks in this building for a very long time.

"Worth the car ride?" Shay asked as her fingers tangled around mine.

"We drove an hour for this, so it better be."

I held the door open for us, and Dex pranced inside like he'd been here every day of his life. And maybe he had.

"Shay!" the woman behind the counter called out just after the jingly bells announced our entry.

"Hello, Leigha, how's life in the rock world?"

"Taking nothing for granite!" she yelled across the shop, and Shay let out a loud groan.

"Did she really just say that?" I laughed as I stopped to touch an amethyst geode large enough for me to climb inside. I closed my eyes to let the energy fill me.

"Every time I stop in." Shay turned around to look at me, and I felt her hand rest on my hip right before her chin touched my shoulder. "Feels good, right?"

"It feels very good."

She kissed my cheek. "Come on." Shay was like a child in a toy store, and she nearly skipped to the service counter.

"Is this her?" Leigha asked with a dimpled smile.

She wore her hair cropped short, and her tall frame was covered with a rock shop t-shirt under rolled up flannel sleeves. She had a powerful energy, but I couldn't tell if it was for the rocks or from them. Either way, I was curious.
~~~~~~~~~~

"It is," Shay said, nodding. "Leigha, this is my girlfriend, Wildwood. Wildwood, this is Leigha."

"Nice to put a face with the name," Leigha said as she stretched out a hand.

I wiped my glove on my pants before shaking. "Good to meet you." My hand fell away, and I couldn't help admiring the stone hanging at her throat. "That's lovely."

She grabbed it. "Lapis lazuli."

"The stone of wisdom," Shay added.

"Exactly." Leigha smiled, and I noticed the blush to her cheeks.

There was definitely a story here, a bond between them, or at least a common interest, and on the car ride home, I'd have a few probing questions about their connection.

"What are you looking for today?" she asked, interrupting my musing.

"A meteorite," Shay replied.

Leigha pointed at her and giggled. "Didn't you just buy a piece?" She stepped out around the counter, and we followed her across the room to a locked display case. "It was a beautiful one if I remember. Antarctica, right?"

I hadn't known the origin of the fragment in my pocket, but somehow knowing it'd been found in that polar desert made it feel more unique.

"Absolutely spot on." Shay smiled.

Their exchange was sweet if not a little odd, but I set that aside as we approached the wall of cabinets.

"This is what we have right now," Leigha said. "A little from all over the globe. Does the location matter?"

I looked at Shay, and she looked at me. Would it matter where it was found?

"Wil?" Shay put the answer in my hands.

"I don't think it's going to make a difference for us. As long as it's available, that's all that matters to me."

"And as long as it's iron and not stone," Shay added.

"How big?" Leigha asked. "Keep in mind that these are sold by weight."

As I looked inside the cabinet, I realized that meteorites weren't cheap, and I wondered if maybe a different material would be a better idea for this damascus steel project.

"Woo, you're not kidding."

Leigha unlocked the cabinet. "That's why we lock it up."

The largest specimen in the case weighed three pounds and had a hefty price tag. "I'd prefer smaller pieces." I held up my fingers, making a circle about the size of a pea.

"We've got fragments down here." She unlocked the drawer at the base of the display. "Most people want a showy piece like Shay bought for you. So we keep the little bits down here." She held the box near her body as I poked around at the contents. "These aren't priced, but they're about ten dollars each."

"I'd need to spread it throughout the container," I thought out loud. If I was going to make a composite weapon, it was important for the meteorite to span the entire billet. "This might sound weird, but do you have anything smaller?"

"What are you thinking?" Shay asked.

But before I could answer, Leigha shoved the box back in the cabinet and removed two clear glass canisters.

"We also have this." She held them up for us to see. "The owner makes all the jewelry in the shop and collects the shavings when she cuts rings with a meteorite. These are forty dollars each."

"Sold!" I said a little louder than necessary.

That made Leigha jump. "Oh, good. You want both?"

"Please." I said, and I understood how Shay could get so excited in this shop.

"Anything else?" Leigha asked.

I shook my head, and Shay answered for the two of us. "That's all we need."

~~~~~~~~~~

"So tell me about Leigha, the rock shop lady?" I said as Shay pulled out of the parking lot.

I was excited about the meteorite shavings in the paper bag on the seat, but I was beyond curious about the flirting taking place during our shopping excursion.

"She's a geologist." Shay kept her eyes on the road, almost too much, as she turned the corner.

"Uh huh. And…"

Her cheeks flushed. "And she's really into rocks. I mean *really* into rocks."

"Uh huh."

"Stop uh huh-ing. There's nothing."

"She's adorable," I said.

Shay finally turned to look at me. "What?"

"I mean, if you're into rocks." I winked.

Shay swatted at my shoulder. "Stop, just stop. She's a very kind person who loves what she does, and that's it."

I smiled at her, solidly confident about my place in her heart, and we rode in silence for a few moments.

Then she said, "I'm scared, Wil." Her hand dropped from the steering wheel and stretched across the seat.

I removed my glove so my skin would touch hers. "Yeah, me, too."
~~~~~~~~~~

CHAPTER XX

PENULTIMATE

"So you're just going to mix it all together?" Dani asked.

She was sitting in the workshop with me, Shay, and Amelia. Tonight I had an audience of three–four, if you counted Dexter–but our fairies were still missing.

"I've already mixed the meteorite and the alicorn powder." I picked up the bowl on the table to show them. "And I've got bits from every billet Benton left us."

"Now the fun starts?" Dani asked.

"Exactly. As long as I can swing Brigid's hammer, we'll have the perfect weapon."

"We get to test it, right?" Dani leaned forward, crossing her forearms on the tabletop.

"Cart before the horse, Forrest. Cart before the horse." Shay patted her shoulder as she walked up with two beers. She handed one to Dani.

"Yeah, yeah. Just tell me we get to test whatever all of that becomes." She fanned her beer hand over the table.

I nodded. "We get to, alright."

~~~~~~~~~~

"This is kinda boring," Dani said as she watched me move the container back into the forge for the thousandth reheat.

"It's a process," Amelia told her, taking a sip from her wife's third beer.

"You know I can get one for you." Shay flicked the bottle in front of her.

Amelia smiled as she took another sip. "Hers is always better." She set it in front of Dani.

"Quality control or some bullshit like that, right, love?" Dani tipped the beer to her lips, leaning farther back than she'd planned to get a taste.

"Absolutely. Can't have you sipping on inferior quality beer."

"Hey, I'll have you know that nothing in this carriage house is inferior quality," Shay protested.

The smile on my face was wide. As ridiculous as they were, they were the family I always wished for.

~~~~~~~~~~

"Now that's exciting!" Dani stood behind me, yelling as I used the angle grinder to cut away what was left of the mangled cuboid container.

"Kinda fun, too!" I yelled back as the cutting wheel broke through the last edge. I hooked the grinder on the wall and, with gloved hands, pried the shrapnel from my demon damascus billet.

"Now what?" Dani asked. It was adorable the way she rocked on her feet with anticipation.

"Back to the forge." I used the tongs to move the billet into the flame.

"More waiting?" Her disappointment was adorable.

Shay patted Dani's shoulder. "Pretty suspenseful, isn't it?"

"How can you stand it?" Dani dropped back in her chair.

"I mean, my lady is kinda hot all decked out in her leather apron with that hat turned around." Shay winked at me.

"Really, Pierce." She waved a hand around the workshop. "In here?"

"I'm almost certain everywhere, Danielle." Amelia patted her wife's chest. "I'm pretty sure you and I covered every surface in that cabin our first year together."

"Yeah, Amelia." I gave her a gloved high five. "You go, girl!"

Dani cleared her throat. "It's getting late." She rotated her wrist to check the time. "Some of us have to work tomorrow."

"About that..." Shay said as she walked her friend to the door. "We need to talk to the chief about the portal."

"I guess that's my signal to go," Amelia said, and I followed them to the door.

"Thanks for coming to the show." I hugged her.

She patted my back before moving away. "Thank you for the invitation. And as much as Danielle jests, she enjoyed it too."

<center>~~~~~~~~~~</center>

"It looks like a taco." Shay's head tilted to the side, confused but curious.

It looked like a taco because it kinda was. To double the amount of meteorite steel, I'd sandwiched it around what would become the striking edges of the weapon I was making. After the fight at the mine and the damage caused by the demon in the unicorn barn, I wanted to arm Shay with a weapon that would also create distance in a fight. I separated enough material to forge a few arrowheads and some pellets for my own Last Resort shotgun shells. I understood now why Benton had them, and if I did it correctly, I could produce three of my own.

"The technique is called san mai, and it's going to make this a demon killer like you've never held before." I placed the billet into the forge and took a minute to draw a quick sketch of the weapon on the face of my anvil. "It's a poleaxe."

"Three weapons in one, nice." She touched the sketch, smudging the soapstone lines. "And you know how much I like axes."

"Yep."

Her arm hung over my hip, drawing me next to her. "And a hammer. Very appropriate."

I nodded.

"But the spear," she whispered in my ear. "I really like that."

My hand flew up to my heart. "I thought you might."

"I approve of your murder taco," she said, stepping back out of my reach.

"Wait, what? Oh, baby, please don't call it that." I shook my head. "Please, I can already hear Stout—" I paused, realizing what I'd said. She looked up at me with sadness in her eyes. "He'll be alright," I promised. "He's a fairy in the fairy realm. They wouldn't hurt him. Would they?"

"I don't know, and part of me wants to send Dexter to find them, but I want to keep the dragon close to home."

Her tone betrayed how conflicted she was. "It's hard to choose, isn't it?" I asked.

"Sometimes, yes," she said, with a small smile. "But never when it comes to you."

~~~~~~~~~~~

"Like a hot taco through butter." Dani stabbed the straw-stuffed dummy again. Whether accidentally or on purpose, Shay had referred to my poleaxe as the "murder taco," and Dani had latched on to the name.

Glowering, I said, "You're a bunch of–"

Shay's hand covered my mouth as she embraced me from behind. "Remember that whole TMOB thing?" she whispered in my ear.

I licked her hand until she pulled it away and reminded her, "We stopped."

"You high-fived each other."

I made a deep voice, joking, "And thus the legend of the murder taco was born."

Dani turned, and using the full momentum of her body, she sliced the dummy in half. "Killed that bitch!"

"If it was only that easy." Shay stepped from behind me and walked to Dani. "Any movement in the mine?" She reached for the poleaxe.

"There's definitely seismic activity. Maybe an earth crevice opening and closing?" Dani said as she picked up the dummy by the shoulders, releasing the stuffing left inside.

Shay laughed, then became serious, taking the poleaxe from Dani. "We have to go back in there again."

"We can't fight your demon in those tunnels. You'll never swing this in there." Dani flicked the spear tip with her finger.

The motion of Shay's body was fluid as she turned, tucked the spear to her shoulder, and launched it through the
~~~~~~~~~~~

workshop and into the axe wall. She buried the murder taco deep into the wood, and the only sound we could hear was the side-to-side sway of the handle teetering in the air.

"Not just for swinging." Shay smiled.

Dani stared, slack jawed, and I felt a powerful sense of pride in my creation. "Hell yeah!" I pumped a fist.

Dani cleared her throat. "That'll work just fine." She walked across the shop, and with the full force of her shoulders and one foot against the axe wall, she removed the poleaxe. She looked like a feral warrior as the butt of the handle tapped the floor. "Now what?"

Shay picked up the Rasavatam from the table. "Now we free our fairies and we find our doppelgänger."

~~~~~~~~~~

Shay stood at the foot of the bed, rolling t-shirts to fit into our backpack. The weapons test in the workshop fueled her need to retrieve Stout and, if she desired to return to our realm, Clia. I was behind this new mission mostly because I wanted to get the hell away from the inevitable confrontation with evil.

I yearned for a life with Shay, a life free from the chaos of the last year, but as she turned the emptied backpack over the trash can, spilling rocks and rubble into the receptacle, she reminded me that the Magick and the Maker of Bannock almost always had a bumpy happily ever after.

"Maybe I should sprinkle some extra demon sift in the bottom," she joked.

"Maybe you should zag instead of zig, and you wouldn't need the sift."

She chuckled. "I'll keep that in mind."

"Are you sure you're strong enough to go after Stout?" I reached for her hand, hoping to still it.
~~~~~~~~~~

If there was one thing to know about Shay, it was that when she was frightened, she kept busy. The unknown also frustrated her, and since the day Benton had handed over the demon steel, we'd been spiraling through an endless cycle of unknowns.

"I'm steady." She pulled her hand away and held it out in front of us. She was cool as could be, but that was her greatest trait.

"What about in here?" I pressed my palm over her heart. Through the entire exchange, she'd avoided my eyes, but when she looked at me now, I saw the words she didn't want to say etched in the lines around her eyes.

"I need to find him." She covered my hand. "He's our family."

~~~~~~~~~~

"Do you think it makes him want to puke?" I asked, looking over at Dexter.

I rested my head between my knees as I tried to get my own nausea in check. To preserve energy, Dexter had shifted us from the carriage house to the portal at Grant's Pass. I loved the idea, in theory, but each trip seemed to increase my motion sickness.

"Stout said Dex didn't like shifting, but he seems to be getting better at taking us exactly where we want to go." She handed me a peppermint.

"Thanks, honey." The plastic wrap crinkled as I opened it. "Yum, nothing like associating a wonderful flavor with the fight to keep down bile."

She planted the poleaxe handle in the ground as she squatted beside me. "Do you need more rest, or can we move through the portal?"
~~~~~~~~~~

"I can move," I assured her. "Passing through feels good. But I'll need a little break before we shift to the fairy realm portal."

Shay nodded. "I was planning to talk with Helms. I think we need to know what's going on in the fairy realm before we move forward."

"Magick of Bannock, we receive you well!" The sound of Helms' voice startled Shay and me.

"Helms of Passofgrant, thank you," Shay said.

She held her arm to his, and their forearm shake warmed my heart. He eyed the poleaxe with an appreciative smile.

"Maker of Bannock, we receive you, but it appears you are not so well." He was in human-sized form as he walked closer to me.

"Helms of—" I covered my mouth to hold back the nausea.

"She is ailing?" He looked over his shoulder at Shay.

"Just sick from the trip here."

"We shall stop at the blamberry patch."

I thought about the odd fruit that grew here in the land of giants, the one that'd tricked our fairy into believing he was drinking beer, and wondered if a magick berry could remove this queasiness.

"It'll help?"

Shay lowered her hand to help me to my feet. "Can it hurt?"

"Well, yeah, I don't want to puke while I'm dodging fairies, but I also don't want to be high when I do it."

"Good point." Shay handed me another piece of peppermint.

"Right, I'm ready to move." I pushed myself up to my feet.

"Helms, how is it in the realm?" Shay asked.

"It is wonderful to have my love back with me. He is learning how our world has changed, but their freedom came at a cost." As we walked toward the portal his body morphed from human-sized to the giant form we expected.

She gave him a concerned look. "What's happened?"

Helms waved a hand to command the portal to activate. The spiraling debris' glow was still beyond belief. "You will soon see," he said as he waved us forward.

There was a bond between us, born of trust and magick, and it felt wonderful to pass into the realm of giants. The tickle on my skin soothed much of the disorientation from Dexter's shifting travels.

Dexter's barking brought me back to reality as my body adjusted to the realm.

"What's happening?" I asked as I tried to sort out the circumstances in front of me. The dog, morphed to dragon, was making noise, scratching and clawing at the dirt where two fairies were drawing something animatedly.

It was a relief to see Clia, but Stout was nowhere to be seen.

Shay dropped to the ground beside Dex. "Clia, are you alright?"

Clia no longer wore the shabby garments Andrea had locked her away in. Her once green skin was now a glowing yellow, and I thought it might be from her time with the fairies.

"You should not have returned." Clia stepped back. "It will come for the Magick of Bannock."

Shay shook her head, clearly confused.

"What is happening?" I asked again.

Shay was distracted by the drawings in the dirt and the fairy trembling behind Clia. "Where is Stout?"

"It's taken him." She flew close to Shay's face, whispering, "Freeing the fairies angered the great evil, and that act, which is on your hands, must be avenged.

Something came for us. It looked like you, and it acted like you, but Stout knew it was not you."

"The evil has come to the realm?" Shay looked up at Helms. "How can this be if you keep the portal?"

"There are countless ways to move through the realms," he said. "This is but—"

Clia interrupted. "Evil has been waiting, feasting on the alicorns, watching for the mantle to pass and for Brigid's power to awaken. The goddess split Evil in two, and all it wants is to make those parts whole again."

"Because of me," Shay whispered.

Clia was quick to reply. "It is because of evil, which you are not, and it knows that." She settled on Shay's hand, which rested on the poleaxe. "Your powers, the Magick and Maker abilities in their purest form, is what every realm needs to push back and lock the monster away."

"Where did it take him?" I asked, but Shay was already standing, shuffling her feet across the scrawling in the dirt.

"It's in the Earth realm." Shay pounded the butt of the poleaxe to the ground.

Both Helms and Clia agreed. Dexter remained in dragon form, which set me on edge. He only did that on his own when there was a threat. His taloned feet made it clear that there was no safe place for us right now.

"We're going back to Bannock?" I asked, but I knew the answer, and I also knew where we'd end up.

"It's there," Shay said decisively, "and if it has Stout, I'm going to get him back."

CHAPTER XXI

DÉJÀ VU

"I've got one in my hand and twelve in the quiver." Amelia laid the demon bow on the table in the workshop.

I poured out the damascus arrow tips I'd held cupped in my hands, in front of her. "Put these on."

Amelia studied the barbed broadhead tips. "Looks like a flying bird." Her finger tapped against the barb. "In any other circumstance, I'd say these are overkill, but I guess that's what we're going for."

"Great penetrating wound in," I said, "and ferocious gore coming out." Amelia stared at me, knowing, remembering the fight at the mine, the place we were gearing up to return to. "It's only going to rip it out once." She rotated the arrow tip onto the shaft and ran her hand across the fletching before sliding it into her quiver. "I'm going to shoot every single one of these into that thing."

"We don't even know what it looks like." Dani said, cradling the shotgun shells, trying to guess their weight from the load of damascus buckshot.

"Wherever Stout is, that's where we'll find it," Shay said.

She ran the poleaxe head across the foot pedal honing wheel. The act was positively primeval, and if we weren't in crisis mode, I'd have given her a few more weapons to sharpen.

"And what's the plan?" Dani put the shells in the buttstock holder. The elastic band wrapped around the gun stock held six standard issue shells on the outside and the magickal three on the inside.

"Go in, get our guy, mess up the ultimate evil, and get out." Shay's foot stopped pumping the pedal. "Murder taco gets the bad guy," she whispered, flicking her thumb against the blade for a sharpness test.

"Murder taco and three hits from these." Dani patted the gun stock. "Sure wish my ammunition specialist was here to help."

She frowned when the realization hit: Stout was her specialist. He'd delivered the Last Resort shells that'd stopped Andrea from manifesting as a demon. We didn't even know if our fairy was still alive.

My arm hitched around Shay's duty belt. "We'll get him back." I kissed her cheek.

"If we don't," Shay said, "that thing is going down in a thousand different ways."

"From the way you described it, I only want to get close enough to kill it once," Amelia said as she laid the full quiver on the table.

"We're going to take it down like we took down Andrea," Shay vowed. She sheathed the poleaxe and laid it beside the rest of our gear. "But this time we'll have Dex." She looked over her shoulder at the circle on the floor in the workshop, only to see it empty. "Dexter!" Shay called him but he did not appear. "Where the hell is he?" Shay walked up to the apartment, calling him again, but this time with a K-9 service command. "Dexter, *reditus*!"

When he didn't appear, Dani, Amelia, and I stared at one another, not knowing what to do.

"When did you see him last?" Amelia asked.

"He was curled up when we got here. I gave him a belly rub." Dani walked around the shop and stopped in the circle. "Clia was buzzing around, and that's the last…" She trailed off, worry heavy on her face.

I'd have thought Shay had wings the way she descended the stairs. "He's not up there," Shay said, panic in her voice.

"He's gone, but so is Clia," Dani said.

"You don't think they shifted to–"

"No," Dani interrupted. "They wouldn't do something so stupid. Especially without telling us first."

Shay circled the room, her hand stretched at her side, chanting words I'd never heard before. "What are you doing, Shay?"

"I'm tracking that fur-ball."

At first, I thought it was a spell or a Tome of Trouble incantation, but then I realized she was whispering the longitude and latitude numbers where Dexter and Clia most likely were.

"We sure they aren't drinking beer in the bar?" I asked hopefully.

Shay typed numbers into her phone. "Damn it!" She held the screen, and although it wasn't a satellite image, I knew what that gold and green patch represented.

"They're at the mine," Dani said.

The brightness of Shay's phone screen reflected in her eyes. Dexter was our boy, and without us even knowing, he'd gone off on his own to find his best friend.

"What the hell was he thinking?" Shay grabbed the satchel and the poleaxe. "Without him, we have to drive, and any*thing* around the mine will hear us coming from miles away."

Dani followed Shay to the door, her shotgun in hand. "We'll roll in slow. Walk the last half mile. It'll be good, Pierce."

The tone was there, like a light switch kicking on in the dark. I loved watching them use cop-to-cop communication with all those intuitive glances and hand signals. They were best at this part, at being the superheroes we needed.

"Maybe he'll sense us when we're closer." Shay opened the carriage house door and stopped cold when the flash of bright orange met her. For a moment her palm pressed against it, then she moved on.

"You take the lead." Dani's trunk was already open, and before she could secure her shotgun, Amelia had the takedown bow cradled inside.

"Good."

It was the last word spoken between them until we arrived at the gravel drive leading to the abandoned mine. Shay and Dani had been here many times since the attack by Andrea Peters. I, like Amelia, never wanted to return.

But here we were, once again, headed directly into the fires of hell.

"Talk to me, Shay," I said. "You're too quiet."

"Just running through scenarios." Her voice was soft, just above a whisper.

I turned to look at her, my hand resting on her forearm. "I'm stronger than I was last time."

"It's not your abilities I'm worried about." Shay's fingers steepled into mine, and the power that passed between us was better than any energy drink ever invented. "The last time we tangled with one of these, it nearly killed me. For the first time in as long as I can remember, I'm worried about *my* magick."

I turned to look at her as she put the car into park. "You're clad in Maker armor from your chest to your belly." I plucked at the velcro on her shoulder. "You have the gauntlet. Use it even if every one of us is left in the dirt." She tried to speak, but I held a finger to her lips. "We will be at your side, armed like never before, because I'm better than I was before."

"You are the Maker of Bannock and impressively so." She kissed me and rested her forehead against mine.

"Bet your ass, TMOB," I joked, and although she wanted to fight the nickname, it reminded both of us about Stout and about what we were here to do.

"I should have punched the two of you for that when I had the chance."

I gasped. "And ruin your superhero reputation?"

"Would've been worth it." She turned away and secured the keys in the lockbox under her seat. "You ready to go in?" The look in her eyes transformed from lover to cop, and I knew her answer to the question.

"As ready as I'll ever be." I opened the door and tucked the axe into the holster on my back, then threw my cutoff gloves on the seat, rolled my fingers around the handle of the hammer of Brigid, and fixed my eyes on Shay.

The absence of our dragon and the fairy he called friend was like a huge dark void as we stood with Amelia and Dani.

"Same plan as last time but no death, magickal or otherwise, unless it's Shay's doppelgänger," Dani said as she racked three rounds into the shotgun. "That thing doesn't make it out alive."

The butt of the poleaxe dug into the ground as Shay stood ready. "I'll take point. We're going in silent. Wil, get in my head."

Dani snickered, and Amelia smacked her shoulder. With a finger to her lips she silenced her wife. Amelia nocked a demon broadhead arrow, preparing to fire, and the four of us advanced into the mine.

"*Ish fa lia dua,*" Shay whispered, and a bubble of silence swallowed us. "Just doubling our chances to sneak in." The rest of us gave her a thumbs up.

The ground beneath our feet carried an echo we'd hoped to prevent. Step by step we inched through the darkness, trekking into the tunnels Shay and Dani cleared of demon embryos months ago.

"*No sign of Dexter,*" Shay thought to me.

"*He'll be here,*" I thought back to her, but part of me worried what we might discover when we found him.

Dani gestured to Shay, and we turned down a tunnel with repetitive switchbacks. It wasn't just dizzying, it also triggered memories of Andrea, of the wound to my shoulder, of Stout's wings being ripped off and Dexter's near demise. I stumbled to the ground, gasping, beads of sweat dripping from my forehead. The struggle for air overshadowed everything else at the moment. I felt the piercing of my flesh and heard the screams of Stout's agony. But that last one was more than a memory.

It was Stout, screaming somewhere nearby.

"*Wil?*" Shay's knees crunched in the dirt as she knelt beside me.

She was in my head, and although I loved her deeply, her voice created confusion and disorientation.

"Stop," I said out loud, and everyone froze where they stood.

"What's going on?" Shay asked.

I put my finger to my lips, shushing her. Like a banging gong, we heard voices echoing in the absolute silence.

"Stout?" Shay whispered.

"But where?" Dani asked. "I don't hear him."

Shay nodded, knowing that somehow our fairy was communicating without sound. The four of us moved toward each other, closing the gaps between us. As our bubble of protection tightened, the echo of Stout's voice became clearer.

Shay waved her hand toward the split in the tunnel, and Dani asked, "Separate or stay together?"

"Together," Amelia and I said at the same time, and the four of us moved down the path on the right.

It was the wrong move, and I knew it the second we stepped through the darkness. The puddle at our feet wasn't water but resin–thick and black with a stench that knocked us to the ground. The puddle was a living force, an extension of the evil growing more powerful in this mine. I knew where they were. I knew deep in my heart that the only place to unite the evil living in my hammer with the evil creeping in this mountain was the cavern of my goddess. Every scrolled etch on my hammer illuminated, glowing brighter the closer we got.

"I know where to go, but whatever you do, don't stop moving," I told them.

Before they could respond, I charged through the resin, letting it cling to my shoes and pants but never stopping for a second because I knew what would happen if I did.

"Is this alive?" Amelia asked.

"Your leg," Dani said, pulling her along as she kept walking. "The resin isn't attacking your prosthetic."

"It knows; it's collecting life force," Shay explained.

"For what?" Dani asked, all the while hurrying through what I guessed would be the first trap of many.

"'If you know the enemy and know yourself, you need not fear the result of a hundred battles,'" Shay recited.

"'If you know yourself but not the enemy, for every victory gained, you will also suffer a defeat,'" Dani finished.

"One fish, two fish, red fish, blue fish?" I said, and the three of them laughed.

Shay smiled. "Not quite, baby. But I get what you did there."

"It's Sun Tsu," Amelia explained. "From *The Art of War*."

Shay stopped walking once we made it through the resin, and we attempted to remove the material clinging to us.

"Recon resin," I joked. "Nifty. So our enemy knows a little more about us?"

"Exactly."

Shay started to lead us off again, but I put my hand on her shoulder to stop her. It was impossible to ignore the magick inside of me rising in harmony with the power inside the hammer.

"They're this way." I jerked my head in the direction the energies pulled me.

"By the looks of that," Shay said, pointing at the full glowing hammer head, "the goddess is here, too."

The others let me take the lead. It was more empowering than I'd imagined, walking through the dark with three extraordinary, capable women behind me. Twelve months ago, I would've balked at the idea, would've deferred to Shay, but here I was now, leading us into the unknown.

Shay reached for my shoulder. "Something is ahead of us."

"Something? Or some*thing*?"

I felt it then, the force of air cooling off like a burst of heat just before opening a door to the winter cold.

"Everyone up against the wall!" Shay ordered, and the barrier moved with us.

The hammer of the goddess rested on my hip, lit up like a holiday parade. I heard the butt of the poleaxe knock the tunnel stones. Amelia set her body, bow drawn to her cheek, poised to strike whatever came into view.

Dani saw it first, and her hand pushed the bow toward the ground. It was a fairy–Clia, to be exact. Or, at least, it *looked* like Clia. It bounced against the barrier protecting us, and for a moment, I wasn't certain if it was a fairy at all.

"This way," it said.

Shay shook her head and mouthed the words, *"Not Clia."*

My heart raced, and my hands trembled as realization struck. If I swung the hammer at this creature, I could kill the great evil threatening the realms, and we could go home, but would we ever find Clia, Dexter, or Stout? Our doppelgänger was here, leading us toward whatever they had in store for us.

"Are we actually going to follow this?" I thought at Shay.

"Yes."

It was the only word she said as she tipped the poleaxe toward the fairy, and we crept deeper into darkness. Shay waved at Dani to get on her left, and we all walked shoulder to shoulder.

I heard the screaming before we saw him, instinctively I knew what was happening. Stout was hooked to the slatted boards blocking the entrance to the tunnel. This was the path to Brigid's cave, and all the powers of the Magick and the Maker prevented entry.

"Stout!" Shay yelled, and the bubble around us fell away as the poleaxe raised, a shotgun racked, fletching touched a cheek, and I arched my hammer to strike.

"Go," Stout rasped. "Tear it down before it kills us all."

My hands touched his fragile wings, torn and tangled, pierced in place by demon barbs. "Are they poisonous?" I asked him as I released the final barb tacking him in place.

His body fell into my palm, and I turned just as the poleaxe flamed to pierce the framework.

"Sift," was all he could say and then Amelia was there, holding her flask of demon anvil dust out to me.

"This is going to hurt." I pinched a small amount to sprinkle on his wounds, knowing that more was better on my lover but not understanding how much might cause our fairy to go into shock. I was less familiar with what the healing energies would do to him.

"Just do–"

His body writhed against my palm, and without me calling it, my sigil flame burst around him. The goddess moved through me into Stout, and the pain struck him unconscious.

"*Ignis*," I heard Shay say, and the walls illuminated. It was not a fire of smoke and flame but of love and light, and anything evil in our presence was blown away.

"What do I do?" I asked as Amelia took the fallen fairy from me.

"I'll put him here." She tucked his body into the hood of Dani's coat. It was the best we could think of as we heard the howl of Shay's K-9 partner.

"Dexter," Shay said through clenched teeth. "It has Dex."

"Hold back, Pierce." Dani grabbed her shoulder. "We stay together."

I could feel her energies bubbling over to join with mine, and my breath hitched. "Slow down, Shay."

"I can't let it happen again," Shay insisted.

We moved forward, breaching the barrier constructed to prevent what we'd just done in the name of saving our dragon. I knew exactly where we were as the thick resin faded and the jagged edges of crystals appeared. The evil hidden for so many years would fight the goddess now, but she was on our side. The chamber, usually gorgeous to my eyes, was not like before. Gone were the glistening gemstones, and in their place were shadowed hues of black and gray.

"What's happened here?" I asked. Shay's hand rested on the wall, which was lifeless and void of Brigid's magick. "Where is the goddess?"

I heard the howls of pain echoing in the chamber ahead. Shay didn't pause; she just fit her way through the crevasse, and we followed. There was nothing but the spiraling void of a portal to an unknown realm.

"That wasn't here before, I swear." I stepped closer, palm flat to reach inside.

"Stop!" Shay and Dani yelled at the same time.

"Holy hell!" My hand hit my chest as I felt the rush of adrenalin. "I wasn't going in. I was just feeling the energies."

"Whatever it is, Dex is through there," Shay said.

"And so is the evil that took him," Dani added.

I leaned against the crystal wall, drawing energies from Brigid's cave. "He's taken her, and we need to go through."

Shay's hand played over mine. "The goddess is speaking to you?"

I nodded. "She's in danger."

Shay looked over her shoulder at Dani and Amelia. "I'm sorry we have to leave you here."

"Leave us?" Dani gripped Shay's forearm. "Together, remember."

"The fairies blocked your–"

Amelia interrupted. "The giants of Grant's Pass gave us the right to move through."

"They did?" Shay and I asked at the same time, the revelation strengthening our resolve.

"It's a long story," Amelia explained, "but Helms and Belos had a *lot* to do with it."

Shay wasn't waiting any longer, and the look that passed between her and Dani was full of understanding. They both knew what was to come.

"We go through in pairs," Shay said. "First Wildwood and me, then Dani and Amelia. Wait for a ten count and then you come ready to fire. When you hit, it's like jumping out of a moving car. Roll with it."

Amelia's chuckle reset the mood. "It's been a minute since I've rolled with anything, but we've got you."

In the heat of the moment, I saw the power behind us, two strong, willing warriors ready to give everything for the unknown ahead.

"On three, Wil." She squeezed my hand, which was resting on her shoulder. "Ten, D."

Silence followed. Dani raised a thumb as Shay and I stepped through the spiraling debris.

As we hit the ground on the other side, I thought about how perfect a description "spiraling debris" really was. This wreck of a portal wasn't the pleasant tickle we'd experienced in the past, and the sting of evil magicks worked to prevent our movement through. I lost my grip on Shay's shoulder as we landed, and three things were clear: Dexter lay tethered to the ground, Evil was here, and the goddess in corporeal form was the most heart stopping beauty I'd ever seen. My eyes could barely take all of her in, even with the monster pinning her to the ground by her throat.

"*By the throat?*" I thought, and without hesitation, I advanced toward the fight. With the full force of my body, I tucked my shoulder and tackled the monster. No one was more surprised than me when the two of us crashed against the boulder.

I scrambled to my feet, and within seconds, I had surveyed my surroundings. This was the field from our dreams. I spotted the tall grass and the shadowed rocks and boulders, remembering them vividly. This evil force had brought us here to a place we'd only known in nightmares.

"Wildwood!" Amelia's call snapped me into the fight as the force of a spired hand met the power of my wrist cuff.

Silence followed as I flew backward, the evil blasting in the opposite direction, landing in the tall grass. The hammer of the goddess remained in my clenched hand, and I felt her energies move from the ground up through my body.

"Get down, Wildwood!" Dani called, and I heard the discharge of her shotgun, saw the monster stumble before regaining a foothold.

"Stupid earth-realmers," the evil growled. "That witch gave you the hammer of a goddess, and yet you come at me with powder weapons? I'll take her power, and then I'll strip you of yours."

I turned to look for Shay and saw her trying to free Dexter. He was in his K-9 form, anchored to the soil by the same chains that bound the unicorns. They were pinning him so tightly that all he could do was whimper.

The goddess stumbled to her feet, staggering with her hand at her throat, unable to speak. I double fisted the hammer, extending the blade enchanted by the being I called my goddess. The flash of orange flame shot through the hammer's head, and I ran full force to attack the monster who threatened us all.

The realization that I am not a sword fighter dawned on me as the monster deflected the blow. "Foolish Maker." It waved off my magick. "I am it, and it is me." The backside of the hammer's head illuminated the pixel image, portraying the face of the monster before me.

"*You cannot strike him down with our hammer.*" Brigid's voice entered my head, and the emotional impact of that tangled with the vibrations of her majesty. It was more than I could bear.

I heard my name as the flash of a spire struck my forearm, knocking me backward and making me release my grip on the goddess' blade. As soon as it was gone from my hand, I felt the absence of magick and scrambled closer to Brigid.

Shay and Amelia struggled with the chains binding Dexter while Dani pumped another round from her shotgun.

We needed our dragon; clearly he was essential to defeating this monster or else he wouldn't be imprisoned right now.

"Maker of Bannock, sister to my soul, we shall fight him as one," Brigid called to me.

I didn't know what she meant, but I watched as the monster took hold of my hammer, his eyes flashing with the darkest cruelty I'd ever seen.

Everything happening around me moved in slow motion. Shay drew the alicorn blade, forcing it into the links of Dexter's chains one by one until they snapped free. Amelia dropped her quiver to her hip, taking position to loose her arrows. Dani's stance behind Shay shifted from defensive to offensive just in time to confront the handful of demons who looked identical to Andrea's form. Evil had minions, and the assault divided our attention.

"The realm of Balthork will be all." His screech blew wild across the trim of the tall grass. "Brigid, you bring me humans with mortal weapons?"

She did not speak.

"Have I stolen your voice?" He laughed. "I am keeper of the Maker of Bannock, and nothing forged with earthen wares will stop me." He slammed the hammer to the ground, splitting it open wide, releasing more of his monsters to attack Shay. "Now I will keep the Magick of Bannock, too!"

"NO!" I screamed.

Amelia launched the broadhead arrows one by one, popping the demon minions like rubber balloons, stopping their advance. She only had twelve damascus arrowheads, and I knew Shay needed to get in this fight.

"Not possible." Balthork said as he watched our archer take out the attackers one by one. "Not possible."

"You underestimate my children." Brigid's voice was gruff as she choked out the words. "No one keeps the Magick and the Maker."

I saw it in slow motion, the flash of steel moving through the air. Shay's full force lifted from the ground, throwing all of her body into swinging the poleaxe toward Balthork. His arm came up, blocking the weapon just below the damascus head. The power of Shay's vest threw her into Dani, knocking them to the grass. I saw the German Shepherd body feather from fur to scales as his growl became a roar of flames.

Balthork laughed. His hand waved at the dragon as he teased him with embryo pustules. "This is how you tame a dragon," he joked, watching Dexter lick at the growing pile. "Like my own." He hammered the ground again, releasing more demons at Amelia.

She only had twelve arrows...or so I thought. As I watched, the fletched shafts drifted up from the ground, floating in space until they dropped into her quiver once more. Clia's tiny wings glistened in the sunlight as she sped to retrieve every arrow after it had hit its mark.

The poleaxe lay at my feet. Balthork stared at the weapon, laughing at my Maker's mark on its cheek. "Your Maker has a pretty little axe, Brigid," he taunted.

"Ego sum lux, quad es lux, sums lux."

Brigid chanted the words over and over as she stepped behind me. Her hands fell to my shoulders, and energy pierced through me, surrounding me until I was her and she was me. Power, magicks like I've never experienced before, touched the tips of my fingers as the sigil of my hand arced with unyielding fire.

Brigid moved my body as if it were her own, effortlessly, like the warrior I wasn't. She kicked the poleaxe into our united hands, and never in my life had I ever turned a weapon so fluidly. Balthork wasn't laughing now as he charged forward.

Amelia's arrow struck his calf as Dani's damascus buckshot scattered across his back. The look of horror on his face filled me with renewed hope. His spire arm stabbed at me, while his hammer hand swung toward my face. With a hip twist, the axe head sliced through the spire, and on the backswing, the spear's tip penetrated his wrist, the axe head catching the flex of his forearm. The deadly dance knocked the goddess' hammer to the ground.

Brigid moved my body one full step back, dragging Balthork off balance. My shoulders rotated, my forearms flexed, and the spear head penetrated his skull. He howled in agony as the axe and spearhead sliced him down the center. I felt it all, the invigoration of victory, the energy of the goddess, and the realization that this fight was coming to an end. As quickly as she'd merged with me, she was gone, and I felt her absence like losing a part of myself.

I fell to my knees, gasping and trying to balance out the magick lingering through me. I looked up, desperate to know who had survived.

Dani stood beside Amelia, frozen in awe, jaws open wide, staring at me. An arrow fell to the ground, breaking the sudden silence in the valley, echoing off the soil.

It was Shay, kneeling beside the drunken dragon, who spoke first. "By the goddess."

"Of the goddess." Brigid's whisper fell across the open field.

A buzzing echoed behind me. "What did you do?" I heard Stout's voice before I saw him. "What did you do?" I wanted to grab hold of our fairy and hug his tiny body, but he was down on the ground spitting fairy magic all over the corpse. "You did it."

My eyes scanned the people in front of me. Shay and Stout, Amelia and Dani, and when my magick pulsed for each of them, fear turned to relief, and the world faded to black.

~~~~~~~~~~~
~~~~~~~~~~~

"I've got her. Let him take you to the carriage house." Shay was ordering someone, but all I wanted to hear was the sweet words confirming that we'd won.

"You can't take her like that." Dani. It was Dani fighting with Shay.

"I'll stay until she's awake." Her arms tightened, and I could hear the rhythm of her heart, quickened by her obvious concern for me.

"It could be hours," Dani argued.

As much as I wanted to speak, I wasn't ready to let go of the peace I'd found in this lingering unconsciousness.

"We'll be safe."

I heard the ruffle of animal paws on gravel.

"Don't wait longer than necessary."

Our bodies shook, and seconds later, the world fell silent. Shay rocked us, and the sway of our bodies was the most peace and comfort I'd felt since our first encounter in the carriage house.

"You are my world, Wil. Please wake up."

Her chin arched over my head, a tight connection drawing me to her breast. But I was tired, and I only wanted her to hold me. I wanted to live happily ever after. I raised my hand to cup her neck.

"Wil?" Her arms relaxed as I looked up to see her face.

"Hi." My voice scratched.

"Oh, love."

I climbed into her arms, fully encircled by her body, never wanting to let her go. "Did we do it?"

"Yeah, baby. We did it." I felt Dexter crawl up beside me until his nose rested on my hip.

"We should finish up here."

My arms tightened around her torso. "I don't want to move."

Shay laughed. "I know how you feel."

I didn't know how long we laid there, rocking back and forth in the dirt. We held one another, silently celebrating our victory over what had felt like an impossible foe. Then Shay's stomach rumbled.

"Hungry, superhero?" I pushed to sit up.

"I am so many things right now." She paused for a moment and said, "I think *you* earned superhero status today."

"Yeah?"

"Oh, very much so." She got up and helped me to my feet. I felt unsteady and was glad for her arm encircling my waist. "I don't think I've ever seen magick like what happened here today."

"The goddess was inside of me," I whispered, hesitant to say the words out loud.

Her thumb hooked my belt loop. "It was gorgeous. *You* were gorgeous and breathtaking. And I think you might have fulfilled a few fantasies."

"Really?" I didn't try to hide the smile.

"I'll give you all the details later."

Dexter's body rubbed against my hip, and before I could kiss Shay, I was in Brigid's cave. Dexter left me there to bring Shay, too, and we stayed long enough to ask for a blessing before shifting to the cars.

"Dani and Amelia aren't here?"

"You've been out for a while, love. They're waiting for us at the carriage house."

"Oh." My head was fuzzy.

"We won, baby." She kissed me. "We really won."

CHAPTER XXII

EPILOGUE

"It's not possible." I stared at the cards on the table, counting once more in my head. "I can't believe I did it!" The proclamation was louder this time, and it got the attention of Dani and Shay standing at the table, checking targets and loading ammunition magazines.

I looked into Amelia's eyes, deep wrinkles appearing around the edges. Time and happiness had left traces of a life well lived.

"You really did." Her voice was firm, as it had been the first time I met her over twenty-five years before.

She held the cards in her aged hands, steady, ready for whatever the universe would bring. Her aim was still true with a bow, and that kept competition alive in her heart. She wore contentment as a cloak of joy.

"What, did you finally cave and let her win?" Dani's body was much the same after twenty-five years, strong and not quite as agile, but she was still Shay's right hand, even after retirement.

"My lady doesn't need charity," Shay bragged.

She jogged toward the porch of the old cabin, her form hardly changed in all our years together. The power of Brigid and the mantle she carried as the Magick of Bannock made her more lithe than ever. I shared that same agelessness and wondered if she saw me the same way I saw her. Twenty-five years had gone by like pages in the wind.

"The two of them have probably played this game a thousand times, and not once did Wildwood win." Dani climbed the stairs and took the seat beside her wife. The markers on the cribbage board told an interesting tale. "One peg? You only–"

"A win is a win!" I interrupted before Dani could harsh my vibe.

"Oh, don't spoil it for her." Amelia touched Dani's cheek before giving her a kiss. "After twenty-five years, I think she's earned it."

~~~~~~~~~~~

"You know, that game felt like something else."

I stood at the edge of the river, watching Shay's muscled arms tip back and forth as her fly rod swished through the air. Tasks as mundane as fishing were the norm for us as we continued sharing life as the Magick and the Maker of Bannock.

"Dani was adorable, defending Amelia like you'd tossed her to the ground." When I didn't answer, Shay turned to look at me. "What?"

I was feeling on top of the world with my little victory, and fishing and camping were great fun, but once in a while it was good to visit someplace new. "You feel like making a little mischief?"
~~~~~~~~~~~

The question came often since we'd conquered Balthork and I'd merged with the goddess. Call-outs for The Magick and The Maker of Bannock came in from realms I once thought impossible, and today was no different.

"I love making mischief with you." She stripped her line, casting out one more time so she could reel it in. "Is that even a real question?" She giggled.

"I was thinking it's been weeks since Dexter got to visit his bestie." The giants of Passofgrant had adopted our dragon, spending year after year trying to coach him to fly. When he shifted from one location to another faster than their wings could carry, they surrendered to conversion, and Dexter encouraged their shifting instead.

Shay removed the reel from her fly rod and disassembled it into the storage case. "Visit the giants?"

Dexter's head popped out of the water, a fish hanging from his mouth. "I think he heard you," I joked as the splashing destroyed any chance of catching fish.

"His vote is a yes." Shay reached to pick up the fish. "Right after we eat."

The fire crackled and popped from the embers as the pan rested over the heat. The small covered side pot confused me. "What's in there?" I asked, reaching to open the lid.

"It's a surprise." Her eyes shone with more joy than any human should hold. When she looked at me, it was like going back in time to that grassy field outside of our foster home. It was true that love could be like this, that it could grow and endure and be that safest place.

But it could also be mischievous, and Shay was very good at that, too.

"No." It was a twenty-five-year-old game, this noodle and meat special.

"Come on, baby."

I was determined to die on this hill. "Every time we go camping, you try to feed me that mush."

"And every time you say no."

I summoned the flame of my sigil hand to balance the heat of the fire as I lifted the lid. "That has—" I pinched my nose. "–not one time ever—" My gag reflex was hard to fight. "–smelled good enough to eat." I dropped the lid on the rock beside me and turned away.

Shay stepped in with a long-handled camping fork. "It's delicious." Every time I refused, she took an enormous bite, then made a face that looked like she'd just tasted the worst thing she'd ever eaten.

"Baby, that is *not* the face of someone eating something delicious."

She poked the fork toward me. "And you would know this, how? You've never tried."

I looked her up and down, my eyes stopping obviously on her torso as they traveled to meet her smile. "I know delicious when I taste it."

"Do you now?"

I scooped her into my arms. "Yes, I really do." I took the fork from her hands, dropping it on the pot lid just before kicking the mess of noodles and meat into the fire pit.

Her lips were close to mine as she whispered. "Did you just kick that pot?"

"I may have."

Her laugh trembled our bodies as she kissed me. "One day, Wildwood Blackstone, I'm going to get you to try it."

"Do what you must, but it's definitely not going to be today." I arched my back, circling us around to face the river.

I turned in her arms until she was standing behind me, her chin resting on my shoulder as she said, "Can you believe it's been twenty-five years, love?"

"It feels like only yesterday."

I held my sigil hand out, the flame bursting with thoughts of the past. There was no longer a gap in confidence with my use of magick. The moment the goddess moved into me, all doubt had faded, and I knew what was real and true about my maker powers.

"How about another fifty years?" Shay whispered into my ear.

"I'll take a thousand if I get to spend every day of it with you."

"Every day, plus one." She kissed my cheek.

"I kinda like that, superhero." My lips touched hers.

"Mmm, yeah. I kinda like that too."

Thank you for reading book Four of the Maker Series, the continuing story of Wildwood Blackstone, a lady blacksmith who finds adventure, demons, magick and love in the small ghost town of Bannock.

<u>The Maker Series</u>
MARK OF THE MAKER
(BOOK 1 OF THE MAKER SERIES)

Wildwood Blackstone believed her dream of being a country blacksmith was coming true. When the town of Bannock hires her to restore their abandoned carriage house built in the 1800s, she can't wait to begin.

But there are more than ghosts in Bannock and shortly after her arrival, she discovers this truth. When a childhood friend answers a call for help, Wildwood finds a part of her past that she longed to rediscover. Together they reveal Bannock's secret and uncover the Mark of the Maker.

THE MAGICK AND THE MAKER
(BOOK 2 OF THE MAKER SERIES)

Wildwood Blackstone longed for a life as a small-town blacksmith. She didn't imagine monsters or magick, and she never expected to fall in love with Shay.

Book two of the Maker Series finds the two women tangled together in the dark secrets buried deep in Bannock's small-town history. Is their commitment strong enough to carry them through? Who is the keeper of the Magick? When will Wildwood and Shay uncover the mystery behind the Mark of the Maker?

ORIGIN OF THE MAKER
(BOOK 3 OF THE MAKER SERIES)

Wildwood and her girlfriend Shay have uncovered Brigid's secret hidden deep in the earth.

Who is the stranger in the carriage house? How are they there? What do they know about the secret and the power it holds? Can Wildwood and Shay find the answers and keep fighting the monsters hunting them night and day?

LEGACY OF THE MAKER
(BOOK 4 OF THE MAKER SERIES)

In a secret world filled with magick, Wildwood Blackstone has encountered unbelievable mysteries. As the blacksmith in her new hometown, she's survived and endured the call to wield the hammer of the goddess Brigid, but to what end?

Celebrating a year with her girlfriend, Shay, the two continue their search for answers. What lived inside Andrea Peters? How did the entity survive for hundreds of years? Who controlled her all this time?

Their call to be The Magick and The Maker of Bannock comes with more questions than ever, but it might also come with answers to their past. Wildwood and Shay are drawn into endless realms, all of which lead to the Legacy of the Maker.

MORE BOOKS FROM SHARON K. ANGELICI

BEHIND THE EYES

Theirs was a love story for the ages: Rasabel, the captain of the guard, and Isolde, the woman of the territory. In a world of swords and arrows, love could not defend against a cruel curse. For years, they searched for an end.

When the alarm bells of Acadia ring, Rasabel goes home, but she is not welcome. Her path collides with Bylyn, a young thief on the run from the executioner's axe. Their lives are forever entangled.

Can Rasabel and Isolde find hope in the hands of a girl who will do anything to keep her freedom?

<u>The Alice and Violet Stories</u>
YULE BE HOME FOR SOLSTICE
Alice and Violet Book I

Violet and Alice's December road trip is definitely a trial by transport as they set out to deliver the perfect Yule log for the Solstice celebration. This cross-state drive commemorates twenty years of sapphic bliss and three hundred thousand miles on their Subaru Outback named Bess. What happens between home and Aunt Eunice's house is a romantic comedy of errors. Sit back and enjoy this *Planes, Trains, and Automobiles*-style adventure to deliver the perfect Yule log for Winter Solstice.

Available now in print, eBook, and audiobook.

DOUBLE DYNO
Prequel to Yule Be Home For Solstice
Alice and Violet Book II

On a two-week hiking and climbing tour, Al Hadley guides a small team toward high adventure. With her best friends PB and Britt making up the Extreme Adventure Group, the goal is to build confidence and experience for each client. What they weren't counting on was Violet Crest and her amateur adventuring ways.

Weeks of planning and detailed maps can't tame Violet's curious nature. She's determined to make every moment count by capturing as many as possible through her camera lens, testing the boundaries and the patience of AEG's team leader, Al.

Dig into the story before the love story, in this slow burn, opposites attract, adventure and the prequel to *Yule Be Home for Solstice.*

Available now in print, eBook, and audiobook.

<u>Rage Room Romance Series</u>
Book 1
CONNED

For Ella Eastman, firefighting is life. She's devoted her body to being the best, but everyone needs a break from reality once in a while. For Morgan Hail, art is life, but she has to make a living. Their lives collide when television fandoms intersect at The Blacktree Comic Palooza.

Morgan's captivating fanart leads to a heated misunderstanding, and a cosplay contest brings these two women together–though only one of them knows the truth. This unlikely pair heats up when their real-world lives collide, but what will happen to their budding romance when Ella reveals her secret identity? And can they find a way to make things work when Ella's job hits a little too close to home? Conned is a story of love, loss, new beginnings, and fandom.

Book 2:
DECONSTRUCTED

After eight years, Ella Eastman has a plan to create the perfect marriage proposal for her partner, Morgan. Inspired by Morgan's to-be-read pile, Ella struggles to incorporate her favorite romance tropes while asking the big question. The ideas pile up, as do the failed attempts to create their once-in-a-lifetime memory. How do you give the perfect partner the perfect memory of a perfect proposal? For Ella, it all seems to come together quite imperfectly. Revisit the Rage Room Romance's chosen family as they unite for Operation Perfect Proposal.

DEAR KANE;
WHAT I WISH WE WOULD HAVE SAID

Do the words that we say in front of our children build them up or tear them down? This short story explores the consequences of hatred and bigotry when it applies, unknowingly, to someone that you love. There's a time in every relationship when a parent must let go of the dreams they have for their child, so the child can chase what they dream to become.

IMMORTAL HUMAN TRUTH

Immortal Human Truth is a collection of poetry written by the author as she traveled to promote her first book
Dear Kane; What I wish we would have said.
Each section explores experiences with love, injustice, loss, and triumph of the spirit.

SHE BELIEVED SHE COULD

What can you do in a single day? Why haven't you done it yet? Jump out of your comfort zone and dive into life as you follow the author on her journey to achieve 365 new experiences in 365 days.

ABOUT THE AUTHOR

Sharon K. Angelici, she/her, was born in the American Midwest, but her heart and soul belong to the mountains of Colorado.

She began writing as a child, using words to recover from trauma-induced depression. As a member of the LGBTQ+ community, she's an advocate for depression awareness and suicide prevention. In 2016, she published her first book dealing with both subjects, *Dear Kane; what I wish we would have said.*

Sharon is a full-time lover of life and all things Pagan and Magick. She's an artist and blacksmith, which inspired her to create her Maker series.

ABOUT THE AUTHOR

 Sharon K. Angelici, she/her, was born in the American Midwest, but her heart and soul belong to the mountains of Colorado.

She began writing as a child, using words to recover from trauma-induced depression. As a member of the LGBTQ+ community, she's an advocate for depression awareness and suicide prevention. In 2016 she published her first book dealing with both subjects, Dear Kane; what I wish we would have said.

Sharon is a full-time lover of life and all things Pagan and Magick. She's an artist and blacksmith, which inspired her to create her Maker series.

Legacy
of the
Maker

Sharon K. Angelici

© 2023

Book 4 of The Maker Series

www.ingramcontent.com/pod-product-compliance
Lightning Source LLC
Chambersburg PA
CBHW070618300726
48975CB00006B/1848